Praise for #1 *New York Times* bestselling author Linda Lael Miller

"Linda Lael Miller creates vibrant characters and stories I defy you to forget."
#1 *New York Times* bestselling author Debbie Macomber

"The versatile and surprising Miller is back dishing up romantic suspense liberally laced with humor and the offbeat . . ."
RT BOOKreviews on *Arizona Heat*

"[A] marvelous contemporary western trilogy launch . . . fraught with amazing chemistry."
Publishers Weekly (starred review) on *Once a Rancher*

"All three titles should appeal to readers who like their contemporary romances Western, slightly dangerous, and graced with enlightened (more or less) bad-boy heroes."
Library Journal on the Montana Creed series

"Miller's prose is smart and her tough Eastwoodian cowboy cuts a sharp, unexpectedly funny figure in a classroom full of rambunctious frontier kids."
Publishers Weekly on *The Man from Stone Creek*

Together

Linda Lael Miller

AVONBOOKS

An Imprint of HarperCollinsPublishers

"Switch" originally appeared in the anthology *Purrfect Love*, published in 1994 by HarperPaperbacks, a division of HarperCollins Publishers.

First Avon Books mass market printing: August 2017

Print Edition ISBN: 978-0-06-200590-8
Digital Edition ISBN: 978-0-06-267760-0

17 18 19 20 21   QGM   10 9 8 7 6 5 4 3 2 1

Contents

Together

In All
Seasons

Prologue

They were little more than children, he fourteen, she twelve, when they stood beneath the arbor of overgrown roses in a forgotten garden of Wellingsley Castle on that midsummer eve. Their hands were clasped, palms together, their fingers interlocked, like their gazes.

It was, to their young hearts, a marriage as true and everlasting as any forged in heaven, on earth, or in any dimension between.

I, Christian Lithwell, swear to love you, Melissande Bradgate, through joy and grief, in minutes and in hours, in all seasons of my life, and to protect and honor you always.

And I, Melissande, make these same vows to you, my lord; I will love you truly, exchanging my soul for yours, and always be your friend, your confidant, your defender.

Chapter One

Five years later
Cornwall, 1508

*B*y some mercy—or some cruelty—of Fate, it fell to Melissande Bradgate (who had decided to be called Sister Pieta, should she ever be allowed to take her final vows) to find Christian Lithwell lying broken, bleeding and bruised, just outside a postern gate on the seaward side of St. Bede's Abbey. It was a chilly night, and rainy, though the month of June was well along and, in keeping with the Abbess's wishes, Melissande had been sent with bread and cheese for any beggars or wayfarers who might be in want of succor.

There were none waiting, but for the shadowy form on the cobblestones, wet with rain and blood, as dirty as if he'd already been buried once, like Lazarus, and then brought out of the tomb again. Melissande recognized him instantly, though whether by the faculties of her mind or her heart, she could not guess, and with a little cry dropped the basket and knelt at his side.

She took his hand gently in her own, and willed him to open his eyes.

He was deeply unconscious, barely alive, in fact, and did not awaken or even stir.

Seized by panic, Melissande nearly broke her solemn vow of silence—she was desperate to convince the Abbess she would make a fine nun—and cried out. Instead, she smoothed the fair, shaggy hair back from the beloved face, willed Christian to hold on to life, and bolted back inside the Abbey walls. In the center of the main courtyard, Melissande grasped the thick, frayed rope of the alarm bell and pulled it hard—once, twice, a third time.

The sisters of St. Bede's Abbey, an elite group because of their exquisite educations, scurried out of the chapel, the infirmary, the dining hall, and the large chamber where many of them spent long and diligent hours copying and illustrating not only the Holy Writ, but secular volumes as well. The Abbess herself, Mother Erylis, was first to arrive.

"What is it, child?" she demanded, firmly but with kindness.

Melissande, her habit and wimple sodden now, let go of the bell rope, from which she'd been quite literally hanging by both hands, and gestured toward the appropriate gate, before bolting in that direction. Mother Erylis and all the sisters followed.

A chorus of exclamations was raised when they reached the scene, and the Abbess knelt beside the long, inert frame on the ground to touch the base of his throat. "He is yet alive," she said, meeting Melissande's imploring gaze after a few moments, "but only barely." Mother Erylis went into action, clapping her hands once and then spouting orders. "Bring a litter, immediately. Someone must heat water and find clean linens and set a chicken on to boil for broth."

Sister Elizabeth, who could ride quite well, was dispatched to put a bridle on the Abbey's one means of transportation, a small brown donkey named Butterpat, and ride the five miles to the parish of St. Paul's, there to fetch Brother Nodger. The monk was an expert with herbs and medicines, but he was being summoned to St. Bede's at such an hour, on such a night, because he was male, and therefore more suited to discern the needs of an injured man.

Melissande followed, both hands clasped to her mouth to keep from screaming, as the visitor was maneuvered onto a litter and carried into the infirmary by a contingent of four nuns.

Christian, she cried in silence, as she stumbled alongside the litter. *Oh, Christian! They said you'd perished, all of them, Queech and Lord James and my father and stepmother, and I believed them. Heaven help me, I believed them.*

Inside the infirmary, lamps were lighted, and the fires were built up to ease the dank chill inherent to an ancient stone structure. Christian was hoisted onto a cot—he was a large and unwieldy man, though slender—and Melissande, shivering now, was hauled gently out of the way so that he could be ministered to, at least superficially.

Those of his wounds that were visible, and they were many, so ragged was his once-fine linen shirt, so torn his breeches, were cleaned with warm water, and he was covered in the roughly woven blankets that were all the Abbey had to offer.

Melissande dragged a stool close to the head of the cot and sat there, one hand resting on Christian's shoulder as she tried to will strength into him. Tears trickled down her cheeks, and she was trembling with cold, but she could not be persuaded to leave him.

Memories of an earlier time flooded her mind and filled her bruised heart. She and Christian had fallen in love as children, and sworn to cherish each other forever, but only weeks before they would have been duly wedded, Christian had been lost at sea whilst carrying a message to Eire for his elder brother, James, Lord Wellingsley.

Or so Melissande had believed.

"You know this young man," Mother Erylis interjected softly, after she had dismissed the other sisters. She and

Melissande sat keeping their vigil alone now, waiting for Brother Nodger, who was old and had some distance to travel to reach the Abbey.

Melissande nodded. There was no point in breaking her promise never to speak, though her heart was so full she could hardly contain all that she needed to say. Giving voice to her feelings would not help Christian.

Oh, yes, Mother, was her inward reply. *I knew him once. His soul was mine, and mine his. And now, even if my beloved survives, he is surely still lost to me, for I see he has suffered wounds I cannot mend or even soothe.*

She crossed herself and offered a silent prayer, her lips moving with the comforting rhythm of the familiar words.

Mother Erylis sighed heavily. It was no secret to anyone that she had her doubts about Melissande's calling, and for this reason the young woman had not been permitted to take her final vows. Melissande had undertaken the pledge of silence, and honored it for a full year, in the effort to prove herself worthy, but still the Abbess, a reasonable woman in every other way, remained unsatisfied.

Perhaps she suspected that her charge had not been completely honest with her.

"You may speak, Melissande," she said now. "I release you from your oath."

Melissande bit her lower lip. She was not certain she could utter a sound, now that a twelve-month had gone by without so much as a single word passing her lips, even if she chose to do so. Moreover, Christian's precarious state made her afraid of incurring the displeasure of heaven by failing to honor her promise. Even the Abbess, in all her piety and wisdom, could not set Melissande free from this troth, for it was a deeper matter, a spiritual pact between a bumbling supplicant and the Holy Mother Herself.

The Abbess did not look pleased when Melissande gave no response, but neither did she press the subject.

On the cot, Christian writhed and called a name Melissande remembered, that of his servant and friend, Robert. She smoothed his hair back from his forehead with one hand and wiped a stray tear from her cheek with the other.

"Sit with him as long as you like," Mother Erylis told Melissande, as Brother Nodger trundled into the infirmary sometime later. Then the older woman departed, for there was no more that she could do, besides pray.

Melissande remained, wide-eyed, throat painfully tight, afraid to look away from Christian even for a moment, lest he slip over the invisible river into the next world, leaving her behind. Losing him once had nearly been her undoing; bidding him a second farewell would certainly destroy her.

Brother Nodger, a small, simple man, with gray tonsured hair and a nose so bulbous as to be nearly comical in its dimensions, glanced at the girl curiously but did not attempt to send her away. Instead, he set his basket of supplies on a nearby tabletop, opened the lid, and began taking out the items he would require.

First, Christian's boots were tugged off his feet and tossed aside, then his breeches and shirt were methodically cut away and discarded.

"There, now," Brother Nodger murmured once, when Christian shifted on his bed, caught in some deep undercurrent of pain. "Peace be unto you, my brother. You are in kindly hands, and no further injury shall befall you."

Melissande heated water and brought it when the monk so instructed her, and watched in breathless hope while he applied various ointments to Christian's wounds and bound them with linen bandages the sisters had prepared.

What in God's name has been done to him, she wondered, now that her mind was calmer and she could focus on a single, coherent thought.

Presently, his work finished, Brother Nodger put away his

medicines, closed his great basket, and regarded his ghastly-pale patient in somber reflection.

"God's blessing be upon you, my son," he said softly, making a graceful and sacred gesture with one hand. Then, raising his benign gaze to Melissande's tormented face, he added, "And upon you as well, child."

Melissande felt a foolish, almost overwhelming urge to fling herself into the monk's arms and sob against his chest, but at seventeen she was a woman grown, and comforts of that kind were for children. Besides, it would not be seemly to display such private emotions.

Brother Nodger took his leave, after one last, despairing look at Christian, and Melissande sat down on a stool, still wearing her rain-soaked clothing, unwilling to leave him even long enough to change into her spare habit and wimple. The lamps sputtered out, one by one, and had to be refilled, reminding Melissande of a favorite passage she'd copied recently, from crumbling sheepskin to heavy parchment, the story of virgins awaiting their bridegrooms by night. Some had kept their lamps trimmed; others were careless and had been left out of the wedding for their negligence.

Sometime in the depths of the night, Christian finally opened his eyes. He looked at Melissande for a long time, his handsome, battered face blank with disbelief at first, then hard with resentment. In a voice so raspy that it did injury to Melissande's own throat to hear it, he ground out, "It is as I prayed, then. I have—indeed died, and gone to hell—for surely that is a better place than I've been these two years past. How then—can it be otherwise—for here you are—the devil's own mistress." He paused, drew a long, ragged breath. "Pray you, Melissande—where is Lucifer, your master?"

Chapter Two

She was indeed real, and not a dream, a vision or a specter as he'd first thought.

Christian stared up at her, through a fog of fury and pain, the latter both physical and emotional in nature, the former an elemental thing, rooted in the very core of his being.

Melissande Bradgate—his lover, his friend, his ideal.

His betrayer.

Tears glistened in her cerulean eyes, and her dark hair escaped its wimple to cling to her fair, flawless skin in damp tendrils. Her lower lip, full and soft, quivered.

He could not help recalling the sweet consummation of their love, in a garden draped in twilight, three full years after they had first declared themselves, but he put the image out of his mind as quickly as he could. He would sooner be tied to a mast and whipped than face the mockery of that memory again.

"If I had my sword," Christian whispered, "I swear by all that's holy that I would run you through." *And after that, myself, for I could not live, having done you violence.*

Melissande raised her chin, squared her small shoulders, dashed at her eyes with the back of one paint-stained hand. She'd always been a stubborn little creature, and Christian's elder brother had warned him that she would not be easy to manage.

Foolishly, callow lad that he was, Christian had told James he did not mean to "manage" Melissande, but only to love her. They were to be wed on a Saturday morning in June, in the vast hall of her father's grand house at Taftshead, near London, but she'd sold him into slavery instead. He'd been two torturous years in the stinking belly of a merchant galley, a ship that Melissande herself would inherit, rowing back and forth between the coasts of England and France. Because of her he had known hunger and humiliation, had suffered brutal beatings on a regular basis, and had inherited sorrows so deep he dared not put names to them.

"What are you doing here?" he demanded, with the last of his strength. "Surely you—even you—dare not lay claim to purity?"

Hot color pulsed in her cheeks, but she would not be goaded. She set her jaw and raised his head onto a hard pillow to spoon broth into his mouth from a crude wooden bowl, but she did not answer his question. Of course, she wouldn't.

Christian accepted a quantity of the thin but flavorful soup and then spewed it unceremoniously onto the front of her gown.

Melissande stiffened momentarily, and another flush climbed the length of her slender neck, but she did not rebuke him. Instead, with a trembling hand, she plunged the spoon into the bowl again, and brought more soup to his lips.

Christian had used the last of his strength to defy her, and so accepted the nourishment, too weak now even to swallow. He let the stuff trickle down his throat, into his long-empty and probably shriveled stomach, and tried to remember how he'd gotten here, to this place. His last clear recollections were of the ship, his prison for twice a twelve-month, and of the cloaked and hooded men who had come aboard to buy him for fifty florins.

Even though he had longed to leave the galley forever, to

stand on solid ground and breathe fresh air instead of the fetid stench belowdecks, he had been wary of his mysterious rescuers, who were careful not to show their faces or to speak.

Christian had been led off the vessel, still in chains, and along a darkened wharf, lit only by the occasional torch tipped in flaming pitch. There was something familiar about the leader of these half-dozen men, and yet Christian could not place him.

Finally, Christian had stopped—they were in an alleyway then, an odious, rat-ridden place almost as bad as the ship they'd just left—and refused to take another step until he'd been told where they were bound.

For an answer, the ringleader of the group had backhanded him across the face—he had recognized his brother's man, Queech, in that instant—and Christian, hands bound behind him, feet in irons, could not defend himself. He had been set upon by all the men at once, and the beating that followed was more savage by far than any he had had at the hands of overseers. He'd refused to utter a sound throughout and, finally, mercifully, he'd lost consciousness.

Only to awaken here, wherever it was, with Lucifer's beloved dribbling broth past his swollen lips.

"What is this place?" he whispered, for he hadn't the strength to put force behind the words. He'd been vaguely aware of a priest working over him earlier, setting his bones, pouring stinging solutions into his open wounds, but there was no sign of him now. "Is it truly what it seems—a convent?"

For an answer, Melissande lifted a small, silver crucifix out of her habit and held it out to him with a brisk nod.

It was true then. She, this female Judas, this she-devil, had taken refuge in a nunnery. Or perhaps she had been imprisoned there, in a desperate effort to salvage her treacherous soul.

Who, then, had brought him to her?

Who had saved him, and why?

He had no ready answer to these questions, though something niggled at the edge of his mind, begging to be brought into the light. A face, looming over him like a dirt-smudged moon, after his assailants had gone. A face he knew, and yet did not know . . .

It was no use, and Christian had enough to think about for the moment.

He stared at Melissande, wondering why he was surprised even though he'd already drawn the correct conclusion on his own. Her wimple and somber robe had not struck him as odd at first, for most women covered their hair and Melissande had ever favored simple garments, despite the fact that her father, now surely dead, if she had come to live in this place, had been an exceedingly wealthy man.

"Good God," he breathed, raising himself a little way off the pillow again and wincing as sharp, sudden pain struck him with the motion. "Have you actually—are you—?"

She shook her head, with a wispy, sad smile, and tucked the crucifix back into her robe.

Christian closed his eyes, unable to admit even to himself that he was, in some poignant measure, relieved by this news. He hated Melissande as one can only hate someone they have loved with the whole of their heart and mind, and yet it was as jarring as a bludgeon blow to think for so much as a moment that she belonged to heaven.

Melissande laid a cool hand to his forehead, and though she did not speak aloud, Christian would have sworn he heard her say, *Sleep*.

MELISSANDE WAS NODDING on the stool when Sister Domina awakened her for Matins, or midnight prayers. Christian was sleeping soundly, and Melissande's heart ached anew at the sight of him lying there, splinted and bandaged, his face so bruised and swollen that she wondered how she had ever recognized him the night before.

But then, Melissande would have known Christian anywhere, she guessed, even if she'd been blind. He was the heart of her heart, and after her father had told her he was lost at sea, she had not wanted to go on living. She had, in fact, fled on horseback to Wellingsley Castle, to visit once more the hidden place where she and Christian had exchanged their vows and then, three years later, given themselves to each other in the physical sense as well. In sorrow, not in shame, she had tried, after that pilgrimage, to hurl herself off one of the keep's towering walls.

It had been Christian's brother, James, who had interceded, grasping her from behind, hauling her down into his arms and murmuring words of comfort, offering to wed her himself and make her happier than she had ever dreamed of being . . .

James Lithwell, seventh Earl of Wellingsley, her father's great friend.

She had refused him, out of hand, and he had been coldly angry.

"Go now," urged Sister Domina quietly, bringing Melissande back to the present. "Mother will be looking for you."

Reluctantly, Melissande took her leave, hurrying off through the predawn darkness to her cell, there to wash her face hastily at the basin, rearrange her wimple, and smooth her hopelessly crumpled habit with both hands. Then, with a heavy heart, she went to the chapel to join the others. More services would follow: Lauds at three or so, then Prime at sunrise. Vespers would be said at eventide, and Compline just before bed.

Breakfast generally was a plain repast of porridge and coarse bread, sometimes with ale or cheese—and then the residents of St. Bede's would be about their daily tasks. Some tended the garden, some cooked, others mended and sewed, and still others, the privileged ones, trained from earliest childhood by tutors and blessed with particular talents, sat upon high stools in the great chamber next to the chapel, copying manuscripts, prayer books, and Holy Scripture for the use of the Church, as well as secular volumes that would be sold in the outside world. Melissande, who had always drawn and painted and had learned to read and write when she was four, was an accomplished illuminator.

That morning, however, she had no heart for her work, though normally it was her greatest solace. She was especially good at depicting angels in beautiful, flowing robes, languishing on the top of a giant, elaborate letter or offering Great Tidings to a band of spellbound shepherds. She enjoyed depicting Adam and Eve in the Garden, too, and the twelve virgins with their lamps, but had never once used Noah and the Ark, even though she adored animals.

Because she'd believed that Christian had died by drowning, Melissande had not been able to draw any sort of seagoing vessel.

After taking a quill, a vial of ink, and a scrap of discarded parchment from her slanted worktable, she proceeded to the infirmary. Christian looked worse than he had the night before, although he was sitting up, his back braced by pillows. He was feeding himself from a bowl of porridge and glaring at Sister Domina whenever she made the slightest, most timorous move to help him.

At the sight of Melissande, he set the wooden dish aside with a thump and scowled. "Get out," he snapped.

Melissande hesitated in the doorway for only a moment, while poor Sister Domina stood stricken at his bedside. At a gesture, the devoted but shy nun fled the infirmary.

Christian flung the porridge bowl after her, scattering cereal across the smooth stone floor.

Melissande shook her head in barely disguised disgust and moved toward him, a female Daniel entering the lions' den.

Chapter Three

Melissande tried to look imposing as she stood at Christian's bedside, but that objective was nigh unto impossible, for she was not a tall woman, and small-boned as a bird. She had retrieved the porridge bowl on her way across the room, and set it down on the table next to him with a reverberating crash, just to let him know he wasn't going to have the upper hand.

He did not flinch, but glared at her, his blue eyes ferocious. Of the two of them, Christian was by far the more beautiful—or had been, before the beating that had brought him to the postern gate of St. Bede's Abbey—his patrician features perfectly aligned, his body fit and strong. He was, for all his fallen-angel appearance, not in the least womanly. No, he had ever been the most manly of men, and that, Melissande could well see, had not changed, despite his private ordeal.

She trembled a little, recalling the way he'd kissed her, the sweetly sinful wantings he'd aroused in her untried body. She had lain with Christian, in celebration of their love, just before he had gone away to sea, and even though the indulgence had caused her grief, she had never truly regretted it. There could be no other lover for Melissande, now or ever.

A tear welled and slipped down Melissande's cheek. He

was not the same man she'd known and loved so well, from childhood. No, that Christian had been lost to her, and another had come back in his place, irrevocably altered by whatever he'd experienced during their time apart.

He plainly despised her, and blamed her for what had befallen him. She could only guess at what that had been.

Remembering the quill and parchment she carried—the small vial of ink was in the pocket of her robe—she spread the materials on the side table, dipped the point, and wrote, *I have promised not to speak.*

"A blessing, no doubt," Christian grumbled, once he'd read her neat, square letters. "Tell me—do you seek to expunge your sin by cloistering yourself in this place?"

Melissande wrote furiously; her script would not have been accepted in the chamber where books were made. *I have committed no sin.*

Christian expelled a harsh breath and sank back onto his pillows again. He was pale, his beautiful eyes hollow and haunted. "I loved you," he said, "and you made me a slave."

She stared at him. Even without the vow to restrain her tongue, she would not have been able to speak. Her eyes must have blazed with the questions burning in her mind though, for Christian answered as though she had denied his wretched charge verbally.

"One day, Melissande," he ground out, "you must face the courts of heaven. And then you will be required to account for your treachery."

She wrote, *I have done no treachery! Why do you accuse me?*

Christian read the words, but the strength was draining visibly from his battered muscles. "Liar," he said, and then he closed his eyes and slept.

Melissande wanted to shake him awake, demand an explanation for the terrible charges he had made—nay, an apology!—but of course she did not. Christian still was in danger, for all that he'd awakened and shown his legendary temper. And the Lord most often used restful sleep, Mother Erylis always said, to do His healing.

Brother Nodger entered the infirmary just as Melissande was fleeing; he greeted her with a nod and a curious look as she passed, then went inside to examine his patient. Silently, Melissande wished him better luck than she'd had and hurried back to her desk in the writing chamber.

It was only when she reached that place that she realized she'd left her quill, ink, and parchment behind on Christian's bedside table. She might not have gone back, were it not for the words she'd scrawled on the heavy paper. She didn't care to explain them to anyone.

Alas, she was too late, for when Melissande reached the infirmary again, Mother Erylis was there, holding the parchment in one hand even as she conferred with Brother Nodger. Christian, evidently undisturbed by the monk's visit, was still sleeping.

At Melissande's appearance in the doorway, Mother Erylis looked at her with a stern and yet wholly tender expression. "Ah, it is you, my child," she said, with resignation. "Your appearance is fortuitous, for it saves me the trouble of seeking you out."

A blush scalded Melissande's cheeks. She felt like a child in the nursery, being called to task by a tutor, but there was no defiance in her. She inclined her head in acquiescence and waited on the threshold for instructions.

"We will speak in the garden, beside the fountain," the Abbess said quietly. "Or, at least, *I* shall speak. You, I fear, will only listen."

Melissande made a little bobbing motion and went off to the appointed place, there to settle herself. It was a bastion of peace, the rose garden next to the chapel, with the sky arching overhead like a blue vault and the leaves of the maple and oak trees whispering silver-green songs of summer. Last night's rain, it seemed, had washed the world clean.

Mother Erylis arrived only moments after Melissande had taken a seat on the stone bench facing the chattering fountain.

With a reassuring smile, the older woman sat down beside her and folded gnarled, hard-working hands in an ample lap. "You have been with us for twice a twelve-month," she said, watching the sparkling waters as they danced in the sunlight, like living diamonds constantly changing shape. "For the first year of that time, you were full of sorrow. For the second, you did not speak. Now, child, I charge you, as your spiritual adviser, to turn from your vow. I do not think God or the Holy Mother require silence from you any longer."

Melissande bit her lip. If anyone could have gotten her to utter a word, it was the Abbess, whom she loved, respected, and admired, but she was afraid to try. Afraid she would never stop talking, or not be able to talk at all. She wasn't entirely sure she hadn't forgotten how.

Mother Erylis produced the bit of parchment, which had been rolled and tucked into the pocket of her habit. There, in progressively worse handwriting, was Melissande's side of the conversation with Christian.

I have promised not to speak.

I have committed no sin.

I have done no treachery!

Why do you accuse me?

"Why *does* this man accuse you, child?" the Abbess asked.

Melissande stood up, sat down again, spread her hands wide then, just as quickly, clasped them over her face and began to weep softly. Her sobs, other than the soft gasp she'd uttered upon recognizing Christian there by the postern gate, were the first sounds she'd made in a twelve-month.

The Abbess laid a hand to Melissande's back and patted her. "There is no sin in loving, lass," she said.

Melissande cried harder. She did not know what to do now, or where to go. She had thought Christian dead, and had buried all womanly feelings with his memory. Now, those feelings were back, in full force, making it impossible for her to dedicate herself to the Church as she'd planned. She had no family to turn to—her father and stepmother had perished of the plague, and all their household had disbanded. Christian obviously hated her; there would be no help or forgiveness from that quarter.

She looked imploringly into the Abbess's plain but radiant face, and all her thoughts and fears must have been apparent in her eyes, for that good woman patted her shoulder and said, "You need make no decisions today. And remember, you are not a pauper. You have the means to make a good marriage for yourself."

All was decided, then. Melissande would never be Sister Pieta. In time—probably a very short time—she would no longer be welcome at St. Bede's Abbey.

How to explain, even if she were ready to speak even the most awkward words, that she could not marry just any man, no matter how eminently suitable? Not after loving, and being loved by, Christian. She dared not confess that her body belonged to him as well as her soul.

No, she would not be wed, nor could she ever be a courtesan.

The Church was her only refuge.

She got to her knees on the cobblestones, clasped both the Abbess's hands in her own, and looked up at her pleadingly.

But Mother Erylis shook her head sadly. "You are not suited, child. It is for you to serve elsewhere, most surely as a mother and a wife."

The words stabbed Melissande in the heart. She would never know the particular joys of holding her own babe in her arms, for none could sire her children but Christian. Christian, who would sooner spit on her—who had *indeed* spat upon her—than take such as she to wife.

He wanted to kill her.

She lowered her head to Mother Erylis's knees, still weeping.

"Shh," the Abbess said, with tender amusement in her voice. "It is the work of heaven, that this young man has been brought to us. Do not despair."

Melissande considered the way Christian had looked at her, the dreadful things he'd said, the bitter accusations he'd made, and she wailed aloud.

Chapter Four

The words came hoarse and raw to Melissande's throat as she looked up at Mother Erylis again. "Please," she begged. "Permit me to stay!"

Gently, the Abbess touched Melissande's cheek. Then she tugged the wimple off the girl's head, allowing her dark, unruly hair to tumble free. "I am sorry, my child," the older woman said. "You are not meant for this life."

"But I paint beautifully and write a very fine hand. You've said so yourself!"

"Your heart is rebellious, full of earthly passions. Your body is as a fertile field, awaiting the seasons of planting and harvest, and your mind, though quick, tends to wander far beyond the confines of these humble walls. No, your place is outside St. Bede's Abbey." Mother Erylis urged Melissande to her feet, squinting against the June sun as she looked up at her. "You needn't fear being cast out into the world with nowhere to go, my dear. You may remain with us until God has revealed His will where you are concerned."

Melissande felt a thrill of hope, then plummeting, crashing despair. On all the earth, only Christian truly knew her, and he abhorred her with the whole of his heart. Was it God's will that she be spurned, disgraced? She could see nothing else in an alarmingly long future.

"Go to your friend, in the infirmary," the Abbess pressed

quietly. "Speak to him. Whatever went wrong between you, make it right."

Melissande cast a longing glance toward the chamber where Christian lay, being tended by Brother Nodger. For all her sorrows, Christian's suffering had been much greater. He'd been a slave, he'd told her, and that probably meant he'd been kidnapped by knaves and sold to work aboard one of the hundreds of galleys constantly making their way between the ports of England, France, Flanders, Norway and Denmark, Italy and Greece, even Africa and vast, frozen Russia. Christian, then, had been a galley slave.

And she owned such ships herself. Ships rowed to and fro by men who served against their will.

Because Melissande was not a person who thought about wealth, she had given little consideration to the inheritance left by her late father and his calculating young wife, Eleanora, who had hardly been older than Melissande herself. Now, as she realized at last what it meant to possess trading vessels of that sort, she was overwhelmed by shame. The force of it caused her to sway on her feet, one hand clasped to her mouth in horror, and Mother Erylis jumped up to grasp her arm.

"What is it?"

"My—ships—" Melissande whispered. Words came hard to her; to speak again would take practice, and the price, like that of so many things, would be measured in pain.

Mother Erylis shook her head, not understanding. "You must go to your cell and lie down, child. You look unwell."

Melissande, nearly too stricken to stand, could only nod her acquiescence. She went to her chamber, as she had been charged to do, but she did not rest. Instead, she knelt on the timbered floor, her gaze fixed on the small square of the heavens revealed by her tiny slit of a window. Her hands clasped, she begged forgiveness for her ignorance in the matter of her four trading galleys. If she did nothing else, she would order those ships into port, free the men on board, and give each one ample gold to start over or make his way home.

Her steward was certain to complain vociferously, as were the retinue of notaries and clerks she employed in addition, but she would not be turned from her course. She owed the slaves mercy and restitution, and she would give it or perish in the effort.

Resolution restored her strength. After some time, Melissande stood, smoothed her rumpled habit, and tried to restrain her hair by running her fingers through it, comb-like. She splashed her face with water from the ewer on her wash table, the one piece of furniture in her box-like quarters, besides the cot against the opposite wall, and returned to the writing chamber.

There, she borrowed fresh ink, took a quill from the cabinet, and appropriated a suitable scroll. With much thought, Melissande began drafting the first command she had ever issued as the true owner of the Bradgate Company. The galleys were to be brought home and refitted as sailing ships, if that were possible. (She had no idea whether it was or wasn't, but since the only alternative was sinking them, it seemed prudent to attempt salvage.) The slaves aboard were to be paid ten florins apiece and sent, unmolested, on their way. She promised to travel to London at the first opportunity, there to either sell the business or personally undertake the running of it.

She smiled, for the first time since finding Christian the night before, as she considered the stir her message would cause when it reached the offices of the Bradgate Company.

That done, Melissande felt better, though she wished she could put her orders into effect that very moment.

Once she had poured sand over the document to absorb the excess ink, then carefully shaken that off into a pail reserved for the purpose, Melissande rolled her brisk decree into a tight cylinder, tied it with a string, and hurried off to find the Abbess.

Without questioning her about the scroll's contents, Mother Erylis promised that the letter should be sent on its way that afternoon, when a coach passed through the nearby village of Gilly. By relays, the missive would reach London in good time, barring any sort of disaster, of course.

Reassured, Melissande looked in on Christian—Brother Nodger was gone and the patient was slumbering peacefully—then returned to the writing chamber. Her hair was uncovered, and the nuns looked at her curiously, but none ventured an inquiry. In many ways, Melissande realized, she had always been something of an enigma to them, taking off her shoes to wade in the surf where it foamed against the shore, climbing a tree to fetch down a village child's mewling kitten, teaching Butterpat, the little donkey, to count to five with his hoof and make low bows like a mummer acknowledging the cheers of a crowd.

After fetching a paint box and brushes from the cabinet and settling herself on her stool, she bent diligently to sketch the Annunciation. She'd worked on it for days and now added blue for the Virgin's robe, a pure, vibrant shade, so rich that it almost leaped off the page. For a time, she did not think of Christian's hatred, or of the fact that Mother Erylis meant to send her away from the Abbey, her only home, forever. Her work absorbed her totally.

CHRISTIAN AWAKENED IN the darkest hours of the night, surprised and, at the same time, *not* surprised, to find Melissande there beside him, perched on a stool, her chin on her chest. She had removed her wimple, and her hair spilled over her shoulders, gleaming like polished ebony in the moonlight, rousing a grinding ache deep in Christian's groin.

From the moment his odyssey of suffering had begun, on that night two years before, when he'd been knocked senseless on the dark street in front of John Bradgate's elegant house in Taftshead and dragged away to the London docks, Christian had kept his grief, his frustration, his fear inside, where no one else could catch so much as a glimpse of them. Now, temporarily safe in this nunnery near the sea—he could hear the distant whisper of the tide over the sound of his own breathing and Melissande's and catch its too-familiar, briny smell—it seemed that his iron control had finally failed him.

He wept silently, under the cover of the night, because he had loved Melissande so well, and she had repaid him with treachery. Because he had been beaten and starved and made to sleep in a foul, vermin-fraught hold, when indeed he was allowed to rest. He had been spat upon, kicked, and generally treated as something less than an animal. Finally, someone had come to collect him, someone whose mien and manner he'd thought he should know, only to subject him to more of the same.

Queech.

James had sent him, of course. James, who had wanted Melissande for his countess.

Christian shifted his thoughts to the present, which was more tenable, for all its failings. He knew he was vulnerable, even within the walls of the Abbey, for he still was too weak to protect himself, and the sisters could not be expected to stand against men with swords or daggers. He would die before returning to the life he'd endured during his captivity, but he might not be given that choice.

He dried his face furtively with the back of one hand. He'd seen other men brought back to the galley after brief stints of freedom, watched them give up, refuse to row or to eat or to sleep. They went willingly to the whipping post, there to be lashed to death, their shredded bodies thrown overboard afterward, as food for the fishes.

Still, that wasn't the worst of it, knowing he might be

forced to return to hell. No, what devastated Christian was the certainty that Melissande, of all people, had sold him into that life. Melissande, whom he had adored so completely, so purely, so foolishly, that there was no room in his heart for another woman, even now.

As though she'd overheard his thoughts—Christian knew he hadn't made a sound, for silence was a skill one learned quickly and well in the hold of a galley—Melissande awakened and slid off the stool to approach the bed.

"Where is your wimple?" he demanded, fearing to say anything else. A part of him, after all of it, longed to pull her into his arms and hold her close against him. "Not that you'll answer me."

She simply looked at him, her eyes dark in the gloom of that medicinal chamber, where he was the only patient. That in itself was a luxury, that he should have so much space to himself, he who had slept like a dog, curled on piles of rags and rotted cattle fodder, in a cell so crowded that he could not move without touching someone else.

"Tell me why," he said. "You owe me that much."

She bit her lower lip. Attempted to speak, and fell silent again.

"Then I shall tell *you* why," Christian bit out, and they all poured out of him in a single, vile torrent, the ugly beliefs that had swelled and festered in his soul during two years of torment, of uncertainty, of almost intolerable loneliness. "Because you decided to marry my brother instead of me, and become a countess. Never mind that he didn't have a stone to strike a flint against, you had gold enough for all of England, did you not? But there was the problem of poor Christian—the hapless second son, who could not offer you a proper title to go with your provincial prosperity. What to do with that poor fool? Ah, yes. Arrange that he be set upon by thugs, clubbed to the ground like a mad cur, and hauled off to one of your own galleys. Masterful. Absolutely masterful."

Melissande's face was a study in surprise. She went pale, and her eyes widened. "You cannot truly believe—" she managed to rasp.

Christian wet his lips, his gaze never wavering from hers. "Before I left your father's house that final night," he ground out, "he told me that you no longer wished to marry me. Other arrangements had been made, he said. I demanded to see you—indeed, I searched the house for you—but you were gone, already with my brother, no doubt. I was standing in the street, trying to decide what to do, when I was taken prisoner."

Melissande stared at him for a long time. Then, calmly, slowly, she replied. "You are not only faithless, sir, but quite wrong. For I would not be here at St. Bede's if I had wed the Earl, would I?"

Chapter Five

Gazing upon Christian's furious face, there in that moonlit room, Melissande wondered if it would do any good to tell him the truth—that she had had nothing to do with his abduction, had indeed thought him dead all this while, and had mourned him with all her might.

She suspected that it was this very hatred Christian so cherished now that had sustained him while he was held captive aboard her galley, and he was reluctant to let go of it even though the worst was surely over. Perhaps he needed it still.

She poured water from the ewer on Christian's bedside table and took a long swallow to ease her dry, unpracticed throat. He stared at her the whole time, but she could not read his expression, for the light, scant in the first place, had dimmed with the passing of some cloud high overhead, and his face was draped with shadows.

As before, she spoke with excruciating slowness. "What say you to that, Christian Lithwell? Why am I not a countess, even now, if that was the fate I sought?"

Christian narrowed his eyes; she sensed the motion because she knew his features so well. Better, in fact, than her own. "Mayhap James suffered an attack of conscience—especially if he'd guessed what you'd done—and you were spurned."

"James once saved my life," Melissande said, after another draught of water. "As it happened, it wasn't a noble gesture on his part. He wanted me for himself. And he had no conscience."

Christian, weary and contemptuous only a moment before, was suddenly, sharply alert. "Had?"

She looked down. "Your brother perished, Christian, of the plague. As did my father and stepmother."

He was silent. He and James were never close, being very different men and James so much older than he, but still, Christian's elder brother had been his only blood kin. Christian was, for all intents and purposes, as completely alone in the world as Melissande herself, though that would probably change little or nothing, where his aversion to her was concerned.

At long last, Christian asked, "Did he have pain?"

Melissande took more water. "It was a sweating sickness, and there was a flux, as well as fever, but the victims did not linger overlong. James was gone within two days, as were Father and Eleanora."

Christian sighed. "Dear God. I never guessed—"

"You had no way to know."

He turned his head away for a moment; she knew he was struggling to maintain his composure.

"Christian." She laid a hand to his matted hair, like silk even in its current state of uncleanliness, longing to wash it with scented soap and clear water, to comb and trim the pale locks and feel them between her fingers.

"Leave me," he said, without looking at her again. "I cannot bear the sight of you."

Melissande did not argue, nor did she hesitate. Her throat was sore and Christian's rebuff, though entirely expected, had dealt her a mighty wound. She bent, kissed his temple lightly, as much to defy him as to lend comfort, then turned and fled the infirmary.

She did not sleep that night, but tossed and turned upon her narrow cot, torn between fury that Christian believed her capable of such treachery and a humiliating need to prove herself.

In the morning, after Prime, Melissande learned that she was to look after Christian until he was well enough to leave the Abbey. A table and supplies were brought to the infirmary so that she could continue the illumination of the Annunciation she had begun.

"I don't want you here," Christian said flatly, that sunny morning after Brother Nodger had been and gone with his potions and ointments.

"That," replied Melissande, without looking up as she dipped her best brush in cerulean paint for the Virgin's gown, "is unfortunate."

"Who manages James's estates, now that he is dead?"

"I wouldn't know," Melissande answered, still absorbed. It was easier to speak, but still painful, and she had to grope through her mind to find the simplest words.

"Probably that rogue, Queech."

Melissande suppressed a shudder at the recollection of her few encounters with James Lithwell's clerk and trusted confidant. She had never liked or trusted the man. "Probably," she agreed, in a distracted tone. "If you keep talking to me, I shall not be able to do proper justice to this illumination."

"You were always clever with a quill or a paintbrush."

Melissande raised her eyes and gave Christian a piercing look.

"You're welcome," he said mockingly, when she let him go unthanked for his compliment. If indeed that was what the remark had been, which seemed unlikely. The silence stretched taut between them, ready to spring back on both sides and send each of them reeling, it seemed to Melissande, like a defeat at tug-of-war. "You were his mistress," Christian said at last.

Melissande's cheeks and neck pulsed with color. She laid the brush down, for fear of smearing the Virgin's garb, with its delicate folds and elegant cut. "I was no man's courtesan, nor will I ever be," she said, through her teeth.

He sighed and settled deeper into his pillows. "So you claim," he replied blithely. Christian seemed to be recovering very rapidly, and Melissande hoped she would be forgiven for wishing he had not regained his powers of speech so quickly.

"So I swear before God," she said.

Christian turned his head, studied her. "What brought you here?"

"I had no place else to go."

"A lie. You had my brother's house, and vast holdings of your own."

"But here I was loved," she told him sadly. "Here, I was wanted for no other reason than that I am a child of God."

"Surely you have contributed to the coffers of this Abbey."

"I have not," Melissande insisted, "though I offered more than once. Mother Erylis welcomed me because she believed I had something worthwhile to give to others." Sadness nearly overwhelmed Melissande in the wake of that statement. Clearly, the Abbess had lost whatever confidence she might have placed in the woman who had hoped to become Sister Pieta.

Christian closed his eyes. His bruises looked worse, not better, even though the healing process had obviously begun. With luck, he would recover and be gone soon. "And now what will you do? Where will you go?"

She blinked back fresh tears. "To London," she said. "I would have dealings with my father's notary."

"I can imagine. You will want fine gowns for snaring a

new husband. And jewels, no doubt, to show that you are a wonderful catch. Except for an unfortunate habit of selling besotted swains into slavery, of course."

Melissande sat perfectly still until the desire to scream in rage and frustration had passed. Mostly. "I seek no husband," she snapped. "They bring naught but trouble and heartbreak, as far as I can see."

"Then why bestir yourself to London? 'Tis a despicable place, full of thieves, with sewage in its streets and rats in every loft and cellar."

"Aye," agreed Melissande, who had always held a similar opinion. "But my business is there, and I have a house nearby, at Taftshead."

"Your galleys." The words were spoken so coldly, so brusquely, that they sent a chill spiking down Melissande's spine.

She rose from the desk at last and went to stand beside him. "Oh, Christian," she whispered, laying a hand to his shoulder. He tried to pull away, but in the end he was not strong enough, and had no place to go. "How can you think I would do you any harm? I was a maiden when I gave myself to you, and I loved you truly."

He studied her face for a long moment. The reply he gave shocked her so much that she was temporarily speechless again. "After I was whipped the first time, about six months after I'd been taken captive," he said evenly, grimly, "the captain had me brought to his quarters. He showed me a letter, signed by your hand, ordering that I be taken aboard the *Eleanora* as a slave."

Chapter Six

. . . *He showed me a letter, signed by your hand, ordering that I be taken aboard the Eleanora as a slave . . .*

Melissande gaped at Christian, stunned by this latest revelation. "I made no such order!" she cried, and then put one hand to her throat because the pain of speaking went through her vocal cords like a thin-bladed knife. And because even as she'd spoken the words, she'd recalled all the documents she'd signed, without benefit of reading, at her stepmother's request. It had been some weeks before Christian's "death," and her father had been away on one of his journeys.

No emotion showed in Christian's bruised face—neither disbelief, nor trust, nor anything else. He simply watched her.

The truth of what had happened, of how both she and Christian had been betrayed by the people they most trusted, besides each other, was beginning to take shape in her mind. James had wanted to marry her, and thus gain partial control of her fortune. Her father and Eleanora had wanted the title only James could confer, being the firstborn son. They had joined forces, the three of them, to achieve their ends and, in the process, destroy a love as elemental as starlight.

She struggled against tears—those would be shed later,

in the privacy of her cell, where no one need see her weakness. Finally, she turned away, her back trembling as she drew deep, shuddering breaths in a vain attempt to calm herself.

"If you didn't do it, Melissande," Christian interjected reasonably, "then who did?"

She did not face him, but instead squared her shoulders and raised her chin. She had been a child for too long; now it was time to become a woman. She had a company to manage and a new vow to fulfill—the one she'd made to make redress to each and every man who had been enslaved aboard her ships.

"Look in your heart," Melissande replied. "The truth is there, whether you want to acknowledge it or not."

"You lie."

"I would not," Melissande insisted, without turning around. "To lie is to sin."

"And so is selling your lover into slavery," Christian said, in a deceptively mild tone. "Come now, Melissande—here is your chance to cast stones. Was it my brother, mayhap? Or did your father decide at the last minute that he might have made a better match for his only daughter?"

It was then that she rounded on him, her pulse thundering in her ears, her breathing shallow and rapid. "What if they were conspirators? Does that mean I was involved?"

Christian was as cool as if she hadn't spoken. "He was an ambitious man, was John Bradgate," he mused. "And his dear wife, Eleanora, aspired to great things as well. Did you know that she and James were lovers?"

Tears sprang to Melissande's eyes. Whatever she thought of her father at the moment, whatever she thought of his feckless wife, she had loved John Bradgate and it did her injury to hear that he had been cuckolded. "You are cruel!" she hissed.

Christian laughed, though there was no mirth in the sound. "Oh, she would never have married my brother. He had no gold, and she, of course, was a common whore. No, my beloved, James wanted you."

"Well, I didn't want him!"

"So it was true?" Again that deceptively gentle tone.

Melissande hugged herself, remembering James's attempts to kiss her after he'd pulled her down off the castle wall. She wished, not for the first time, that he'd left her to jump. "Yes!" she cried. "He asked me to marry him."

Christian's face was hard as granite. "I was right, then."

"No! I had no part in this plot, if there was one!"

"It seems impossible that there wasn't," Christian reasoned, his eyes cold, measuring. "And of course you would deny everything now, wouldn't you? Since there is no one present to refute what you say."

"I loved you more than any woman should love a man," Melissande said. She stood a little straighter, though her chin wobbled and she felt sure her eyes were glittering with tears. "That was before I learned how bitter and mean-spirited you are. It would appear that losing you was not the curse I took it to be, but a blessing instead."

"Go back to your painting, if you must linger. You exhaust me."

"I did not begin this conversation; you did." She would not break down. *Would not.* "If you don't like looking at me, hearing me, then close your eyes and stop up your ears."

Having so spoken, Melissande turned, with great dignity, and returned to her desk. With some difficulty, which she hoped was not apparent, she calmed herself and fixed all her powers of concentration upon the illumination waiting to be completed. The task soon absorbed her, and when she was too fatigued and too hungry to continue, she raised her eyes to find that Christian was sleeping once again.

Sister Domina arrived with bowls of rabbit and turnip stew for both Christian and Melissande, and inspected the slumbering patient with a sort of unnerved fascination.

"He is very tall, isn't he?" she whispered to Melissande.

Melissande smiled and accepted the offered bowl with both hands, moving to a window seat to take her meal. "Yes," she agreed. "And he is agile, a fine horseman, and an expert with the sword and lance."

Sister Domina set Christian's ration of food on the night table and stepped back quickly, as though expecting him to draw a broadsword from beneath his bedclothes and brandish it like a pirate or an executioner, severing heads.

Amused by her colleague's timid curiosity, Melissande hid a second smile behind a spoonful of the savory dish prepared in the Abbey's well-stocked kitchen. At that moment, beggars and poor villagers were gathering at the gates of the nunnery, there to be given a generous helping of that same delectable mixture. Most of the funds earned by the scribes of St. Bede's, through the copying and illuminating of secular manuscripts, went to feed and clothe the unfortunate, by Mother Erylis's own decree.

"Christian has ever been a tall man. Even as a boy, he towered over everyone else." She was remembering other things about Christian, too. How lonely he'd been. How often James had cuffed him, leaving bruises on his face.

"You have known him all your life?"

"His father and mine often did business together. Christian and his elder brother, James, the late Earl of Wellingsley, accompanied their sire to our house at Taftshead, and we spent summers in the village near one of their estates."

Sister Domina was still watching Christian warily, out of the corner of her eye, and she raised a hand to shield her words, lest they carry across the chamber to his ears. "He is most ill-tempered. When I brought him porridge, he flung the bowl at me."

"He is indeed ill-tempered," Melissande agreed sweetly, hoping that Christian was only pretending to sleep, and thus hearing every word. "And that is only one of his weaknesses."

Sister Domina, who had been at St. Bede's since she was a girl of thirteen, was an innocent of the first water. Her brown eyes went wide. "There are others?"

"Terrible ones," Melissande confided, in a whisper contrived to carry. "Christian has a great penchant for gaming, and for drink as well. And—" She paused, mostly for effect, before finishing with, "he has been known to make cuckolds of honorable men."

Sister Domina gasped and raised a hand to her mouth, though Melissande wasn't entirely certain that her friend even knew what a "cuckold" was. As the nun scurried outside, to avoid the company of sin, Melissande murmured a prayer for forgiveness.

Every word she'd said, at least where his "weaknesses" had been concerned, had been a lie, although she had no doubt that Christian, when he returned to Wellingsley as a free man, would have no trouble finding women to fawn over him. Indeed, he was now an earl, and rich in lands and manors if not florins, though even if he'd been a penniless troubadour, he would never lack for female companionship. Proper or otherwise.

"Stop pretending," she said, between bites of stew, still curled up on the window seat, with the light of midday washing, mullion-patterned, over her. "I know you're awake."

Christian dragged himself upright, reached for his stew, and sniffed at it critically. "You were deliberately baiting me," he accused, tucking into the food with encouraging appetite. "The devil has taken your tongue as well as your scruples, it would appear."

"I was jesting," Melissande said, refusing to take offense. "That poor woman believed you."

"Do you care what she—or anyone else for that matter—might think? You never did before."

"You are wrong," he said quietly. "I cared very much what you thought, at one time."

Melissande gave a long, weary sigh. "Can we not declare a truce?" she asked. "The Abbess has seen fit to ascribe your care to me. Must you make every moment that passes a torment?"

"You know nothing of torment," Christian retorted coldly.

There was no suitable response to that. What he said was true; Melissande had led a sheltered life. Her mother had died when she was yet a babe in arms, but her father, if he hadn't doted upon her, had been generous and fair. Although there had been no love lost between herself and Eleanora, his second wife, the two women had managed to be civil to each other. Melissande had been well educated by private tutors, hence her ability to paint and write, and she had never lacked for anything in all her life.

Until Christian Lithwell supposedly perished at sea, that is. When that news came to her, she had been undone by it, had wanted only to die and be finished with the never-ending pain.

"What will you do when you leave here?" she asked, in what she hoped was an idle tone, finishing her food and returning to the desk to take up a fresh brush. She had decided to use a rich chestnut brown, highlighted with traces of gold, for the Virgin's lovely, flowing hair.

"Return to Wellingsley," Christian replied bluntly, "and throw my brother's man Queech into the moat. If I don't decide to kill him first instead."

So much, Melissande thought, *for the customary period of mourning.*

Chapter Seven

A s he lay in his nunnery bed, watching Melissande paint, hurting in every muscle and bone and especially in the most secret regions of his heart, Christian felt his resolution of undying hatred beginning to slip. He clutched at it, the way a workhouse wretch might grasp a ragged blanket on a cold winter night, for the hostility he cherished toward this woman was his only defense. Without it, his very soul would be stripped naked, his every nerve exposed.

And yet he found himself thinking about kissing her and, inevitably, bedding her again. His manhood, having lain fallow for more than two years, rose hard against his belly at the thought.

He suppressed a groan, but not, it seemed, quickly enough.

Melissande looked up from her efforts. The afternoon sunlight transformed her into an angel, more beautiful than any illumination in any book of days. "What is it?"

"I want a bath," he said. It was true enough, though only a small part of what he truly desired. He would have Melissande administer that washing, would feel her deft, gentle hands on his flesh—flesh that had known no tender touch until he'd been brought to this Abbey and abandoned at a postern gate.

He still wondered who had carried him there, and why

they had done so, of course, but he was a long way from being able to physically seek the answers to those vexing mysteries, and he knew it. His left hand and right ankle both were splinted, and most of the rest of him was bound or bandaged. He would not be setting out on a quest of any kind in the near future.

"You want a bath," Melissande echoed, her cheeks turning a fetching shade of apricot pink. He noticed that her fingers trembled slightly as she dipped her paintbrush in some solvent, wiped it on a cloth, and laid it carefully aside.

"Yes," Christian replied. He'd nettled her, and it was the high point of his day.

So far.

"I'm sure Brother Nodger will be happy to oblige when next he comes to visit you."

"I don't wish to wait."

Melissande looked mildly exasperated for a moment, then recovered the placid countenance she had no doubt learned from the nuns. "Then you must practice self-denial," she said, in moderate tones. "Surely it will be to the benefit of your soul to wait."

He almost laughed. Here was the Melissande he'd known and loved—and trusted, God help him. The saucy, playful minx with a wickedly subtle tongue. "Mayhap it will be to the benefit of *your* soul to serve a poor, battered wayfarer in his time of greatest need. Rather like the Good Samaritan. Or even following the example of Our Lord, who washed the feet of the unworthy ones."

A small muscle twitched wildly at the base of her throat, and Christian felt her fury roar through the room like an unseen, silent storm, crackling with all the energy of an impending cloudburst. "Mayhap," she said carefully, for she knew as well as he did that Mother Erylis, bless her guileless and charitable heart, would see bathing a patient as a simple nursing task, rendered proper by its merciful nature.

Christian sighed contentedly. "I should like scented soap if you have it. And very warm water—yes, a great deal of that."

"You are insufferable!"

"I am also filthy, and most uncomfortable in my own company."

"There, sir, I can sympathize with you."

He smiled. Melissande, Melissande. How he had missed her, for all her perfidy. "Good," he said.

Melissande nearly overset her stool, so quickly did she rise from it. "I will see if Brother Nodger can visit," she said, "or perhaps send one of the novices to see to the task."

"Thank you," Christian replied melodiously.

"Despicable," Melissande muttered, but she went out, without a backward glance, to attend to her errand.

IT WAS AS Melissande had feared it would be.

"We cannot bother our brothers at the monastery with such a trivial request," the Abbess said flatly, when Melissande had begged audience with her and entered the small chamber from which St. Bede's was managed. "It was enough that we brought poor Brother Nodger over these terrible roads as many times as we have already done. You are Lithwell's nurse. It falls to you to minister to him."

Melissande felt a rush of damning pleasure, immediately followed by an equal share of abject horror. To lay back the blankets and see Christian's naked frame . . . to perform such an intimate service as washing him . . .

"I do not think I can, Mother," she said lamely.

"You must," replied the Abbess, without looking up from the papers on the plain table before her. "Now, leave me to my accounts, child. There is much work to do before Vespers."

Melissande took a hesitant step forward, another protest forming on her lips, saw the futility of it, and withdrew. In the kitchen, she asked that water be heated and taken to the infirmary, then fetched a basin, a cake of the Abbey's own soap, made with beeswax, and some cloths from the cupboards where such sundries were stored.

Then, telling herself she would steel herself against all feeling, sinful or otherwise, while she bathed Christian, she returned to his bedside. It would be a small offering in the cause of humility, she decided, penance for her unwitting part in the suffering of an untold number of galley slaves in general and Christian in particular.

Christian grinned when he saw the accoutrements of bathing. "I'm feeling better already," he said. "A bath will surely make a new man of me."

"You ask too much of mere soap and water," Melissande replied, in a taut tone. While Christian most certainly needed laundering, not to mention barbering, for his hair was matted and by now he'd sprouted a golden beard, she knew he was making the request mostly to irritate her. It was galling that she had no choice but to comply.

Two wide-eyed novices carried in wooden pails full of steaming water, plunked them down beside the bed without so much as glancing at the man resting upon it, and fled.

Christian chuckled and rubbed his bearded chin with his unsplinted hand. "God's blood, I must look worse than ever I dreamed."

Determined by then to make the best of a bad situation, Melissande filled the basin from one of the buckets, dipped the cloth, and began to lather it with the soap. "You are truly horrible to look upon," she lied. Her hand trembled only a little—she hoped—as she gingerly drew back Christian's blankets.

Her gaze went directly to his member, which throbbed against his belly like the tool of a stallion shut away with a mare. She blushed again and raised her eyes quickly to Christian's face.

As she'd feared, he'd noticed her lapse. He smiled, showing his sturdy white teeth.

Melissande pointedly raised the covers to his waist and moved the pillow behind his head, putting the basin in its place. She would wash the rest of him later.

Christian sighed and closed his eyes as she soaked his hair and began to cleanse it gently, lathering the soap between her hands. With some effort, the silken, pale gold locks came clean, and Melissande toweled his head with a damask cloth and replaced the pillow with a fresh one.

After that, it was easy. She felt a strange detachment and, at the same time, a sweet fascination with what she was doing. Tenderly, emptying and refilling the basin over and over again, Melissande scrubbed every inch of Christian's body, where it bore scrubbing. Then, deftly, without his rising from the bed, she exchanged the sour sheets for fresh ones and covered him again.

He looked like the old Christian, except that he was harder now, and of course far less trusting. He was but nineteen, but in those two years since his abduction, he had aged in more subtle ways than the sharper planes of his face and the guarded expression in his blue eyes.

"Thank you," he said, rather hoarsely.

Melissande could not reply. She merely nodded and began clearing away the clutter of buckets and discarded sheets. She had emptied the basin in the dooryard as she went along.

The bath marked the beginning of Christian's real recovery, or so it seemed to Melissande at least. He began to get out of bed and hobble about, supported by a crutch he'd improvised himself from a discarded broomstick. He sat for short periods in the garden, wearing a monk's robe and thin leather shoes borrowed from one of Brother Nodger's colleagues, and made Melissande bring him manuscripts from the Abbey's comprehensive library. These he devoured as eagerly, as hungrily, as he did his food and drink.

He and Melissande talked, but only of superficial, ordinary things, and although he was calm, even serene, she felt less like an erstwhile postulant and more like a harlot with every passing day. As the cuts on his lips healed and the swelling went down, she could only think of kissing him. When the splint was removed from his hand after a month, she yearned to be touched once more by those long, elegant fingers.

She finished the painting of the Annunciation and began a new illumination, with Mary Magdalene for a subject, and prayed without ceasing that all unseemly thoughts might be removed from her mind.

Then, at long last, a message arrived by courier, bearing the seal of the Bradgate Company. The notary respectfully found Melissande's "suggestions" unsuitable and, with regret, refused to honor them.

Chapter Eight

Melissande was in the garden, weeding the flower-beds, when the missive was brought to her. Christian, much mended now that a month had passed, sat upon the marble bench, his fine brow furrowed as he deciphered a volume of ancient poetry, translated from the Greek into French.

He watched, without comment, as Melissande rose from the dirt, dusted off the skirts of her habit, and accepted the leather pouch from Sister Annetta. Melissande felt nothing but anticipation as she broke the elaborate wax seal bearing her late father's personal insignia—he had always wanted a crest, she knew—and took out the heavy parchment page within.

Her sweet mood soon soured.

"How dare he flout my commands in such a manner?" Melissande burst out, flushing as she read the document through a second time. "Who does he think he is?"

Christian smiled. "No doubt the poor man believes himself to be the head, titular or otherwise, of the Bradgate Company."

"I shall disabuse him of that notion immediately," Melissande said, rolling up the parchment and waving it at Christian like a switch. "I mean to go to London and have Henry Renford *removed* from my employ!"

"Renford is by no means stupid," Christian pointed out reasonably, setting the manuscript carefully on the bench beside him before turning his complete attention to Melissande. "Your father surely made some stipulation that entitled him to take over the company in the event of just such a disaster as befell the Bradgate household."

Melissande sagged inwardly. Christian was right, of course—not that she liked him for it. Although John Bradgate had provided well for his daughter, he would never have left the management of his enterprise to a young woman. He had been too ruthless for that—how else could he have made slaves of free men? What other dreadful things had he done, in the making of his several fortunes?

"Sit down," Christian instructed, not unkindly, and made room for Melissande beside him. "It isn't so terrible as all that. I'm sure Renford has done a fine job of multiplying the loaves and fishes in your absence, Sister Pieta."

Melissande might have toppled Christian backward into a flowerbed if it hadn't been for the time and effort she had spent looking after him these past weeks. She glared at him, her hands on her hips, the rolled letter jutting out to one side like a spike. "And how many lives have been ruined in the process? How many spirits have been broken?"

Christian clearly knew she was referring to the galley slaves that provided power for her ships whenever they were becalmed. Which was often, she suspected.

"Do you care?"

"Of course I do. I was an innocent girl, Christian. I never knew how my father acquired his gold." She drew a deep breath and released it. "Believe me, I would sooner have begged in the streets than profited by the suffering of those hapless souls. And I will do exactly that before I allow the travesty to continue."

Christian's gaze was curious and a bit wary. "I think you're serious. You really mean to go to London."

"Did I not say so before?" Melissande asked, with no little

impatience. She glanced up at the sun, trying to gauge the approximate time. "I'm too late for today's coach," she said after a few moments, "but if I set out tomorrow, I should be in the offices of the Bradgate Company by week's end."

Grasping his crutch, Christian raised himself to his feet and stood swaying for a moment. His blue eyes were narrowed, his jawline tight. "You *will not* travel to London. The roads are not safe for women alone."

"I am going," Melissande said, folding her arms. "And I shan't be alone in any case. The coaches are always full."

"Yes. Full of blackguards, brigands, and rogues. And as likely to be set upon by highwaymen as not!"

Melissande carefully picked up the messenger's packet from where she'd dropped it, folded the parchment, and tucked it back inside. She watched Christian through her lashes as she spoke. "If you are so worried, then perhaps you should come with me."

"Oh, I will," Christian replied.

And thus it happened that, when the coach left Gilly the following afternoon, both Christian and Melissande were aboard it.

Christian was grimly silent and dressed in garments Melissande had paid for with Bradgate gold—fawn-colored breeches, a loose-fitting shirt, soft leather boots, and a belt sent to St. Bede's from the only shop in the village. She'd given him a dagger as well, though against her better judgment, because he'd insisted that they could not make such a journey without a means of defense.

Some injury had plainly been done to Christian's pride through all this, for he had not a farthing to call his own, having been stripped of everything but the clothes on his back when he'd been pressed into service aboard the *Eleanora*. Circumstances forced him to accept help from Melissande, but nothing could make him do so gracefully.

After bidding tearful farewells to Mother Erylis and the

other nuns at the Abbey, Melissande had donned the dark mourning gown she had been wearing when she'd first arrived, seeking solace in the arms of the Church, and a veil that could be drawn over her face should the need arise. They had walked the short distance to Gilly, Christian moving rapidly in spite of his crutch, to meet the coach in front of the public tavern, an unappealing establishment called the Rooster and Fiddle.

They had the carriage to themselves for the first leg of the trip, and Melissande was most grateful, since it was not only unbelievably small, but filthy in the bargain. The debris on the floor did not bear identification.

"You are aware," Christian said, once the coach was underway, jostling over the rutted road that led to the next village, "that when we get to London, you will be welcomed at the threshold of the Bradgate Company with protests of joy, given spiced wine and sweets, then guided quietly out from underfoot?"

"I will not be patronized," Melissande insisted, though in truth she wasn't so sure. She had no experience in business, after all—only the certainty that she did not want to draw her sustenance from the blood and sweat of other human beings. "After all, I am the legal heir."

"Don't be surprised if it isn't that simple," Christian said, with a sigh. Then he turned his head and gazed out at the lovely countryside. Or was he watching for bandits? Melissande noticed that his hand never strayed far from the hilt of the dagger in his belt.

All that afternoon, they traveled, stopping in one village for a change of horses, and then driving on to another, where they tarried again, to collect messages bound for other places. An enormously fat man, some sort of wandering friar by his dress, joined them there, and tried in vain to engage Christian in conversation. Melissande, forced to share Christian's seat or wedge herself between the friar and the wall of the coach, drew the veil over her face and kept her own counsel.

She and Christian might have been stitched together, for they were joined at the thigh, the shoulder, even the hip. The close proximity stirred still more wanton feelings in Melissande, who was heartily grateful that no one could know what she was going through. Unseemly dreams had begun to torment her nights, and she ached for the sensation of Christian's mouth on hers. It would be tentative at first, his kiss, and then more demanding . . .

She shivered and risked a sidelong glance at Christian, who was close enough to see her face through the veiling. He was smiling.

Chapter Nine

At nightfall, the cramped coach rattled to its final, and therefore most merciful, stop of the day, at a nameless inn set in the middle of a bleak and windswept moor. It was a desolate place, grim and seamy, and Melissande admitted to herself, if not to Christian, that she was glad she had not attempted the journey alone.

They ate roast quail and shared a cup of wine near the fire, keeping well away from the friar and the other patrons of the tavern, who looked a hard lot to Melissande.

The floor of the establishment was scattered with dirty straw, and more than once Melissande saw a small rodent scurry by, making a rustling sound as it passed. She shuddered to think of closing her eyes and sleeping in such a place, and yet she was incredibly weary. Though she was young and very strong, the coach ride had been a trying experience indeed.

When she had traveled from Taftshead to St. Bede's nearly two years before, Melissande had been accompanied by a sizable escort, and had slept comfortably each night in the homes of family and friends along the way. She had never seen the inside of such a place as this grim little inn, let alone stayed in one.

Christian, having finished his meal, stared contemplatively into the peat fire, idly cleaning his fingernails with the dagger at the same time. Melissande watched him for a while, through her veiling, and then turned her gaze to the friar, who had consumed a platter full of quail and more than one mug of ale during the course of the evening.

Finished at last, the holy man hoisted himself off the coarsely planed wooden bench at the trestle table where he'd taken his supper, emitted an enormous, rolling belch, and turned to lumber outside. After a few minutes, he returned, gave the innkeeper a coin for the use of a blanket, and made a bed for himself in the straw on the tavern floor.

Melissande shuddered slightly, and Christian chuckled.

"Don't worry, my lady. You shall not be asked to share your bed with the mice, although I daresay you might find me hardly less objectionable."

She stared at him through the veil. "What?" she whispered.

"You will have to sleep with me," Christian said easily, as though there were no impropriety in it.

Melissande blushed hotly, not so much because she was scandalized, but because she found the idea so wretchedly appealing. What was happening to her?

"I won't," she replied, in a firm whisper. "We are not wed, sir."

Christian raised one golden eyebrow, his fair hair gilded by the firelight, and she thought she saw his fine lips twitch with quickly curbed mirth. "No," he said. "But I have no intention of sitting up all night long, and the only way we're going to get a bed in this place is by sharing one."

"We could each have our own."

"Do you truly want even so much as a wall between us? Here?"

Melissande bit her lower lip, hesitating even though she knew there was no need to deliberate over the answer. She wanted Christian and his steel-bladed dagger, close enough to touch.

In a manner of speaking.

"No," she said, at long last. As accepting garments and a blade from her had stung Christian's pride, this admission stung hers.

With an exaggerated sigh that said she should have simply listened to him in the first place, instead of dragging the whole thing out, Christian got to his feet and, using the crutch, hobbled over to speak with the innkeeper. A few moments later, they were shown into a room beneath the stairs.

Almost every inch of space was taken up by a hammock-like bed, fashioned of rope and slung between the slanting wall and the straight one. There was one musty blanket and a window that would not open, and Melissande would sooner have slept in the stables, but she was not about to complain. She was sure to face greater challenges than this when she reached London, and set about putting the Bradgate Company to rights.

"You'd better lie down first," Christian said. "I want to be on the outside, nearest the door."

Melissande removed her veils and nothing else and scrambled awkwardly onto the swaying berth, slamming her head and one shoulder hard against the wall before the thing stopped swinging. There was no light in the room, but for the moon glow gleaming at the dirty little window, but she saw the flash of Christian's teeth as he grinned at her dilemma.

"It's quite comfortable," she lied, to spite him.

He did not reply, but simply rested the crutch against the wall, laid the dagger on the windowsill, where it was within easy reach, and joined her. His weight and warmth awakened all the sensations Melissande had been trying, by force of will, to suppress.

After spreading the blanket over them both, he gave a great, lusty sigh and turned onto his side, causing Melissande to roll into him.

It was like lying against a rock wall, impervious and yet warmed through and through by the summer sun.

Melissande gasped.

"Is something wrong?" Christian asked. The innocence in his voice was a mockery; he knew full well what was wrong.

Melissande heartily wished she believed in violence, because then she could have slapped him across the face. As it was, she could do nothing. "No," she said. "I am quite all right."

"You're trembling. Are you cold?"

"No," Melissande said. A truth, for indeed she was fevered, ready to fling off the blanket. Feelings stirred and awakened in hidden parts of her, and her heart pounded. She hoped Christian hadn't noticed how swift and shallow her breathing was. "I'm—I'm quite warm."

"So am I."

Melissande did not know what to say to that.

Christian draped his left arm, no longer splinted but still supported by a sling, over her side. Their foreheads touched, and she felt his breath on her face. Softly, briefly, he brushed his mouth over hers.

"I used to dream of lying beside you like this when I was aboard the galley," he said presently, in a low, husky voice.

Melissande knew she should pull away from his embrace, but she couldn't make herself do it. "I thought you hated me."

"Oh, I did—when I was awake."

She wanted to weep for what he'd suffered, but of course it would do no good now. Mayhap, by setting the other galley slaves free, she might in some small measure make restitution to Christian as well. "And do you hate me now?"

"I'm not sure," he said.

Melissande was glad he could not see her face, for then he would surely have guessed that his words had wounded her sorely. She'd known he could not love her, of course, but she'd hoped that, in the time they had spent together, Christian had come to know her for the person she was, and to trust her just a little.

When she did not speak, he took her chin gently in his hand and, with a low groan, turned her head and kissed her.

Melissande felt a thrill so sharp it was almost painful, and responded with all the eagerness of her relative innocence. In those moments, she forgot the bitterness that lay between her and Christian, the distrust and sorrow and cold fury. All that mattered, all that existed, was the love that had never died.

Christian was breathless when at last he drew back. "God forgive me," he muttered, and then he kissed Melissande again, even more passionately. If she had not been lost before, she surely was by then; her young body arched against his, seeking a union she did not fully comprehend, even after that other experience, and her soul was torn asunder by the force of her longing, like a tree struck by lightning.

Presently, Christian kissed and nibbled his way down Melissande's neck to the upper swell of her small, firm breasts. He untied the laces of her bodice with his teeth and when she was bared to him, took a nipple boldly into his mouth.

Melissande cried out softly, stunned by this fresh intensity of sensation. Her hands found their way into Christian's soft, shaggy hair, and buried themselves there, pressing him closer.

He suckled and tongued and nipped at her with his teeth, and within a few minutes, Melissande was delirious with the need to be joined to him. He raised her skirts to her waist—she was wearing nothing but a chemise beneath—and then shifted, setting her astride him. Her well-tended breasts spilled out of the open bodice of the gown and her hair was a wild tangle down her back and over her shoulders and arms.

"If you would refuse me, my lady," Christian warned hoarsely, "do so now."

Melissande moved upon him in silent reply, seeking to take him inside her.

He found the warm, moist entrance to her body and thrust hard, wringing a gasp from her.

"Have I hurt you?" he asked, sounding stricken.

She had forgotten how large he was, how he filled her, and there was pain, but there could be no turning back for Melissande. Instinctively, she began to raise and lower herself upon Christian's staff, and soon they were both caught up in a rising storm of passion.

Chapter Ten

Long after Melissande had fallen asleep in his embrace, Christian lay awake, pondering what had happened between them that night, upon a rope bed in a rude country inn. They might have been Adam and Eve, tumbling happily together in the Garden, before the Fall from Grace, so purely and so beautifully had they loved each other.

He twined a silken tress of her hair idly around one finger as he reflected; she stirred and snuggled against him with a contented little sigh, her head resting lightly on his shoulder.

She had betrayed him, he reminded himself, as surely as Judas had betrayed the Christ. Why then did he feel this extraordinary tenderness toward Melissande, this passion?

She denied having ordered his kidnapping, of course. And Christian supposed it was possible that she was telling the truth. Though always intelligent, Melissande had never been particularly practical, and she might very well have signed the order for his captivity without knowing what it was. In those days her father and Eleanora had been putting all manner of documents before her, requesting her signature, and it would be like that Melissande of yore, youthful and full of trust, to endorse some official-looking missive without reading its contents.

Christian told himself he was dancing with shadows. She had wanted to be rid of him, so that she could marry James and become the Countess of Wellingsley. Now that he was, for all practical intents and purposes, the heir to his brother's estates and rickety fortune, she had set out to snare him.

The idea filled Christian with rage, for he wanted so much to believe in her. He dared not give in, of course. Trusting Melissande, letting her hold his heart in her hands, would make him a prisoner again, as surely as if he'd been bound and shackled and taken back aboard the *Eleanora* to serve at the oars. No, he would take his pleasures with Melissande— she owed him that much after what she'd done—but allowing himself to truly care for her again was out of the question.

He might just as well have taken an asp to his breast.

She opened her wonderful eyes and blinked, yawning a little. "Christian?"

"I'm here," he said, and the tenderness in his voice was not entirely feigned. He would have to work on his emotions, he decided. Put them right, lest he fall into a second trap and find himself shorn, like Sampson, with the walls and pillars and roof of some temple crashing down upon his head.

She wriggled against his side, and he remembered how she had ridden him, in the night, with all the abandon of a maiden racing across a meadow upon a palfrey's back. The recollection made him hard again, but he did not turn Melissande onto her back and enter her as he might have done with a whore or a mistress. She was not a practiced lover, and she would be sore for a day or so.

He should have known that, but jealousy and fear had ruled his thoughts.

During the five and twenty months of his imprisonment, the worst torture of all had been imagining Melissande in James's bed, willingly giving herself up to the man who had made her a countess. He had pictured them laughing together over the clever and lasting way they'd dispensed with him, and had been convinced that they were proud of their treachery.

But now he knew that James, along with Bradgate himself and his wife, Eleanora, was dead these two years. And on top of that, Melissande had spent the intervening time in St. Bede's Abbey, doing her best to persuade Mother Erylis to allow her to take final vows as a bride of Christ.

What did it all mean? Had he been wrong about Melissande—wrong about his brother and prospective father-in-law? And if James was dead, why had Queech come to kill him, Christian?

In the darkness, Christian shook his head. He had learned a number of things during his time in the belly of hell, and the foremost lesson was that no one can be trusted. Brothers, future wives, friends—all could be persuaded to sell out if the price was high enough.

Christian willed himself not to weep for the loss of the woman he'd once believed Melissande to be. Better to remember, every moment of every night and every day, that for all her pretty ways and sweet, fiery passions, she had the heart and soul of a cobra.

MELISSANDE AWAKENED IN time for Matins even though they were far from the Abbey by that time. Christian lay beside her in the hammock bed, nay, half wrapped around her, one leg flung over hers, his slinged arm resting across her shoulder. His breathing was deep, rhythmic, and even.

She nudged him. "Christian?"

"Arr-ugg," he said, his thick lashes fluttering as he opened his eyes halfway. "Whaaa?"

"The coach will be leaving soon."

"The coach is leaving in five hours," he pointed out, none too charitably. "Go back to sleep, Melissande."

"I want to talk."

"Fine. Talk to yourself. Silently."

"You made love to me tonight." She said the words matter-of-factly. "Or were you just relieving yourself, the way you might with a tavern wench or some poor servant girl?"

"I don't make a practice of 'relieving myself' with 'poor servant girls,'" he replied. "I took you because I wanted you."

She stiffened. "And that, by your lights, was reason enough?"

"Don't put words in my mouth. I didn't hear a breath of protest from you, if I may be so rude as to point out the fact."

"What if I'd refused you?"

"I would not have pressed the argument. Again, may I say that you *didn't* protest?"

"What are you going to do, when we get to London? Will you abandon me there?"

Christian sighed. "I have business of my own to conduct. The Wellingsley estates are mine, and I want them."

"You will wish to marry and produce at least one heir."

"Yes. No doubt I will."

"You will be wedded to someone you do not love?"

"I no longer believe in love," Christian replied. "And all I truly know about the woman I shall marry is this: She will not be anything like you, Melissande Bradgate."

Chapter Eleven

The rest of the journey, three days and nights, was made, stitch and fiber, of the same fabric as that first evening upon the road. Each night, Melissande and Christian shared a bed in some tawdry inn peopled with thugs and scoundrels, and each night they made love.

Melissande had no illusions that Christian's feelings toward her had changed, although he was unfailingly tender when they were alone. She supposed he wanted her because he was starved for the attentions of a woman. Her reason for surrender was equally simple: She knew that, in all her days, she would never love again. She was trying to store enough memories to sustain her for a lifetime.

On the fourth day of traveling, Melissande and Christian at last reached the bustling city of London, standing staunchly, brashly on the banks of the River Thames, its all but impervious White Tower looming tall against the sky.

London was a noisy, dirty city, and yet Melissande felt a rush of excitement as she looked out at it through the coach window. If she could not have Christian, there was still her business. She would turn all her energies to making the company thrive in a just and honorable way.

At a tavern in the center of town, they disembarked from the muddy coach and hired another conveyance, a cart drawn by two gray mules, to carry them to the offices of the Bradgate Company.

At least Melissande was carried. Christian insisted on limping along beside the cart, making his way between piles of manure and puddles of mingled rainwater and sewage. He was, by Melissande's reckoning, the stubbornest, proudest man in all creation, and yet she loved him beyond all sense and reason.

To say the occupants of the two-story wooden frame building on Carstairs Street were surprised to see Melissande, let alone Christian Lithwell, would be an understatement of the gravest proportions. An immediate and thunderous silence descended upon the Bradgate Company as the new arrivals stepped into the room full of high, slanted desks where the clerks and bookkeepers plied their trades.

Henry Renford, left in charge of the business after John Bradgate died, came out of the inner offices straight away, smoothing his expensive green-velvet doublet and looking quite annoyed at the interruption. He was a slender man with bulging eyes and an oily thatch of brown hair. His gaze scooted over Melissande to rest, with rising horror, upon the unreadable face of Christian Lithwell.

"Well," he said, and that single word tolled through the room like the dolorous peal of a funeral bell. He cleared his throat and nodded abruptly at Melissande. "Demoiselle." Another nod for Christian. "My lord."

Melissande felt Christian shift restlessly beside her. Did he sense, as she did, that her late father's man of business was not only irritated by their unexpected appearance but frightened as well? No doubt Renford had known of her father's plot to dispose of Christian—if indeed there had been a plot.

"My lady," Christian said, in tones at once dulcet and dripping with acid, giving a little bow in her direction to indicate that Melissande would do the talking.

Melissande was certainly nervous, but the power of her convictions spurred her forward. Blushing, she swallowed hard, folded her arms as she had seen the Abbess do in times of stress, and raised her chin. "Your services will not be required after today," she told Renford bluntly. "I mean to manage the company myself."

A nervous twitter moved through the rank and file.

The little man made a sound that was at once a snuffle and a snort. "I beg your pardon?" he said, but the glint in his bird-bright eyes told Melissande he'd understood her perfectly.

"You will gather your things and leave this establishment before the close of today's business," she said, more confident than she might have been otherwise because Christian was beside her. "I have no need of you."

The twitter gave way to a stunned, vibrant silence that throbbed through the cold but spacious room. The clerks bent their heads over ledger pages and piles of gold coins, not daring to look but plainly hearing every word that passed between Melissande and Renford. And wondering, no doubt, if they too were to be turned out into the streets.

"This is an outrage," Renford said coldly, "and I shall not abide it. Your esteemed father left *me* in charge of this enterprise, knowing full well that a fey girl could never manage anything so complex and far-reaching. I have papers to prove my assertions, signed by Bradgate's own hand and duly witnessed!"

"Mayhap you have," Melissande agreed, with a smoothness she surely didn't feel. "Alas, I have his will and testament, making me the owner of all his holdings. Indeed"—she did not dare to glance at Christian when she went on—"indeed, some of Father's trading vessels were legally transferred to my possession even before he died."

Color rose in Renford's jowly cheeks, but he did an admirable job of restraining his temper. "May I remind you, Demoiselle, that I was appointed your guardian and given full control of all the company's various interests until such a time as Lord James or myself deemed you ready to manage such a vast enterprise?" His gaze shifted uneasily to Christian. "Unless you mean to marry, of course." This last was barely audible, so quietly did he utter the words.

Christian smiled winningly. "And here I am, a sea-going Lazarus, roused from my watery grave. I might offer myself as a bridegroom at any moment, who knows?"

Renford paled slightly, and Melissande felt a surge of hope rise within her. Of course Christian wasn't about to marry her, for all their lovemaking on the road to London. He'd said as much, straightout. Still, Renford didn't know how things stood between the Bradgate heiress and her erstwhile beloved, and it was obvious that his confidence was shaken.

He directed his next words to Christian, ignoring his remarks of a moment before. "I fear I have ill tidings to relay to you, my lord. Your brother, James, has perished of the plague."

"Yes," Christian said, "I know. I mean to ride to Wellingsley, once my lady and I have concluded our business with you, to take over my inheritance."

"You'll find things in a sorry state," Renford observed. He did not sound overly sorrowful. "Walls crumbling, roofs fallen in, servants and vassals gone to find other lords to serve."

"I shall relish the task of setting my holdings to rights," Christian said, undaunted. His hand cupped Melissande's elbow, in ever so loose a grasp. "Mayhap I will be wedded soon, and have a wife and the prospect of babes to spur me on to greater effort."

Renford's face had gone from red to a pale shade of purple.

"You must sit down, Mr. Renford," Melissande said, genuinely concerned, dragging over a stool for the notary. "You appear to be unwell."

He sagged onto it, wrenching a lace-trimmed kerchief from the wide, slashed sleeve of his doublet and blotting his gleaming forehead. "Do you mean to marry Christian Lithwell?" he asked of Melissande, in a plaintive tone, as if they were alone in the room.

"No," Melissande replied, folding her arms. "I fear my lord will not have me to wife, for he thinks me untrustworthy. Nevertheless, I shall have my business back, even if I have to rouse some tavern lout from his cups and drag him before a priest to accomplish it."

Christian gave no word of protest, which was a disappointment in and of itself.

Melissande was, to a degree, bluffing. She did not wish to wed anyone other than her own Christian, of course, but she was too proud to admit as much in his presence. How much better, and fairer, it would be if she could simply *inherit,* being her father's sole living heir. Had she been male, there would have been no difficulty; as it was, she might have to take Renford to law in order to rid herself of him.

"You will force me to approach the magistrates?" she asked, when Renford held his tongue.

The notary started to smile, glanced at Christian, and apparently thought better of it. "Demoiselle Bradgate—" he began, in an unctuous tone that was somehow even more insulting than his patent refusal to recognize her right to manage her own holdings.

Christian slipped his good arm around Melissande's waist, sending an embarrassing thrill shooting through her, scattering its fire like a star tumbling from the night sky. "Melissande was quite wrong earlier," he said. "I would gladly take her to wife, if she will accept my suit."

Melissande gaped up at Christian, astonished and unable to hide the fact. What was he saying? Was this a jest, some cruel trickery meant to raise her hopes so that he might have the pleasure of dashing them?

"Will you?" he asked, looking down into her shock-widened eyes, his own expression as inscrutable as ever. "Be my lady, I mean?"

She swallowed. Her mind was reeling, skeptical and wary; it was her heart, her impulsive, dreamer's heart, that caused her to speak as she did.

"I will," she said.

Chapter Twelve

Some hours after the confrontation in the offices of the Bradgate Company, Christian and Melissande set off for her home at Taftshead, a thriving village just outside London. Upon their arrival, while Melissande was hurrying through the rooms, quietly exulting in being home again, Christian pondered what he had done in offering marriage to the very woman who had probably consigned him to hell.

What, exactly, had prompted him to do something so rash?

It could not have been their lovemaking, though God and the angels knew lying with Melissande Bradgate, bless her treacherous little heart, had proven to be the sweetest aspect of his recent resurrection.

Once, of course, he had loved her, but he had changed, hardened toward her and, for that matter, toward all humanity. No, he had claimed Melissande because he needed, even craved, the fiery solace she offered. And he supposed he had proposed marriage because it would take a great deal of gold to make the estates James had put to ruin to pay their way again.

He shoved his unsplinted hand through his hair. A long time ago, when he'd been able to afford the luxury, Christian had subscribed to more elegant principles. Now he knew all too well that only fools married for love, and yet it troubled him, this stark and cold decision he had made.

He sighed. He would be kind to Melissande, in his fashion. He would sire children on her—daughters, he hoped, as well as sons. Once the nursery was filled, however, Christian meant to take a mistress, mayhap two, and never lie with his lady wife again. A heart could be disciplined, schooled, just as a sword arm could, or a fine horse.

No one knew that better than he did.

"Why are you doing this?" a familiar male voice demanded.

Christian turned from the window, where he'd been gazing out at the neglected grounds of Melissande's home, to see Henry Renford standing in the doorway. So he'd followed them here, then, instead of taking his leave from the company in a timely and dignified manner.

Not surprising, really.

"I hope you don't mean to beg," Christian said. "That would be most disconcerting in a man of your stature."

Renford flushed. He was wearing a cape over the same doublet and hose he'd had on when Christian and Melissande paid their fateful visit in London, and his hat, which sported a sweeping feather, was askew. "Do not flatter yourself, you penniless, landless galley slave—"

Christian suppressed an urge to strangle the man and leaned back against the wall, his arms folded indolently. "You were in it, then, as I suspected. Along with Melissande's father and the others."

"The others?" Renford gave a snort of derisive laughter. "I might have been privy to a secret or two. I will say, Lord Wellingsley, that your late brother and his man Queech were the instigators."

"I should kill you." Christian spoke calmly, because he knew that was more frightening, more unnerving, than a shout.

Renford retreated half a step. "You can't prove any of it."

Christian studied his fingernails speculatively. "I think I could," he mused. He studied the man through narrowed eyes, but decided not to pursue the point further. Yet. Privately, though, he had concluded that there was someone who knew the truth, someone who might be persuaded to tell. The person who had carried him to St. Bede's after his latest beating.

"Bradgate believed you had cuckolded him, with the Lady Eleanora." Renford was red again, though he spoke coldly.

Christian felt a muscle tighten painfully in his jaw and willed it to go slack. Eleanora had wanted him for a lover, it was true, but he'd turned aside her approaches and said nothing of them, adoring Melissande as he had. "Well, he was mistaken," he replied at last.

"You do not care for John Bradgate's daughter, sir," Renford accused, in a low hiss, "and I shall tell her so if you force me to it. You want her gold, as your brother did, and naught else."

"I want a great deal else," Christian said.

"You are aware that she was probably one of your betrayers?"

For a moment, Christian could not speak. When he did, his voice was a lethal rasp. "Will you prattle now of love, Renford? Since when are noble marriages made on the basis of so fatuous an emotion? The union will serve us both well."

"It will serve *you* well, methinks. I am not so sure about the Lady Melissande."

"As if you gave a damn. You're only interested in saving your own hide." Christian drew in a deep breath, let it out in a long, weary sigh.

"While your motives are purely altruistic, of course."

Christian smiled. "Of course," he said. Then he took Renford forcibly by the arm, led him to the front door, opened it, and thrust him over the threshold and onto the marble steps. "I bid you good eventide, sir."

MELISSANDE PAUSED ON the stairs, her heart thumping in her throat. She told herself not to be silly, that she'd *known* Christian wasn't marrying her because he loved her. All the same, she'd cherished the fantasy, and now that she'd over-heard the conversation between Renford and the man who would have been her lord and husband, she could no longer pretend.

She descended to the entry hall, trying hard to keep her determined smile from slipping. "Once I've engaged a staff of servants," she said to Christian, who was looking at her with a slight frown creasing his brow, "I should be quite safe and comfortable in this house."

"What is the matter, Melissande?" Christian asked. He must have guessed that she'd heard him speaking with Mr. Renford, and that made it hurt all the more, the knowledge that he thought her so tractable, so weak, that she would still marry him when he had done everything but slap her across the face with the truth.

"I think I don't fancy being wed on the morrow after all," she blurted out. "Or ever."

Christian took a step toward her. "Melissande, listen to me—"

Humiliating tears had sprung to her eyes; she dashed them away angrily with the back of one hand. "Damn you, Christian," she whispered. "You wanted to hurt me—you wanted revenge. Well, you've certainly triumphed. Are you satisfied?"

He caught hold of her elbow when she would have turned and fled up the stairs, holding her fast. "If you do not marry me," he said quietly, evenly, "you will not have control of your galleys. Slaves will continue to squire them over the seas, giving their life's blood to fill your coffers with gold!"

Melissande felt as though he had struck her. Until that moment, she had half expected some reassurance, some protest that she had misunderstood the exchange between him and Renford. She jerked her arm free. "I shall free those men if I have to set fire to the ships myself," she vowed, in a tone that chilled her own heart and, by the look of him, Christian's as well. "And I will burn with them before I share a bed and a name with the likes of *you*, Christian Lithwell, eighth Earl of Wellingsley!" With that, she spat full in his face, turned on one heel, and stormed out of the house.

Wisely, Christian did not follow.

WELLINGSLEY CASTLE, CHRISTIAN'S nearest holding, was a long ride from Taftshead, and he had neither horse nor gold to buy one. He took himself to the village tavern—a man could oft have an ale in such a place, in return for the telling of tales, and he had those in abundance.

He had barely entered when he was approached by an old friend—Robert, once his servant.

Robert's greatest strength, besides a certain physical prowess, lay in his steadfast and worthy nature, not a comely face. There were several new gaps between his teeth as he stood in front of Christian's table, beaming. "You've recovered, then," he said.

Christian gestured for Robert to join him. He remembered now, for the blood-red haze that had fogged his mind parted suddenly, and Christian knew that this was the man who had saved him after Queech and his men were through mashing him into the broken cobblestones of a London alley.

"You," he said.

Robert nodded, looking sorrowful as he took the bench across from Christian and signaled for an ale. Unlike his former master, he had coin to spend.

"It grieved me no little bit to see them beat you that way, Chris," Robert murmured, "but if I'd spoke up they'd have killed the both of us. So I let them have their way and came back for you when they was finished."

The cold and pain and fear and fury of that night echoed

through Christian's spirit. "You did what you could. I'm grateful, Robert."

Robert ducked his head for a moment. He was unaccustomed to praise, as were most men of his station. "I couldn't let you die, sir. You've always been good to me. I brought you to St. Bede's because I knew 'twas a good place, with your lady there."

Christian reached across the table to slap Robert's shoulder affectionately. "Tell me why Queech wanted to put an end to me. James couldn't have sent him that time—being already dead."

The ale was brought; Robert noticed that his companion had no cup and ordered a second mug. "He figured you might escape or get free some other way, and come cut his throat."

"I still might."

Robert shook his head. "He's gone, is Queech. Stole what little Lord James had left, after the plague came to Wellingsley Castle, and took to his heels."

"But it was James and Bradgate who had me enslaved, wasn't it? With some help from a certain lovely lady."

Robert looked grim. "A lady, sir? Well, I wouldn't have called Dame Eleanora 'lovely,' given the evil she had in her—"

"I meant the Demoiselle," Christian said. "Melissande."

"Your own lady love, my lord?" Robert was pale with shock. "You can't think she'd do such a vile and craven thing! Why, she grieved herself near to death after word came that your ship had been sunk before it reached the coast of Eire."

Christian's ale arrived, and he drank deeply, his gaze fixed on the fire in the grate, saying nothing. Robert sat comfortably across from him, waiting.

After a while, Christian began to talk, slowly, thoughtfully, laying plans.

The hour was late when Christian, having said good night to his friend and made arrangements to meet with him in the morning, returned to the dark house where Melissande slept. Much had gone awry between them, and he was still not wholly convinced of her innocence in the matter of his enslavement, but he could not bring himself to leave her alone and unguarded. He well knew, did Christian Lithwell, heir apparent to a largely meaningless title and a handful of rubble piles scattered over half of England, that the world was indeed a perilous place.

Chapter Thirteen

The morning after her arrival at Taftshead, while going through the papers secreted away in a special compartment of her father's desk, Melissande found the poems. Apparently, John Bradgate had been telling the truth when he'd claimed, long ago, that only she knew about the hiding place.

The verses were passionate, heartfelt avowals of love, and they had been written in Eleanora's compact, rounded hand. Christian Lithwell was the subject of every one.

Feeling the color seep out of her face, Melissande sagged into the chair. The poetry revealed Eleanora's passion, then her growing spite. Christian, it seemed, had never returned her sentiments, and over time she had grown angry with him, and sworn to take vengeance. Melissande had never guessed that such a drama was unfolding under her very nose, but her father had known. Oh, yes, he'd known, all right—or he wouldn't have appropriated the poems and tucked them away for safekeeping.

Mayhap Bradgate had meant to blackmail his errant wife with them—they could be construed as adultery, which made them grounds for a termination of the marriage contract. A divorce, thus sanctioned, would of course have freed Melissande's father to remarry immediately, and attempt to sire a male heir by another woman.

Melissande settled back in her chair, deeply troubled. It had probably been Eleanora, or even John, who had arranged for Christian to be pressed into service aboard one of the company's merchant galleys—with Lord James's complicity, of course. She hadn't wanted to believe it before, when Christian had raised the idea, but there were no other viable explanations.

"My lady?" Even his voice had the power to startle her.

She looked up quickly, rubbing one temple in the vain hope of assuaging an impending headache. Christian loomed in the doorway, unshaven and rumpled. He'd slept on a pallet in the upstairs passage the night before, the dagger she'd bought for him clasped in his good hand, and when she'd awakened him and rather rudely insisted that he leave, he had refused.

"Yes?"

"If I may borrow a horse, I shall ride to Wellingsley Castle today."

Melissande swallowed. "Eleanora loved you," she said, raising the sheaf of awkward, oversentimental poems in one hand, as an exhibit. "Why didn't you tell me?"

"She was misguided," Christian replied. He came no closer, but neither did he retreat. "I did not tell you because I did not want to make matters worse between you and your stepmother."

"You were right," she said simply. "It was my father, with Eleanora and James urging him on, both for their own reasons. They wanted you to disappear."

Christian's jawline tightened almost imperceptibly, and his dark-blue gaze fell to the papers in her hand. "What do you have there that would prompt such an admission?"

"My stepmother's very soul," Melissande said sadly, handing the poems over to him when he crossed the room to stand before the desk. "Why are you so certain that *I* was the one who had betrayed you, Christian? Is it because that is the worst thing that could happen, and you want to be prepared for it?"

He tossed the poetry onto the surface of the desk. "You forget, Melissande, that your signature graced the letter instructing the *Eleanora*'s captain to make a prisoner of me."

Melissande felt a sharp, sour rush of shame. "Mayhap I did sign that damnable decree, thinking it was some innocent document. I took other people's word for truth in so many things back then."

"I have no doubt that you did," Christian said. "Now, will you lend me a horse, or not?" She knew he would have preferred supping on hot coals from the grate to asking.

"Yes," she answered, hiding the hurt he'd done her behind an expressionless face as she took a pouch from her belt and tossed it, so that it landed on the desk in front of him. "You may serve as my agent, if you will, and buy a proper steed to carry you to Wellingsley. When you have settled yourself there, and purchased horses of your own, you may send the creature back to me."

"Melissande—"

"Just leave, Christian. Take the gold and get out."

He looked at the pouch as though it would sear his hand, should he cause himself to touch it. His eyes revealed some deep, nameless emotion as he looked at Melissande.

"I cannot abandon you here, unguarded," he said, after a long and awkward interval of silence had fallen. "Come with me, I pray you."

Melissande looked away, not wanting Christian to see how much she longed, even in the face of his contempt and mistrust, to travel at his side, to be his helpmate and true wife. "I did not sell you into slavery," she said softly. "I thought you were dead."

Christian's voice was hoarse as he looked away. "I know that," he said. "But I have changed, Melissande. I have lived as an animal for too long—I no longer have a heart or a soul, and I would make you no fit husband without those things."

"Perhaps, then," Melissande said quietly, willing herself not to dissolve in grief before his very eyes, "we can be partners."

Christian met her gaze, his eyes narrowed again. "What are you saying?"

"Even if I manage to wrest the company from Renford's hands, I cannot run the enterprise properly without your help," she replied. "Not until I've had time to amass some experience. I will sign over half of everything I own to you. All I ask in return is that you serve as my adviser and steward."

He stared at her, stunned. "You have changed your mind, then, and decided to marry me after all?"

Melissande shook her head. "No," she said. "I would not wed you now unless you came to me on bended knee and swore your love and devotion by all that is on earth and all that is in heaven. What I propose is strictly a practical alliance, and nothing more."

Christian dragged up a chair and sank into it, utterly silent.

Chapter Fourteen

Christian and Melissande set out together, the following morning, mounted on newly purchased geldings and bound for Wellingsley Castle, which stood a half-day's ride from the village of Taftshead. Christian said little along the way, except to Robert, his friend, who accompanied them, and Melissande wondered what he was thinking, though she would not have inquired to save herself from the hottest fires of hell. Love Christian though she did, she was through groveling and weeping over a man who did not care for her in return.

Her mind was busy, in any case, as they traveled through the gentle countryside, with its sheep-cropped pastures and broad forests of oak. If she failed to wrest control of the Bradgate Company from Renford's grasping fists, so be it; she would never lack for gold or anything else she needed. But she would not know true peace until she had freed the galley slaves who labored under flags bearing the colors her father had adopted. What she didn't know was exactly how to go about accomplishing this worthy aim—she was only one woman, after all, and a small one at that. Though she'd vowed to Christian to burn the ships herself if need be, that had been mostly bravado, for Melissande couldn't begin to guess how one set about making a ship burn. For one thing, there were bound to be people aboard, the very slaves she wished to save. For another, the crew wasn't likely to stand idly about while she, who had trouble getting a brazier lighted, tried repeatedly to fan a blaze from a spark.

No, she must have help to achieve her purpose, and the logical choice was Christian. He, knowing the plight of those men as few others could, surely would be willing to lend a hand.

At midday, the little party reached the largest of Christian's holdings, and was greeted on the creaking drawbridge by a few faithful retainers, a slat-ribbed hound, and a pack of filthy children. One of the men stepped forward, his eyes wide, and then gave a great wailing cry that might have been rooted in either joy or sorrow. He grasped at Christian's wounded leg.

Robert, mounted on one of the fine new horses, beamed down on the scene, as though he'd been in some way responsible for bringing the reunion about.

"My lord Christian!" the elderly retainer sobbed. "It is a miracle—the Virgin has heard our prayers and sent you back to us—"

"Hello, Willy," Christian said, very quietly.

"We've had naught to eat in many a day, my lord," Willy babbled. "Our stores are empty, and what few crops we was able to plant were ridden down by knaves—"

Christian loosed the bag of provisions, bread and dried meat and a bit of cheese purchased that morning in Taftshead, from his saddle horn. He tossed the food to Willy, who scrabbled to open the bag, while all the children rushed forward.

"Why did you stay?" Christian asked, watching with abject sorrow in his eyes as Willy and the others ate. Melissande took some cheese from the pocket of her gown and threw it to the hound.

"We had nowhere else to go, my lord," Willy said, speaking around a mouthful of coarse brown bread.

"Have a care," Melissande put in quietly. "You'll make yourselves sick if you eat too fast."

"What of Queech, my brother's man?" Christian inquired, his face tightening. "Has he returned?"

Willy spat in the dirt. "Gone to hell, I hope," he murmured. "And may the devil roast his toes like chestnuts!"

With that, the servant grasped the bridle of Christian's mount and led the animal through the open gates and into the outer bailey. No more would be said of Queech, at least in Melissande's hearing.

Wellingsley, once one of the finest castles in England, was in a state of total disrepair. There were no chickens or geese in evidence, of course, and certainly no swine or cattle. The granaries were empty, as were the wine cellars and the dairy.

It was only when they reached the great doors of the keep itself that Willy took any notice at all of Melissande, and then he said exactly the wrong thing. As he was helping her down from her mare's back, he looked into her face and blurted, "Why it's you, the same lass as tried to hurl herself from the southern parapet—"

Melissande flushed—she was not proud of that episode and had not wished to remind Christian of it. All hope that he had not taken note of Willy's words was quickly dashed, however.

He turned a sharp glance in her direction and took her arm in a firm hold. "See to the horses, Willy," he said, for command clearly came easily to him. Then, when the servant took the reins of both mounts and led them off toward the stable, Christian hustled Melissande into the privacy of the great hall. "You tried to leap from the battlements? *You?*"

Did he not remember? She'd admitted as much, at St. Bede's Abbey, in a rash moment.

Melissande bit her lower lip and nodded.

"Why?" The word was honed to a lethal edge, like the dagger Christian carried so near to hand.

"Because I thought you were dead." She drew a deep breath and let it out. "Christian, we discussed this—"

"I have no memory of that," he said, and she knew by the look in his eyes that he was telling the truth. His injuries had been such that he was lucky he could remember anything at all.

He cursed under his breath when she said nothing more. "That you would do something so foolish—"

"I was a child. I believed the man I loved to be drowned at sea. Had I known the whole truth, that you would return with no heart in your breast and despise me for a crime I did not commit, no one could have stopped me from ending my life!"

Christian stared at her in mingled fury and anguish. "Who interceded?"

"James. He grasped me from behind and held me until I ceased struggling. Then he held me in his arms and stroked my hair and asked me to marry him."

Christian was silent now, absorbing her words.

"Are you satisfied?" Melissande demanded, and tried to move past him to escape into the courtyard outside, where the sun might warm the chill from her bones.

He stopped her. "I could not have borne it," he ground out, "if you'd perished because of me. Better you had wedded yourself to James."

Melissande gazed up at him. "Oh, Christian," she whispered, "what are we going to do?"

He held her close against his chest, his hand buried in her hair, which fell free beneath a pearl-trimmed cap. "This," he said, and tilted her head back that she might receive his mouth upon hers.

There was desperation in that kiss, and fire, and glory.

"God help me," Christian rasped, when that first skirmish

had ended. "I have always and will ever love you, Melissande Bradgate." He put an arm around her waist, guided her quickly inside the neglected great hall, there to press her into a dusty alcove and kiss her again.

"What," she asked breathlessly, "has possessed you?"

"I've been an idiot," he said, one hand smoothing her wind-tumbled hair. "A fool."

"I could have told you that," Melissande replied.

He laughed.

"Forgive me," Christian said, when he had sobered again. His eyes glistened as he looked down at her, searching her face. "You were right before, Melissande," he confessed gently. "Losing your love was the worst thing I could imagine happening. I tried to be ready, to steel myself against it."

Tears stung Melissande's eyes. "Oh, Christian—"

He touched her lips with one finger and smiled. "I love you, my lady. Say you will allow me to court you again." Before Melissande could reply, or even nod, he dropped somewhat gracelessly to one knee, taking her hand in both of his. "Let us make this madness right at last, my lady," he said. "Marry me."

Chapter Fifteen

The Lady Melissande accepted, and that was only the beginning of Christian Lithwell's good fortune. It soon was discovered, in the process of starting the renovations to the castle, that while James Lithwell, seventh Earl of Wellingsley, had left behind nothing more than a few hungry servants and four equally neglected keeps, an earlier earl had shown more foresight.

Hidden under the half-rotted floor of an ancient garde-robe, in a part of the structure long since fallen into disuse, were several bags of gold, along with a wooden chest containing a collection of jewels passed down by bloodline from the days of the First Crusade.

Christian placed no sentimental attachment on either the gold or the jewels, and promptly made arrangements to invest the former and sell the latter.

With the proceeds, food and livestock were purchased, along with tools and stone and other supplies, and skilled workmen were engaged to begin the restoration, in earnest, of Wellingsley Castle. Servants bustled once more through the chambers and along the passageways, sweeping and scrubbing and laying fresh rushes on the floors, and crofters returned to the weed-grown fields beyond the walls, reclaiming the fertile ground with their spades and hoes.

The marriage of Christian Lithwell and Melissande

Bradgate was to take place within a fortnight, but first there was the matter of the galleys, with their slaves. Neither Melissande nor Christian was willing to rest until the situation had been made right.

They left the work at the castle in Robert's charge and journeyed on horseback, first to Taftshead, then to London, where they found the offices of the Bradgate Company operating as before, under the charge of Mr. Renford's chief clerk. Melissande might never have been there, never have announced that she was now the head of the business, as well as its owner.

She demanded to see the ledgers and spent the afternoon poring over them, while Christian busied himself with other inspections.

Melissande soon learned that one of the vessels, the *Eleanora* as it happened, was of course still at sea, on a voyage to Flanders, but the other three were anchored in the Thames, being loaded with fresh cargo for trade in Spain, Italy, and Greece, respectively. The profits, even with the ever-present dangers of piracy and shipwreck factored in, were bound to be enormous, and they would be entered into the accounts of heaven in numerals of blood.

Melissande closed the last book with a clap and marched out into the large counting chamber, where all the clerks sat hunched over their ledgers, their pens making a steady *scratchety-scratch* sound on the parchment. Christian, his rounds completed, leaned indolently against a doorjamb, his eyes on the floor.

Melissande's heart swelled with love at the sight of him.

"Gentlemen," she said clearly, addressing the room at large.

The clerks laid down their quills and looked at her expectantly. Their pale faces revealed neither malice nor goodwill, but only curiosity. She knew they had no power and thus could be assigned no blame for the sins of their employers.

"Mr. Renford is no longer in charge of this company," she reiterated clearly. "It is mine—and Lord Lithwell's. Those of you who wish to do so may remain in our employ, those who are loyal to my late father's notary are hereby dismissed."

There was a humming silence, but no one moved. Melissande wasn't surprised; whatever their feelings about having a woman at the head of the company, the men had families to support. Some of them did glance in Christian's direction, as if seeking confirmation. He seemed to take no notice, though of course he was listening to every word, assimilating every nuance.

Presently, the clerks turned back to their ledgers, and Melissande, smiling to herself, gathered up her skirts and made for the door.

The harbor was not a savory place, and when Melissande arrived there, escorted by a watchful, silent Christian, night had already fallen. Torches burned along the wharves, and drunken men laughed raucously.

Christian hadn't wanted Melissande to accompany him on this particular mission, but she had insisted, and in the end, knowing that nothing short of tying her up and locking her in a cupboard would stop her from following, he had given in and assented. He wore a cloak with the hood raised, and carried his father's sword in a scabbard at his side, along with the dagger.

Melissande was also armed, at Christian's insistence, though she wondered if she'd actually be able to plunge the thin blade of her knife into living flesh.

"Leave the overseer to me," Christian said, as they boldly boarded the first ship, the *Serena*.

"Hold, there!" exclaimed a guard.

Melissande presented a scroll. "I am the owner of this vessel, and I would speak with the captain," she said.

The captain was summoned, and upon reading the document, the grizzled old man peered at her through rheumy eyes and murmured a curse. "You're Bradgate's lass, then," he said. "I thought you'd gone to a nunnery."

Melissande smiled. "I'm back," she answered.

With that, Christian drew his sword, and the mariner took a stumbling step in retreat. "What's this about? You've brought pirates aboard your own ship?"

"This is Christian Lithwell, who served aboard the *Eleanora* these two years past. He has business in the hold, with your overseer."

Christian was already on his way belowdecks. Several sailors moved to stop him, but at a grumbled order from the captain, they receded.

There was shouting below, and then, after some minutes, men began pouring up out of the hold, mere skeletons most of them, clad in rags and unutterably filthy. At a word from Christian, they trooped past her, one by one, and Melissande placed ten gold florins in each grubby, calloused palm.

Some fled immediately, intoxicated by the suddenness of their freedom and their newfound wealth, but the majority remained, following Christian and Melissande to the next ship and the next, unlocking chains and fetters, flinging overseers and their whips overboard into the dark water.

At the end of the evening, only the *Eleanora,* upon which Christian had been a prisoner, still carried galley slaves. On her return to England she would be met by another of the Bradgate ships, boarded, and quickly divested of her crew of slaves. The vessels of Melissande's small but valuable fleet were to be fitted with sails and carried along the trade routes by no other power than the wind itself.

Near midnight, Christian and Melissande arrived, both exhausted and exhilarated, at the house in Taftshead, where they found lights glowing in the windows and a lavish meal set out on the board, courtesy of the newly hired staff.

They had no time or interest for food.

In the entry hall, Christian scooped Melissande up into

his arms. His eyes shone and, for the first time since he'd been dumped at the postern gate of St. Bede's Abbey, he looked happy, and at peace. "Thank you," he said gruffly.

Melissande slipped her arms around his neck. "Let us go above stairs, my lord, and discuss the exact degree of your gratitude."

He laughed and flung her over one shoulder, and the servants, like the mice, took care to stay out of sight as the Earl of Wellingsley and his soon-to-be countess mounted the steps in that most unorthodox fashion.

The Scent
of Snow

Chapter One

Cornucopia, Washington
December 1892

elicate, silvery fans and curlicues of frost decorated the windows of the farmhouse that morning when Rebecca lit the bedside lantern, arose, and hastily donned a wrapper and slippers. Since the room was far too cold for washing, she took the light and the calico dress she meant to wear that day and hurried down the steep, narrow stairway to the first floor.

Reaching the large kitchen, with its many shelves and cupboards, she set the lantern in the middle of the scarred oak table, draped the dress over the back of a chair, and took a handful of kindling from the woodbox beside the stove. When the banked embers of the fire flared around the dry, pitchy pieces of pine, Rebecca smiled and lifted the lid on the reservoir at one side of the massive black Kitchen Queen. The water inside was tepid, perfect for quick morning ablutions.

After washing, Rebecca fed more wood into the stove, then quickly exchanged her nightgown and wrapper for the calico, one of the three dresses she owned. She warmed her bare toes in front of the stove while unplaiting her waist-length, chestnut-brown hair, brushing it thoroughly, and then winding it deftly back into its customary thick braid. Once that was done, Rebecca put on her stockings and practical shoes, went out onto the back step, and tossed the contents of the washbasin into the snowy yard.

She carried her nightclothes back upstairs to her room while water for cornmeal mush heated on the stove. She made her bed—at least, she'd certainly come to *think* of it as her own—and tapped at the twins' door as she passed along the hallway.

"Annabelle, Susan," she called, as she did every morning. "It's a new day."

Her ten-year-old half sisters groaned so loudly that she heard them from the hall—and that, too, was part of the routine. A smile touched Rebecca's mouth as she made her way to the stairs. Annabelle and Susan were young, so it was easy to forgive them for a lack of perspective. It would be years before they fully realized how fortunate they were to be living in that solid farmhouse, with plenty to eat, warm clothes to wear, and the opportunity for an education.

Rebecca's smile faded as she reached the kitchen and began preparing breakfast. As dawn spread across the sky, turning the frost patterns on the windows to glorious shades of pink and apricot, a sense of uneasiness troubled her. Over the past two years, she'd made a place for herself and the twins, there on that patch of land just outside the small town of Cornucopia, in the wheat country of Washington State. They were an accepted part of the community, a family, the three of them, and by sewing and taking in the occasional roomer, Rebecca managed to make an honest living.

She put three broad slices of bread into the oven to toast and then cracked a trio of brown eggs into a pot of boiling water. Annabelle clattered into the kitchen, hopping on one foot while she tried to pull on the opposite shoe. Her bright, honey-gold hair was tousled from sleep, and her woolen dress was misbuttoned. Susan, the more graceful of the pair, glided into the room fully and correctly clad, her hair already brushed and neatly tied with a ribbon.

She gave Rebecca a pained look and started to set the table, while Annabelle struggled, muttering, into her coat.

"Such a big fuss over a little task like feeding a few chickens," Susan remarked.

Annabelle glowered at her sister. "We'll see who makes a fuss tomorrow, Miss Priss, when it's *your* turn to see to those cranky birds."

"Wash up and have your own breakfast first, Annabelle," Rebecca interceded gently. "I don't want you to be late for school."

Minutes later, the three of them sat down to eat. The dawn was still struggling against the darkness, and the light of kerosene lanterns flickered cozily in the warm kitchen.

"Mary Alice Holton is getting a doll for Christmas," Susan announced. "Her brother sent it all the way from San Francisco. He works on the docks."

Rebecca felt a pang. She'd managed to give her half sisters food and shelter and a great deal of love since her ne'er-do-well father had dropped them off at her door back in Chicago nearly three years before, when she herself had been but nineteen. Luxuries like store-bought dolls, however, were out of her reach.

Annabelle, the less fanciful of the two, made a face. "Mary Alice Holton is a crybaby. Her brother probably sent that doll just so she'd quit her sniveling and give her mama and papa some peace."

Although she smiled at this observation, a lump thickened in Rebecca's throat. Whatever Annabelle might say to the contrary, and despite the fact that she was an avowed tomboy most of the time, Rebecca knew she wanted a pretty doll every bit as badly as Susan did.

"It cost two whole dollars," Susan went on, ignoring her

sister's comment. "It has glass eyes and a china head and real hair. Mary Alice named it Jeanette."

Annabelle gave a long-suffering sigh. "If this doll is supposed to be a Christmas present, how come Mary Alice knows what it looks like? It's only the first week in December!"

"She peeked, of course," Susan replied loftily.

"Hurry, now," Rebecca said in a brisk tone, rising from her chair and reaching for her empty bowl, her silverware, and the plate that had held her toast and poached egg. "You'll be late for school. And don't you dare forget to feed those chickens, Annabelle Morgan."

Annabelle and Susan looked at each other—although they often squabbled, the twins had an uncanny way of communicating without words when they so desired—then followed Rebecca's lead and carried their dishes to the cast iron sink. Soon they were bundled up in coats and boots, hats and scarves, school books and lunch tins in hand.

Rebecca watched from the back step as they trudged through the deep snow, sunlight pooling around them, to the chicken pen. Susan dutifully held Annabelle's things while her sister attended to the chore of feeding the squawking birds.

The schoolhouse was just down the road and around the bend—the smoke from the building's wood-burning furnace curled gray against the dove-gray winter sky—but Rebecca kept an eye on the children until they had disappeared from sight.

A strange sense of apprehension dogged her as she went about the morning tasks of tidying the kitchen and chopping more wood for the fire. For some inexplicable reason, her gaze kept straying toward the quiet, snow-shrouded road.

She had work to do, she told herself, and tried to shake off her troubled state of mind as she spread the lush red velvet for Miss Ginny Dylan's Christmas dress on the table. She'd made the pattern pieces herself, devoting a full afternoon and part of an evening to the task, using a page torn from a fashion book as a guide. Even though she'd checked the paper panels carefully against Ginny's measurements, Rebecca inspected each one again before pinning them into place. The velvet was costly, and she could not afford to make a mistake.

The sunlight grew brighter as the morning passed, and the frost portraits melted from the windowpanes. Despite her concentration on the task at hand, Rebecca still felt nervous and fitful. Once she even wrapped her shabby woolen cloak around herself and walked down the path to the very edge of the road to look long and hard in both directions.

She was glad, as she returned to the house and her sewing, that there was no one around to see her odd behavior and ask for an accounting.

LUCAS KILEY HAD bought his wagon and team in Spokane, within an hour of stepping down off the westbound train, but he'd waited to purchase the other supplies he needed. Since Cornucopia was going to be his home from now on, he thought it was only right that he do as much commerce with the local merchants as possible.

He was chilled to the bone when he finally reached the small town he'd thought about so often—during the long years in that factory in Chicago and then, afterward, while he was recovering from the accident—but a sense of celebration lifted his heart.

Lucas took a long look around him, taking in every detail of the small town that would be his home from now on. God knew, the place wasn't much—just a general store, a bank, a church, a livery stable, and a couple of saloons, huddled together on the prairie. A few sturdy little houses flanked the main street buildings, but because of the cold, there was no one out and about except for one skinny yellow dog.

He reined in the two big sorrel draft horses and set the

brake lever with one foot, sparing a second glance toward the Green Grizzly Beer and Pool Parlor. It was late afternoon, surely a proper hour for a glass of whiskey to melt the icy splinters in his blood. But he was going to need every penny of the money he'd saved to stock his farm and woodshed and see himself through the winter.

Lucas entered the general store instead, and felt strengthened by the blast of warmth from the large potbellied stove that stood in the center of things. Two old men sat with their feet toasting on the chrome rail, and a pretty dark-haired woman with a gracious manner swept out from behind the counter. She was in her forties, Lucas guessed.

"You're a stranger here," the lady observed kindly, her wise eyes full of friendliness and humor. She held out one hand, just as readily as a man would have done, and Lucas liked her instantly. "My name is Mary Daniels, and I run this store."

He shook her hand. "Glad to meet you, Mrs. Daniels. I'm Lucas Kiley and—"

"Lucas Kiley!" the storemistress interrupted, beaming. The minor impoliteness seemed almost elegant, coming from her. "Well, it is *about time* you showed your face in Cornucopia! That delightful little family of yours has been carrying on without you quite long enough!"

The wind seemed to rush from Lucas's lungs, just the way it had once in Chicago, when he'd gotten into a fight and taken a hard punch in the gut. *What delightful little family?* he wondered stupidly. For a moment, he almost believed he'd married at some point and then forgotten both the woman and the ceremony, but then he overcame his shock enough to begin, "But I don't—"

"She's a trooper, that Rebecca," Mrs. Daniels butted in again. She stood with her hands on her narrow waist, looking up at Lucas with bright eyes. "Why, she's taken that rundown old place and made it into something, all on her own. You ought to be proud of her, Mr. Kiley."

Lucas swallowed any further protests. He was tired, hungry, and confused, and ever since he'd lived at Mrs. Ella Readman's boardinghouse in Chicago, several years before, the name "Rebecca" had had a stunning effect on him whenever it came up in conversation.

Obviously, this wife business was a misunderstanding. Lucas was a methodical man, not given to tangents or impulse. He would sort the matter out soon enough.

He bought a wagonload of groceries—mostly staples like sugar and flour and beans and coffee—and set out through the snapping cold of that pristine winter afternoon for the farm he'd purchased, sight unseen but completely furnished, just a few months before the factory accident that had set him back for so long. He didn't need to look at a map; Lucas knew the road by heart, having traveled over it a thousand times in his imagination. The landmarks were like old friends.

There was the abandoned Halley place, just as the last owner had described it, and there was the single oak tree jutting up in the middle of the field—two hundred years old if it was a day. Beyond that was the schoolhouse, a one-room structure.

Lucas smiled as he passed. Class was just letting out for the day, and children were bursting through the doorway like gravel from a shotgun, shouting and laughing and pelting each other with snowballs. Lucas's tired heart rose another notch, and he turned his light green eyes toward the next bend in the road.

Although the homestead itself wasn't quite visible, he saw smoke twisting slowly against the sky, and considered Mrs. Daniels's mention of a wife. He frowned and urged the horses into a trot, even though the snow was fairly deep and the going was hard.

The storemistress's warning and the spiral of wood smoke notwithstanding, Lucas was surprised when his house and barn came into view and he saw a woman wrapped in a cloak standing on the step, one hand shielding her eyes from the sun as she watched his approach.

Curious as he was for a look at the place itself, it took some doing to tear his gaze from the figure of the woman. He gazed with approval on the solid-looking barn and whitewashed two-story house. There was a wellhouse, too, and a fenced pasture, and the fields looked smooth under their mantle of snow.

He turned his attention almost resentfully to the woman.

There was something familiar about her tall, slender figure and that rich fall of red-brown hair, and Lucas rubbed his beard-stubbled chin thoughtfully as he drove closer. It was almost as though she'd been expecting him, this trespasser standing so brazenly on *his* back porch.

As he pulled the wagon to a stop in the dooryard, she lifted her skirts a little and stepped gracefully down the stairs. Her cheeks were bright crimson—and not from the cold, Lucas reckoned—as she made her way toward him.

Recognition crackled between them as he looked down at her from the wagon box and she gazed up at him from the ground. For an instant, it seemed they were back in Chicago, at the boardinghouse, sitting across the dinner table from each other.

"Hello, Rebecca," he managed, his voice raspy. "I understand you and I have tied the knot, though I confess I don't recall the first thing about the ceremony."

The blush on her beautifully-shaped cheekbones intensified, but her maple-brown eyes, glowing as if lanterns burned behind them, regarded him steadily. "Come inside before you catch your death," she said, with resignation.

Chapter Two

*E*ven though Rebecca had had a premonition that something disturbing was about to happen, and even though
she kept her back straight as a poker walking ahead of her
"husband" into the farmhouse, she was in a state of inner
turmoil. She would have been less surprised if a plague of
locusts had descended on the snowy landscape than she was
by the arrival of Mr. Lucas Kiley.

After all, she'd had every reason to believe he was dead.

Lucas paused on the narrow porch to shake out his hat
and stomp the snow from his boots. Rebecca bustled to the
stove, unable to meet his gaze, at a distinct loss for a proper
explanation for her presence.

"I suppose you're hungry," she said, using all her considerable willpower to keep the words light and steady.

"As a bear," Lucas agreed. His voice was deep, just the
way she remembered it.

She poured coffee from the small blue enamel pot at the
back of the stove—like everything else in that solidly built
farmhouse, she'd come to think of it as hers. And she'd been
fooling herself the whole while, because the homestead belonged to Mr. Kiley—lock, stock, and barrel.

"Please sit down," she said, blushing when she realized
she'd just invited the man to take a seat at his own table. He
accepted the mug with one hand, and out of the corner of her

eye Rebecca saw that he was looking at the bright scraps of red velvet littering the table.

"You've come up in the world since I saw you last," he observed. There was no rancor in his tone, no sign of an accusation, and yet Rebecca felt defensive.

"I don't wear velvet, Mr. Kiley," she said crisply, turning away to go to the pie safe for the leftovers from last night's supper. "I sew for those who can afford such things, to make a living."

Lucas gave the cold meat and vegetable pie she set before him an appreciative glance, then pulled off his muffler and shrugged out of his heavy sheepskin coat. The brief, slanted smile he offered Rebecca caused a warm, spilling sensation inside her. "I'm waiting for an explanation," he said, taking up the fork she gave him and tucking into his dinner without further ado.

Rebecca might have told Lucas exactly what had brought her to Cornucopia and that modest farm, if the door hadn't burst open just then. Annabelle and Susan hurried in, cheeks red from the cold, eyes bright with curiosity as they sought and found Lucas.

"That your team and wagon, mister?" Annabelle inquired, bouncing from one foot to the other while she separated herself from her boots. At the same time she used her teeth to pull off her mittens.

"Yes." Lucas's green eyes twinkled with quiet amusement as he regarded the child. He wasn't a handsome man, Rebecca reflected, but there was something solid and appealing about him all the same.

Susan, who had managed to shed her winter garb with easy grace, kept her distance. "Are you a boarder?" she asked. "If you are, you got here too late, because Mr. Pontious always takes the room in the barn on Friday evenings, on his way back to Spokane for more supplies. Once he stayed a whole week."

Lucas arched one eyebrow at Rebecca—who promptly went as red as the scraps of velvet she was scooping up from the tabletop—then answered Susan's question. "I don't reckon I'm exactly a boarder," he said moderately, pausing to take a sip from his coffee. "In other words, if anyone around here sleeps in the barn, it isn't going to be me."

Rebecca put a hand on each of the twins' backs and shooed them toward the parlor. "Go on, now, and do your lessons for tomorrow. There's a nice fire going."

Annabelle and Susan obeyed the command, but they weren't tractable about it. They dragged their feet and kept looking back at Lucas in curiosity and concern.

Once they were settled by the hearth, in the shadow of the big potted palm Mr. Pontious had once given Rebecca in lieu of rent on the room in the barn, she returned to the kitchen.

Lucas had finished his pie and coffee and carried the dirty dishes to the sink. He stood with his strong, work-worn hands braced against it, gazing out the steamy window into the gathering twilight.

Rebecca paused in the doorway, taking advantage of this opportunity to study him unobserved. He wasn't an especially tall man, but his shoulders were broad and powerful, and his light brown hair curled over his collar. There was an air about him of dignity and quiet strength, the qualities Rebecca had first noticed when they'd met three years before in Chicago.

"Looks like more snow," he said, without turning around.

Rebecca thought she'd been silent, entering the room. "Not surprising, since it's December," she replied. There was a cheery, optimistic note in her voice, but it rang false.

Lucas turned, folded his arms, and leaned back against the sink, regarding Rebecca with an unreadable expression for a long moment before he spoke. "What are you doing, living in my house and telling folks you're my wife?" he asked.

She sighed, crossed the room, took her cloak down from a peg on the wall. His coat hung next to it, smelling of fresh air and snow. "I have to see to the chickens," she hedged, taking a colander full of potato peelings from the work table and proceeding outside. "If you would care to join me, Mr. Kiley—?"

Lucas snatched down his coat and followed her out. In the middle of the yard, where his team and wagon still stood, he gripped her arm and stopped her.

A muscle clamped briefly in his jaw, and she saw frustration in his eyes. Huge snowflakes began drifting down, catching in his rumpled hair. "Damn it, Rebecca," he breathed, "I am at the end of my patience! What's going on here?"

Rebecca swallowed hard, and unwanted tears stung her eyes. She and the girls would be destitute after this, but she would always be grateful for the warmth, comfort, and safety they'd enjoyed up until Lucas's return.

"One day while you and I were both living at Mrs. Readman's boardinghouse," she began gravely, "my drunken, no-account father turned up with Annabelle and Susan." She paused, sniffled. "His second wife, their mother, had died, and he was going to abandon them if I didn't take them in. They were near-starved and scared to death. Mrs. Readman fed them a good meal, but she made it clear she wanted no children in her establishment, so we left. I found a shack near the factory where I worked and—and—" She had to stop again, remembering those days, reliving the hopelessness, the chronic cold and hunger, the bone-deep weariness. "I went back to the boardinghouse to fetch some things I'd left with Mrs. Readman, and she told me you'd been hurt in an accident, and that you'd very likely died. She gave me some papers that belonged to you and asked me if I'd drop them off at the hospital, to be forwarded to any kin."

Lucas just stood there, silent and stern, still holding Rebecca's arm fast in his fingers. "Go on."

"I went to the hospital nearest the mill where you'd said you were working, and they had no record of you. Then I called on your employer, and a clerk in the office said you were dead, that you'd been crushed when some crates fell from a platform, and that as far as they knew, you didn't have any family."

The memory of the accident was visible in his face for an instant, then it faded. "Obviously," he said, "I'm not dead."

"Obviously," Rebecca retorted. The word came out sounding a little tart; she was cornered, the game was up, and the resultant fear made her testy. She drew a deep breath, tried vainly to pull free of his grasp, and went on. "I finally went through your papers, hoping to find the address of a friend. Instead, I came across the deed to this farm."

Lucas's tone was deceptively soft. "And you just decided to come out here, take over my land and my house, and tell everybody you and I were married? How did you explain my absence, *Mrs. Kiley*?"

Rebecca looked away for a moment, unable to bear the accusation in his eyes. The snow was falling thicker and faster, and the wind was bitter. She wondered where she and Annabelle and Susan would sleep that night if Lucas ran them off his property—something he had every right to do.

"I told them you were working back east," she replied miserably. Rebecca had made plenty of fresh starts in her life, but in those moments things looked impossible to her, and she felt as if she'd aged a century since morning. "I said we wanted to buy more land—the Halley place—and that you'd be joining us as soon as you'd saved enough of your wages. I . . . I said you planned to adopt my sisters once we got settled in."

Suddenly, he released her and, to Rebecca's great surprise, she nearly fell. She'd thought he was holding her prisoner, but now it seemed he'd been keeping her upright instead.

"What did you tell those children in there?" He cocked a thumb toward the house. "Or did you get them to lie, too?"

Rebecca lowered her head, but Lucas cupped her chin in his hand and made her look at him. "They think I have a husband in the east, same as the townspeople," she managed.

Lucas turned away—in frustration or disgust or perhaps both—and muttered a curse. Then he stomped over to the wagon and began unloading the supplies.

Afraid to speak at all, let alone ask Lucas what he meant to do about her trespassing, Rebecca hurried off to toss the potato parings into the chicken pen. Then she went inside to see about supper.

Lucas didn't say a word to her all the while he was carrying in bags and crates and stacking them in the pantry, nor did he join Rebecca and the twins when they sat down for the evening meal.

"That's him, isn't it?" Annabelle asked, wide-eyed, as the sounds of Lucas driving the team toward the barn seeped through the walls of the kitchen. "The man you married to get us this place?"

Susan dropped her fork to the table with a clatter, and the color drained from her cheeks. "You said he'd never come out here and bother us!" she breathed.

Rebecca broke one of her own rules then, set her elbows on the table, and dropped her forehead to her palms. "Well," she answered, on the verge of weeping, "I was mistaken."

On orders from Rebecca, Annabelle and Susan went to bed early that night—Rebecca was hoping Mr. Kiley wouldn't be hard-hearted enough to throw sleeping children out into the snow—and then went upstairs for her wrapper and slippers. Lucas had already said he wasn't going to pass the night in the barn, which meant he'd want his room. Rebecca planned to stretch out on the parlor settee. Heaven knew she wouldn't get a moment's rest, so she'd spend the time trying to think of a solution to her obvious problem.

She had just turned away from the tall bureau—like the other furnishings, it had come with the place—folded night-dress in hand, when the door opened and Lucas quietly entered the bedroom.

Rebecca's heart slammed against her backbone. For the second time that day, she was utterly and thoroughly stunned.

Lucas favored her with a tired, crooked smile and hooked his thumbs under the straps of his suspenders. "I think I'm going to like having a wife," he said, running his gaze over her person just as if he had the right not only to look, but to touch in the bargain. "I've been alone a long time."

A hot feeling surged through Rebecca's body, and her strong legs suddenly felt weak. She even wondered what it would be like to be kissed by that impudent mouth, and that fact troubled her more than anything.

Resolutely, she moved toward the door, chin high, but when she went to pass Lucas, he stopped her.

"Get into bed, Mrs. Kiley," he said, reaching out and clutching her.

"I'll scream." She whispered the threat, struggling—even though she didn't really want to get free—but he held her fast.

"Who will rescue you?" he asked reasonably. His eyes danced with an enticing wickedness that caused her heart to beat still faster. "Those two little girls across the hall?"

Rebecca's temper was flaring, and she was scared, but there was an even worse emotion to deal with. She was as attracted to this man as she had been when they'd lived in the same boardinghouse, and the idea of sharing his bed, innocent as she was, made her light-headed with wanting.

Still, her pride would not let her give in. "You wouldn't dare force yourself on a decent woman!" she hissed.

He leaned close, his nose a fraction of an inch from hers. "I wouldn't force *any* woman, decent or otherwise. But I worked for years to buy this place, lady, and the thought of it was all that kept me going after the accident, when I was laid up in the storeroom of a two-bit tavern on the waterfront. In the meantime, you've been right here, living off the fat of *my* land, wearing my name just as if you were entitled to it. I think, Mrs. Kiley, that if I want the softness and warmth of a woman lying next to me in my bed—and I sure as hell do—you owe me that comfort."

Rebecca opened her mouth, closed it again.

Lucas gave her a little push toward the bed and, to her own amazement, she didn't balk. He blew out the single lantern, plunging the room into total darkness, and she listened with her heart in her throat as he undressed.

"Do you promise not to take advantage?" she asked shakily, unable to believe she'd been reduced to such a situation.

"Yes," he answered, and the bedsprings creaked as he stretched out. "I presume I can expect the same promise from *you*?" And he smiled in the darkness.

Chapter Three

*N*ightdress buttoned to her chin, Rebecca lay stiffly on her side of the bed, so near the edge that any sudden movement would almost certainly send her toppling to the floor. She was only too aware of the heat and scent and substance of Lucas's unclothed body next to her; his weight tilted the mattress.

"I thought you were dead," Rebecca said.

"That's obvious," Lucas replied, with a sigh.

"What happened?"

He spent some time settling in. "There was an accident in the factory where I worked. I spent more than a year recovering, and used up a lot of my stake. Once I was up and around, I had to earn some more money."

Rebecca absorbed his words thoughtfully. "All things considered," she allowed, after a pause, "I'm glad you're not dead."

"Thank you," Lucas replied, in a wry tone.

She sighed. Once again, she and the girls were going to have to make a new start in a new place. "The twins and I will leave tomorrow," she said, near tears at the thought. She loved the farm, and Cornucopia, and all its people.

Lucas shifted, stretched, gave a long, decadent, and purely masculine yawn. "Um-hmmm," he said. "There's no need to dangle off the side of the bed like that, Mrs. Kiley. Like I said before, I don't take women who don't want taking."

Until that day, Rebecca hadn't blushed more than two or three times in her life, by her private accounting. Just since Lucas's appearance that afternoon, however, she'd felt her face flood with stinging color at least half a dozen times. It happened again as she assimilated the outrageously frank words he'd just uttered.

She bit her lip in an effort to get a grip on her temper, then said, "You're making me stay here just to torment me."

He chuckled, and the low, rich sound set things to tumbling and melting inside her again. "To 'torment' you? Great Scott, Rebecca, is your passion that intense? I'm shocked."

Rage flooded Rebecca's being; if she hadn't been afraid of the repercussions, she would have clouted him with her pillow. "You flatter yourself," she said evenly, when she could trust herself to speak. "Let me assure you, Mr. Kiley, you most certainly do *not* inspire my—my passion."

Lucas settled deeper into the feather mattress and let out a rather theatrical snore.

Rebecca lay rigid, staring up at the dark ceiling, wondering what to do. After a seeming eternity had passed, and she felt certain that Lucas was truly asleep, she started to rise, intending to follow her original plan and make a bed downstairs on the settee.

Before she could sit up, however, Lucas reached out, spread one hand over her stomach, and pressed her gently but firmly back to the mattress. Although the weight of his palm and the strength of his fingers lingered against her for only a few moments, Lucas's touch sent ripples of alarming sensation flowing from Rebecca's center into every extremity.

"Good night, Mrs. Kiley," he said pointedly.

After that, Rebecca didn't try to get out of bed again, not even when she needed to use the chamberpot. She just lay there, thinking that she had indeed woven a tangled web of her deceptions.

Somewhere near dawn, she drifted off to sleep from pure nervous exhaustion, and when she awakened she was alone in the room and the house felt unusually warm. The light at the window was thin, and small flakes of snow were swirling in a busy wind.

Quickly Rebecca jumped up, dressed, brushed her hair, and hurried downstairs. Since it was Saturday, their only day to sleep late, she didn't awaken the twins.

Lucas was in the kitchen, standing near the stove and sipping from a steaming mug of coffee. He gave Rebecca one of his slanted grins.

"'Morning, Mrs. Kiley."

It was a glorious luxury, rising to a warm house and finding the coffee already brewed, but Rebecca could not afford to enjoy the pleasure. She and the twins would soon be out in the cold, with nowhere to go and very little money to sustain them.

"I think it's about time you stopped addressing me as 'Mrs. Kiley,'" she said, taking a cup from the shelf and pouring coffee for herself. "The joke is beginning to wear thin."

His eyes danced with amusement as he watched her over the brim of his mug. He was wearing trousers, a plain woolen work shirt, suspenders, and boots, and although his unruly hair had been brushed, he needed a shave.

"May I point out that this whole situation is your doing, and not my own?" he asked.

"I was desperate!" Rebecca whispered angrily. "Can't you see that? I didn't mean any harm. I was just looking for a way to put a roof over my sisters' heads!"

Lucas raised one eyebrow and pondered her thoughtfully before asking, "If you were so destitute, how did you scrape together the money to come out here from Chicago?"

Rebecca turned away quickly, afraid her aversion to that question, not to mention its answer, would show in her face.

"I had saved a few dollars," she said, and that was true enough, though it wasn't the whole of the story. "And I borrowed from a friend." That, in contrast to her first statement, was an unadorned lie. Duke Jones certainly hadn't been her friend by any stretch of the imagination, and he had taken part of her soul in return for the small amount of money he'd given her.

Silence pulsed in the cozy, lantern-lit kitchen, while Rebecca struggled to assemble an expression that wouldn't betray her. Finally, after much effort, she was able to face Lucas squarely. "I am truly sorry, Mr. Kiley, for taking advantage of your name and property. My sisters and I will be out of the house before noon." There was only one small problem: She had nowhere to go. But she would worry about that later.

The look of amused puzzlement in Lucas's eyes turned to one of concern. "There's no need for that. As I said yesterday, I sort of like the idea of having a family."

Rebecca set her coffee cup aside with a trembling hand and said coldly, "I've told lies, and I've trespassed, but I am not a whore. I won't pay for our food and shelter by sharing your bed!"

He shoved the splayed fingers of one hand through his hair, mussing it, and uttered an exasperated sigh. "How many times do I have to tell you, Rebecca? I won't so much as kiss you unless I have your permission."

She put her hands on her hips, and blood pounded in her ears. "And yet you insist that I lie beside you at night, just as a wife would do!"

"Keep your voice down," Lucas said sternly. "Do you want the children to hear you talking that way?"

Rebecca made a strangled sound of immense frustration, but at the same time hope was pulsing inside her bosom like a second heartbeat. Maybe she wouldn't have to uproot her sisters after all. At least, not before Christmas.

"Will I or will I not be required to sleep in your room as I did last night?" she hissed.

"Yes," Lucas replied flatly. "You will."

"And you promise not to . . ."

"Make love to you?" he finished, when Rebecca hesitated. "Yes, Becky, I promise. But I'm ready to wager you'll be behaving like a real wife before the month is out."

"What a scandalous thing to say!"

He toasted her with his coffee mug. "Scandalous," he agreed, "but true." He sighed philosophically. "Now I could do with some breakfast, if you don't mind. There's a lot I want to get done today, and a man needs his nourishment."

Rebecca's mind was spinning. Under other circumstances, she probably would have told Mr. Kiley exactly what he could do with breakfast, but it was freezing outside and she had very little money and two little girls to provide for. She couldn't afford to turn down this man's hospitality, much as it nettled her to comply with his wishes.

She got out a kettle and set it on the stove top with a *clank*.

EARLY THAT AFTERNOON, after the house had been put to rights and she'd basted the sleeves of the red-velvet dress into place, Rebecca changed into her going-to-town dress, pinned her braid up into a coronet, and put on her bonnet.

"I don't understand why we can't stay here with Lucas," Annabelle complained, watching as Rebecca resolutely tied the ribbons of her bonnet under her chin. "It's no fun sitting around the church while the choir practices!"

Rebecca turned from the kitchen mirror and reached for her cloak. "You can't stay here with *Mr. Kiley* because— because he's busy. Now, get your coat on and let's go. Mrs. Fitzgillen will be upset if I'm late."

Susan was already wearing her winter gear. "Couldn't we visit Mrs. Daniels at the store while you're singing with the choir?" she asked sweetly.

Despite her situation, Rebecca had to smile. Susan was the diplomat of the family. "I think that's a very good idea, and I'm in favor as long as you don't make pests of yourselves."

Annabelle scrambled into her coat and boots, anxious to cooperate now that she wouldn't have to sit quietly in a pew for upwards of an hour and a half. "Maybe Mrs. Daniels will let us touch that doll with the blue dress, the one that's in the window."

Rebecca's pleasure over the prospect of an outing was tinged with sadness at the mention of the longed-for doll, but she didn't let her feelings show. "You'll keep your grubby hands to yourself, Annabelle," she said briskly, "or I'll know the reason why."

A hammering sound echoed from the barn as Rebecca and the twins crossed the yard, headed toward the road leading into town.

"I could run inside and tell Luc—Mr. Kiley that we're going to town," Annabelle volunteered, a bit too eagerly for Rebecca's tastes. It was plain that the child already had come to like her elder sister's alleged husband, and Rebecca couldn't help wondering how that exasperating man had won the canny Annabelle's esteem so quickly.

"There's no need to tell him anything," Rebecca replied, with a sniff.

Susan put in her two cents' worth. "Maybe he'd hitch up the wagon and give us a ride into town if we asked him," she ventured uncertainly.

Rebecca's patience was strained. "We would be imposing," she said, with finality, and led the march toward the road. Annabelle and Susan had little choice except to follow.

The walk into town took a full half hour and, by the time the twins had descended on the general store and Rebecca had made her way to the church, her feet were numb with cold.

Since firewood was at a premium—having to be brought from some distance by wagon or train—the small sanctuary was chilly. Like the other members of the choir, a stalwart group of scant numbers, Rebecca kept her cloak on while she sang.

As always, the music lifted her above the cares and worries of the normal world. While practicing her joyous solo for the special community service scheduled for Christmas night, she was able to forget that she'd gotten herself into a situation.

When the rehearsal was over, she said good-bye to the other choir members and walked slowly back to the general store. Normally, she looked forward to her chats with Mary, since the older woman always gave her tea with sugar and lemon and made her feel welcome, but that day she dreaded facing her friend.

Like everyone else in Cornucopia, Mary believed that Lucas Kiley was Rebecca's husband. Thus, Rebecca would be expected to behave like a happy wife just reunited with her mate, full of news and blushes and secrets.

As it happened, there were customers lined up along the counter, and Mary was much too busy for idle conversation. She smiled and waved at Rebecca, but went right on with her work.

Rebecca lingered by the stove for a few minutes, to warm herself for the walk home, and looked around for the twins. They were unpacking a crate, setting brightly painted toys on a shelf for Mary to sell.

There was a wooden replica of Noah's Ark, complete with a dozen different kinds of animals, all in pairs, and tiny, painted people, as well as a miniature fire wagon pulled by a metal horse, a storybook with cloth pages, and a lovely fair-haired doll wearing a pink dress.

Briefly, Rebecca considered dipping into her small savings to buy the doll as a Christmas gift for the twins, but she didn't dare give in to the impulse. The pitifully few dollars tucked away in the bank's vault were all that stood between the three of them and a very difficult world.

She turned away, only to find herself unexpectedly face-to-face with Mary.

The older woman held out a well-worn copy of a Spokane newspaper; she always saved them for Rebecca to read.

Accepting the folded paper, Rebecca allowed herself a moment to sorely regret stepping inside the store. Now Mary would ask about Lucas, and Rebecca would be forced to make up some story about how happy she was to have him home.

Instead, however, Mary whispered, "I'll put the doll back for you, and you can pay for it later, a little at a time."

Pride straightened Rebecca's spine and brought her chin up. She'd never bought on credit before, and she wasn't about to start then. "There's no need," she said, with quiet dignity. "I can manage Christmas presents for my sisters."

Mary sighed with affectionate exasperation. "That good-looking man of yours must not mind having a hardheaded woman for a wife," she observed. "Or have the two of you been apart so long that he remembers you as a sweet and pliant thing?"

"Hush," Rebecca scolded, embarrassed, but Mary only chuckled.

Chapter Four

Lucas was waiting in the kitchen when Rebecca and the twins arrived home again, just before sunset. He sat astraddle a chair, his arms resting against its back, within close range of the stove. There was a pipe clamped in his teeth, and in one hand he held a small book bound in blue cloth. *Everyman's Astronomy.*

He took the pipe out of his mouth and grinned cordially, but he didn't rise from the chair. "The wolves didn't get you after all," he commented.

Rebecca wanted to ask whether he was pleased by this outcome or disappointed, but she did neither. She took off her cloak and bonnet and sniffed the air. "Have you been cooking?"

Lucas nodded and gestured toward the oven door, pipe in hand. "I'm roasting one of the hens," he said. "Hope she wasn't a favorite."

Annabelle and Susan were staring at Lucas, round-eyed. No doubt they were as surprised as Rebecca to encounter a man who would cook when there was a chance of foisting the task off on some hapless female instead.

"Wash your hands and set the table," Rebecca said to the twins, since she couldn't bear the silence and had no idea what to say to Mr. Kiley.

The children hastened to obey, but Rebecca wasn't mollified. She suspected they were out to please Lucas, not their tiresome elder sister.

She watched him in bemusement as he pushed back his chair, set aside his book, lifted one of the stove lids, and tapped the contents of his pipe into the flames.

He caught her staring and winked, and Rebecca flinched as though he'd reached out and touched her with one of his calloused hands.

During supper—there were boiled potatoes and canned spinach to complement the roast chicken—the girls chattered about school, Christmas, and the dolls on display in Mary Daniels's store. Rebecca kept her eyes on her plate and contributed next to nothing to the conversation, her thoughts all a-tangle.

Night was creeping across the land, and soon she would lie beside Lucas again, painfully aware that his body was a natural counterpart to hers. Perhaps, she reflected, his presence was God's way of punishing her for all the times she'd pretended Mr. Kiley was reclining next to her, and imagined herself to be his real wife.

Once the meal was over, Lucas appropriated the newspaper Mary had given Rebecca and retreated to the parlor. Rebecca set the girls to washing dishes while she heated water for their weekly baths.

When the tub was positioned in front of the stove, full of steaming water, Susan balked. "I'm not taking off my clothes with a man in the house," she said.

"Me neither," Annabelle agreed.

Rebecca sighed. She'd hoped to avoid having to speak to Lucas any sooner than necessary, but she clearly had no choice. She went into the parlor, where she found him stretched out on the settee, his stockinged feet dangling over one end. A fire crackled on the hearth, and he was reading the newspaper with an expression of solemn concentration.

"Mr. Kiley."

He looked up, grinned. "Mrs. Kiley?"

Rebecca would not stoop to correct him. "The twins are about to have their baths, and we would appreciate it if you would avoid the kitchen until they're through."

He turned his attention back to the newspaper. "Call me when they're decent," he said distractedly, "and I'll carry out the water for you."

First Lucas had cooked supper, and now he'd volunteered to haul a heavy tubful of water outside. In an odd way, his offhanded kindness nettled Rebecca; she'd been more comfortable when there was a barrier of disagreement between them.

"Thank you," she said stiffly, and returned to the kitchen.

After the twins had been scrubbed and shampooed, and had donned nightgowns and been sent to bed, Rebecca returned to the parlor. This time, Lucas was standing on the stone hearth, gazing thoughtfully into the fire.

"It's safe to go into the kitchen now," she said, and from the way her voice trembled, anyone would have thought she'd made some momentous announcement.

Lucas smiled and started toward her, and Rebecca scrambled to get out of his path. It was herself she was afraid of, however, and not Mr. Kiley.

True to his word, he emptied the tub, and Rebecca wiped it out with a cloth and hung it in its place on the pantry wall. When she came out of that small room, Lucas was waiting for her, his eyes warm with mischief.

"I've got some things I could be doing in the barn, if you wanted to take a bath yourself," he said.

Rebecca imagined herself naked in this man's kitchen, as she had been on many other bath nights, and turned her head to hide another rush of color. "I couldn't," she replied, and went to take her sewing basket from a cupboard in the breakfront.

Hoping Lucas would go on to the barn anyway, she sat

down at the table and took out the two dolls she was making for Annabelle and Susan. The small bodies were formed of wooden spools, with painted faces and yellow yarn hair. Using scraps of the red velvet from the Christmas gown she'd been hired to make, she began to fashion simple dresses.

Lucas joined her at the table, watching her work in companionable silence.

Rebecca kept fumbling, but she persisted. She would make other clothes for the spool dolls, from the scraps of other projects, and on Christmas morning Annabelle and Susan would have something in their stockings.

The clock on the breakfront ticked ponderously through minute after minute, until an hour had passed. Then Lucas gave a yawn.

Without a word, unable to face the mirth she knew was twinkling in his eyes, Rebecca carefully put her handwork away, smoothed her skirts, went over to bank the fire in the stove. Once she'd finished, Lucas took the lantern from the table and led the way through the center of the house and up the stairs.

Rebecca checked to make sure the twins were covered and sleeping soundly, and when she entered Lucas's room, he was already in bed. His muscular chest was bare, since the sheet and blankets barely reached to his waist, and his arms were folded behind his head. Rebecca averted her eyes and crossed the room to turn down the lamp.

She ached with strange longings and wild embarrassment, and silently prayed Lucas wouldn't guess that—for all her brave, defiant words—she felt a lewd attraction to him.

Rebecca took off her dress in the darkness, praying Lucas's eyesight wasn't too sharp, and pulled on her nightgown. Beneath it, she wore her camisole, drawers, and, for good measure, a petticoat.

Even through all that muslin and flannel, she could feel Lucas's warmth as she lay carefully in bed, keeping as far to her own side as she could. And for all those precautions, she thought she would surely die if Lucas didn't take her in his arms and kiss her.

She whispered his name, without meaning to.

He rolled easily onto his side, encountered the fullness of the petticoat, and chuckled. "What is it, Becky?" he asked, with gruff gentleness.

"I've never slept with a man before."

His tone was wry. "I'd guessed that, somehow."

"Do you think I could be sent to hell for this?"

A smile lingered in his voice, and his hand came to rest on her middle, fingers splayed. Her nipples pushed against the soft fabric of her camisole in response, even though he hadn't touched them. "No. There's no sin in just lying there, wearing every last stitch you own." He paused, sighed. "And clothes or no clothes, what a temptation you are, Miss Becky Morgan."

He'd remembered her last name. Somehow, the knowledge warmed Rebecca. Not that her temperature wasn't soaring already.

"What if you kissed me and I didn't try to stop you?"

Lucas chuckled, even though she was entirely serious, and traced the outline of her cheek with the tip of his forefinger. "I don't know. Let's find out."

In the next instant, Lucas's mouth was teasing hers, shaping it, persuading her lips to open for him. For Rebecca's part, she was suddenly rocked with alarmingly sweet sensations. She opened herself to Lucas's kiss, and he took full advantage, his groan of desire echoing against her throat.

He moved over Rebecca, letting her feel his hardness and power without crushing her beneath his weight, and still he kissed her. She whimpered softly when he finally left her mouth to nibble at the side of her neck. Although she didn't fully understand what he had to give her, she wanted with all her soul to accept.

Lucas moved downward a little, cupped one flannel-and-muslin-covered breast in his hand, and scraped the hidden nipple lightly with his teeth.

Rebecca bit her lower lip to keep from crying out in startled pleasure, and she yearned to be bared to him, to let him initiate her into all the secrets of her own flesh. "Lucas," she whispered again.

To her surprise, he shoved himself away and gave a great, despondent sigh. "Not yet," he breathed, after a long time, in answer to the question she didn't have the nerve to ask. "I won't have you saying I seduced you."

Rebecca's heart was pounding so hard that she feared Lucas would hear it, and the feminine parts of her either ached or felt like so much melted wax. Lucas's kiss, and the sensation of his weight resting against her, had combined to make matters much worse, instead of easing her discomfort as she'd hoped. Lying next to him, throbbing with the unfulfilled promise he'd awakened in her, was sheer torture.

The next morning, she awakened early, and once again the house was deliciously warm. This time, however, Lucas had returned to the bedroom, bringing coffee for both of them.

Rebecca had never had anyone wait on her that way in her life, and she was completely taken aback. For all her unsettled emotions, however, she didn't miss the fire burning in Lucas's eyes.

It gave her no little satisfaction to know that he wanted her as badly as she had wanted him the night before, and now that the sun was up and there was more space between them, she was struck by a reckless impulse. Perhaps there was a way she could repay him for the sweet suffering he'd subjected her to the night before by poising himself over her and kissing her until she'd thought she'd die of need.

She set her coffee aside on the bedstand, climbed out of bed, and brazenly pulled her nightgown off over her head.

Lucas fell back against the closed door of the bedroom, staring at her in amazement.

The old Rebecca was gone for the moment, replaced by a brazen, mischievous imposter. She stepped out of her petticoats, humming softly under her breath, and then removed her camisole—and drawers, too.

Lucas's Adam's apple moved the length of his neck, and he swallowed hard. His eyes were round as he watched her take out fresh undergarments and put them on, then pull her Sunday dress from its peg on the wall and step into it.

"Would you fasten the buttons, please?" she asked sweetly, approaching Lucas and turning her back to him. That would teach him to make sport of her innocence the way he had the previous night.

She felt his fingers fumble against her spine as he worked the tiny buttons through their loops of fabric. She was not immune to his touch, or to the sense of him standing close behind her, but she didn't let her reactions show.

Not, at least, until Lucas finished with her buttons and bent his head to kiss her lightly on the side of the neck. "I wouldn't tease if I were you," he warned, in a gruff whisper. "The next time you flaunt that delectably lush body of yours, Mrs. Kiley, I may just call your bluff."

The practical Rebecca returned in exactly that instant, bristling with mortification. She whirled, glaring up into Lucas's laughing eyes. "Kindly get out of my way," she said. "I don't want to be late for church."

He gave a grunt of amusement and laid his hands on either side of her waist. "Think about tonight, Becky," he taunted. "Think about how it will be, lying beside me, wanting the kind of loving that will shake your soul. Think about *this*." With that, Lucas hauled Rebecca against him and kissed her hard.

Chapter Five

*R*ebecca was most inattentive in church that morning, and the fact that Lucas insisted on accompanying her only made matters worse. She sat up front, with the rest of the choir, and for the whole of the sermon, Mr. Kiley watched her instead of the preacher.

When the pastor publicly welcomed Lucas to Cornucopia and said what a good thing it was that a family had been re-united, Rebecca thought sure the Lord would send a bolt of lightning right through the shingled roof of that little church to strike her dead. Lucas beamed, delighting in her discomfort, and during the social hour following the worship service, he called Rebecca "dear" and made a point of slipping an arm around her waist whenever he got the chance.

He was popular with the townspeople, too. By the time the members of the small but dedicated congregation were ready to return to their homes, Lucas had garnered no less than three invitations for supper. Of course, he was supposed to bring Rebecca and the twins, too.

Graciously, he refused the offers, saying he was still re-newing his acquaintance with "Mrs. Kiley's" cooking and promising to be more sociable once the honeymoon was over.

"The honeymoon?" Rebecca protested later, mortified, when she was settled beside Lucas on the seat of his wagon. Annabelle and Susan were riding in back, absorbed in some discussion of their own. "Lucas, how *could* you embarrass me that way?"

He grinned as he bent to release the brake lever, then urged the team into motion with a light slap of the reins. "I was only doing my part to shore up your story, Becky," he said reasonably. "When a man's been away from his wife as long as you claim I have, he naturally feels a need to make up for lost time. Fact is, folks will be looking for you to have a baby in the next year or so."

Rebecca's cheeks flamed, but she held on to her dignity. "Then 'folks' will be disappointed."

Lucas chuckled, and there was no doubt in Rebecca's mind that he was thinking of her scandalous responses to the kisses he'd stolen, not only the night before, but just that morning. "Maybe," he said.

The implication made Rebecca livid. Yes, she'd lied, and trespassed. And there was no denying that she'd behaved like a shameless hussy that morning, deliberately taunting Lucas with her nakedness—dear God, what had possessed her? But she wasn't an immoral person. She was pure, and she'd never stolen in her life, even though she'd often been hungry. She tried to live in a proper and upright fashion, working hard for what little she had, and she was kind to others. Mr. Kiley had no earthly right to imply that she would ever surrender her body to him or any other man.

"You are quite arrogant," she said loftily, and a new snow began to fall, dusting the horses' broad, strong backs and rimming Lucas's hat with fat, fluffy flakes. A blanket of stillness covered the land. "Furthermore, you have vastly overestimated your charms."

Lucas smiled, clearly unruffled by her comment, and pushed his hat back with a practiced motion of one thumb. "You grew up poor in Chicago," he observed, "that's plain. But I can tell you've had schooling by the way you speak. How did you manage to get an education, Becky?"

Rebecca kept her gazed fixed on the pristine landscape. Lucas had pulled her soul close to the surface, and she didn't want him to see the pain that remembering caused her. In fact, showing him her body had been far easier.

"My mother died when I was seven," she said softly. "Pa couldn't manage, so he left me off at his sister's gate. Aunt Martha was an invalid, and I had to take care of her day and night to earn my keep, but she did teach me how to read. I consumed every book I could beg or borrow, and I guess some of what I took in must have stuck." When she could, Rebecca looked at Lucas. "What about you? Did you go to school?"

Lucas adjusted his hat again, glanced at the road, and turned his attention back to Rebecca. "For a while. My mother was a schoolteacher before she married my father, and she taught me what she could. Like you, I just sort of gathered up the rest, from books mostly."

A curiously comfortable silence fell between them. The wagon jostled over the rutted road, the twins chattered and occasionally bickered, and the snow came down harder and faster.

When they reached the farmhouse, Lucas drove the team straight inside the barn. The twins lingered to pester him, and Rebecca went into the house to see to Sunday dinner.

She'd found a ham among the supplies Lucas had brought with him when he arrived, and it filled the kitchen with a mouth-watering aroma as it roasted.

Rebecca exchanged her sateen church dress for a serviceable calico, tied a dish towel around her waist for an apron, lit several lanterns against the thickening glower of the winter afternoon, and set the table. While she waited for the potatoes to boil, she set a blaze in the parlor fireplace and sat down to read the newspaper Mary had given her the day before.

One item in particular, an advertisement on the back page,

caught her attention. According to the bold print, the men of Seattle and Alaska were desperate for wives, and transportation would be provided for suitable candidates. Even as she shuddered at the idea of marrying a stranger, she fetched her sewing scissors and clipped the panel out, folding it and tucking it into her dress pocket. Then, frowning, she tossed the remainder of the newspaper into the fire.

When the twins came in from the barn, their cheeks were bright with color and their eyes shone with excitement.

"Lucas is making a workshop in the barn," Susan blurted, with uncharacteristic enthusiasm. "You should see all the tools he has!"

"He's going to make tables and bureaus and bedsteads and sell them to people," Annabelle added, with admiration. "He's a carpenter."

"And whatever we do," Susan put in, "we're not to set foot in that workshop between now and Christmas."

Rebecca smiled, but she felt a certain resentment, too. Lucas was a stranger, after all, and already Annabelle and Susan thought he'd descended straight from Mount Olympus, trailing clouds of glory. "Wash your hands and faces," she instructed her sisters, "and next time you come in from the barn, wipe your feet first."

Susan and Annabelle looked at each other and shrugged, then scampered off to do as they'd been told.

When Lucas came in, he brought with him Mr. Pontious, the peddler who sometimes boarded in the hired man's room out in the barn.

"Look what the wind blew in!" Mr. Pontious cried, grinning and spreading his hands for drama. He was a tall, slender man, bald beneath the bowler hat he invariably wore, and always full of good cheer. For all his bluster, though, there was a troubled expression in his blue eyes.

Rebecca greeted him warmly, wondering if he'd somehow guessed her deception and reasoned out that Lucas

Kiley wasn't really her long-lost husband. She put another place at the table and poured coffee for her boarder, and all during the meal he and Lucas talked about farming.

It generally was agreed that wheat was the best crop to grow around Cornucopia, and now that the train came through once a week, marketing wouldn't be a problem. What the town needed, Lucas and the peddler decided, was a flour mill.

Rebecca cleared away the dinner plates, when most of the food had been consumed, and put out a dried apple pie.

"I don't mind saying I'm glad Mrs. Kiley and the children won't be alone out here anymore," Mr. Pontious said, chewing appreciatively even as he spoke. "The way folks are today, what with all the crime and everything, it just isn't safe."

Lucas tossed Rebecca a mischievous glance. "Don't worry," he said, "I'll look after my wife."

Maybe so, Rebecca agreed silently, but who was going to protect her from her so-called husband? Although he'd promised not to seduce her, Lucas was doing a pretty good job of making her want him all the same, and without any apparent effort.

That night, by the light of the kerosene lanterns, Mr. Pontious and Lucas played cards until late. The twins were sound asleep, and Rebecca had long since consigned herself to Lucas's bed, when her "husband" finally entered the room.

Rebecca pretended to be asleep and, to her combined relief and disappointment, Lucas didn't touch her. He just undressed, crawled under the covers, and let out a yawn loud enough for a bear getting ready to hibernate.

It irritated her to no end that he only had to lie there to make her scandalously conscious of his strong arms, his hard chest and muscular stomach, his powerful legs . . .

Morning caught Rebecca by surprise, since she had expected to suffer instead of sleep. Lucas was already up and hammering away in the barn, and the twins had gotten ready for school on their own.

"Lucas made pancakes," Annabelle explained, when Rebecca said she'd fix toast and fried eggs for their breakfast.

"Mr. Pontious said he'd never eaten better flapjacks," Susan remarked. Then she squinted at her elder sister in concern. "Are you feeling all right, Rebecca? You look sort of peaky."

"I'm fine," Rebecca replied, and if the words came out sounding a little snappish—well, she couldn't help it. Taking care of Annabelle and Susan was her responsibility, not Lucas's, and she didn't appreciate his interference. "Don't forget to put on your boots and button your coats before you start for home this afternoon. And whose turn is it to feed the chickens?"

"Lucas did that," Annabelle said, and then the two were gone, racing through the snowy morning.

Mr. Pontious came in just as Rebecca was washing the last of the breakfast dishes. "That's a fine man you've got there," he said, but the look in his road-weary eyes was a somber one.

Rebecca offered no comment on Lucas's character. She poured a cup of coffee for her favorite boarder, and he sat down at the table.

"Something's been troubling you ever since you got here," she said gently. "What is it?"

Mr. Pontious cleared his throat and wrapped his long fingers around his cup to warm them. "Maybe you'd best sit down, Mrs. Kiley."

Before, Rebecca had only felt curiosity, but now there was a flash of alarm. She joined the peddler at the table, and he glanced nervously toward the door, as if expecting Lucas to appear.

After a long interval, he finally spoke again, at the same

time taking a small leather folder from the inside pocket of his tattered woolen vest. "As you know," he said hoarsely, "I get up to Spokane fairly regular, so's I can pick up new merchandise to bring out here to the farm country. Last week, I met a feller there, and he sold me this."

Even before Rebecca reached for the object Mr. Pontious so reluctantly pushed toward her, she knew what she would see when she raised the cover of that folder. Still, her heart all but stopped when she saw the photograph inside. It was one of the images Duke Jones had taken, during those desperate days just before Rebecca and the twins had left Chicago, and her own eyes stared back at her from the tintype.

That wasn't the worst part, though. She'd posed in just a thin camisole and a pair of scanty drawers, and her hair tumbled loose down her back, like a harlot's. Her face obviously had been painted, and she'd assumed a seductive expression, at Mr. Jones's insistence.

Rebecca rubbed her nape, where a headache was stirring. She knew little enough about Lucas Kiley, but she was well aware that he held shameless women in very low esteem. Once, back in Chicago, she'd heard him speak contemptuously of an actress who had stayed at the boardinghouse for a short time. When that same woman had flirted openly with Lucas at the dinner table, he'd cut her dead with a cold stare.

Now, in the warmth and decency of Lucas Kiley's kitchen, Rebecca felt more like a trespasser than ever. She covered her mouth with one hand and uttered an involuntary groan.

Mr. Pontious looked at her pityingly. "I guess you must have had a good reason for what you did," he said. "Still, I don't suppose folks around here would take kindly to a likeness such as this one."

Rebecca closed the folder and kept it covered with one trembling hand, as if she could guard her secret that way.

"The man who sold you this," she whispered brokenly. "What was his name?"

"Jones, if I remember correct-like," Mr. Pontious said. "He was fixing to set up a studio in Spokane. I ran into him in the—er—the Rusty Spur Saloon one night, and that's when he showed me your picture. I bought it for ten cents."

Rebecca knew without looking in a mirror that she'd gone pale as the snow mantling the land for miles around. Shaking, she went to the breakfront, took a dime from the tin box she kept in the top drawer, and offered it to Mr. Pontious.

He refused the payment with a shake of his head and pushed the photograph toward her.

Stricken, Rebecca studied the image once more, then carried it resolutely to the stove, dropped it inside, and watched in grim silence as it curled into ash.

Chapter Six

After Mr. Pontious had gone out to the barn to bed down in the spare room, Rebecca went to the pantry, moving like a woman in a trance, to get the washtub. Her mind was filled with the image of herself posing for Duke Jones's scurrilous photographs; she didn't see the kitchen around her, the kettles she filled with water and set on the stove to heat, the tub itself.

She was startled out of her reverie, at least briefly, when the back door opened and Lucas came in, along with a rush of cold air.

He looked at the bathtub and the kettles and raised an eyebrow. "I thought you'd decided your virtue would be in peril if you bathed while I was around," he said. He took off his coat and hat, and hung them on the pegs next to the door.

Rebecca still was in shock, and seeing that awful picture had left her feeling dirty. Even though she knew she couldn't wash away what had happened back in Chicago, in Jones's studio, she was sure she would go mad if she didn't strip, step into a tubful of hot water, and scrub herself from head to toe with strong soap.

"Becky?" Lucas prompted, when she didn't say anything in reply. He came to her, took her chin in a hand fragrant with the scent of new lumber, and made her look at him. "What is it?"

She wanted to tell him, she truly did—but in that moment, she came to the cataclysmic realization that she loved Lucas Kiley. That was the reason she'd tried to find him after hearing about his accident in the factory in Chicago, and why she'd come to live in his house, posing as his wife. He was enjoying the game of pretending to be married now, and he had been kind and generous.

Once he learned that Rebecca had sold herself the way she had, however, he would hate her. It wouldn't matter that no man had ever made love to her, that she'd only posed for the pictures to get the money to start new lives for herself and the girls. Lucas wouldn't see past the fact that she'd sat for a photograph in just her dainties—no good, decent man would.

It was just too much to ask.

"I'm—I'm all right," she finally said, twisting free of Lucas's gentle hold on her face. "A little bit tired, that's all. If you'd just agree to let me have my privacy—"

Lucas nodded and stepped back, but his eyes were full of questions. Clearly, he knew Rebecca was a whole lot less than "all right." He put on his hat and coat again, lit the lantern he'd been carrying when he came in, and went back out into the cold.

Rebecca went upstairs for a nightgown and wrapper, and then sat in the dark kitchen, staring numbly out the window, while she waited for the water to finish heating. When it was hot enough, she filled the tub, took off her clothes, and sank gratefully into her bath.

She scoured every inch of herself, scrubbing until her skin stung. But as she'd expected, the feeling of being filthy would not be washed away. Finally she reached for a towel and dried off, then put on her nightclothes.

Lucas knocked politely at the back door, after some time had passed, and Rebecca's voice was hoarse when she called, "Come in."

He set the glowing lantern on the table, gave Rebecca one unreadable look, and hoisted the heavy tub. While he was carrying the water out of the house, Rebecca fled upstairs to the master bedroom and plunged under the covers. She was still wearing her wrapper.

Lucas appeared presently, carrying the lamp. "Stop pretending to be asleep," he ordered, in a kind but firm tone. "I know you're not."

Rebecca felt as though all her nerves were outside her skin, exposed and vulnerable. She wasn't naive enough to think she'd solved her problem by burning that one tintype; there were surely other pictures circulating in and around Spokane. Frantically, vainly, she searched her mind for a solution.

"Thank you for going to the barn while I bathed," she said woodenly. God in heaven, why did she have to love this man? When and how had his opinion of her become a matter of life and death?

The mattress gave as Lucas sat down on its edge and began pulling off his boots. "Think nothing of it," he replied cordially. He undressed completely, as casually as if he and Rebecca had shared a bed for half a century, and got under the covers before reaching over to turn down the wick in the lantern. "I'm getting pretty tired of washing in a basin myself. Maybe tomorrow I'll have a nice hot bath. Feel free to stay right there in the kitchen and wash my back, Mrs. Kiley."

He was only teasing, and Rebecca knew that, but something in his words or the gentle, humorous tone of his voice broke down the flimsy barriers she'd been hiding behind all evening. Without warning, without so much as a sniffle to foretell the onslaught, Rebecca began to sob.

Lucas was taken aback for a few moments—she could sense that—but then he reached out and pulled her close to him. "There now, Becky," he said, somewhat helplessly. "There now, don't take on so; you might hurt yourself."

Rebecca would have laughed if she hadn't been so full of despair. As it happened, all she could do was let out a low, miserable little wail. She was a strong woman, and she'd endured more than most, but she'd finally reached her limit.

He kissed the top of her head, entangling his fingers in her hair, and held her very tightly. "Whatever it is," he assured her, "I want to help."

She wailed again, muffling the sound by clutching the edge of the quilt and bunching it against her face. Her spirit was in terrible turmoil—and at one and the same time, her body was betraying her. Lucas felt so strong, so hard, pressed close to her like that. He was a brick wall that could protect her from any danger.

Rebecca put her arms around his neck, laid her cheek against his chest, felt his heartbeat, steady and fast. Soon the photographs would turn up in Cornucopia—maybe they already had—and when Lucas saw them, her world would end. Her time with him was limited, and it was precious.

"Make love to me," she whispered.

He pressed her onto her back and leaned over her, his face no more than a shadow in the darkness of the bedroom. "What did you say?"

"I—I want you, Lucas. You said I would ask for—for intimate relations, and you were right. I'm asking."

Disbelief echoed in his voice. "Are you sure?"

Rebecca nodded. And she *was* sure. When she had to leave Lucas and the farm and Cornucopia forever, in disgrace, she would at least have one special memory to look back on. "Yes," she managed to say.

His mouth fell to hers; he kissed her long and hard, and they were both breathless when he finally broke away. "It's your first time?"

Tears burned in Rebecca's eyes, and she was glad he couldn't see them. Physically, she was untouched, but a deeper part of her had been conquered long ago. "Yes, Lucas," she told him. "You're the first."

He muttered something, then gently raised her nightgown over her head and tossed it away. She flushed when he lit the lamp, and tried to cover herself, but Lucas wouldn't allow that.

He straddled her thighs and looked at her face and her breasts, her belly and her most private place, as though she were a glorious painting, or a never-to-be-forgotten sunset. "Ever since I first saw you, way back when we both lived in the boardinghouse, I've wanted to see you like this, to touch you."

Rebecca felt shy, and attempted to hide her breasts under her hands, but Lucas gripped her wrists and held them easily against the mattress. "Will it—will it hurt?" she asked.

Lucas reached out to touch one of her nipples, and it hardened obediently beneath his fingertip. "Just this once," he replied. "I promise I'll make it all worthwhile, though, if you'll just trust me."

She closed her eyes, arched her back slightly, and moaned as he continued to caress her breast. "I trust you," she said.

He lowered his head, took a well-prepared nipple into his mouth, and began to suck softly. At the same time, he pressed the heel of his palm to the moist delta between Rebecca's thighs and made a slow, circular motion.

The more he suckled and teased, the more she pitched beneath him, wild as a mare with her stallion. When he trailed a path of kisses down over her belly and then burrowed through and took her femininity just as he'd taken her nipple, she pushed her knuckles between her teeth to keep from crying out in stunned pleasure.

When he eased a finger deep inside her, Rebecca's body buckled in a delicious spasm. Lucas reached up and covered her mouth with his free hand, and he was just in time, for her shouts of surrender vibrated against his palm.

The response seemed to go on and on, and Rebecca was damp with perspiration when the wild, sweet convulsions finally ebbed away. She lay snuggled against Lucas, unable to speak, dazed by the glory of all he'd made her feel.

He held her for a long time, until his own need became too great. He parted her legs and mounted her.

"This is your last chance," he whispered. "If you're going to refuse me, for God's sake, do it now."

Instead, Rebecca spread her hands over the taut muscles of his back and urged him closer.

Lucas sighed and then, very, very slowly, he glided inside her. She felt a stretching sensation, and then a brief, sharp stab of pain. He held his body still while she adjusted to him, kissing her eyelids, whispering raspy words of comfort.

The first twinge of pleasure surprised Rebecca so much that her eyes flew open. She gasped and arched her neck, and Lucas kissed the underside of her chin.

"Shall I stop?" His voice was like distant thunder.

"No," Rebecca whimpered. "No—*please*—don't draw away—"

He chuckled and began to move upon her. Her womb contracted in the first sudden and startling throes of renewed passion.

"Lucas," she murmured, as her body began to flex beneath his, meeting every lunge and parry of his hips. "Lucas—is it supposed to be like this?"

Lucas laughed and nipped at her earlobe, sending another storm of sensation raging through her system. "Yes, Becky," he answered. "It's supposed to be *just* like this. And I always figured it would be, if you and I ever found ourselves under the same blanket."

Rebecca was breathless, fevered. She twisted and writhed in obedient rebellion, and her fingers delved deep into his shoulders. "It's—oh, Lucas, I can't bear it—it's too much—"

He tasted her lower lip, captured her mouth with his, lined the underside of her jaw with soft kisses. "Let it happen," he told her, and when she curved her back and stiffened, he kissed her again, swallowing her cries of satisfaction.

The pleasure was so intense that Rebecca was only half-conscious when Lucas finally reached his own pinnacle. He plunged deep and moaned, and she felt his warmth spilling inside her. In some ways, that was even better than the flurry of frantic delight he'd caused her minutes before.

She held him, comforted him, when he collapsed beside her, recovering from the force of his release.

"Now I'll go to hell for sure," she said forlornly, when a long time had passed and her breathing had settled back down to its normal rate.

Lucas chuckled. "Not likely," he replied. "They wouldn't have the first idea what to do with you down there."

Rebecca wasn't sure whether she'd just been complimented or insulted. "I'd probably have exactly the same problem in heaven," she said sadly. "Wherever I go, it seems like I turn out to be the onion growing in the petunia patch."

He kissed her lightly and caressed her cheek, then pushed her hair back to trace the shape of her ear with a fingertip. "Oh, Becky, believe me, you're not an onion. You're a wild rose, beautiful and fragrant and so thick with thorns that it takes all a man's courage to touch you."

A tiny muscle tightened in Rebecca's throat. "You talk in poetry sometimes, even though the words don't rhyme. Has anybody ever told you that?"

Lucas cupped her breast in one hand, bent his head to idly brush its tip with his lips, touched it with his tongue when it hardened for him. "No," he answered. "But it doesn't necessarily take words to make a poem. When you move under me the way you did a little while ago, trying to take me deeper and deeper inside you, that's poetry, too."

She plunged her fingers into his hair and held his head to her breast while he suckled, and even though she was silent for a long time to come, her body gave an eloquent recitation of its own.

Chapter Seven

All Rebecca's doubts and fears returned with the morning, and she wondered at this duplicity in herself that allowed her to fluctuate so wildly between bluestocking modesty and a distinct inclination to behave brazenly. She supposed there was some flaw in her nature that kept her from being like other women; no doubt it was a legacy from her unscrupulous father.

Mr. Pontious joined the household for breakfast, and there was a certain awkwardness between him and Rebecca. He hastily left, after settling up with Lucas for the cost of two nights' lodging. Lucas headed for his workshop in the barn, and the children crunched happily through the deep, crusted snow, schoolbooks and tablets in hand.

Rebecca had finished the red-velvet dress, except for final alterations and putting up the hem. At noon, Ginny Dylan arrived for the last fitting. She was a lovely young girl, with dark hair and bright green eyes, and in that splendid gown, she was a vision.

Just as Rebecca was putting the last pin in Ginny's hem, around noon, the back door opened and Lucas entered the kitchen, along with a wintry breeze. Rebecca felt an absurd fear that he would look at the beautiful Ginny and forget all that had happened in the night.

He greeted the visitor with a cordial nod, hung up his coat

and hat, went to the stove for coffee, and then wandered into the parlor. Rebecca was embarrassed by the depth of her relief; it appeared that Lucas had barely noticed Cornucopia's most celebrated beauty.

Ginny was used to charming men of all ages, and she sulked a little as she sipped her tea and waited for Rebecca to finish hemming the dress. When the task was completed, and deemed acceptable, Ginny paid Rebecca the sum agreed upon and left, driving herself back to town in a small, fancy surrey with spindly wheels.

Rebecca might have mourned the lovely gown for an hour or two, if her mind hadn't been so full of the damning photograph Mr. Pontious had showed her the night before. She stared down at the money Ginny had given her—she *had* been planning to add it to her modest savings—and knew she must use it instead for stagecoach fare to Spokane. Her only chance of finding peace of mind and true happiness lay in locating Duke Jones and persuading him to destroy the photographic plates that held her image. She wouldn't be able to track down all the copies he had made from the plates and she could only hope there weren't many, but once the plates were destroyed, the chance of a photo turning up in Cornucopia would be much less.

Her heart rushed into her throat when she turned and saw Lucas leaning against the woodwork of the parlor doorway, arms folded. His expression was speculative, somewhat worried, and his words came as a total surprise.

"You should be wearing velvet dresses yourself, instead of sewing them for other women."

Rebecca found Lucas's kindness nearly intolerable, given the fact that she was keeping a secret from him. She managed a faltering smile and tucked the money into her apron pocket before turning away to begin assembling the midday meal. "I'd look silly in such a gown," she said. "Silly and pretentious."

Lucas caught Rebecca off guard by stepping up behind her, laying his hands gently on her shoulders, and turning her to face him. "No," he said, his voice gruff. "You must have looked into a mirror a thousand times, Becky. How could you have failed to notice that you're beautiful?"

Sweet anguish filled Rebecca; she tried to pull away from Lucas, but he held her fast. "Please, Lucas—" she murmured. She knew what he was going to tell her, and with the entirety of her soul she longed to hear the words, but at the same time, she dreaded them.

"It's time we made things right between us," he insisted. "We ought to be married. For real."

Tears brimmed in Rebecca's eyes, but she blinked them back. Lucas had not offered her a flowery, poetic declaration of devotion, and yet she knew he cared for her in his way. If he hadn't been at least a little smitten, he would have thrown her and the twins out of his house the first day after his return.

"You don't understand," she faltered. "I'm not—I have a past."

Lucas's smile was crooked and painfully endearing. "We all do," he replied. "What did you do, Becky? Set a brush-fire? Hold up a stagecoach?"

Life had made Rebecca practical. Much as she would have liked to indulge in the delusion that Lucas might see the fact that she'd posed for a stranger's camera—practically in the altogether—as a mere lapse of judgment, she knew better. Men were proprietary creatures.

"It was nothing you need to know about, Lucas Kiley," she said stiffly. "Now, if you don't mind, I'd like to get the midday meal on the table before it's time to start supper."

Still puzzled, Lucas released her, but it was clear that he wasn't willing to let the subject drop so easily as that.

"I know you don't have a husband or a lover tucked away somewhere; I was definitely the first man to have you." He must have seen the blush glowing in her nape, though he said nothing about it. "Tell me, Becky—are you running from the law?"

"No," she said, stirring the pot of beans she'd put on earlier, then moving on to slice the accompanying cornbread. "I've committed no crime."

She heard the legs of one of the kitchen chairs scrape against the floor as he slid it back to sit, and he sighed.

"Your father's in prison," he guessed, sounding weary and not a little frustrated. "Or maybe one of those places where they put crazy people."

Rebecca bit her lower lip for a long moment, fighting the urge to say yes, it was one of those things. She'd done enough lying since coming to Cornucopia, though, and another false claim would have caught in her throat. "My father might have wound up in either place, if he hadn't drunk himself to death first."

She spooned beans into a bowl, stacked several slices of cornbread on a plate, carried the light meal to the table. She was careful not to look into Lucas's eyes, fearing that if she did, her soul would go tumbling through them, never to be her own again.

"I need to go to Spokane," she said, in a businesslike voice. "Annabelle and Susan will stay with Mary, at the store."

Lucas caught hold of her wrist, but while she probably could not have escaped his grasp, the gesture was in no way threatening. "It's almost Christmas," he said. "How can you go away now?"

Misery filled Rebecca. While other women were making last-minute preparations for the holiday, roasting geese and keeping wonderful secrets, she would be jostling along on the hard seat of a stagecoach. She would be searching for Duke Jones, begging him to destroy the pictures that might well ruin her life.

"I have to," she told Lucas simply.

"Then I'll go with you."

"No!" she cried out, startling herself as well as Lucas. "No, this is something I have to do for myself."

"Will you come back?"

Rebecca wouldn't meet his gaze. "Yes," she answered, failing to add that, if she was unsuccessful in dealing with Jones, a prospect that seemed likely, she would return to Cornucopia only long enough to collect her sisters from Mary Daniels.

That afternoon she packed. When the girls came home from school, she immediately presented them with a large satchel, containing everything they'd need for several days. They looked at her in heart-wrenching bewilderment, probably remembering the uncertainty of their days with their father, and how he'd finally abandoned them in someone else's care. Still, they asked no questions.

Lucas drove the three of them to town in his wagon, grimly silent throughout the trip, and Rebecca sat rigidly on the seat beside him, keeping her eyes on the road. Reaching the general store, he unloaded their baggage onto the wooden sidewalk and then left, a brief touch to the brim of his hat his only farewell.

"Where are we going?" Annabelle asked, in desperation.

"You're staying right here in Cornucopia, for the time being," Rebecca answered. "I have business in Spokane."

"But it'll be Christmas soon!" Susan wailed. "What if you miss it?"

Rebecca sighed as she pushed open the door of the shop. A cheery little bell tinkled overhead. "It wouldn't be the first time," she answered, a bit irritably. In truth, Rebecca had been looking forward to the holiday herself, mainly because of Lucas. Although, as usual, there would have been few presents, she'd planned to cook a special meal and decorate the parlor with paper angels and strings of popcorn.

Mary's bright smile faded when she saw the satchel Rebecca carried. "What is happening here?" she asked, her tone full of polite insistence.

"I'd be obliged if the girls could spend a day or two here with you," Rebecca said, speaking carefully in an effort not to burst into tears. "I promise they'll make themselves useful when they aren't at school."

Annabelle and Susan looked at each other, but neither spoke.

"And where will you be during this time, pray tell?" Mary inquired, rounding the counter to stand facing Rebecca. The purposeful storemistress took hold of her friend's arm and led her back between rows of boots and garden hoes and flour barrels to the main storeroom. "Start talking, Rebecca Kiley."

Rebecca lost her battle with tears and, in a frantic whisper, began to pour out her story. She told Mary how she'd met Lucas in Chicago, when they'd lived in the same boardinghouse, and that she'd been in love with him even then, although she hadn't known it. She confessed that she'd come to Cornucopia believing he was dead, and pretended to be his wife so that she and the twins finally would have a decent life.

Mary smiled when Rebecca got to the part where Lucas returned unexpectedly, to find himself with a wife and family, but she didn't interrupt.

The smile faded to a look of sympathy when Rebecca explained how she'd earned the money to travel west and take over Lucas's farm. "Last night," Rebecca finished, "Mr. Pontious spent the night in the barn room. Mary, he had one of those dreadful pictures, and he said he'd bought it in Spokane, from Duke Jones himself."

Mary sighed and embraced her friend briefly before asking, "What do you expect to accomplish by confronting this man, Rebecca? He clearly has no scruples, or he wouldn't engage in such pursuits in the first place."

"I have to try," Rebecca said, standing stiffly in the crowded storeroom. "I love Lucas, but if he ever sees one of those pictures, he'll despise me."

"Maybe not," Mary replied, with gentle uncertainty. "Wouldn't it be better just to tell him the truth, and hope he understands? You wouldn't be the first person to come out west with a secret or two buried in their past. Why, lots of folks are here to make a new start of one kind or another."

Rebecca only shook her head. Lucas was a good, decent man—and a proud one. He wouldn't be able to bear the knowledge that her charms were on display to any man who could pay a dime to view them.

She and the twins spent the night in Mary's spare room, the girls sleeping deeply, Rebecca sleeping not at all.

Early the next morning, the stagecoach came through town, and when it headed north toward Spokane, Rebecca was aboard it. She was grateful to be the only passenger, since she couldn't have made polite small talk to save her immortal soul.

The ride was long and extremely wearing. Rebecca could see her breath, and her feet were so numb that she couldn't move her toes.

When at last she arrived in Spokane, night had fallen, and the small city seemed very loud and decadent to Rebecca, now that she'd become accustomed to Cornucopia. Resolutely, she straightened her Sunday bonnet, lifted her reticule from the floor of the coach, and climbed out with as much grace as possible.

Being too embarrassed to ask for directions to the saloon Mr. Pontious had mentioned, she simply followed the sounds of badly tuned pianos, gunshots, and revelry until she came upon a row of scurrilous establishments.

As she stood on the sidewalk in front of the Rusty Spur

Saloon, peering over the swinging doors, flakes of pristine snow began to fall all around her, white as goosedown. Rebecca took a deep breath, squared her slender shoulders, and proceeded bravely into the smoke-filled den of depravity where she hoped to find Duke Jones.

Chapter Eight

*J*ones had not changed much, really. He was still handsome, in a smarmy sort of way, and when he saw Rebecca, he chuckled with delight, folded the hand of cards he'd been playing, and tossed them into the center of the saloon table.

The men seated there with him were too busy staring at Rebecca to grumble over an early end to their game.

Mr. Jones stood, for all the world like a gentleman, and scolded indulgently, "Rebecca, my dear—for shame! This is no place for a lovely lady!"

Rebecca narrowed her eyes at him, remembering how he'd taken advantage of her desperate need in Chicago, how he'd promised that no one west of the Mississippi would see those disgraceful pictures he'd taken. And she'd been fool enough to believe him!

She caught herself, just as she would have spit on his sawdust-coated boots, and summoned up a milder expression, a smile being quite beyond her. "I would like to speak to you privately," she said, with cool dignity.

He clamped a cheroot between his teeth, lit it with a wooden match, and then gestured grandly toward the back of the saloon. "As you wish," he told her. "I have an office in the back."

Just the thought of what probably went on in that place

made Rebecca's flesh crawl, but she straightened her spine and preceded Jones along a dimly lit hallway. Everything depended on her ability to reach a satisfactory agreement with the man who held her future in his hands.

Jones opened a door, using a large brass key, and went in before Rebecca to light a lamp. She was relieved—to some extent—to find a desk and chair, a bookshelf and some photographic equipment in the room. At least there wasn't a bed.

"Sit down," he said, gesturing graciously toward the chair facing his desk. "What a wonderful surprise it is to see you again, Rebecca."

Rebecca smoothed her skirts as she sat, with as much dignity as if they were silk and not well-worn calico, and willed her hammering heart to settle into a calmer beat. "I can't imagine that you're surprised," she said. "When you sold my photograph to Mr. Pontious and saw his reaction, you must have guessed that he knew me."

Jones tapped his chin with one finger, feigning deep thought. "Pontious . . . Pontious. Oh, yes—the peddler." He paused to smile around the cheroot he'd lit earlier. "You should have seen him, Becky. He went pale as milk when he recognized you."

His inadvertent use of the nickname "Becky," heretofore reserved for Lucas, stung Rebecca's heart and sent hot venom flooding through her veins. Still, though she knew her color was high and she was definitely trembling, she managed somehow to keep her composure.

"I want you to destroy the photographic plates and give me any copies of those pictures you might have in your possession," she said.

Jones laughed and drew on his cheroot for a few moments before countering, "Oh? You may be the subject of the photographs, my dear, but they belong to me. What do you have to offer in payment?"

Rebecca struggled against the currents of fear and fury

that would pull her beneath the surface of reason and smother her, along with all her hopes and fragile wishes for the future. "Nothing," she answered. "I'm depending on you to do the honorable thing."

This statement seemed to amuse Jones even more. "Great Zeus!" he boomed, spreading his hands in jovial mockery. "Look around you, Becky. Is this the sort of place an 'honorable' man would frequent?"

She clutched the handle of her reticule tightly in both hands. "What do you want?" The words came out in a whisper.

Jones smiled, opened a drawer in the battered desk, and brought out two photographic plates and a handful of pictures. "Not so much, really," he said. "You compromised yourself once. What do you have to lose by doing it again?"

Rebecca's blood turned to ice. "What are you saying?"

With a shrug, Jones responded, "It's quite clear that you have little or no money. But money is not all a beautiful woman like yourself can offer in trade."

She stood, shaking with rage and humiliation. "I can see I've wasted my time in coming here. Good evening, Mr. Jones."

He rose rapidly from his previously languid position in the other chair just as she turned her back. "One night in my bed. That's all it would take to persuade me to destroy these plates." Jones slithered to her side, silent as a snake, and handed her one of the sepia-tinted photographs.

Rebecca felt light-headed, and she thought for certain she was about to throw up, but somehow she managed to pretend that she still possessed her dignity. "I would sooner pass the night with the devil himself," she said, and then she walked out, taking the damning photograph with her.

Now, she thought forlornly, as she walked through the main part of the saloon, taking little notice of her surroundings, and stepped out onto the sidewalk, there was nothing to do but go back to Cornucopia, show Lucas the photograph, collect the twins, and leave. She still had the advertisement she'd clipped from Mary's newspaper, the one calling for wives for men in Seattle and Alaska.

Rebecca began to walk, heedless of the ever-deepening snow. Perhaps the twins could board at a mission school until they were old enough to be on their own. Their well-being was all that would matter to Rebecca after this; she would get through her own life by rote.

She had walked some distance before she became aware of angelic voices echoing through the cold, snowy night. The familiar words of Christmas carols penetrated her despair, and when she saw the lights of a church ahead, her step quickened.

Rebecca slipped into a back pew, hidden by the shadows, watching and listening in singular misery as a choir practiced Christmas hymns. The words of the songs soothed her like balm, and eventually she stretched out on the bench, lulled into blessed sleep.

When she awakened, chilled to the marrow, it was morning and the small, rustic church was empty. Rebecca sat up, righted her hat and smoothed her rumpled skirts, and hurried out, praying no one would see her and decide she was a derelict.

As she stepped out onto the sidewalk again, and a rush of icy air struck her, she shoved her hands into the pockets of her thin cloak. On the right side, she found the photograph, a brutal reminder of the hopelessness of her circumstances.

She made her way back to the stagecoach depot and purchased a return ticket to Cornucopia. Then, to bolster herself for the difficult journey, she bought an apple and a thick slice of buttered bread from a grocer and dutifully choked them down.

Once again, she was the sole occupant of the coach, and once again, she was thankful for that. Rebecca could not have borne the effort of making conversation just then; she felt like one big bruise, inside and out, a magnet for all the pain of the universe.

The ride was bumpy and frigidly cold, just as Rebecca had known it would be, and when the coach finally came to a stop in front of Mary Daniels's store, darkness had fallen. "A happy Christmas to you, now," the stage driver said, as he helped Rebecca down.

Rebecca's heart constricted; until that moment, she hadn't realized it was Christmas Eve. She returned the man's kindly wishes and took her reticule. A light snow was drifting down from a black sky, filling the air with a clean scent, a fragrance of hope and purity.

She approached the entrance of the general store, but when she went in, there was no sign of Mary. Instead, Lucas waited beside the stove, warming his hands, coatless and as much in need of a shave as he'd ever been.

"What are you doing here?" Rebecca asked, not in challenge but in honest bewilderment. She'd been so conscious that their love was over—before it had had a chance to start—that she'd assumed Lucas knew it, too.

"I was hoping you'd be on the evening stage," he said. "Let's go home, Becky. The girls are waiting for us."

"But—"

He came to her, touched her lips with one finger, effectively silencing her. "Whatever it is, it can wait until Annabelle and Susan have had their Christmas," he said. "Now, let's get ourselves home, Mrs. Kiley."

The team and wagon were just outside—Rebecca had been so distraught that she hadn't seen them before—and Lucas hoisted her into the high seat as easily as if she were a child. Once he'd lit the lanterns that hung on either side of the rig, he climbed up beside her. Then he carefully covered her legs with a woolly blanket.

Rebecca had never known such tenderness before Lucas, and now she sorely wished she hadn't experienced the sweetness of it for even so much as an hour. For the rest of her days, while she toiled beside some man she didn't love, in faraway Seattle or even the frozen north, she would have to remember the magnitude of her loss.

A single tear stung its way down her cheek.

"We'd best wrap your throat as soon as we get home," Lucas said, as matter-of-factly as if there were nothing wrong between them. "I'll make you some hot lemon juice and honey, too. It would be a shame if you couldn't sing your piece tomorrow at the church party."

Rebecca lifted both hands to her mouth, but the small sob escaped anyway. She wouldn't be able to sing the next day or for a long while to come. Her broken heart wouldn't let her.

Lucas put his arm around her shoulders and squeezed lightly, but he didn't say anything more, and Rebecca was wildly grateful. Even the sound of his voice, deep and certain and strong, was a torment to her then.

Soon they arrived at the farm, where the windows were all alight. Lucas drove right up to the back step, climbed down, and lifted Rebecca after him, refusing to let her so much as carry the reticule.

"Go inside and sit by the parlor fire," he ordered. "I'll be in to look after you as soon as I've put the team and wagon away."

Rebecca had no strength, no desire, to argue. She simply nodded and did as Lucas had told her to do.

Annabelle and Susan had been playing checkers in the parlor, and they were beside themselves with delight when Rebecca appeared. She embraced them, wishing she had splurged and bought the pretty dolls they'd admired at the general store. After all, this very likely would be the only real Christmas the three of them would ever spend together.

"Look!" Annabelle crowed, her small frame fairly vibrating with delight. "We have a Christmas tree, just like Prince Albert and Queen Victoria!"

The potted palm was bedecked with strands of popcorn, plus painted paper stars and angels. There wasn't an evergreen growing within twenty miles of Cornucopia, which was why the houseplant had been elected, and Rebecca was secretly glad that no tree had been chopped down for brief glory.

"Theirs is probably a noble pine," Susan said, with a little sniff, but from the gleam in her eyes, Rebecca knew she was as pleased as her twin.

Rebecca wiped away tears with the heel of her palm.

"Here," Annabelle said, taking charge of her wayward sister. "Sit here by the fire. Susan and I will bring you some supper."

Rebecca laughed, though the sound was peculiarly like a sob, and sank into the appointed chair because Annabelle pushed her, not because she'd chosen to sit. "I'm not an invalid, for heaven's sake."

The girls ignored her protests and ran off to the kitchen, returning shortly with a bowl of savory chicken and dumplings and a mug of spiced cider.

"Lucas cooked supper, and he made the cider, too," Annabelle chirped, clearly amazed at the feat.

Rebecca began to eat, realizing only as she picked up her spoon that she was desperately hungry. "I thought you two were going to stay with Mrs. Daniels until I returned from Spokane," she said.

That was when Lucas appeared in the parlor doorway, his presence as warm and elemental as the fire crackling on the hearth. "Children belong at home at Christmas," he said quietly. Then he shifted his attention to the twins. "You'd better finish that round of checkers soon. It's almost time to hang your stockings and go to bed."

Annabelle and Susan returned to their game, chattering with excitement, and Rebecca's heart splintered as she watched them. She supposed it was a mercy that they couldn't know the future, and that they would have this happy time to remember, but for the life of her, she couldn't manage the merest prayer of gratitude.

Chapter Nine

*O*nce Annabelle and Susan had hung their patched woolen stockings from the mantel of the parlor fireplace and gone off to bed, Lucas made good on his earlier promise to take care of Rebecca. He wrapped her throat with a warm scarf, brewed a soothing potion of hot lemon juice and water sweetened with honey, and then he knelt on the hearth to remove her shoes.

Rebecca's heart ached with despair. All her life, she'd yearned for one person who would give her tenderness, who would search for her if she was lost and pamper her if she was hurt or ill. Now she'd found that person, only to lose him again.

Lucas set aside her sodden shoes, rolled down her stockings, and rubbed her feet, first one and then the other, gently restoring the circulation. He might have pressed her to explain her strange behavior, and her absence, but he did not.

Instead, he talked quietly about planting crops in the spring, and buying a milk cow, and building good furniture to sell when he wasn't plowing fields. He found the spool dolls and put them into the twins' Christmas stockings, along with oranges he'd evidently purchased for the occasion. Citrus fruit was a rare treat, and expensive, but Mary had gotten in a special shipment for the holiday.

When Rebecca's great weariness finally overwhelmed

her, Lucas lifted her into his arms and carried her upstairs.

There, as tenderly as if she were a child, he undressed her, helped her into a nightgown, and tucked her under the covers.

"Sleep," he told her. "Just put everything out of your mind for tonight and get some rest."

Rebecca's eyes filled with tears. "Oh, Lucas," she whispered, unable to stop herself, "I love you."

He bent, kissed her forehead. "And I love you."

With that, Lucas put out the lantern he'd lit and left the room. Despite her exhaustion, Rebecca lay listening as he moved around downstairs, imagining him banking the fire in the kitchen stove, putting out the parlor lamps, perhaps sitting down in the chair Rebecca had occupied to smoke his pipe.

The bumps and thumps continued, but it was a long while before Lucas finally came to bed. When he did, he gathered Rebecca close against him, making no other demands, and held her fast. She finally slept, heartbroken, in the temporary safety of his embrace.

Morning brought shrieks of delight from downstairs, and it was several moments before Rebecca was able to shift her mind from the murky depths of slumber to the reality of a new day. Then she realized that it was Christmas, and a certain bitter joy filled her heart.

She sat up, imagining the girls emptying their stockings. She hadn't expected them to be quite so thrilled with a pair of homemade dolls.

Lucas was standing with his back to the bed, gazing out the window, wearing trousers and his undershirt, his suspenders hanging down over his hips. His strong, woodcarver's hands were braced against the framework surrounding the frosted glass.

"What do you see?" Rebecca asked softly.

"Snow," he answered, without turning around. "Oh, but

it's beautiful, Becky, so perfect and clean. Looking at it, I can almost believe that the sins and mistakes of the world have been covered in purity, that we're all being given a new start."

Rebecca let her forehead rest against her updrawn knees for a moment, while she dealt with the pain of all she faced. "There you go," she said brokenly, looking up at him, "talking like a poet again."

At last, he turned to face her. The expression in his eyes reflected her suffering and his own, but he smiled.

"I'll go down and see what all the fuss is about," he said, and then he left the bedroom, pulling up his suspenders as he went.

Numbly, Rebecca rose, hastily dressed, brushed and rebraided her hair, then followed.

Annabelle and Susan crouched in front of an enormous dollhouse with real glass windows and a shingled roof, walking their spool dolls through the spacious rooms. Against the wall, a beautifully simple wooden sled awaited their attention.

Rebecca looked at Lucas, who was leaning against the mantel, watching the children with a smile in his eyes. In that brief, glittering moment, Rebecca's pain doubled and redoubled, because it was so obvious that this man loved her sisters as if they were his own children. Their loss, when the truth came out, would be as great or greater than hers.

Trembling, she took a packet from the branches of the decorated palm and extended it to Lucas. The gift was small, a half-dozen handkerchiefs embroidered with his initials, but he looked delighted.

After admiring the handkerchiefs and carefully folding one to tuck into his back pocket, Lucas disappeared into the kitchen, returning a few moments later with a large, varnished wooden box.

"Happy Christmas," he said, setting the object in Rebecca's lap.

She had received small gifts in the past, oranges and peppermint sticks, and once a sweet-smelling sachet, but no one had ever given her anything so splendid.

"I thought you needed a place to keep your sewing tools," Lucas said, sounding shy as a schoolboy offering some personal treasure to a favorite teacher.

Rebecca was too moved to look at him. She lifted the hinged lid of the box and the scent of cedar perfumed the air. "Thank you," she whispered, overcome.

Moving like a woman entranced, she carried the sewing chest with her when she went into the kitchen to get breakfast started. Lucas soon joined her, putting his arms around her waist from behind, bending to kiss her ear.

"How do you feel today, Mrs. Kiley?"

The use of that precious title stabbed Rebecca's heart. "Well enough to sing my solo at the church party tonight," she answered, marveling that her voice could come out sounding so normal when she was dying inside. Suddenly, it was imperative to pretend everything was right with the world, that all her sins had indeed been covered up and absorbed by the snow. "I don't know what we'll have for Christmas dinner," she fretted. "I quite forgot to prepare a chicken."

With obvious reluctance, Lucas released her, and she heard her own brittle merriment echoing in his deep voice. "I've got a goose hanging in the springhouse, ready to roast. I bought it from a farmer yesterday."

"I guess you'd best bring it inside, then," Rebecca said, with fragile good cheer. "If I don't get it into the oven, we'll be up 'til midnight waiting for our supper."

Lucas hesitated for a few moments—Rebecca felt this rather than saw it—and then he put on his coat and hat and went out. She watched him from the window as he moved toward the barn, marking the perfect snow with his passage, and she tucked the image away in her heart as a keepsake.

Later, Rebecca served breakfast, and the kitchen was warm and fragrant with the roasting goose. The moment the dishes had been washed, Annabelle and Susan bundled up and rushed outside, taking their new sled with them. The small knoll west of the house would be perfect for sliding.

"You've spoiled them," Rebecca said, sitting at the kitchen table and making sure not even to glance at Lucas as she carefully arranged her collection of thread in the box he'd made for her.

Lucas was smoking his pipe and reading from his volume on astronomy. "They haven't had enough spoiling," he replied, "and neither have you."

Rebecca bit her lip and looked away, her vision blurred. She'd spent her life fighting for survival—her own and then that of her twin sisters—and she had never been pampered until this man. "You've been so very kind, Lucas," she finally managed to say.

He reached out, covered her hand with his own. She felt the calluses on his palms, the might of his deft fingers. "Let me love you, Becky," he said. "Stop trying to put up fences between us and just let me look after you like a real husband."

Such a tangle of emotion whirled up inside Rebecca at his words that she was shaken by it. She could lie, and hope that Lucas never had occasion to see the photographs Duke Jones had taken . . .

Rebecca dismissed the idea before it had time to take root. A lie would poison her life with Lucas.

"You won't want me, once you know the truth," she said miserably, after a long, torturous interval of silence had passed.

He tightened his grasp on her hand, but the moment conveyed only affection, not anger or impatience. "Tell me your terrible secret," he said.

She had meant to wait until the next day, but now Rebecca realized she wouldn't be able to carry the burden that long. It was already crushing her.

"All right," she agreed, meeting his eyes at last. She reached into the pocket of her skirt, brought out the photograph Jones had given her in Spokane. "Here's the reason."

Lucas picked up the image, stared at it in consternation at first, then with obvious shock. The color drained from his face, and when he looked at Rebecca at last, she saw cold anger in his eyes.

"Why?" he asked. The word was ragged, and it echoed in the warm kitchen like the report of a cannon shot.

Rebecca had expected his condemnation, had tried to steel herself for it, but nothing could have prepared her for the stunned way he was staring at her then. "He paid me," she said, the words a bare whisper. "I needed the money so the twins and I could come west."

Lucas looked at the photograph again, and a series of unsettling emotions moved in his face. "How many of these are there?" he asked, after a long time. "How many men are looking at your body, Becky?"

She leaped from her chair, propelled by pain and shame and helpless rage. "I don't know," she said, when she could speak, careful to keep her back turned to Lucas. "Jones has the plates, so he can make as many as he wants."

The room seemed to tremble with the force of their joined emotions. Then Lucas went to the door, not even troubling with his hat and coat. "That's why you went to Spokane?" he asked, as the kitchen filled with a wintry chill that didn't begin to match the coldness of his fury. "Because Jones is there?"

"I wanted him to destroy the plates," she said.

"I see. That way, you could fool me just the way you've fooled the townspeople all this time—"

Rebecca whirled, wild in her desperation and her anguish. "No, Lucas!" she cried. "I was going to tell you, no matter what. I would never have tried to deceive you that way!"

Lucas's contempt and disbelief were plain in his face; there was no need for him to speak of them. He turned and walked out, slamming the kitchen door behind him.

After a long time had passed, and Rebecca could hear over the frantic pounding of her own heartbeat, she caught the echoing ring of a hammer striking over and over. Lucas had taken refuge in his workshop.

The girls returned after an hour of sledding, chilled and full of Christmas laughter. They drank hot chocolate and ate the sandwiches Rebecca made for them, then went back to the parlor to play with their dollhouse. When Rebecca looked in on them, they were curled up on the hearth rug like a pair of kittens, sound asleep.

She covered them with a blanket from upstairs, then went back to the kitchen. Because she didn't know what else to do, she peeled potatoes for the meal and baked a dried apple pie for dessert. Then she sat by the stove, still as death, holding her cherished cedar sewing box in her lap and staring sightlessly out at the cold perfection of the day.

Late in the afternoon, she served the Christmas goose, along with a tableful of other carefully prepared foods. Lucas returned from his workshop, but he was very quiet throughout the meal and wouldn't meet Rebecca's gaze. Fortunately, Annabelle and Susan were so busy chattering that they didn't notice the hurt and anger of the adults.

When the time came, Lucas hitched up the team and wagon, and the four of them set out for the church building in Cornucopia, looking for all the world like a happy family putting the finishing touches on a truly spectacular

Christmas. Rebecca feared she wouldn't be able to sing, but at the same time she hadn't the strength to decline the task and stay home.

Buggies and wagons were crowded around the well-lit church, and the sounds of music and laughter rolled out onto the snow to greet Lucas, Rebecca, and the children as they arrived. The twins raced inside, carrying their spool dolls in mittened hands, but Rebecca stubbornly lingered while Lucas secured the team.

They entered the church together, and even managed to smile and return the greetings of the merry crowd. The humble sanctuary had been decorated with pine boughs, and the festive scent was a stab to Rebecca's heart.

Chapter Ten

ucas sat in the last row of pews, while Rebecca took her place with the choir at the front of the church. After the factory accident in Chicago that crushed his body, he'd thought this was the worst thing that could ever happen to him. It had even been something of a relief to think he'd paid his dues, so to speak.

He was a man of simple integrity, and the thought of other men leering at photographs of Rebecca tore at his spirit like the teeth of an animal. It was as if she'd *sold* some part of herself.

Now Lucas had learned only too well that a soul—as well as bone—could be broken, and this new pain, this searing sense of betrayal, was wild inside him.

The minister got up, led a prayer, and then spoke eloquently of the meaning of Christmas. The words went straight through Lucas, as though he had no more substance than a mirage, and he never once took his eyes from Rebecca.

She was beautiful, though not in the fragile way of some women. No, Becky was a practical beauty, sturdy and strong, full of spirit and courage.

And lies, Lucas reminded himself.

Her turn to sing came and she stepped in front of the choir, her hands trembling slightly under the hymnal she held. There was a flush on her high cheekbones, and the first words of the old song were shaky, but then Rebecca got a grip on her emotions and let out all the music that was inside her.

She sounded like an angel.

The image of her, posed for Jones's camera, filled Lucas's mind, and he wanted to weep with grief. She was so unbearably lovely—and damn it, she was his. The idea of other men looking upon the secret glory of her was pure anguish.

Somehow, Lucas got through the rest of that evening. When the services were over, he talked with other members of the community and even managed to sample some of the baked goods the townswomen had brought.

The sky was clear, and the North Star shone bright against it, when the time came to get into the wagon and drive home. Exhausted by the excitement of the day, Annabelle and Susan slept in back, on beds of hay, covered with warm quilts brought from the house. Rebecca sat rigidly beside Lucas, her hands folded in her lap, keeping her gaze fixed on the starlit road leading back to the farm.

Once there, Lucas awakened the twins, and he and Rebecca helped them inside. There were so many things he wanted to say to Becky, but as it happened, he couldn't even bring himself to look at her. He was afraid to lose control of his raging emotions for so much as a second.

He was restless, though, and when he returned to the barn, intending to put the team and wagon away for the night, something was released in the deepest, most hidden passages of his heart. He looked back at the house for a long moment, imagining a life with Rebecca, thinking of rich crops of wheat, flocks of children, and all the Christmases to come.

Lucas unhitched the team only long enough to feed and water them. Without a word to Rebecca, with barely a silent word to himself, he took what remained of his savings from a hiding place in his workshop and climbed back into the wagon box.

For a long moment he just sat there, the reins resting in his gloved hands, looking up at the fiery silver star that seemed to fill the sky. Then, with only the merest whisper of hope in his heart, he began to follow it.

REBECCA WIPED STEAM from the kitchen window to watch as Lucas's wagon disappeared into the night. She wanted to run stumbling after him through the deep, crusted snow, beg him to understand and forgive, but she didn't. Even if he gave in to her pleas and stayed, things never would be the same.

Too injured to cry, Rebecca turned away from the window, banked the fire in the cookstove, took up the one lantern burning in the room, and made her way through the house to the stairway. Sleeping in the bed she'd shared with Lucas would be too painful, so she went into the twins' room instead.

Despite a sadness that ran deeper than any she'd ever felt before, Rebecca smiled at the sight of her sisters. Annabelle slept in a sprawl of unconscious abandon, her arms and legs going every which way, while Susan rested in a tidy alignment of limbs, graceful even in slumber.

Rebecca turned down the lantern wick until the flame went out, then undressed to her camisole and drawers and crawled in beside Susan. One by one, she went over the cherished memories of the day, the things that had happened before she'd shown the photograph to Lucas.

For the rest of her life, she would remember the smile in his eyes while he watched the twins enjoying the dollhouse he'd built for them with his own hands. No matter what happened, or where she went in future travels, she would keep the sewing box with her. Whenever she raised the lid, Lucas's image would rise out of it, along with the scent of cedar.

Rebecca awakened early the next morning, to a house

chilled with winter and with Lucas's absence. She left the twins sleeping soundly and crossed the hallway to the other room, staying just long enough to fetch fresh clothes. Though she tried not to look left or right, not to remember how it was to be held and cherished, or driven wild with pleasure, the very walls seemed to exude Lucas's scent and personality.

She hurried downstairs, built up the fire, then put on her cloak and went out to feed the chickens. The sunlight glared off the hardened snow, scattering the landscape with diamonds, and there was a frigid bite in the air.

After breakfast, the twins washed the dishes, then scrambled outside to take turns sliding down the knoll on their new sled. At a loss, Rebecca went into the parlor, cold without the fire and merriment of the day before, and carefully removed the homemade decorations from the potted palm fronds, putting them away in a box.

She didn't think about the future, for it was so bleak she could not bear to face it. She put away the stockings the twins had hung from the mantel and removed all signs of Christmas.

After a midday meal of sandwiches and soup, when the twins had once again succumbed to fresh air and exhaustion and collapsed on their beds for a nap, Mary Daniels arrived, riding her dapple gray mare. She wore a hooded cloak and carried a basket over one arm.

There was only one person on earth Rebecca would have been happier to see, and that was Lucas. She hastily brewed tea while Mary warmed herself by the kitchen stove.

"I came to look at the furniture Lucas has been building," the visitor said. "There are new people settling around here all the time, it seems, and I believe I could sell tables and chairs and the like through my store."

Rebecca spooned tea leaves into the crockery pot, carried it to the table, fetched cups and sugar and milk. "Lucas is a fine craftsman," she said, hoping her voice didn't reveal too much of what she was suffering. "He made a dollhouse for the twins, and a sled as sleek as any you could send away for."

Mary came to stand beside Rebecca, gently grasping her arm. "Did you tell Lucas about the photographs?"

Tears burned in Rebecca's eyes, sudden and blinding. "Yes," she answered hoarsely. "And it was just as I expected. He can't bear the sight of me, Mary. He got in the wagon last night and drove away, and I don't have any idea where he's gone—"

"There now," Rebecca's friend said quietly. "He'll certainly be back, once he's worked the matter through and realized you only did what you had to do. Why, if you'd stayed in Chicago, the twins would have been working in that factory right alongside you by now."

Rebecca nodded miserably. "I wanted to give them a better life," she whispered. "Now, instead, I'm going to have to give Annabelle and Susan up to some school or orphanage."

"Nonsense," Mary interrupted. "I'd take those children in myself before I'd see that happen. Just what are you planning to do with *yourself*, by the way?"

Sniffling, Rebecca left Mary's side, lifted the lid of the sewing box, and took out the well-worn newspaper advertisement she'd clipped days before. "I'm going to get married," she said, with shaky resolution. *And I'm never going to allow myself to dream again.*

"Dear Lord," breathed Mary, after reading the advertisement. "You can't do such a thing, Rebecca! I won't let you! Why, you could end up at the mercy of some monstrous man—"

"It's decided," Rebecca said briskly, snatching back the bit of paper.

"But you could stay on in Cornucopia—maybe open a little dress and millinery shop."

Rebecca shook her head. "Even if that were possible—

and I don't have the money to set up a business—I couldn't bear to stay on here. I wouldn't be able to stand being so close to Lucas, seeing him take a real wife, and bringing her here to live."

"You're getting a little ahead of yourself, it seems to me," Mary said, in practical tones. "Any fool can see that Lucas Kiley loves you, and that you love him. Wait a while, Rebecca. Give him time."

Recalling the look in Lucas's eyes after he'd seen the photograph, Rebecca sighed. He might as well have caught her whoring, he'd been so shocked.

There wasn't enough time in all eternity to heal the wound she'd dealt him. "Were you serious about keeping the girls?" she asked, hardly daring to hope. "They're of an age to help out around the store, and I'd send as much as I could toward their board."

Mary hugged Rebecca. "Yes, I was serious, but I still don't think it's going to come to that. You give some thought to what I said, and don't be too quick to give up the fight."

With that, Mary went to the parlor to inspect the dollhouse. Then she put on her cloak. "There's fruitcake in that basket I brought," she said, "along with a special kind of tea I ordered from back east and some little treats for the children."

A moment later, Mary was gone.

Lucas didn't return that night, and when the girls went off to school in the morning, there was still no sign of his team and wagon on the road.

Just after noon, however, Rebecca heard the creaking of harnesses and axles, and rushed to the back step to see Lucas drive in.

He jumped down from the wagon box and came slowly toward her, carrying a small parcel in one hand. As he drew close, Rebecca could see that his lower lip was swollen and cut, though the look in his eyes was quietly triumphant.

"Here," he said, extending the packet.

Rebecca tore away the paper and plain twine, and found two photographic plates inside. She raised her gaze to Lucas's face, hardly daring to believe, to hope.

"It cost me almost half what I had saved for spring planting," Lucas told her, "but I bought back those plates and all the pictures Jones had in his possession."

Rebecca was so moved that most of a minute passed before she could find words. "Wh-what happened to your face?"

Lucas grinned. "After Jones and I had finished the transaction, I couldn't resist knocking him on his—knocking him down. He fought back, but he only landed one punch before I thrashed him proper and left him sitting on the floor of his office."

She looked down at the photographic plates, then back at Lucas's face. "You've forgiven me, then?"

He stepped closer and cupped her wind-chilled face in his strong, carpenter's hands. "It damned near killed me to think of anybody else seeing you in your unmentionables," he said, "but after I thought about it for a while, I realized what a fine woman you really are. Lord, Becky, but you've got more grit than most of the men I know, and I love you so much that it's like a fever burning inside me. Please say you'll marry me right and proper, and stay right here where you belong."

Rebecca gave a hoarse cry of joy and flung the photographic plates against the woodpile, where they shattered with a satisfying tinkle of glass. Then she hurled herself into Lucas's waiting arms and laughed as he lifted her off her feet and swung her around in the glittering snow.

Finally, he set her down again, though she was still crushed against him, and kissed her thoroughly.

She looked up at him with all her soul showing in her eyes. "I love you so much, Lucas," she vowed, "and I swear you'll never know a moment's sorrow for marrying me."

He slid an arm around her waist, propelled her toward the waiting wagon. "The greatest sorrow I could know would be losing you," he told her, hoisting her easily into the box and climbing up beside her to take the reins. He kissed her lightly on the mouth before releasing the brake lever with one foot. "Let's get to the preacher's house and make our promises, Becky. I want to spend tonight making love to my wife."

Rebecca said nothing. She just scooted closer to Lucas, laid a hand on his thigh, and smiled to think of all the miracles that lay ahead.

That Other
Katherine

Chapter One

Seattle, Washington
1991

Katherine Hollis. Her name was Katherine Hollis.
She thought.
Katherine listened to the steady beeping of the hospital machines, the low murmur of the nurses' voices as they attended her. *Poor creature . . . terrible accident . . . coma . . .*

She became aware of the pain suddenly, the crushing, ceaseless pain, and at the same time, she realized it had been there all along. She seemed to be climbing some kind of inner stairway, with each step bringing her closer to full consciousness.

Katherine tried to remember the accident, but not even a flicker of memory lighted her way. She had no idea who would be standing there if she peeked behind the name she'd recalled.

The pain was agonizing, and Katherine wanted to cry out, but she couldn't. For all its suffering, her body felt lifeless and cold, as rigid as a statue, while her spirit seemed to be gaining strength with every passing moment, a flame burning brighter and brighter. An explosive sensation of joy flared within her, completely separate from the misery of traumatized bone and muscle.

She felt a tear pool along the lashes of her right eye.

The voice Katherine heard then was masculine and hoarse with emotion. "Look—she's crying. She could be waking up, couldn't she?"

Katherine felt a strong hand close around one of her own while the voice caressed her soul. Jeremy. A few ragtag memories trickled back. That was her brother up there in that other dimension, that place of wakefulness and reason, trying to hold on to her.

Her heart constricted. She would have given practically anything for the chance to say good-bye, but her lips might as well have been made of marble. She couldn't even manage a flutter of her eyelids.

I want to live, Katherine thought desperately, with the last strength left to her. *There are so many things I didn't get a chance to do!*

The machines began to make strange noises, and then there was a burst of activity all around her.

"I'll get the doctor . . ."

". . . crash cart . . ."

"Please, Mr. Hollis . . . no time . . . waiting room . . ."

"No! Kathy . . ." That was Jeremy's voice, frantic and young. Jeremy, whom she'd pulled behind her in a red wagon when they were both children, over a bumpy sidewalk with weeds growing between the cracks . . .

In the next instant Katherine was enveloped in light more brilliant than the dazzle of a thousand spring suns. It was a moment more before she realized that a subtle change had taken place in the form and substance of her body.

She was the same and yet different, standing on an arched bridge that seemed to be fashioned of multifaceted crystal.

"I don't want to die," she said firmly, knowing there was someone in the light to hear her argument and weigh it. "I never fell in love, or made a wreath of spring flowers for my hair, or wore a long dancing dress, or had a baby . . ." She paused, then finished plaintively, "Oh, please."

That was when Katherine heard the other voice calling, pleading, storming the very gates of heaven. It was a lusty feminine shriek.

"No more . . . please . . . oh, God, help me . . . let me die . . ."

There was an interval then of fathomless peace, followed by a wordless answer from the glorious, unutterably beautiful light. *I have heard.*

Immediately after that, Katherine was caught up in a spinning storm of iridescent fire. She tumbled end over end through a crystal tunnel and then landed with a sudden, solid thump.

Joy filled her. She was back inside her body; she could feel her heartbeat, the moist tension of her skin, the movement of her fingers. Even better, she was fully conscious, and she could see.

A frown creased her sweat-dampened forehead. She wasn't in the hospital; this room had high ceilings with plaster molding and pale pink wallpaper striped in silver, and instead of the standard railings on the sides and foot of the bed, there were huge bedposts with carved pineapples on top.

Her stomach was bare, and it resembled an overripe watermelon with skin stretched over it. Her bare knees were drawn up, her legs apart, and there was an old man standing in the V, looking ponderous.

She decided she was having some kind of crazy dream, fraught with Freudian meanings.

She didn't recognize the body or the room. None of what she was seeing could possibly be real . . .

Except the pain. She screamed. That was totally authentic.

"What the hell is going on here?" she cried when she got her breath back.

The white-haired man looked up from whatever medical intimacy he'd been performing, his florid face a study in Puritan disapproval. "Now, Katherine, there is no need to use profanity. I should think you would be trying to redeem yourself, rather than make things worse."

"This hurts," she babbled, panting. "This whole situation was sprung on me with no warning . . . no preparation . . . I never got to go through Lamaze training . . . I want morphine!"

"Mrs. Winslow," the doctor replied with testy patience, "during the war, I treated men who'd had their legs and arms shot off. Not one of them carried on the way you have today."

"They weren't having babies!" Katherine blurted, and then she screamed again. It seemed that the whole lower half of her body had become one giant muscle, about as much under her control as a runaway train would have been. "Oh, God . . . nobody told me it would feel like this!"

"Kindly stop bothering the Almighty," said the man. "It would have behooved you to consult Him a little earlier, it seems to me."

Katherine recalled the voice she'd heard from the crystal bridge, calling out to heaven for mercy.

Her body . . . this body she didn't recognize . . . tensed again, violently. Her cotton nightgown clung to her skin, transparent with perspiration.

"Push," the doctor instructed crisply, his face taut with concentration. "Mary!" He barked the name over one shoulder, and the door popped open, revealing a pale young woman in long skirts.

"Yes, Dr. Franz?" The girl's eyes were the size of soccer balls, and she was wringing her hands nervously.

"Fetch Gavin," ordered the physician. "Immediately. Tell him his child is about to be born, just in case he's interested!"

The fitful maid rushed off to obey.

Katherine was braced on her elbows, tears streaming

down her face. "Why are you people in costume?" she managed to gasp out, after her next contraction. "Who's Gavin?"

Dr. Franz arched one bushy eyebrow. "There is no need to add insult to injury, Mrs. Winslow, by pretending you don't know your own husband."

"I don't have a husband." Katherine panted, clutching the bedclothes as another pain began to gain steam on the inside of her pelvis. "And my name isn't Winslow. It's Hollis. Katherine Hollis."

"Nonsense," said the doctor briskly. "You're Katherine Simmons Winslow. I've known you since you came to Seattle—heaven help the hapless place."

The thrusting sensation in Katherine's abdomen was building to another crescendo, and yet the tears on her face were ones of happiness. She was alive! She didn't know where she was, or how she'd gotten there, but *she was alive!*

An impatient knock sounded at the door, but Katherine was too busy with the current contraction to pay much attention. When a dark-haired man appeared beside the bed, however, she was thunderstruck by his good looks and by her own sense of shattering recognition. She'd seen his face in her dreams a thousand times—she recalled that, if little else.

"Nice of you to make an appearance, Gavin," grumbled Dr. Franz. "There now, Katherine, one more good push."

Reluctantly, it seemed, Gavin reached down and took her hand between both his own. Even in that state of great confusion and greater pain, she felt a jolt at his touch.

Her torso arched high off the mattress, taking no command from her mind. She clung to Gavin's hands, and her primitive cry, half groan and half scream, echoed against the walls of the strange, old-fashioned room. The anguish of childbirth peaked, and then there was relief, a sensation of something slipping from her. Soon after that she heard the angry squall of an infant.

She saw Gavin's steel-gray eyes dart toward the newborn, then shift away. He looked down at her with what seemed to be a mingling of contempt and furious hurt.

"You have a son, Gavin," Dr. Franz announced, as though Katherine had had nothing to do with the process.

Gavin's strong jawline flexed, relaxed again. His gaze scored her face. "Kathy has a son," he corrected, and then he let her hand fall to the mattress, turned abruptly, and left the room.

"Let me see the baby," she pleaded hoarsely. Later, she would try to reason things out. For now, she just wanted to see this child she'd given birth to but never conceived.

He was tiny and red and messy, and she couldn't imagine even a Christmas angel being more beautiful.

"Hello, handsome," she said, feeling joyous exhaustion as an infinitesimal hand closed around her finger. The far side of the crystal bridge already seemed more dream than reality now, something imagined. "I hope we can be friends. In case you haven't noticed, I'm not very popular around here."

Dr. Franz was doing painful things, things it seemed better not to think about. An Indian girl in a drab calico dress, long like the maid's, took the baby and left the room. Katherine suddenly was too drowsy to protest.

Several women came in, all looking like fugitives from an episode of *Little House on the Prairie*, with their hair upswept and the hems of their dresses brushing the floor, and helped Katherine from the bed. Brisk hands washed her and pulled a clean nightgown over her head, and the sheets were crisp and fresh when she lay back down on them.

"You're to take this," one of the women said, pouring liquid from a brown bottle into a spoon. "Dr. Franz left it for you."

Katherine obediently opened her mouth and accepted the medicine, which tasted like lawn mower fuel smelled. Then she settled back against the fluffy pillows, barely able to keep her eyes open. "Gavin hates me," she said, sighing and yawning at the same time.

There was only one woman in the room then; she had gray-streaked brown hair and pale green eyes, and although her expression was stern, there was a softness about her mouth. "It isn't as though you haven't given him cause," was the answer. "But you've also given him a son. A man will forgive a great deal for such a gift."

Katherine closed her eyes, too weary to go on, and was soon dreaming. Although she caught glimpses of the light and the crystal bridge, she didn't wander close, and when she awakened it was to see her son sleeping in an ornate antique cradle next to her bed. Her heart caught when she noticed Gavin crouching on the hearth, lighting an early-evening fire.

"Gavin?"

His broad shoulders tensed beneath the fine white fabric of his shirt, and he did not turn to look at her. He rose to his full height, well over six feet, and gripped the mantelpiece with strong, sun-browned hands. The light from the gas-fed fixtures on the walls flickered in his dark hair and on the shining black leather of his riding boots.

Katherine phrased her question carefully. "What will you name the child?"

Slowly he turned to meet her gaze, his pewter eyes cold and wary. He couldn't entirely hide his surprise at the inquiry, though Katherine could see he was trying. "Name him?"

"He is your son, after all." How she wished that she too could lay just claim to that beautiful infant boy. She remembered little of her old life . . . if indeed it really had been a life and not just an illusion . . . but she knew she'd longed for a baby from the day she was given her first doll.

Gavin's answer was a quietly brutal chuckle. "Is he?" he countered, turning back to the fire.

Katherine felt tears well up behind her eyes, but she refused to shed them. Somehow, through an instinct that seemed oddly like memory, she knew this man would not respond well if she wept. "Your wife was unfaithful to you," she said.

Another chuckle, sardonic and wicked. "Yes," he replied, turning to face her, his arms folded. "You were. Are."

"Then why haven't you divorced me?"

Gavin smiled cordially. "Believe me, darling, I would love to, but even in the grand and gloriously modern year of 1895, such things simply aren't done."

Katherine sat bolt upright as a series of mental puzzle pieces dropped into place. The primitive birth, the gas lamps on the walls, Gavin's oddly formal clothes, the long dresses the women had worn. "In 1895?" she echoed, awed.

"Please," Gavin said skeptically. "None of your little dramas. You know exactly who you are, where you are, and what you did. And if I have anything to say about it, you're never going to forget."

Chapter Two

Katherine was unaccountably wounded by Gavin's dislike and troubled by memories that could not have been memories. Her emotional reactions to him during their first encounter had been ones of recognition, not discovery.

She averted her gaze for a moment, fingers plucking at the elaborate lace trim of the top sheet. "Suppose I told you I'm not the Katherine you knew," she ventured hoarsely. "Suppose I said I'm really another woman, from another time?"

Gavin clasped his hands together behind his back and rocked slightly on his heels. "I would respond that pretending to have lost your grip on sanity won't save you from my revenge," he said, and the tone of his voice made the otherwise cozy room turn chilly. "Instead it might just land you in an asylum."

"Revenge?" Katherine swallowed. Just the *suggestion* of a nineteenth-century mental hospital brought on instant wariness.

His smile was callous. "I loved you on our wedding day, Kathy," he said. "Perhaps if I still cherished tender feelings toward you, I would simply send you away somewhere, with an allowance and a maid, and get on with my life. Alas, my fatal flaw is that I want you to know the same humiliation, the same sense of betrayal, that I did." He came to stand at Katherine's feet, his knuckles white where he gripped the bedpost. His gray eyes glinted like frost over steel as he looked at her. "This time, Kathy, you'll be the one people pity and hold in contempt."

Katherine's throat constricted. She didn't love this man, didn't even *know* this man, and yet his words were like hard-flung stones, bruising her soul. "Gavin . . ."

He gave a low, mocking laugh. "How tenderly you speak my name," he said, going to stand beside the cradle. His expression grew softer as he looked down at the sleeping baby. "Were you as sweet to your lover as you are to me?"

Katherine fell back against her pillows and put both hands to her face for a moment, struggling to gain some composure. "I don't know," she said, in all honesty.

When she looked again, she caught Gavin watching her with naked sorrow in his stormy eyes. The expression was so quickly sublimated, however, that she wondered if she'd imagined it.

"Good night," Gavin said without emotion, and then he turned and strode from the room, closing the door briskly behind him.

Katherine lay shaking in that other woman's childbed for a very long time, watching the shadows gather in the corners of the room and the fire die to embers on the hearth. Finally, when she felt strong enough, she rose and went to kneel carefully by the baby's cradle.

Her son slept, his thick dark hair like ebony against the white blankets, and she touched him ever so gently, marveling that so beautiful a creature could exist in such an uncertain world. He was a miniature Gavin Winslow, this tiny soul, and Katherine already loved him, already thought of him as her own.

"You look just like your dad," she said in a whisper. "One of these days, he'll notice that. Might take a while, though, because as you can see, he's a very hardheaded man. We'll have to be patient, you and I."

For a long time she lingered beside the cradle, admiring the child, marveling. Then, when she began to feel the strain in her weary body, she stood awkwardly and made her way to the bureau.

There was a mirror above the dresser, framed in dark, heavy wood, and Katherine's first glimpse of herself had all the shocking impact of a body slam by a major league quarterback.

Her knees weakened, and she raised one hand to her chest in an unconscious effort to modify the pounding of her heart. She did not remember who she had been before the accident, before crossing the crystal bridge and finding herself in 1895, but she knew she hadn't looked at all like the woman reflected in the glass.

In fact, she could almost see her previous self, standing beside this stranger she had become.

In that other life, she'd been small and slight. The woman looking back at her was tall, with a lush hourglass figure.

Before, Katherine had had short brown hair, worn in a smooth, bouncy cut. Now, dark auburn tresses tumbled, thick and wavy, around the bodice of her nightgown. Her eyes were green, her cheekbones high and well defined, her lips full, her skin flawless and very creamy, like fine ivory.

Katherine stared at herself for a long time. Then, when the weakness grew too great, she turned and made her way back to the bed.

She had barely settled beneath the covers when a woman entered the room carrying a tray. It was the same girl Dr. Franz had sent to bring Gavin when it was clear that the baby's birth was imminent.

"Supper, missus," she said without meeting Katherine's gaze.

Given that this was 1895 and that the mistress of the house had obviously had an affair, Katherine supposed the maid saw her as a scarlet woman and preferred not to associate. The thought only made Katherine feel more isolated, confused, and afraid.

"It certainly smells good," she said in an attempt to make conversation.

"Yes, ma'am," the maid answered. "Cook does have a way with biscuits and gravy. The doctor likes that dish more than anything."

"Dr. Franz?" Katherine asked. She was so grateful for the sound of a civil human voice that she tried to keep the chat going.

"Dr. Winslow," the maid corrected, turning startled blue eyes to Katherine's face. "Your husband, ma'am."

So Gavin was a doctor, too. "Oh," Katherine said quickly, brightly. "Yes, of course. He's had a lengthy practice here in . . ."

"Seattle," the maid said, frowning.

Katherine was ravenously hungry, and the food on her tray was fragrant and appealing. "Seattle," she confirmed. That was a relief. Maybe she'd changed centuries, but at least she was still in the same city. "Your name would be?"

The young girl took another step toward the door, as though she expected Katherine to lunge at her, wild-eyed and foaming at the mouth.

"Mary," she whispered. With that, Mary turned and bolted from the room.

Katherine ate, trying to figure out what was happening to her.

Maybe it was the food that restored her. She seemed to recall that her blood sugar tended to fall when she got too hungry . . .

She remembered lying in a faraway hospital bed, remembered the nurses talking and the grasp of her brother's hand and the earnest way she'd begged the light surrounding the crystal bridge to let her live. Evidently, she concluded as the pleas of another woman echoed in her mind—*oh, God, help me . . . let me die*—she and Gavin's real wife had somehow exchanged places.

That was too much to credit, Katherine thought, setting her tray on the bedside table and leaning back against her pillows, and yet here she was, in another woman's body. A body she liked far better than her old one, for all the problems inherent in the situation.

Presently the Indian girl came in to take away her tray, and that made Katherine smile. Mary must have been afraid to venture near her again after that little encounter earlier.

"What's your name?" she asked pleasantly when the young woman had set the tray in the hall and returned. The baby awakened and gave a small, fitful cry.

"Maria," the visitor replied, unruffled, bending to lift the infant from his cradle before Katherine had managed to swing her legs over the side of the bed. Maria sat down in the rocking chair near the dying fire and opened the bodice of her plain dress to nurse the baby.

Again, Katherine felt envy. She didn't like the idea of sharing this child, or his father, with any other woman.

Maria was conscious only of the baby, humming a soft, rhythmic tune as she held him to her breast and stroked his downy head with a light finger. The firelight flickered over the pair, gilding them in crimson and shadow.

A deep loneliness overtook Katherine; she felt as though she'd been abandoned in some unknown galaxy. She remembered only the merest details about her other life, and in this one everyone seemed to dislike her.

Presently Maria finished feeding the child and brought him to the bed for changing. She handed him to Katherine, who gently raised him to her shoulder to be burped.

"Thank you," Katherine said, mesmerized by the bundled miracle in her arms.

"What will you call the little one?" Maria asked, regarding Katherine with placid dark eyes that revealed nothing of her inner thoughts.

Katherine ached with love as the child squirmed against her shoulder, and she longed to be able to feed him herself. "I don't know," she answered. "Perhaps we'll name him for his father."

The silence that followed felt awkward to Katherine. Remembering the accusation her husband had thrown in her face, she blushed and blurted out, "Gavin. He'll be called Gavin, of course."

Maria did not react, and her manner was neither friendly nor unfriendly. "Is there anything you'd like, Mrs. Winslow?" She went to the hearth without waiting for Katherine to reply and added a log to the fire. "The kitchen kettle is still on. I could brew you some tea."

Katherine shook her head. "No. No, thank you. But if you'd please put the baby to bed . . ."

The Indian girl assessed Katherine with narrowed eyes for a moment, then collected the infant and carefully put him into the cradle to sleep. "Good night, Mrs. Winslow," she said after turning off the gas that fed the lights.

Only the glow of the fire and the strained silver shimmer of the moon lit the room after Maria closed the door behind her.

Cautiously, Katherine lay down flat on the feather mattress. This body she had borrowed was very sore, and she felt like weeping with exhaustion and confusion, but beneath all these things ran an undercurrent of sheer exultation. She had been given another chance at life, and she meant to make the most of it.

Watching the firelight waver against the dark ceiling, she wondered if Gavin had ever laughed in this room or made love to his wife here. Surely he hadn't always been so grim and solemn!

It seemed to her that as she was just dropping off to sleep, the first solid memory of the other life came to her. She was driving along the Seattle freeway in her red convertible, her dark hair tossing in the wind, on the way to her brother Jeremy's downtown office. They were planning to have lunch together.

In the space of a moment, everything changed. A truck jackknifed just ahead of her, and before she could slow down, her car struck the trailer with a deafening impact. Metal shrieked, pain racked her body, and then darkness exploded around her like a bomb.

"Kathy!" Strong hands gripped Katherine's shoulders, and a firm masculine voice came to her through the smothering fog of fear that surrounded her. "Katherine, wake up!"

Gavin was sitting on the side of the bed, and her longing to have him take her into his arms and hold her was a bleak and fathomless thing. The baby, frightened by the noise, was fretting in his cradle.

Katherine started to get out of bed, but Gavin wouldn't allow her to rise.

"Never mind," he said abruptly. "I'll get him."

At once a stranger and a husband, Gavin lifted the child deftly from the cradle and handed him to Katherine.

"I'm sorry," she crooned, her lips against the infant's cheek. "I'm so sorry I woke you up, sweetheart . . ."

Something made her lift her eyes to Gavin then, and she saw that he was looking at her strangely again, as though he didn't quite recognize her.

She drew a deep breath and made herself smile at the man who so clearly despised her. "Our son will need a name, you know," she said with a little sniffle. "We can't go on referring to this child as 'he' and 'him' for the rest of his life."

Even in the firelight, she saw Gavin's powerful body go rigid. The brief, tenuous peace that had existed between them was obviously over.

"Why not name him Jeffrey?" Gavin asked in a tone that was no less brutal for its softness. "For his father."

Chapter Three

*G*et out," Katherine breathed, glaring at Gavin. She was trembling inside, but she was as strong and agile as a lioness when she sprang from the bed to return the baby to his cradle.

Gavin stood his ground, arms folded. "May I remind you that this is *my* house?"

"I don't care," she spat. "You're nothing but an arrogant bully, and if you're any example of nineteenth-century manhood, it's no wonder there was a women's movement!"

"If we're going to call each other names—"

"Don't you dare!" Katherine clasped her hands over her ears and at the same time maneuvered herself back into bed. "I know perfectly well what you think of me, Gavin Winslow, but I've been through a lot today, and I would appreciate it if you would leave me alone."

To her surprise, Gavin's countenance grew a little less stern. He approached the bed and tucked the covers in around her with a certain brisk tenderness.

"You're right," he said, in a husky voice. "I'm sorry." With that, unbelievably, he bent and kissed her lightly on the forehead, and at that simple contact something deep inside Katherine was changed forever.

Gavin didn't come to her room the next day, or the day after that. Katherine spent her time caring for the baby, whom she could nurse now that her milk had come in, reading the books and magazines Maria brought her, and remembering.

It was that other life that kept unfolding in her mind; she still knew very little about the woman she had become.

As Katherine Hollis, she'd lived in a world of convenience and noise, working for a market research firm in Seattle and slowly paying off a one-bedroom condo overlooking Lake Washington. She'd been on the verge of getting married once, but in the end she'd realized Phillip Hughes was all wrong for her, and she was all wrong for him, and she'd given back his ring.

She recalled that she'd grown up in a modest home on Seattle's Queen Anne Hill, and that her divorced mother, Julia, had taught piano lessons in the dining room to supplement meager child-support payments. Julia had died of ovarian cancer when her daughter was twenty, and after that, there had been only Jeremy . . .

Now, Katherine marveled, she found herself in another world. Here there were no speeding convertibles, no market research companies, no semitrucks to jackknife in the middle of the freeway. Beyond the walls of this house, which she'd had no chance at all to explore, carriages, buggies, and wagons rattled over dirt streets and cobblestones.

The sunlight was bright, the sky so blue the sight of it twisted Katherine's heart.

She was standing at the window, looking out over the garden with its gazebo and its tangle of colorful flowers, when there was a light knock at the door. Just as she would have turned to call out an eager "Come in"—she was so lonely that even Gavin would have been a welcome caller—she saw her husband walk through a gate in the side fence.

He looked so handsome in his riding breeches, linen shirt, tailored charcoal coat, and boots that Katherine's breath caught. Just when she was about to tap impulsively on the glass and wave to him, forgetting all his insufferable qualities in the face of the breathtaking attraction she felt, a woman joined him. Her dress was yellow, like the roses that climbed the walls of the gazebo and tangled on its roof, and her hair was the color of honey.

As Katherine watched, stricken, the woman held out both hands to Gavin, and he clasped them in his own. His strong white teeth flashed in a cavalier's smile as he bent his head to kiss his companion's gloved knuckles.

"There's Caroline Raynes again," a voice beside Katherine announced, and she jumped, startled. "You'd better look out for her, because she's sweet on Gavin."

Katherine turned her head and saw a petite girl standing next to her. Her hair was dark, and her eyes were the same steely-gray as Gavin's, and from that Katherine deduced that this woman was her sister-in-law. The little golden pin affixed to the bodice of her plain but expensive dress shaped the letters of her name.

"Hello, Marianne."

Marianne's attention was fixed on the scene below; she didn't see Katherine study her, or glance at the bare ring finger of her left hand to determine her marital status.

"Look at her," she said, her breath making fog against the windowpane. "What a hussy."

Katherine looked, against her better judgment. Caroline was standing on her toes, her hands resting on Gavin's lapels while she whispered something in his ear. A feeling of such intense, primitive jealousy went through Katherine that she grasped the windowsill to keep from pounding on it with her fists.

"Not that you didn't bring a lot of this upon yourself by stirring up that scandal with Jeffrey Beecham," Marianne added matter-of-factly, taking Katherine's elbow and steering her away from the window. "Come now, it's time to dress for the christening party. You can't very well attend in your slippers and wrapper, you know."

The prospect of leaving that infernal room, even for a short interval, raised Katherine's spirits considerably. Every time she got up to walk around, it seemed, Dr. Franz or one of the maids came to chase her back to bed.

"What will I wear?" she asked, confused.

"What indeed?" Marianne answered, rolling her eyes. She opened a door to the left of the fireplace, which had always been locked when Katherine tried it, and swept through. "As if you didn't own more dresses than any woman in Seattle!"

Katherine hurried along behind her sister-in-law, casting her gaze this way and that, taking in as much of the massive room as she could. "Maybe nothing will fit," she fretted.

An enormous chandelier graced the high ceiling, and the fireplace was fronted in pale marble. The rugs were Persian, the walls were paneled in rosewood, and the bed was bigger than the living room of her apartment in that other Seattle.

She stood in the middle of the chamber, looking around her in awe, while Marianne went straight to a set of double doors, opened them, and disappeared inside.

Her voice echoed. "Nonsense. You were incredibly careful about what you ate, remember?" she called. "I think the dark blue taffeta would be exactly right, don't you? Given the state of your reputation, my dear, there's no point in even *attempting* propriety. No, the occasion calls for something that shows you won't be discounted and forgotten."

Katherine flinched when the main door of the room swung open and Gavin entered, carrying a black medical bag and a riding crop in one hand.

His eyes swept over her rumpled wrapper and tangled hair with a sort of charitable contempt, and Katherine was instantly furious.

"Where's Caroline?" she asked sweetly.

Gavin set his things down on a table that Katherine thought would probably bring a small fortune at a modern-day antique show. "Caroline," he responded, his tone even and cutting, "is too much of a lady to engage in the sort of illicit rendezvous you specialize in, my dear."

Color surged into Katherine's face, and she pulled her wrapper more tightly around her, as if to shield herself.

"Too much of a lady, pooh," Marianne interceded, before Katherine could think of a response. She thrust the aforementioned blue taffeta dress into her sister-in-law's arms and turned to face Gavin, her hands on her hips. "For someone who's supposed to be such a man of the world, Gavin Winslow," she said bluntly, "you are certainly naive."

Gavin looked at Katherine, even though he was speaking to Marianne, and his expression was scathing. "I can't deny that," he answered, "since I once trusted my heart to a woman who probably doesn't have one beating in her bosom."

Tears stung Katherine's eyes, and she swallowed hard to keep from giving full rein to her feelings. There was nothing she could say . . . the other Katherine probably *had* been guilty of flagrant adultery. Yet on every occasion when she encountered Gavin, no matter how rare and volatile those times were, she felt an elemental pull toward him, as though her soul had somehow been magnetized to his.

Marianne popped him in the upper arm, and the gesture was so sisterly that it almost made Katherine smile, despite everything. "Stop being so mean, Gavin, and get dressed for your son's christening. That is, unless you plan on going in your riding clothes."

The look that passed from Gavin to Katherine was a private one, since Marianne was by that time bustling toward the door of the other room. His gaze was as mocking as a slap, and Katherine hurried after her sister-in-law, wondering if Gavin meant to attend the christening at all.

He did, as it happened.

Gavin announced to the assembly, without ever informing Katherine, let alone consulting her, that the baby's name would be Christopher Jennings Winslow, and he looked for all the world like a proud father.

He even took his place beside Katherine after the intimate ceremony held in the house's private chapel, and shook hands with the endless stream of strangers, well-wishers all, who passed by.

The guests clearly admired and respected Gavin, but the looks they gave Katherine were plainly speculative. A wonderful meal was served in the garden, and inside the house, tables were heaped with gifts.

Despite his attempts at keeping up appearances earlier, by the time Maria had taken the properly christened Christopher back inside the house, Gavin was totally absorbed in a conversation with the bouncy Caroline Raynes.

"I hate perky women," Katherine muttered, turning away only to collide with a tall, handsome man in an expensive tweed suit. He had green eyes and chestnut-brown hair, and his sensual mouth quirked into a sad little smile.

"So do I," he said, taking both of Katherine's hands in his, just as Gavin had done with Caroline earlier in the day, when Katherine had been watching from the upstairs window. "How are you?"

His words and tone were so solicitous that Katherine was caught off guard. She still was weak from giving birth to Christopher and bruised from various sparring matches with Gavin, so this man's attentions were like warm sunshine after a dip in a frigid stream.

"F-fine," she said.

"You shouldn't be on your feet." He led her to the edge of the fountain that graced the middle of the garden and gently sat her down. Then he brought her a glass of punch from the refreshment table, along with some small sweet cakes coated in sesame seeds.

Katherine wished she had an inkling of the man's identity. She sipped her punch, thinking it was unfortunate that everybody didn't own a brooch made up of the letters of their name, like Marianne.

"Feel that sunshine," she said, lifting her face to the blue sky, closing her eyes, and smiling. "Isn't it wonderful?"

"Wonderful," her companion said distractedly. "Katherine, about our plans . . . Don't you think we should delay a few more weeks, until you're stronger?"

"Ummm," she answered, not really listening. A violin was playing nearby, and she began to sway happily back and forth with the tune. "I wish we could dance," she said, opening her eyes again, searching the stranger's handsome face. "Will you dance with me?"

A third voice answered, and it was only too familiar. So was the proprietary grip on her forearm.

"It's time you rested," Gavin informed his wife in a taut voice. "Come along, I'll see you to your room."

Katherine didn't try to pull away, though she heartily resented Gavin's tone and manner. She *was* tired, tired enough to faint. Dancing, of course, was out of the question, though it had seemed like a marvelous idea only moments before.

"It was nice meeting you," she said to the other man, without thinking, and then Gavin was propelling her toward the French doors leading to the main parlor.

Just over the threshold, he wrenched her angrily up into his arms. "'It was nice meeting you,'" he mimicked. "What kind of asinine remark was that?"

Katherine rested her head against a hard shoulder and yawned. "Oh," she said, in a tone of weary revelation. "I take it that was the infamous Jeffrey Beecham, with whom I was allegedly indiscreet."

Gavin took the stairs easily, as though Katherine's voluptuous weight was no strain at all to carry. "Allegedly," he scoffed under his breath. "I found the two of you in bed together, my darling. Remember?"

Chapter Four

Gavin's footsteps slowed as he passed the double doors of the master suite—he had carried Kathy through them many times during happier days—but now he proceeded down the hall without hesitation.

Reaching the entrance of Katherine's chamber, originally meant to be a dressing room, he opened the door and crossed the threshold.

Maria, who had been minding the sleeping baby, rose from her chair and left.

Katherine yawned and stretched, lush and kittenlike, when he laid her gently on the bed. Gavin's loins tightened in response. He couldn't have made love to her, of course; only a brute would have expected such accommodation so soon after childbirth. But the knowledge didn't stop him from wanting her, God help him, and neither did the mental image of her lying naked in Jeffrey Beecham's arms that day months before.

Gavin closed his eyes, remembering. Regretting.

He'd gotten drunk, for the first and last time in his life, after finding his wife and her lover in the guest house. And while he hadn't actually raped Kathy in their bedroom that night, he'd used her roughly. The fact that his wife had mistaken his rage for passion and responded wholeheartedly did not absolve him.

Now, stretched out on the bed to which he'd banished her, Katherine looked too angelic, too innocent to betray a husband's love. She favored him with a distracted little smile, her eyelids fluttered closed, and then she was asleep.

Gavin was unable to maintain his stern expression, now that she wasn't looking. He smiled as he gently removed her satin slippers and covered her tenderly with the lightweight wool blanket he found draped over the back of a chair.

She stirred beneath the coverlet, and Gavin felt his heart twist painfully. Some ancient instinct whispered that she was not the same woman he'd known, but somehow drastically changed. He was a physician, however, a man of science, and he couldn't give credence to anything quite so mystical.

He trusted facts, not feelings. It was a lesson he'd learned the hard way.

He resisted an urge to brush a tendril of auburn hair back from Katherine's forehead and turned to leave the room. Then, unable to help himself, he paused beside the baby's cradle, gazing down at the little boy he'd named Christopher that very day.

Gavin could no longer deny, even to himself, that this child was his own; the resemblance was too marked to be discounted.

After glancing in Katherine's direction to make certain she was truly sleeping, he crouched beside the cradle and gently touched Christopher's tiny ear.

"My son," he said, his voice hardly more than a hoarse whisper. Then he rose and walked from the room, closing the door behind him.

In the face of emotional confusion, Gavin generally took refuge in routine. He would change clothes, he decided, then get his medical bag, call for the carriage, and make his rounds.

His work at the hospital would take care of the rest of the night, and tomorrow could look after itself.

THE NEXT MORNING Katherine awakened to a room flooded with sunlight. By the time Maria arrived with a pitcher of hot water, she already had changed Christopher and fed him, and mother and child were sitting in a rocker by the windows, admiring the view of the garden.

"You shouldn't be out of bed, Mrs. Winslow," Maria said, with her usual lack of inflection.

"Nonsense," Katherine responded. "It's not as though I've had major surgery, after all." She raised Christopher and kissed his forehead. "Giving birth is a natural thing, and the sooner I'm up and around, the better."

Maria set the pitcher on the washstand and laid out a damask washcloth, a fluffy towel, and a bar of soap so fragrant that Katherine could smell its perfume from where she sat. "Whatever you say, Mrs. Winslow," she parroted. "I'll bring up your tea while you're washing, and Miss Marianne really thinks you should have breakfast. Shall I take the baby?"

Katherine surrendered her son, but reluctantly, and Maria put him in the cradle. "Tea would be wonderful, but I'll have my breakfast in the kitchen or the dining room or wherever everyone else eats. I'm sick to death of being locked away in this room." She poured some of the water Maria had brought into the waiting crockery basin and reached for the soap and cloth. "Tell me, Maria, how is it that you speak the way you do?"

Maria paused at the door. "You mean, why don't I sound like an Indian?"

Katherine blushed. She hadn't meant her question to sound condescending, but evidently it had. "Yes," she admitted. "That's what I was wondering."

For the first time in their acquaintance, Maria smiled. "My stepmother was white, and she was a schoolteacher until she married my father. She taught me 'Boston English,' but I have not forgotten the tongue of my people. It is very precious to me."

"Unfortunately," Katherine said with a thoughtlessness she had not intended, "the Indian way of life will all but disappear in the coming years." When she glanced in the wall mirror and saw Maria's stricken expression, she knew she had erred.

Maria lowered her head for a moment, but when she looked at Katherine again there was a proud, defiant light in her eyes. "Indian ways will live forever, in the safety of our hearts."

Katherine rinsed away the soap and dried her face and hands thoroughly on the towel provided, giving herself time to think. Finally she turned and faced the hired girl. "Yes," she said. "Maybe that's the only hope any of us have for our traditions—the memories of our children."

Maria swallowed visibly, and she glanced toward Christopher and nodded. "The old ways and stories are too valuable to be forgotten. They are a part of who we are."

"Yes," Katherine answered without hesitation. "I'm going to write down every single thing I can remember." Except for giving birth to Christopher, she hadn't done anything worthwhile since she'd crash-landed in the nineteenth century. Now, at least, she could make some kind of record of her experience. Maybe someone, someday, would believe her.

There was a long silence while Maria hovered in the doorway, silent, not quite able to meet Katherine's gaze. Finally she said, "My stepmother was going to help me write out the old legends, but we always thought we had plenty of time. Two years ago she caught the cholera and died."

"I'm sorry," Katherine said. She knew what it was to lose a mother. Memories filled her mind: waxed floors of chipped linoleum, fresh-baked cookies filling the house with the wonderful aromas of chocolate and sugar and butter, a

Christmas tree bedecked with homemade ornaments and shining colored lights, the sound of scales being plunked out on the piano by some earnest student.

Katherine had lost all those things, and much more, when Julia Hollis succumbed to cancer, and the grief had followed her even into another woman's life.

"I will bring your tea," Maria replied, closing the door.

Katherine began to pace the length of the hearth, feeling wildly restless. She still remembered only a few details of her other existence, but she knew she'd been an active, energetic person, committed to regular exercise.

"This Victorian bird-in-a-gilded-cage number is not me," she confided to the baby, who gave a tiny little sigh in response.

She stopped and looked at her image in the elegant mirror above the small brick fireplace. Although she'd had some time to accept her situation, if not understand it, it still astonished her to see a stranger's face reflected back from the glass.

Deciding she needed to take some action, however small or even ill-advised, Katherine eyed the inner door that led to Gavin's room. If she was going to go out and explore her surroundings, she would certainly need clothes, and they were evidently stored in that closet Marianne had entered the day before.

Katherine tried the knob cautiously, all the while expecting a shout of angry warning from Gavin. The door was locked, as before.

A glance at the clock on the mantelpiece revealed that it was well after nine A.M. Surely a dedicated doctor like Gavin had long since left for the hospital or for an office somewhere.

Securing the belt of her robe, Katherine squared her shoulders, marched out into the hall, and boldly turned the brass handle on one of the towering oak doors leading into the master suite.

She wasn't doing anything wrong, she insisted to herself, zeroing in on the closet without so much as a glance toward the massive four-poster. Ever since she'd seen the bed the day before, she'd been entertaining some very disturbing thoughts and images. In short, she'd pictured herself lying naked on it, surrendering to Gavin, taking him inside her.

Entering the huge closet, she found an array of dresses she could not even have imagined. There were silks and organdies, chiffons and cottons, velvets and laces. The sumptuous beauty of the gowns made her breath catch, and she caught an inner glimpse, in her mind's eye, of a little girl playing dress-up, far off in another century, another universe.

Carefully, she took down a hunter-green dress with a short jacket. The fabric was a very lightweight wool, and both garments were trimmed in black silk ribbon.

She was so caught up in the spectacular magic of that closet that all the breath fled her lungs when she turned to leave and collided with a rock-hard chest.

Gavin was standing in the doorway in riding breeches and no shirt, his arms folded. Even with his dark hair rumpled and his beard growing in, he looked entirely too good to be true.

"Good morning," he drawled, and Katherine could see that her disconcertment pleased him.

Color surged into her face. Deciding that the best defense was an offense, she challenged, "What kind of doctor is still lying around in bed at this hour?"

He chuckled, and while the sound wasn't exactly mean, it grated against Katherine's already jumbled nerves. "The kind who didn't get home from the hospital until five-thirty this morning."

Katherine swallowed, wishing he would let her pass. "If you'll excuse me . . ."

Gavin caught her chin in one hand and lifted, and his eyes were somber all of a sudden as he studied her face. "Where are you planning to go?"

"Out," she responded. "If I don't get some fresh air and sunshine, I'll lose my mind."

His dark brows drew together for a moment. "Since when do you enjoy the outdoors, Kathy?" he asked. Skepticism stole into his features. "Ah. Yes. You're meeting Beecham somewhere."

The insult quivered in Katherine's spirit like a spear. "No."

His thumb caressed her cheek, and the light in his gray eyes was a dangerous one, like a night fire flickering in an enemy camp. He touched her mouth then, as if to prepare it for conquering.

A moment later, with a raw sound low in his throat, Gavin kissed her. The action sent a sensation of delicious violence tumbling through her, and when he pulled her closer it was as though she'd struck a brick wall at high speed.

She could not have imagined more powerful feelings than those, but when Gavin thrust his tongue into her mouth, she was confronted with a whole new level of excitement. Her knees went weak, her heart began to beat so rapidly that she feared it would explode, and there was an achy, melting stir in the center of her womanhood. When Gavin lifted a hand to her breast and caressed her, still consuming her mouth, she was struck with a sweet and cataclysmic seizure of a kind she'd never experienced before.

She whimpered, her body convulsing softly against his, and when Gavin suddenly ended the kiss, she stared up at him in bewilderment.

"Never again, Kathy," he said tersely. "*Never again.*"

Katherine bent to pick up the dress that had dropped to the floor between them, not wanting him to see the hurt and embarrassment on her face. She might not have understood exactly what he was talking about, but she knew rejection when she encountered it.

Shakily, she left the room, her head held high. Gavin didn't need to know that it took all her pride to keep from defending herself to him, and all her courage to take the dress with her when she left.

One thing was clear. She could do nothing to change what had happened to her; she had a feeling there was no going back to that time and place beyond the crystal bridge.

That left the here and now to work with, and she meant to push up her sleeves and shape a life for herself.

With or without Dr. Gavin Winslow.

Chapter Five

Katherine walked around the beautifully maintained yard and gardens, exhilarated by the fresh spring air and bright sunshine. When she grew tired, she sat on the edge of the marble fountain, drew a deep, delicious breath, and closed her eyes.

The light, unexpected kiss made her open them again, wide.

Jeffrey smiled down at her. "Hello, Kathy," he said in a throaty voice.

If Katherine could have wished the man into a parallel universe, she would have done it. She wasn't at all surprised to look up at the second-floor windows of the mansion and catch a glimpse of Gavin as he turned away.

Jeffrey sat down beside her and took her hand; she wrenched free, feeling miserable.

"Your timing could not have been worse!" she hissed, bolting to her feet and smoothing her skirts.

Jeffrey's gaze had followed hers to the row of windows in the master bedroom. "I suppose the good doctor is on his way down to bloody my nose even as we speak."

"I wouldn't blame him if he did," she replied, tightening the black grosgrain ribbons that held her hunter-green bonnet in place. She drew in another deep breath, this time for courage, and then launched into her announcement. "I don't know what happened between the two of us," she said, and blushed as Jeffrey arched one eyebrow and smiled slightly. "All right, I *do* know. But I want to forget it all. I—I love my husband."

Jeffrey's amused expression turned stormy. He straightened his silk cravat and rose to look down at Katherine's face. "You made a promise to me. You vowed that we would leave for San Francisco, just the two of us, as soon as you'd regained your strength."

Katherine frowned. "Just the two of us? Surely I never meant to leave the baby . . ."

A crimson flush moved up Jeffrey's neck. "We agreed that the child would be better off here, with Dr. Winslow and his sister. Katherine, what's come over you? You're not the same woman I knew!"

She sank back onto the marble seat, dazed. She liked having this ripe and womanly body, and she loved Christopher and . . . yes, heaven help her, Gavin . . . but the more she found out about the original Mrs. Winslow, the more quiet contempt she felt. Not only had the other Katherine betrayed her husband, she had actually planned to abandon her own baby.

Katherine's high spirits were deflated. Earlier she had dared to believe it was possible to win Gavin's forgiveness, if not his love. Now the whole situation seemed more hopeless than ever.

"I don't want to see you again, Jeffrey," she said softly but firmly. "Not ever."

Jeffrey glared at her for a long moment, then turned and stormed away. The metal gate made a loud clatter behind him.

The next sound Katherine heard was slow, derisive applause.

She turned to see Gavin standing on the pathway leading to the French doors. He looked as handsome as ever in his tan breeches, linen shirt, and tailored tweed jacket, and every bit as stubborn.

"Stop it," she snapped. "I'm tired of your damnable mockery, Gavin Winslow."

"An excellent performance—the young matron bidding farewell to her lover. You belong in the theater."

Katherine stamped one foot. "Stop being such a jerk and give me a little credit, will you? I meant what I said to Jeffrey—Mr. Beecham. I never want to see him again!"

"What's a jerk?" Gavin asked, with wary curiosity.

Katherine laughed, but the sound was bitter and filled with despair. "Stupid and stubborn would pretty much cover it," she said.

For a long, long moment, Gavin just looked at her, his expression unreadable. There might have been tenderness in his pewter eyes, but there were anger and distrust, too. "I think you'd better go inside," he finally decreed.

She didn't bother to argue; she was suddenly too tired, and the events of the morning had left her feeling a little loosely wrapped. She started toward the house, her eyes averted, and when she passed Gavin he stopped her, catching hold of her arm.

"I won't forgive a second mistake, Katherine," he said.

She did not look at him. "You haven't forgiven the first one," she pointed out.

In her room, a fresh nightgown and wrapper awaited, and a maid had put clean sheets on the bed.

Katherine changed clothes, then sat in the rocking chair to nurse Christopher, who seemed to have a keener appetite with every passing day. When he'd gone back to sleep some minutes later, with that guileless propensity of newborns, Katherine crawled into bed, stretched out on the crisp bed linens, and dozed off herself.

When she awakened several hours later, the floors and corners of the room were shadowed with twilight, and there was a covered tray of food waiting on the bedside table.

Maria was sitting in the rocking chair, nursing Christopher.

Katherine sat up with a sigh and moved the tray onto her lap. Like Christopher, she was ravenous. "Is your baby a boy or a girl?" she asked.

Maria's expression was remote. "A boy."

The dinner tray held a delectable assortment of fare, including a chicken pie and a dish of stewed pears. "I'd like to see him. What's his name?"

Maria gazed down at Christopher as she spoke. "The tribal elders will give my son a name, when the time comes." She lifted deep brown eyes to Katherine's face. "I, too, would like to see him, but he lives with my people now."

Katherine, who had been eager to eat, lowered her fork back to the tray, her food forgotten. "You mean they took your baby away from you?"

"I gave him to them; his father is the chief's son. It is best."

Katherine forced herself to take a bite of her meal. "I couldn't bear to be away from Christopher," she said.

A glance in Maria's direction revealed that the woman was looking at her in confusion now. Perhaps she'd known that the mistress of the house planned to run away with a lover and leave her child behind for others to raise. Perhaps Maria had even hoped to fill the void in her heart by caring for the Winslow baby once Katherine was gone.

"I'll share him with you," Katherine said gently.

Maria blinked, looked away, then met Katherine's gaze again. "You've changed," she said. "And it seems there is much you don't remember."

Katherine nodded. "I have changed," she agreed. "I've changed more than anyone in the world would ever believe. And you're right—there's a lot I don't remember. Did Mrs.—did I keep diaries, Maria? Did I save the letters I received?"

Christopher had fallen asleep at Maria's breast. She laid him ever so gently in her lap, rebuttoned the front of her dress, and then raised the contented infant to her shoulder to be burped.

"There are papers," Maria said. "I will bring them after Dr. Winslow goes to the hospital for rounds."

"Thank you," Katherine replied.

As it happened, Gavin visited Katherine's room before he left the house. She would almost have preferred his scathing temper to the cool distance of his manner.

"I'm sending you to the island house for the rest of the summer," he announced.

Katherine was dismayed. She didn't know what island house Gavin was talking about, for one thing. For another, she hated leaving him in Seattle with the likes of Caroline Raynes. "Do I have a choice?" she asked.

The concept obviously caught Gavin by surprise. "A choice?"

Katherine nodded. These nineteenth-century men were something else. "Suppose I said I didn't want to go anywhere, that I preferred to stay in Seattle with you?"

Gavin gave a long-suffering sigh. "I would reply that your preferences don't carry a great deal of weight," he responded evenly.

Once again he'd used words to slap Katherine, and the blow hurt as much as the back of his hand would have.

"Bastard," she said, angry not only because of the pain he'd inflicted but because tears had sprung to her eyes, and she hadn't wanted him to see her cry over something he'd said or done.

He came to her bedside and bent to kiss her forehead. "I love you, too, my cherished darling," he responded with theatrical politeness. "Good night."

Finally Katherine noticed his formal clothing. "You're

going out!" she accused, picturing him dancing with one beautiful woman after another in some elegant ballroom. The next picture she had was of Gavin and the oh-so-proper Miss Raynes, chatting while they ate an elegant dinner, then clinking their wineglasses together in a toast that excluded the rest of the world.

"Yes," he responded.

Katherine started to protest, then stopped herself. She couldn't ask him not to socialize, especially with the track record the other Katherine had chalked up. "Gavin . . ." She ran her tongue over dry lips. "I don't suppose . . . well . . . would it help if I told you I was sorry for all the things that happened before?"

She sensed his withdrawal long moments before he actually drew back from her bedside. "No," he answered flatly. "It's too late for that."

He turned to the cradle then, and Katherine wished she could read the expression on his face as he looked down at the baby, but the gas lamps and the fire had not been lit, and the room was dim.

"I suppose you've noticed that he looks exactly like you," she dared to say.

Gavin raised his eyes to her face then, and the coldness in them pinned Katherine to the headboard as surely as an Indian's arrow would have done. "Christopher is my son," he conceded, "but that is a happy accident. He could just as well have been sired by Beecham or the man who delivers coal. As far as you and I are concerned, the fact that I'm acknowledging this child changes nothing."

The lump aching in Katherine's throat made speech impossible for the moment, and her mind was reeling anyway. She would not have been able to think of a response scathing enough to match Gavin's words.

That night the house seemed to buzz with activity, but

Katherine was still too stricken by her encounter with Gavin to wonder what was going on.

In the morning she found out.

"We're going to the island," Marianne announced, her face aglow. "I can hardly wait to walk on the beach again."

Katherine loved the beach, and the prospect of spending time in a waterfront house would have thrilled her in her other life, but now she only felt forlorn. Obviously, Gavin wanted his wife and sister out of the house so he could bring his mistress around with impunity.

Katherine and Marianne left for the wharf area at the head of a virtual caravan of carriages. They were followed by Maria and Christopher in another coach, and beyond that was a wagon loaded down with trunks.

Reaching Elliott Bay, where a small boat, part of the mosquito fleet, would take them to Vashon Island, Katherine forgot some of her heartache. There were creaking wharves and shouting sailors and clanging bells everywhere, and the scene was so different from its counterpart in modern-day Seattle that she was amazed. She wanted to remember every sight and sound.

After the passengers and their baggage had been loaded onto the boat, the captain tooted his whistle and the craft slipped bravely out into the harbor. Katherine stood at the railing, watching the land retreat.

The city was so like the one she knew, and so different.

Gavin didn't trouble himself to see them off, and Katherine wondered if he'd ever returned from his dinner party the night before. She hadn't seen him since his visit to her room, or caught the sound of his voice in the hallway.

"I brought the letters and the diaries," Maria said, standing beside her on the deck. At Katherine's immediate frown, the Indian girl smiled and added, "Don't worry. Christopher is with his aunt, being badly spoiled."

Katherine sighed. "Thank you for helping me, Maria—and for not automatically deciding that I'm crazy."

The girl's ageless brown eyes studied Katherine's face placidly. "You are not mad," she avowed. "And you are not Katherine Winslow."

Chapter Six

Katherine looked into Maria's pensive brown eyes and recognized a friend. She was not ready to explain her helter-skelter arrival in this time and place; indeed, she didn't understand the situation herself. Still, it was a comfort to know there was one person who might be receptive to such a strange confidence.

After that, both women watched the shore as the steam-powered boat chugged out into the bay, headed toward Vashon Island. White gulls as well as gray swooped and chattered alongside, and the waters looked like india ink under the relentless blue of the summer sky.

Katherine was entranced by the sight of the receding city. There was no evidence of the towering steel-and-glass skyline of her day, and wagons and carriages moved in the streets instead of automobiles.

She smiled. "It's like a movie," she said.

Maria frowned. "What?"

Katherine patted Maria's hand. "I'll explain some other time," she promised.

After an hour's journey, the boat docked at Vashon Island. There, another carriage awaited the Winslow party, along with a buckboard for hauling trunks and valises.

Katherine was just as fascinated by the island as she had been by the city. As they drove through a small cluster of buildings she spotted a mercantile, a blacksmith's shop, and a lovely lighthouse formed of natural stone. For her, the world had become one big hands-on museum.

The Winslows' summer house, which overlooked the water, turned out to be almost as impressive as the mansion in the city.

It was an enormous white frame house with lots of balconies and porches, and a few feet below the point of the highest gable, an octagon-shaped stained-glass window glowed with captured sunlight. There were rose bushes everywhere, along with arbors and benches and fountains, and two rows of graceful weeping willows towered like an honor guard on either side of the gravel driveway.

Although Katherine was not happy to be exiled to the island, she could not help being charmed by the magnificent house. Just looking at the place gave her a feeling of homecoming so profound that tears came to her eyes.

She sniffled. "It's lovely," she said.

Marianne hadn't even glanced out the carriage window. "You've been behaving so oddly of late, Katherine. You speak as though you've never seen the Haven, and you were married here!"

Katherine glanced helplessly at her sister-in-law, then bit her lip and ignored Marianne's remark. There was simply nothing she could say that wouldn't eventually land her in some grim nineteenth-century asylum.

If Marianne only knew how many things she didn't "remember," Katherine thought. What had happened to Gavin and Marianne's parents? For that matter, what had happened to her own? Had the other Katherine been raised in a happy home, with brothers and sisters, or as an only child? Why wasn't a pretty young woman like Marianne married?

The questions were practically never-ending, and Katherine hoped the letters and diaries Maria had brought along would answer at least a few of them.

As the carriage wheels rattled on the brick cobblestone driveway, Christopher stirred in Maria's arms and began to fuss. Katherine reached for him, astonished at the depth of love she felt. He was another woman's child, conceived and nurtured by the light of a stranger's soul, and yet she could not have been more devoted to him if he'd been her own.

"There now," she said softly, holding the infant against her shoulder and patting his tiny, flannel-swaddled back. "We're home."

The inside of the house was as splendid as the outside, and of the same gracious design. The rooms were all large and bright, filled with solid beautifully constructed furniture, but the pieces didn't loom oppressively over Katherine's head the way some of their counterparts at the mansion did.

There was a screened sunporch overlooking the orchard and, beyond that, the indigo water. Katherine intended to spend a great deal of her time in that quiet, sheltered place, working things through in her mind.

Her trunks were carried to the master suite, which turned out to be the chamber boasting the eight-sided stained-glass window. The suite offered both sitting and dressing rooms, and the floor was of bare wood, polished to a high shine. There was a small fireplace, fronted in gray and white marble, and the mantelpiece was fashioned of a wood so shiny and dark that it resembled ebony.

"There's been a mistake," Katherine confided anxiously to Marianne. Christopher had been fed, and Maria had taken him to the nursery across the hall, and Marianne was supervising the placement of Katherine's trunks.

"What kind of mistake?" Marianne asked as George, the caretaker, and Walter, his helper from the stables, left the room.

Katherine went to close the door, and the color was high in her cheeks when she replied, "This is surely *Gavin's* room. You know he and I don't share quarters . . ."

"More's the pity," Marianne reflected. "It would be better for both of you."

Katherine was impatient. "I think I should move to another room at once."

"Poppycock," Marianne returned airily. "Gavin is not God, however he may protest to the contrary; he has no right to hand down decrees. Besides, we probably won't see him until we return to Seattle in September anyway."

"September?" Katherine loved the island, as little as she'd seen of it, but the idea of not having so much as a glimpse of Gavin for three long months was practically unbearable.

Marianne sighed, spread her hands for a moment, then let them fall back to her sides. "You've finally fallen in love with your husband, haven't you?" she demanded with kindly frankness. "Forgive me for asking, Katherine, but what took you so long? Couldn't you have recognized your tender feelings before you humiliated the man in front of half the city of Seattle?"

Katherine detected no hostility in Marianne's words, only honest puzzlement. "I can't explain," she said, stepping through the French doors that opened onto a balcony. "At least, not yet. But yes, heaven help me, I think I have fallen in love with Gavin. I would do practically anything to win him back."

Marianne stood beside her at the railing of the balcony, and the two of them watched the sunlight dancing on the sound and the pale gulls soaring over the tops of the apple trees in the orchard. "I would like to see that happen," she said with gentle foreboding, "for your sake, and Christopher's, and especially for Gavin's. But the way you flaunted your—flirtation—with Jeffrey Beecham, well, that kind of disgrace isn't easy for a man to live down."

Katherine swallowed, and she didn't look at Marianne when she went on. She didn't dare. "Suppose I told you I didn't remember anything that happened to me before

Christopher was born? No wedding, no adultery, no anything. Would you believe me?"

"I would be very concerned," Marianne replied gently.

Katherine met Marianne's gaze and knew she could not tell her more, not then. "You're so lovely, Marianne. Why haven't you married and started a family of your own?"

Marianne's flawless skin paled slightly, and her mouth tightened almost imperceptibly—not with anger, Katherine thought, but with pain. "You really *don't* remember," she said. "Katherine, I was engaged to Timothy Waynewright, the vice president of the Merchants' Bank. He was shot and killed in a robbery two days before our wedding."

"Dear God," Katherine whispered, sagging against the railing for a moment. "Marianne, I'm so sorry."

Marianne looked more concerned with Katherine's state of health than her own tragedy. She took her sister-in-law's arm and escorted her firmly back inside the house.

"Gavin should be told about this—this memory lapse of yours. It might make a lot of difference." As she spoke, Marianne was maneuvering Katherine onto the big bed and covering her with a creamy cashmere throw.

Katherine shook her head. "None at all," she said. "He would think I was only pretending, in an effort to escape the consequences of Kath—of my mistakes."

Marianne left then, and Katherine slept for several hours. When she awakened, a lavender hatbox had materialized on her nightstand, like something left by Santa or the Easter Bunny. Katherine sat up, smoothed her hair, and set the box on her lap.

It was filled with scented vellum letters, and there were sepia photographs and two thick leather-bound journals as well.

Katherine started with the letters, which were mostly from school friends and family members back East. From the collection of mail, she learned that the other Katherine had been raised by a wealthy maiden aunt in Maine. She'd gone to boarding school in Connecticut from the first grade through the twelfth, then attended a Boston finishing school.

The photographs showed Katherine standing with Gavin, smiling brightly, and the two of them looked so happy. How could things have gone so terribly wrong?

Katherine leaned back against the carved mahogany headboard for a long time, staring at the empty fireplace and assimilating what she'd garnered from the first dozen letters. Only after Mrs. Hawkins, the housekeeper, had brought her tea and fresh strawberries did she tackle the rest.

It was strange, examining the images of another person's life, seeing her hopes and dreams reflected back in the handwriting of an elderly aunt, an understanding friend, a cousin. Even though Katherine learned a lot about the other Katherine in those leisurely hours of reading, the questions multiplied even faster than the answers.

The journals awaited her, promising the most intimate insights of all, but Katherine's mind was already spinning with details. She would save the diaries for another day.

At dinner that night Katherine was preoccupied, pretty much letting Marianne carry the conversation. Her predecessor had been a flighty and somewhat selfish creature, and very spoiled despite her isolation from her family. She must have been a lonely child, though privileged, starved for love and attention.

The next morning Katherine rose very early. She saw to Christopher's needs, then left him with Maria and went out for a walk, carrying one of the journals with her. Following a winding path down through the orchard, she heard the low, summery murmur of the tide, and the sound stirred some long-dormant hope within her.

Katherine walked along the shoreline for a time, delighting in the sights and sounds and smells, the wet, rocky sand, the water-beaten pilings and swaying boat docks. She came upon a bed of oysters, stopping to speculate, one hand shading her eyes from the morning sun, as to whether any of the hoary shells contained a pearl.

When she began to feel tired she returned to the orchard, found a tree with a low, sturdy branch and a clear view of the water, and climbed up. Once settled, her cumbersome skirts tucked in around her, she pulled the first journal from her pocket and started to read.

The diary's author, whom Katherine now thought of as Katherine the First, had visited Seattle after sailing from San Francisco to Hong Kong and back again. She'd met Dr. Gavin Winslow at a party and deemed him "handsome, if dreadfully serious." She'd also recorded that he'd inherited a fortune from his father, who'd been among the first timber barons in the area, a fact that apparently redeemed him a little for practicing the humble profession of medicine.

As Katherine read, her legs dangling from the tree branch, one shoulder resting against its trunk, she confirmed her earlier suspicions. Gavin's young bride had not been a wicked vamp, bent on shaming her husband in the eyes of the world, but a confused, lonely child. She'd needed *everyone's* love and attention, not just her husband's. When people failed to notice her, she'd written, she felt as though she were invisible and sometimes even began to doubt her existence. Often, she'd sunk into "black melancholia" and sincerely wished she'd never been born.

Her name came tumbling toward her on the warm, salty breeze.

"Katherine! Kaaathy!"

It was Marianne.

Katherine closed the journal, tucked it back into her skirt pocket, and clambered down from the tree. Her skill at this endeavor was a holdover from the life she'd lived on the other side of the crystal bridge. There, as a child, she'd been an inveterate tomboy.

When Katherine reached the ground and turned to start toward her sister-in-law, she found the young woman staring at her, openmouthed.

"Katherine, were you up in the boughs of that tree?" she asked incredulously.

"You know I was," Katherine answered pleasantly. "You must have seen me."

"But you *never* do things like that."

Katherine smiled. "I do now."

Chapter Seven

Katherine and Marianne had lunch on the screened porch, with Maria to keep them company. Katherine was preoccupied, as she had been the night before at dinner, and the journal, hidden away in her pocket, consumed her thoughts.

When the new idea bobbed to the top of Katherine's mind, it startled her so much that she dropped her soup spoon with a clatter and even gave a little cry.

"Excuse me, please," she blurted out, shoving back her chair and bolting to her feet.

The other two women looked surprised at her behavior.

"Katherine, are you all right?" Marianne inquired.

She merely nodded hastily and dashed into the main part of the house. In a massive and very masculine study off the main entryway, she found what she was looking for: a desk, paper, a bottle of ink, and a pen.

Sinking into a cushioned chair of the finest Moroccan leather, Katherine pulled several sheets of expensively made vellum stationery from the desk drawer. After arranging the paper on the mirror-bright surface, she opened the ink bottle, dipped her pen, and began to write.

Excitement mounted within her as she penned one non-sensical sentence after another. Only when her hand became too tired to write did Katherine finally wipe the pen's nib clean and put the lid back on the ink.

Without waiting for the pages to dry, she compared them to the flamboyant script in the journals. The letters on the loose papers were narrower, neater, and much smaller.

She had retained something more of that other life than a tangle of memories, then. She had kept her own handwriting.

Within a moment Katherine was so breathless that she dared not rise from the chair, lest her trembling knees refuse to hold her.

She laid her head down on the desk and tried to gather her composure. The other Katherine was almost surely lying in that hospital bed in the Seattle of a hundred years hence, or perhaps she'd even died.

Katherine had sympathy for Gavin's bride, but she also wanted this body, this man, and this life, even though the last tenant had botched things up royally.

She began to shiver, feeling chilled even though the room was warm. Maybe the whole process would reverse itself. Maybe she would be wrenched away from Christopher and Gavin and the elegantly antique world she had come to love . . .

Finally Katherine drew a deep breath and made herself sit up. She would take things one day at a time and deal with trouble when she came across it. In the meanwhile she planned to somehow, someway win Gavin back.

During her first week at the Haven, Katherine read and reread all the diaries and letters, and she must have studied the tintypes and sepia photographs a million times. She tried on all the summer dresses that had arrived with her in the trunks and studied herself in the mirror.

The second week brought a letter from Gavin. Katherine was disappointed if not surprised that it was addressed to Marianne. While the message carried warm wishes for his sister and inquiries about Christopher's progress, Katherine might not have existed at all.

By the time twenty-one days had gone by, Katherine was riding all over the island on horseback. While she enjoyed her adventures, she also knew she was trying to outdistance her own doubts and injured feelings.

After a month, Marianne announced plans for a garden party. Everyone in the Winslow social circle, both on the island and in Seattle, would be invited.

Katherine went through her wardrobe, garment by garment, and prayed that Gavin would attend.

In early August, five weeks after Marianne, Maria, Katherine, and Christopher had moved to the island for the summer, the party was held.

Gavin sent word from Seattle that he was too busy to join in the festivities.

Katherine attended the social event, smiling the whole time, barely able to breathe because her heart was in her throat. She spoke with warmth and graciousness to all the guests but was careful not to behave inappropriately, for she hoped to undo some of the damage the other Katherine had done.

After the last guest had retired, Katherine locked herself in her room and wept because Gavin had stayed away.

On a hot day at the end of August, when Maria went to visit friends on the far side of the island, taking Christopher along, Marianne journeyed to Seattle to attend a wedding. Katherine looked at the roiling charcoal clouds on the horizon and felt a sweet, dangerous anticipation.

There was a storm coming, and Katherine loved storms.

As night fell, the very earth seemed to rock with the force of the thunder. The wind howled around the house, and Katherine knew the water in the sound would be churning, the waves white-capped. Lightning outlined the old lighthouse Katherine had sketched so many times, and the housekeeper and caretaker hurried from room to room, securing the windows.

Katherine's fascination with the natural panorama seemed to confound them, but they offered no comment. Despite her earlier efforts to let the old couple know that she regarded them as equals, they still saw themselves as servants.

"Would you like me to bring you a brandy, Mrs. Winslow?" the housekeeper asked anxiously. She was a sturdy but compact woman with large blue eyes and white hair wound into a coronet on top of her head. "I know you always get a little nervous when the weather gets like this."

"Nervous?" Katherine laughed. "Heavens, no—I'm not afraid of a little thunder and lightning."

But *she* had been, Katherine realized. That was why Mrs. Hawkins was looking at her as though she was turning into a werewolf before her very eyes.

Before the housekeeper could reply, the front door slammed and a voice as domineering as the thunder echoed through the house.

"Marianne! Maria!"

Gavin.

It wounded Katherine that he hadn't called her name as well, but of course she shouldn't have been surprised. From the first, Gavin had allowed her not even the skimpiest illusion that he cared for her.

At least he was consistent.

Mr. Hawkins was busy building a blaze in the parlor fireplace, so his wife went to greet her grumpy master. When Gavin entered the room, he looked through Katherine as if she were invisible and went to stand on the hearth, warming his hands.

The housekeeper and caretaker left immediately, and Katherine herself was edging toward the towering double doors when Gavin stopped her with a brusque "Where is my son?"

The very roof of the house shook with the force of two fronts colliding high in the sky, no more elemental than Gavin's formidable will meeting her own.

"*Our* son is with Maria," Katherine answered evenly, wondering how she could love Dr. Winslow so much when he invariably made her yearn to strangle him. "They went visiting this afternoon, and I'm sure they're perfectly safe."

Gavin assessed his wife with eyes as cold as a frozen steel blade. "You've been well?"

Katherine was secretly thinking how fitting it would have been if he'd snarled and shown vampire teeth, but Gavin was as stunningly attractive as ever. The reflexive pitch and roll in her stomach was proof of that. "Very well."

A blast of thunder rattled the windows, and his gaze narrowed as he stared at her. "I rather expected to find you cowering under the bed in fear, my dear," he said. "You were always terrified of storms."

"You don't know me as well as you think you do," she responded crisply. For all her light words, she had a dizzying fancy that some dangerous enchantment had settled over the big house with Gavin's arrival.

"I know you all too well," Gavin corrected her, shedding his long coat and tossing it aside, then crossing to a teakwood cabinet near the doors and pouring himself a brandy.

Katherine decided to ignore the statement. "What brings you here, Dr. Winslow?" she asked, moving close to the fire because he had abandoned the space. "Did someone tell you I was happy? That would surely account for your hasty appearance and intractable mood." *I'm getting the Victorian vernacular down pretty well*, she congratulated herself.

Gavin was frowning as he regarded her in the flickering glow of the lamps, his brandy like glowing amber in the firelight. "Since when do you use words like 'intractable'?"

"You wouldn't believe it if I told you," Katherine replied. Invisible St. Elmo's fire danced and crackled in the room, and she sensed that Gavin was as aware of the dynamic charisma between them as she was.

He took another sip of his brandy. "You'll be sorry to hear that your Jeffrey Beecham has lit out for greener pastures." The challenge was a quiet one, but nonetheless deadly.

"Good," she said, with light assurance. "I won't miss him." She swallowed, summoning up all her courage. "But I have missed you, Gavin. Very much."

His frigid gaze moved over her—she was wearing a cotton gown, a white background with small lavender flowers scattered over it—and her rich auburn hair was gathered up in a soft Gibson-girl style. When his Adam's apple moved, Katherine felt a certain tenderness toward him, as well as a captivation so powerful that she feared to think to what lengths it might drive her.

"Do not insult me with the inference that you cherish any wifely sentiments toward me," he warned. For all his words, for all that she was standing half a room away, Katherine was woefully conscious of the hardness and heat of his body.

She sighed. She'd never seduced a man before, or been seduced *by* one, for that matter, and she had no idea how to proceed. She only knew that she had been thrust into this century, and the company of this particular man, because his soul was mate to hers.

"You want me, Gavin," she said simply. Quietly.

He turned away and tossed his brandy, glass and all, onto the fire. The glass shattered and the blaze roared up the chimney, but Gavin paid it no apparent mind. He stood with his back to her, his hands braced against the mantelpiece.

He hadn't given an inch of ground, and yet somehow Katherine knew she had the upper hand. "I'll bring you some dinner, if you'd like," she said in as normal a tone as she could manage. She'd been hoping and praying Gavin would come to the island all these weeks, and now he was here and she was more certain of her love for him than ever.

He was silent for a long, long time, but Katherine was just as stubborn as he was, and she waited.

"Bring the tray to my room," he said.

Her heart rushed into her throat. She was both terrified and joyous as she hurried to the kitchen. By the time she climbed the back stairway and entered the master suite half an hour later, after she'd laboriously reheated the leftovers from supper, she was trembling.

It wasn't fear of sharing her body with Gavin that scared her, although she had never been with a man in her life, despite having gone through the experience of childbirth. No, it was the possibility that he meant to reject her, to humiliate her, that frightened her so much.

Balancing the tray on one hand, she opened the door and stepped into the bedroom that had been hers alone these past weeks.

Gavin had built up the fire and was sitting in a wing-back chair, gazing solemnly at the flames. He'd taken off his coat and his collar, and his shirt gaped open to the middle of his chest.

Katherine wished she could believe he was looking so rakishly handsome for her benefit, but it was more likely that he was completely unaware of the image he presented.

She set the tray on the small round table beside his chair, and he didn't raise his eyes to her or acknowledge her in any way.

She decided she'd read him wrong earlier and moved to the bureau, feeling both dejection and relief. "I'll sleep in one of the guest rooms," she said in a voice barely loud enough to compete with the storm outside and the crackling babble of the fire.

"You're my wife," Gavin said gruffly, still without looking in her direction. "You will sleep in my bed."

Chapter Eight

The light of the bedroom fire flickered over Gavin's rain-damp clothes, glimmered on the polished leather of his riding boots, lent a crimson halo to his ebony hair. Katherine was stricken by the joyous love she felt for this husband she'd won by accident; it was as though some ancient wrong had been finally righted, after a long and difficult struggle.

Every tiny fiber in her body seemed to resonate, like the strings of some mellow old instrument that had been lifted from a musty trunk, tuned, and finally strummed with cherishing fingers.

Gavin set his strong hands on the arms of the chair and thrust himself wearily to his feet. When he turned to face Katherine, he took on an aura made up of firelight and the violent, golden lightning that flashed beyond the terrace doors.

Katherine could not read the expression on his face for the shadows that cloaked him, but she felt the barely leashed power in his body, sensed the distant tumult of the battle going on within his spirit. The conflict, she knew, was between the mightiest of human emotions, love and its twin, hatred.

For the first time since she'd landed in this place, she had hope of finding her way into Gavin's heart and making a lasting place for herself there.

Fearful that anything she said might tilt the delicate balance the wrong way, she kept her silence. She lifted her chin and stared straight at his face to show him she wouldn't be intimidated. For all that, the separate impacts of his physical presence, the warriorlike strength of his spirit, the laser-powered reach of his mind, practically overwhelmed her.

He took a step toward her, then another, reluctantly, as though resisting some elemental force every inch of the way.

His hand came to rest on her shoulder, and she turned and lightly brushed his knuckles with her lips.

"God help me," he whispered in the tone of one who expects no aid from any quarter, including heaven. He tilted his head back and closed his eyes, and Katherine watched the play of muscles in his magnificent neck for a long moment, then softly kissed the hollow of his throat.

She felt a shudder go through him, knew a sensation of homecoming that went far beyond the physical when he wrenched her against him. Her hair spilled down her back as he plunged splayed fingers beneath the little knot she'd pinned so carefully into place.

He spread his free hand over the small of her back, pressing her curvy softness against an opposing hardness. When he assailed her with his demanding, masterful kiss, it seemed to Katherine that the elegant room had suddenly turned to a vacuum, like outer space. Only her connection with Gavin allowed her to breathe; when he withdrew, her last contact with the life force would be broken. She would shrivel to a cinder and then disappear entirely.

Just when Katherine thought she couldn't accommodate another sensation, another dizzying emotion, without going into overload, Gavin thrust his tongue past her lips. It was symbolic of the conquering that would come later, she knew, and the sweet warning caused her knees to go weak.

She uttered a desolate little cry when Gavin lifted her into his arms, never troubling to withdraw his mouth from hers, and carried her to the bed. Only when he'd laid her on the coverlet did he draw back so that he could look at her as he stripped her of her clothes.

He made a slow ritual of that process, starting with her shoes. After rolling down each of her stockings, he kissed the tops of her insteps with light, fevered touches of his lips.

He pushed up her skirts and petticoats to bare her knees, and Katherine bit down hard on her lower lip to keep from pleading with him to go ahead and take her.

By the time she was completely naked, her skin glowed with perspiration and her hips twisted on the mattress, betraying her, seeking some contact with him.

He caressed one of her plump breasts as he began taking off his own clothes, and when he was finally bare, as she was, he stretched out over her, letting her feel his daunting manhood against her upper thigh.

Now, she thought, as hot shivers of desire streaked through her. *Now, finally, he'll take me. I'll be his.*

Instead, though, he slipped downward, his coarse chest hair chafing her breasts and stomach in an elementally pleasant way. When he took her nipple into his mouth, she cried out in helpless pleasure and arched against the steely strength of the body that spanned the length of her like a bridge over a flood-swollen stream.

At the same time, thunder and rain slammed against the house, and Katherine had a vague sense that no matter how loudly she called out in response to his attentions, no one else on the planet would hear.

She surrendered, completely and absolutely, reaching back to grip the underside of the headboard in desperate hands. Had she still possessed the faculties to speak, she would have begged, but she was far beyond that now. A storm had broken in her body and spirit, and she was at its mercy.

Finally, finally, when she wanted to weep with the force of her need, Gavin entered her in a long, slow stroke. He was looking into her suddenly wide-open eyes as he took her, watching her responses in the faulty light of the fire.

Katherine had never been so intimate with a man, not in her previous life, and in that other body she would probably have suffered pain. As it was, she felt only a tightness, then electricity as the tempest in her heart and soul gained momentum.

She clutched wildly at Gavin's shoulders, unable to ask for what she needed because she didn't know its name.

Fortunately, he seemed to know very well. He began to move within her, slowly, steadily, strongly, and while he moved, he nibbled at her lower lip, her neck, her earlobes, her jawline.

Each stroke made Katherine more desperate for the next one. Her breath quickened, and her nipples were hard buttons against Gavin's chest, her legs like a fierce vise around his hips.

Finally the pleasure reached an explosive pitch, and Katherine marveled even as her new body did its dance beneath Gavin, curving high to meet his hips. Her husky cries of triumph breached that last barrier of reserve he'd erected, and he uttered a raw shout and then convulsed against her, driving deep, spilling himself.

Gavin collapsed, his head resting against her breast, when it was finally over. His breathing was ragged, like Katherine's own, and neither of them was capable of speech.

Now that the harsh demands of his body had been met, at least for the moment, Gavin could think with some coherence again. And what he was thinking troubled him deeply.

People rarely changed in any lasting fashion. He knew that because of his Harvard education and his personal experience as a man and a doctor. Seeming alterations of personality usually were temporary, except in some cases of religious conversion.

He listened to the heartbeat of the woman whose luscious breasts cushioned his head, not as a physician, but as a man who drew a spiritual sustenance from the sound. This was Kathy, the woman he'd loved to the point of desperation, the mother of his child, the only bedmate he'd taken since his marriage. Yes, even after his wife had betrayed him, he had been faithful to her.

It did seem that Kathy had changed drastically since the day of Christopher's birth, though he feared to believe it. Her much-gossiped-about indiscretions had wounded him to the very well-springs of his soul; he knew he could not endure such terrible pain again.

He closed his eyes, already feeling the temptation to turn his head and feast gently at her nipple, and a series of images flashed through his mind for the thousandth time.

Months before, Kathy had been defiant about her affair with Jeffrey Beecham. She'd said he was more attentive and affectionate than Gavin, more *fun*. She'd made no secret of the fact that she'd rather be Beecham's wife than his.

Since Christopher's arrival, however, she'd brushed the other man off like a speck of dust, and tonight she'd responded to Gavin's lovemaking as she never had.

There was a change in the way she spoke, too. Although her vocabulary had not been limited before, she had a much greater grasp of the language now.

Then there was the way she acted. Katherine was a devoted mother to Christopher, he knew that from what he'd seen and from Marianne's regular letters. And there were still other things.

According to reports from Maria, Kathy had taken to sitting in trees, reading. It was amazing enough that she would open a book other than her journal; it was incomprehensible that she was reportedly working her way through the Haven's well-stocked library. Furthermore, she'd never treated the help with such courtesy.

Gavin's long-starved body was not concerned with the speculations of his mind. He could feel himself going hard against the delicious cushion of Katherine's thigh, and the muscles in his hips and buttocks were flexing involuntarily, preparing themselves to thrust.

He wondered how she would receive him now, she who had never really cared for the strain and messiness of love-making—at least with him.

With a long sigh, Gavin turned his head and brushed a waiting nipple with his lips. The morsel immediately pouted, ready for capture.

He laid a hand on Katherine's belly, made slow, firm circles on the satiny expanse.

Kathy's fingers plunged into his hair, and she startled him by pulling him close for her kiss. Just before she raised her lips to his, she whispered breathlessly, "No preliminaries this time, Gavin. Just take me, hard and fast."

Her words intoxicated him as surely as a pint of good Kentucky whiskey would have done, and again he marveled as he positioned himself to give her what she wanted. What they both wanted.

THE STORM HAD passed when Katherine awakened the next morning, and Gavin had already left her bed. Indeed, Christopher was back, regarding his mother wonderingly over Maria's shoulder as she held him in the rocking chair.

The immediate sense of desolation that had gripped Katherine at the realization that Gavin was gone was instantly displaced by the joy of seeing her son again.

"You're home from your travels," she chimed, sitting up and tucking the sheets underneath her armpits because Gavin had stripped her of every stitch the night before and never given her time to put on a nightgown.

Maria turned to smile. "Yes. I hope you weren't worried—we

were safe with Aunt Nisa and Uncle Tie throughout the storm. Uncle brought us home this morning."

Although Katherine had definitely missed Christopher, she had had confidence in Maria's ability to take care of him, and she had not been overly concerned. "I trusted you completely. Now let me hold my handsome boy before I perish for the longing."

Gently, Maria handed the infant to Katherine, who cradled him against her breast and bent her head to kiss his fuzzy little crown.

"Have you seen Dr. Winslow around this morning?" she asked presently, hoping the question didn't betray too much.

A glance at Maria's face showed that the other woman had already divined the situation, probably from Katherine's lack of a nightgown and the pair of shiny riding boots sitting neatly beside the wardrobe.

"He's gone to the shore, I think," Maria said with a certain friendly smugness. "When something's troubling the doctor, he likes to come out here and walk along the beach while he works it through."

Katherine cuddled Christopher a little closer and stroked his back with her hand. Gavin had made thorough love to her the night before, unknowingly changing her forever, but he hadn't mentioned the word "love." She could only conclude that he was having doubts this morning, and maybe regrets, too.

"You look so sad," Maria said, coming to sit on the edge of the bed and squeezing Katherine's free hand.

A tear welled up in Katherine's eye. "I am," she answered. And then, because she knew this woman was a friend, because she couldn't keep the secret anymore, she poured out her story. Katherine told Maria about that other life, painted the freeway and the speeding sports car and the jackknifed truck into as understandable a picture as she could. She explained about the crystal bridge, the shock of waking up inside someone else's body—someone who was in the middle of childbirth—and the even weirder sensation that she'd known Gavin Winslow for all eternity, that her love for him was as primitive as the stars, and that she belonged with him.

When all the breathless, disjointed words had tumbled out of her mouth, Katherine sat tensing, holding Christopher and waiting to know if there was one person on earth who would believe her.

Chapter Nine

Maria carefully took the baby, who had fallen asleep against Katherine's chest, and laid him in the cradle.

Pressing the covers to her collarbone, Katherine scrambled to the foot of the bed for her paisley silk wrapper, which she hastily donned. She hoped Maria was remembering the day they'd come to the island, when they'd stood talking at the rail of the ferry and the other woman had said, *You are not mad. And you are not Katherine Winslow.*

When Katherine's friend turned to face her, there was a reassuring smile on her face. "We have many strange legends among our people," she said with a little shrug. "Besides, who is to say what is truth and what is not?"

Katherine was so relieved that she sagged to the edge of the bed. "Do you know what Gavin would probably say if I told him that same story? That I'd broken a blood vessel in my brain or suffered a psychotic episode."

Maria's pretty face crumpled with puzzlement. "What?"

"He'd think I was crazy," Katherine simplified.

"Tell me more about that other world. Is it better than this one?"

"In some ways," Katherine answered with a sigh. "There are lots of medical advances." She glanced toward Christopher, sleeping comfortably in his cradle, and felt fiercely protective. "Many of the old-time diseases like whooping cough and measles and smallpox have been almost entirely eliminated. People don't have to work as hard, and everything is much faster. For instance, here, a letter takes weeks to cross the country, but where I come from, there's a machine called a fax that will transmit—send—words or pictures anywhere in the world, in just a matter of moments."

Maria's mouth was open.

If there was one thing Katherine enjoyed, it was a receptive audience. "There are many other wonderful machines, too—airplanes, for instance," she went on, encouraged. "They're like a big metal ship, except that they have wings and fly through the sky instead of sailing on the water."

"I want to see this place!"

Katherine was filled with sadness. "That doesn't seem very likely to happen," she said gently, laying one hand on her friend's shoulder, "but don't worry. I have enough stories to last until we're both very old women. In fact, some of these things will be starting to happen by then."

"They must be written down, those things you remember."

Katherine agreed, and she couldn't help grinning. What a shock some historian would get when he or she opened a dusty old journal dated 1895, and found detailed descriptions of fax machines, computers, airplanes, and video cameras.

"In what ways is this time better than your own?" Maria wanted to know.

"I don't know that 'better' is the proper word," Katherine mused. "Things are generally simpler here. There isn't so much stress." She looked around at the sumptuous room. "It's very romantic, this life, riding in carriages, living in mansions, wearing long dresses that rustle when I walk. But I'm well aware that the vast majority of people don't enjoy this kind of luxury."

Maria's brow was furrowed with a frown. "Don't women wear long dresses in your world?"

Katherine smiled. "Only for very elegant parties and things like that. I spent most of my waking hours in jeans—trousers."

"Women wear trousers there?" Maria's voice was soft with disbelief and wonder.

"Yes," Katherine said. "And they vote and own their own businesses and hold political office."

Raising the fingertips of both hands to her temples, Maria shook her head. "This is a lot to take in."

Katherine felt an even greater affection for her quiet, practical, steady friend. "Yes," she agreed gently. "But don't get the idea that I came from some kind of paradise. The human race still has a very long way to go."

Still looking a little dazed, Maria left her, and Katherine washed, dressed, and groomed her hair. Then, placing the baby in Marianne's capable care, she set out for the beach.

Katherine told herself she wasn't looking for Gavin, but when she spotted him sitting on a boulder in the distance, the salt-misted breeze ruffling his hair, she was overjoyed. She stopped to smooth the skirts of her bright cotton peasant dress with its lace-up front and to pat her hair.

"Good morning," she called when she knew she was close enough to be heard. With one hand, she shaded her eyes from the fierce sunshine, and behind her calm exterior trembled a woman who knew she was betting her soul on a longshot.

Gavin's gray eyes swept from her face to her hem then back again. He climbed agilely down from the rock, slung his lightweight tweed jacket over one shoulder. There was a remoteness in his manner that was even more disturbing than the hostility he usually displayed.

"Was I wrong in thinking last night made a difference?" Katherine asked boldly, facing him on the hard, rocky sand. The tide licked at the hem of her skirt, and the wind made coppery tendrils of hair dance around her face.

His expression was haunted, and Katherine felt an anger as deep as Puget Sound as she realized just how badly his voluptuous bride had wounded him. It was a bitter irony, having to pay the price for the other woman's sins.

"There are times," Gavin conceded after a long interval of pensive silence, "when, if I didn't know better, I would think you are another person entirely."

Hesitantly, Katherine touched his arm, and just that simple contact started a sweet riot of sensation within her. She clung tenaciously to reason, to the sad truth that Gavin would merely think she was insane if she tried to explain how she had come to him. "Isn't it enough that I've changed, Gavin, that I'm genuinely sorry for whatever might have taken place in the past? Can't we go on from here?"

He raised his hand as if to touch her cheek, then let it fall back to his side. His grin was so brief and so sad that the sight of it wrenched Katherine's tender heart. "Yes and no," he finally answered, his tone ragged. "I want you in my bed again, and I want more children by you, but there will always be a part of my soul that I can't share with you."

Katherine longed to be welcome in Gavin's bed, and she wanted even more to bear him other babies, yet the pain his words caused her was so intense that it struck her dumb.

Gavin wanted to *use* her, like a stallion would a brood mare, and with no appreciable difference in concern for her feelings. He wasn't asking her to be a real wife, and he certainly wasn't offering her anything that remotely resembled love.

Her entire body trembled with the effort not to slap him across the face.

"I am not a bitch dog," she pointed out evenly, after a very long time.

Gavin hooked a finger under one of the laces at her bodice and brazenly traced the outline of a nipple, causing it to press toward him. "The response to that, my dear," he said, "is so obvious that I won't even stoop to it." He grew bolder then, flattening his palm against her breast, smiling as it swelled in his fingers, as ripe and succulent as a late-summer melon.

Katherine moved to twist away, her face crimson with rage and humiliation, but he curved one iron arm around her waist and stopped her.

"At last," he said, "I've figured out how to deal with you, Katherine. You need a man who can play your body as deftly as an angel plays a harp, and we both know that, for some reason comprehended only by the gods, I have become that man. I will bed you often and well, and you will behave yourself in the interim or suffer the consequences."

Katherine's defiance drained out of her; she knew all the blood had left her face. "What consequences, Gavin?" The question was barely more than a whisper, for it took phenomenal effort to push the words past her constricted throat.

With an index finger, he lightly traced the line of her jaw, and she hated him for arousing such wanting in her with so innocent a caress. "Very simply," he said, with a regretful sigh, "I will divorce you and ship you off to live in a cottage somewhere, with a maid."

"And Christopher?"

"He would remain with me," Gavin said flatly.

Although she did not want to be sent away from Gavin and, admittedly, from the rich lifestyle he provided, she could have borne both those things. The thought of losing her son, however, filled her with desolation and terror. Where in her own century she would have been able to fight Gavin for custody, in the late 1800s, she had no more legal rights than her husband's favorite horse. She was his property.

"I couldn't bear that," she said, softly but proudly.

Gavin curved a finger under her chin and raised her face so that their gazes met. While his touch was certainly not painful, there was no tenderness in it, either. "Perhaps motherhood has redeemed your black little soul," he said. "We shall see." With that, he walked away in the direction of the house.

Katherine stood on the shore for a long time, feeling an explosive anger build inside her, fueled by frustration and, worst of all, desire.

It was probably despair that sent her rushing after Gavin to angrily grip his jacket, which was still slung casually over his shoulder.

"Damn you, Gavin," Katherine cried, "don't you *dare* drop a bomb like that and then walk away!"

His expression was one of bafflement, rather than anger, when he turned to look at her. "'Drop a bomb'?"

She sighed and shook her head. She had no patience for explaining about World War I and all the succeeding developments that would influence the language. "If you'll just open up to me, Gavin," she pleaded, holding his arm. "If you'll only give me a chance to prove I'm really different . . ."

"I'll visit you here when I feel the need," he said dismissively. "When I return to Seattle, I will live as I should have before."

Katherine's heart plummeted. "You're talking about taking a mistress, aren't you?" she breathed. "Maybe you've already done that, set up some bird in a gilded cage—"

He shook his head, not in denial but again in bewilderment. There wasn't a hint of confusion in his words, however; they were cutting and concise. "Don't tell me you have the gall to object?" he drawled.

She closed her eyes tightly and clenched her hands at her sides, struggling not to outscream the gulls whirling and diving against the blue sky. Finally she trusted herself to speak. "I do object," she said reasonably. "You are my husband, and I won't share you."

He touched her hair and offered her an indulgent little smile. "How refreshing," he said. "And how utterly unlike you." He bent his head to nibble lightly at her lips, but she knew the kiss was not a display of tenderness. It was a challenge.

Again he caught his finger under the laces of her bodice, nestled it in the velvety softness and warmth of her cleavage. "I'm going into the city today to attend to some of my patients, but I will return in time for dinner and your wifely comforts, my dear. Be ready for me."

Even as Katherine's mind shrieked rebellion, her body ached for the pleasures of Gavin's possession. Her nipples yearned to nourish him, her hips and thighs to cushion his weight. In her own time, the talk shows covered problems like hers, but since Sally and Phil and Oprah and Geraldo had yet to be born, she would just have to deal with it on her own.

They separated then, and Katherine went to one of her favorite refuges, a tiny chapel set back in the woods. It was complete with pews, stained-glass windows, and candles to light, and the place seemed somehow eternal, neither of this century nor of her own.

Before her accident and subsequent mystical experience, Katherine had not been particularly religious. She still wasn't too clear on her theology, but she had encountered Someone near that shimmering glass bridge, and she knew now that the universe was not the random place it had once seemed to be. There was a distinct order and logic to events, though for the life of her she couldn't see how her own situation fit into the scheme of things.

As she sat in the soothing silence of that place, a tear slipped down her cheek. Every day her old existence in modern-day Seattle seemed farther and farther away, more and more like a fantastic story she'd read somewhere. This life, here and now, was real and vital, the one she truly wanted to live, and yet the emotional distance between her and Gavin seemed too vast to bridge. They were in accord only when they were making love, and that simply wasn't enough.

Chapter Ten

Gavin did return to the island house for dinner that night. He made love to Katherine later, in the privacy of their room, just as he'd promised to do, and even though her ego demanded it, she hadn't the strength to resist.

Gavin transported her, taking her to new levels of pleasure with every conquering, swallowing her cries of stunned ecstasy so that the whole household wouldn't know what was going on. Between bouts of passion, he kissed and caressed Katherine back to a state of such fevered wanting that she murmured in frantic distraction until he satisfied her.

When Christopher cried, Gavin got up, lit a lamp, and changed the infant, then brought him to bed and watched, propped up on one elbow, while Katherine nursed their son. Never, in this life or the other, had she ever treasured the miraculous secrets of her womanhood as she did then.

She put Christopher back into his cradle when he was full and sleepy again, and stood watching him in quiet awe for a long time. Her body was naked, her wild auburn hair tumbling down her back.

"Katherine."

She turned and watched as Gavin tossed back the tangled sheets on her side of the bed. Incredibly, he wanted her again.

She went to her husband without hesitation.

SHE WAS DIFFERENT. The stubborn thought nagged at Gavin as he stood at the railing of the boat as it chugged across the water toward Seattle. Before the great change, which seemed to have come with Christopher's birth, Kathy had avoided his lovemaking. She'd said he was too big, too fierce, too insatiable.

Yet the night before, she'd bucked beneath him like a mare in springtime, flinging back her head so that the muscles in her neck corded when she climaxed. He'd kissed her to stifle the cries that vibrated from the depths of her moist little belly and burst from her throat to batter against his. Once, while taking her in the way that went back to earliest man, he'd muzzled her with his hand. She'd taken one of his fingers into her mouth, and Gavin had closed his eyes and delved deep, and there had been no one to muffle his moan of triumphant surrender.

Gavin sighed. According to Mrs. Hawkins, Katherine regularly visited the chapel in the woods behind the house, and that was another mystery. The Kathy he knew had recognized no deity other than her own self.

The way Marianne told it, Katherine would spend hours on the sunporch with Maria, laboriously recording "stories." That was another thing that baffled Gavin; the woman he'd married wouldn't have drawn up a laundry list, let alone penned reams of prose.

He shoved a hand through his hair. Katherine wanted him to believe she'd changed, he concluded. It was all just an elaborate scheme to regain his trust, to keep her hold on the sumptuous lifestyle she admittedly loved.

How ironic it all was, he reflected. Just when he'd stopped caring, Katherine had become everything he'd convinced himself she was, back in the days before their marriage. Gavin now thought of that era as a time of foolish bliss; he'd been ensnared by his own illusions, and he had no intention whatsoever of repeating the error.

The passenger ferry came into port, and crew members shouted to one another as they tied the vessel to the pilings and put down the plank. It was a bright, noisy, blue-skied day, and instead of going ahead of him, to the hospital and the patients who awaited him there, Gavin's mind strayed back to the island, and the woman. She had watched him go with red-rimmed eyes, her chin at a proud, obstinate angle, and he knew the image would haunt him until he saw her again.

The door of an especially fine carriage popped open as he passed, intent on finding a cab, and Caroline Raynes peeked out, beaming. "Gavin!"

He wasn't wearing a hat—he hated them because they made his scalp sweat—but he touched a nonexistent brim anyway. Caroline, the niece of the very forward-thinking Dr. Elliott Raynes, a colleague of Gavin's, was a beauty with blond hair and flirtatious brown eyes. She'd offered herself to Gavin on more than one occasion, as though her favors were of no more consequence than a platter of sweetmeats and exotic fruits.

He'd always meant to help himself—some other time. Now, just returned from a fresh baptism in the fires of physical pleasure, Gavin was only too aware of his vulnerability to Katherine, and he knew he'd better do something about it.

Fast.

Dr. Gavin Winslow had finally decided to take a mistress—not because he really wanted or needed anything more than the cataclysmic pleasure Katherine gave him in his own bed. No, what he needed was a defense against the wiles of his lovely wife.

"Hello, Caroline," he said, and returned her smile.

"On your way to the hospital?" Caroline's voice was like chiming cowbells, and Gavin wondered why he'd never taken notice of that singularly annoying fact before.

He nodded, and she offered him a ride, just as he'd known she would. Seated across from her in the elegant, tufted-leather interior of the carriage, he studied the slender lines of her figure.

Katherine was plumper, especially since she'd had the baby, he thought, but he liked feeling her softness beneath him, like a scented featherbed.

"Gavin?" Caroline sounded petulant, and Gavin steered his wandering attention back to the matter at hand.

"I don't think I've ever seen you looking lovelier," he said.

"I'M GOING BACK to the city," Katherine announced, two weeks after Gavin had left the island. In that time, she hadn't had so much as a terse note from him, let alone a visit, and her mind was filled with all sorts of dreadful visions.

"Gavin hasn't sent for us," Marianne pointed out, as though that settled the whole issue. It was a rainy afternoon, and the two women were seated on the sunporch, Marianne stitching a sampler, Katherine writing. She'd been recording memories of her other life as fast as she could, and it was a good thing, too, because with every passing day she could recall less of the place beyond the crystal bridge. Before long, she guessed, she would probably forget it entirely.

"Of course he hasn't," Katherine muttered furiously. "He's too busy entertaining his mistress!" The social column in that day's issue of the *Seattle Times* had linked Gavin with Caroline Raynes, and Katherine had been in torment ever since she'd read it.

Marianne didn't even look up from her sewing. "All men have mistresses, Katherine," she said. "It's a fact of life."

"It isn't going to be a fact of *my* life," Katherine countered. Then she marched upstairs, prepared Christopher to travel, packed her own things, and sent the caretaker around for the carriage.

When the ferry left that afternoon, Katherine was aboard it, along with Maria and Christopher. It was time for action; Katherine loved her man, and she meant to fight for him.

She arrived at the mansion overlooking the harbor only to find that preparations were being made for an elaborate yard party. Colored Chinese lanterns hung from wires, and ribbon streamers decorated the rose arbors and the garden benches. Tables had been set up, and extra servants bustled back and forth, carrying chairs and food and more decorations.

At first Katherine was delighted. Then she realized she not only hadn't been invited to this party, she wasn't supposed to know about it. Her temper bubbled up like mercury in a desert thermometer.

"Take Christopher upstairs, please," she said to a wide-eyed Maria, who obeyed without question. After tossing her gloves onto the marble-topped table in the entryway, Katherine started for the kitchen.

Katherine was not surprised to find Caroline Raynes there, consulting with the cook, and yet her emotions were as volatile as dry gunpowder in hell. "What are you doing here?" she demanded.

The cook backed away and then fled through the dining room doorway, rightly sensing the approach of disaster.

"I might ask the same thing of you," Caroline responded coolly. "It was my understanding that Gavin had consigned you to the island, where you couldn't get into any trouble." She smiled with acid sweetness. "You know. Like you did before."

"Get out," Katherine said with quiet menace.

Caroline evidently sensed Katherine's determination, for some of the color drained from her cheeks, leaving her rouge to stand unaided. "But the party—"

"There isn't going to be any party, Miss Raynes," Katherine broke in. "And you may interpret that statement as you see fit."

"Gavin will have something to say about this!" Caroline snapped, but, nonetheless, she snatched up her little beaded handbag and headed for the door.

"He certainly will," Katherine replied. She was thinking of the eighteenth-century dueling pistols that hung on the wall of his study over the fireplace, and wondering where a person went to buy musket balls. Or whatever they fired.

When Katherine got her wits about her again, she noticed the big cake on the counter, and everything fell into place. Of course. It was Gavin's birthday, and as his wife, she should have known that. *She* should have been the one to plan a celebration.

When Gavin entered his study half an hour later, he looked more than a little surprised to find Katherine seated at his desk, solemnly pondering the dueling pistol she'd taken down from the wall.

"Happy birthday," she said pleasantly, still simmering. Then she frowned at the gun in her hand. "Tell me, does this thing still work? If so, I'd like to change your gender right about now."

Gavin didn't comment. He simply approached the desk and lifted one of the pages from her journal that she had laid there, the one describing the Space Needle. "What's this?"

"Proof that I'm not the same person you knew," Katherine answered, hoping her voice wasn't shaking. "Look at the handwriting, Gavin. Did she form her letters like that?"

He lowered the page to look at her, and she realized she'd gotten through by the stunned expression in his gray eyes. "No," he said, and the word came out hoarse and broken. Here was something Gavin couldn't explain away with scientific babble, and Katherine could see that he was troubled. "Katherine . . ."

She laid the pistol on the desktop and stood to face her husband with tremulous dignity. "Did you sleep with Caroline, Gavin? Is she your mistress?"

He was still staring at her, as though she were some kind of freak. He seemed to be stricken speechless, and Katherine marveled that she hadn't thought to show him samples of her handwriting before. Maybe, she reasoned, she hadn't wanted to, subconsciously, until she was ready to make a full commitment to this time, this place, this man.

"Gavin?" she prompted.

"No," he said. "I planned to, but it just never happened."

Katherine laid her hands on his lapels. "Good, because I love you with my whole heart and soul, Gavin Winslow, and I plan to keep you so well satisfied that you won't need another woman. Ever. And you can trust me, because I'm not the Katherine you knew, and I'll never hurt you."

She felt his powerful shoulders move under her hands in an involuntary shudder. His jawline clenched as he struggled visibly to control his emotions, and once again Katherine was filled with tenderness, thinking how he'd suffered.

"Tell me who you are . . . where you came from . . . how such a thing could happen . . ."

She touched an index finger to his lips. "Not now, Dr. Winslow. At the moment, you have a birthday present to unwrap."

A smile lit his eyes, and he took her hand. "That's scandalous, Mrs. Winslow. After all, the servants are around and there's about to be a party."

"The servants are all deaf," Katherine responded teasingly, "and if there's a party, why, that's all the more reason to celebrate."

They climbed the stairway hand in hand, aware only of each other. Gavin lifted her into his arms and carried her over the threshold of the master suite, his lips already tasting hers.

This encounter was unlike their earlier couplings, however, for there was no leisurely pleasuring, no tempting and teasing. The hunger was simply too great, because of their long separation and their newfound accord, and there could be no waiting.

Somehow, fumbling, now laughing under their breaths,

now kissing playfully, they managed to undress each other. Then Gavin laid Katherine gently on the side of the bed, positioned himself between her thighs, and glided into her.

For Katherine, the sensations were far more profound than mere pleasure; this experience was spiritual as well, something that had been preordained at the conception of the universe. She gave a primitive, guttural cry as Gavin lunged, withdrew, and lunged again, and when her body began its dance of release, it seemed that her mind soared free.

She found herself standing on the crystal bridge again, felt a deep and abiding fear because she knew she could be called away from Gavin forever. Behind her was 1895, Gavin, Christopher, Marianne, Maria. Ahead was darkness, and that was when Katherine realized her old body had died.

"The other Katherine," she asked of the shimmering light. "What happened to her?"

She is at peace, the light answered, without words.

Katherine was relieved. "Let me go back to 1895," she pleaded. "Please. That's where I belong, where I've always belonged."

You have made your choice, the light replied.

Katherine found herself in Gavin's bed again, her face wet with tears, her body still trembling with the aftershocks of her release. Gavin was breathing hard, his muscular back moist under her palms, and she rejoiced because she had a lifetime to make love with him, plenty of time to tell him about the crystal bridge and the world on the other side.

"I love you," he said.

Katherine kissed the top of her husband's forehead. It might have been his birthday, but she'd been the one to get the gift.

Store-bought Woman

Chapter One

Onion Creek, Washington Territory
April 1872

*B*ess Campbell felt a big hand come to rest on her shoulder, noting the gentleness of the touch even in her sleep. For one blissful moment, she thought she was still home in Philadelphia; that Papa, or perhaps her brother, Simon, was waking her so that they could go out for an early-morning horseback ride.

"Wake up," an unfamiliar voice commanded.

Bess, who had been curled up on a pile of empty seed sacks in a corner of the Onion Creek General Store, for want of a better place to sleep, opened one dark blue eye to see a bearded wild-man grinning down at her. She gave a small, involuntary squeal of alarm.

"You Miss Elizabeth Ann Campbell?" the giant inquired. He was obviously a frontiersman, roughly clad in a home-spun shirt, woolen trousers, and suspenders.

Bess, who was fully clothed and had slept the night through clutching her valise and handbag to her bosom, sat bolt upright on her improvised bed. "I might be," she answered, smoothing her tangled blond hair. "Who are you?" He *wasn't* John Tate, the man she'd come all this way to marry, that much she knew.

It was still dark outside, and the little store was lit by a single lantern set on top of a pickle barrel. Mr. Sickles, the proprietor, stood nearby scowling, clearly unhappy that he'd been rousted from his bed at such an hour.

The wild-man chuckled, regarding Bess through pale brown eyes that seemed to dance with humor and mischief. "Well, ma'am," he answered, showing unusually straight white teeth when he spoke, "I reckon I'm not the gent you're expecting, but in the circumstances, I'm afraid I'll have to do for a bridegroom."

Bess stiffened, felt a shiver weave itself from one end of her spine to the other. She had not expected her flight to the Golden West to be as fraught with danger and discomfort as it had been, and she was not only exhausted, but disillusioned as well. Now, this disreputable person was crouched beside her bed, apparently confident of his acceptability as a husband.

"I beg your pardon," she managed to sputter, grappling for her handbag and nearly ripping it open when the strings became tangled. "I'm promised to one John Tate," she went on, plundering for the crumpled, much-read and much-regretted marriage contract that had brought her to this place even God had forgotten. She held out the document. "See for yourself."

The man was looking at her hands, his expression curious and thoughtful. "Do you always sleep in gloves?" he asked.

Bess blushed crimson, and her temper surged to life. "Don't trouble yourself wondering, sir. It is certainly none of your business what I wear when I sleep!"

The whiskey-gold eyes laughed at her and he ignored the marriage contract until Bess finally lowered it, with a shaking hand, to her lap. "I reckon it is my concern, ma'am, since I'm going to be your husband."

Bess had at last gathered enough aplomb to stand, albeit tremulously, shake out her rumpled skirts, and tug at the hem of her trim velvet traveling jacket. "I have already told you," she said coldly, "that I am pledged to Mr. John Tate. Are you deaf, sir?"

He stood, offered her a huge, but as far as she could see in the dim lantern light, *clean* hand. "Yes, ma'am, you were to be my brother's wife," he said patiently. "Trouble is, John has gone north, looking for gold, and it falls to me to fulfill his obligations. Which include marrying you."

Bess paid no more attention to his hand than he had paid to the marriage contract. She tugged at her jacket again, even though she knew it was already about as straight as it could get, and held her chin high. More than anything, though, she wanted to crumple herself up into a little ball on those rough feed sacks and weep until the very angels in heaven wept with her in sheer sympathy.

"Well, then, Mr.—Tate, I assume?—allow me to absolve you of at least one of those obligations. I would not think, you see, of joining myself to a stranger in holy matrimony."

For a moment, Mr. Tate looked disappointed, but he recovered quickly and grinned again. The expression gave him the look of a mischievous choir boy, so incongruous with the rest of his person. "'Course you would," he argued. "You were going to take up with John, and he was a stranger to you—I know that for a fact, 'cause he told me so before he went off chasing rainbows. And you can call me Will from here on out, because I don't hold with silly eastern manners."

Bess bristled again, and she felt color warming her cheeks, which were no doubt less than clean, even though she'd splashed her face and neck carefully at the stream the night before. "That was different," she said. "I met Mr. Tate, and found him personally acceptable." She blushed once more, realizing too late that she had been tactless.

Will Tate arched one golden eyebrow, and his grin wobbled slightly, then held. He gave a great, philosophical sigh, finally remembered that he was still wearing his hat, inside and in the presence of a lady, no less, and quickly snatched the battered thing off his head.

He had more hair than a crazy man Bess had seen once as part of a circus sideshow. She'd pitied that poor fellow to the depths of her soul, but Mr. Will Tate didn't need anyone to sorrow for him. He was big, a full head taller than Bess, and his shoulders were so wide he'd have to turn himself sideways just to get through an ordinary doorway. He was plainly strong, of temperament as well as body, and he exuded some kind of primitive heat that seemed to come from the core of his being.

"I know I'm not as fair of appearance as my brother," he said, holding the disreputable hat close to his bosom, which looked to Bess as though it would be harder than tamarack, were she brazen enough to touch him. "But I'm a good bargain, Miss Elizabeth. I don't drink, nor cuss more than the average man, and I firmly believe in bath-taking and church-going. Fact is, I've been known to break the ice on Onion Creek in the winter time, just so I can get myself some washing water to carry up to the cabin and warm by the fire. And I swear by my own mama's grave that I'd never lay a hand on you in anger."

Bess knew an unwelcome warmth, deep inside, and she fought it. Agreeing to marry John Tate had been rash enough, the act of an impetuous and, all right, *desperate* woman, but this brother of his was another matter entirely. To Bess, he looked fierce and primitive and, besides, all of a sudden she was feeling things and getting ideas that were distinctly un-Christian.

She retreated a step and took refuge in righteous indignation. "I must say it was incredibly rude of your brother to summon me all the way out here to this—this place, and leave me stranded!"

Will smiled, and Bess felt another wrench, for it was even more dazzling than the grin she'd seen before. "But he didn't leave you stranded, Miss Elizabeth," he reasoned patiently, as though speaking to a terrified cow up to its udder in sticky mud. "John knew I'd take up the slack. It's always been that way between him and me."

Bess turned away, arms folded, blue eyes blurred with scalding tears. "Stop calling me 'Miss Elizabeth,'" she said fretfully. "No one has ever called me anything but Bess."

"Bess," he said quietly, and even that was somehow sensual, the way he murmured the name, and seemed to taste and then savor it.

Bess tried to brush away the moisture brimming in her lashes with a surreptitious motion of one hand, but Will took a gentle hold on her other elbow and turned her to face him.

"There now," he said, with a gruff tenderness that made Bess feel a little safer in that foreign and hostile place. "No need for weeping and carrying on. You didn't plan on marrying me, and I certainly didn't plan on hitching up to you, but here we are and we might just as well make the best of things. Fact is, I could use a wife for company of a lonely evening, as well as a helping hand around the farm."

Bess was amazed, not only by his blithe audacity, but by the fact that he could speak so lightly of such a holy institution as matrimony. "You'll just have to look elsewhere," she said, even though a bold and erstwhile unknown part of herself wanted to go home with Will Tate. "I'm returning to Philadelphia."

But even as Bess said the words, she knew she couldn't go back and face the shame and the gossip that awaited her there, and Will was evidently perceptive enough to see the realization in her eyes.

"You have the money and the strength for a trip like that?" he asked. "And once you got back there, you'd just have to handle whatever it is you're running away from."

"I'm not running . . ."

Will held up one hand. "Don't go lying to me, Bess. That's

an unseemly trait in a woman, and I'm no more partial to it than I am to stealing and fornicating."

Bess's face went hot again. No gentleman in Philadelphia would have used such a scandalous word, except for the preacher, of course, and he'd have put it in a biblical context.

At last, the storekeeper, whose very existence Bess had forgotten, put in his two cents' worth. "You two better work this out somewheres else. I ain't done sleepin', and I don't care to listen to your damnable yammerin'!"

It was plain Bess could not depend upon this wretched man for help in a time of crisis, and since the town of Onion Creek consisted of two other buildings, a livery stable and a saloon, there was probably no one else to turn to, either.

"You have the advantage, Mr. Tate," she said bravely, bending to gather up her handbag and her small leather valise. "I was counting on your brother to be here, and I am friendless. I have almost no money, and I haven't had anything to eat since yesterday, when I arrived in Spokane by railway. I must depend, I'm afraid, on your kindness and honor."

Another grin lit Will's face, and Bess wondered fleetingly if he might not be very handsome, if only he were shorn of that awful beard and all that hair. When he turned his attention to Mr. Sickles, however, his features hardened, and Bess realized that Will Tate was not so lighthearted as she'd thought.

"Seems like you could have spared a lady a piece of bread and some dried meat, you tightfisted old geezer," he said grimly. "And some would have given up their own bed, rather than see a female traveler lay herself down on a lot of old burlap."

Bess shuddered at the idea of sleeping on the storekeeper's bed; she was grateful that he hadn't offered that particular courtesy. Putting one gloved hand on Will's arm, which felt like living stone beneath the coarse cloth of his sleeve, she said, "Don't stir up trouble, Will. I'm not about to perish of starvation, and I slept rather well, as it happens." No need to add, she thought, that she'd wept with homesickness and regret, and cursed her own hasty nature.

"I ain't in the charity business, Tate," the greasy man said.

Still glowering at the storekeeper, Will pried a coin from his trouser pocket, tossed it across the cramped, dusty little shop. After that, he lifted the lid from a barrel, appropriated a small chunk of yellow cheese, and held it out to Bess. "Here," he said. "This'll hold you till we get to my place, where there's beans and fatback and the like. It isn't far."

Bess took the cheese and gobbled it in a few bites, figuring she'd work out what "fatback" was later on. In the meantime, Will reached for the handle of her valise.

"You got anything else?"

Sickles snorted at that. "Ain't you got eyes, Will Tate?" He jabbed a thumb toward one of the walls. "My lean-to out there is half-filled with trunks and boxes and gewgaws. Looks to me like it'll take half a day just to load it all."

Bess simmered. All the way across the country, railroad men had given her grief about her belongings, and the freight driver who'd brought her here from Spokane had charged her double and told her she was lucky he'd just emptied his wagon at the train station.

"I couldn't just go off and leave everything I own," she protested.

Will gave her a look of resignation, and somehow that stung more than condemnation would have done. "Come along, Bess," he said, gesturing for her to precede him into the chill pre dawn air. "I've got a farm to run, and I sure as hell can't afford to dillydally around here all day."

Feeling chagrined, Bess stepped outside. The air was indeed crisp, and she heard the rustling whisper of the creek passing by on its way to the low country. She gathered her skirts close and allowed Will to hoist her up onto the wagon seat, a task he managed easily.

"You do understand," she said, smoothing her skirts over her thighs, "that this doesn't mean I'm agreeing to your proposal of marriage."

Will had already turned away to assess the amount of luggage stacked inside the storekeeper's lean-to. He whistled an exclamation and muttered something that sounded like a swear word.

"I thought you said you didn't curse," Bess challenged, feeling stronger now, because of the cheese, and slightly braver.

"I said I didn't do it *much*," Will responded, hoisting the heaviest of her trunks and thrusting it unceremoniously into the back of his weathered wagon.

The whole vehicle shook, and the two horses harnessed to it nickered and shifted uneasily.

The storekeeper's uncharitable prediction notwithstanding, Will managed to load everything inside of fifteen minutes. The sun was just creeping over the mountaintops when he climbed up beside her and took the reins in hand.

"I'm quite sure this isn't proper," Bess said, sensing that he was about to join the ranks of her critics and make some snide comment about her tucking half the city of Philadelphia into her trunks and hauling it right along with her. "My going to your house and all, I mean."

Will released the brake lever with a practiced motion of one foot and made a clicking sound with his tongue to prompt the horses into motion. "No, ma'am, I reckon it isn't, but it appears to me that we don't have much choice for the time being. Ole Harlan Kipps will be passing through any day now. He's the circuit preacher, and we'll get him to say the words over us."

Bess drew in a deep breath, and it restored her as much

as the bite of cheese had earlier. She would think about the prospect of marriage later; for now, she had more immediate concerns. "How do I know you won't take shameful advantage of me, now that we're alone?"

Of all the responses Will could have given, laughter was the one Bess would least appreciate. And laughter was what she got.

"Now's a fine time to start worrying about that," he said, when he'd composed himself a little, his hands idle and easy as he held the reins. "You just spent the best part of a night under the roof of the meanest sinner the Lord ever despaired over. You're a whole hell of a lot safer with me than you were with ole Purvis Sickles, I can tell you that."

Bess was nearly undone by this news, but she did her best to hide the fact and stared straight ahead, as if unmoved. "You swear considerably more than you claimed to when we first discussed marriage," she said primly.

Will laughed again, but he offered no statement in his own defense. He simply settled down, humming to himself, and concentrated on driving the team and wagon over the rutted, muddy strip of dirt posing as a road.

The territory surrounding the community of Onion Creek was a peculiar combination of flatland and timbered hills. Bess took a certain grudging solace in its beauty as the rising sun revealed a clearing of flowing green grass sprinkled with wild flowers, a rugged, rocky hillside too sheer to climb, and trees so tall and so broad that they'd probably already been thriving when the pilgrims stepped off the *Mayflower*.

"Why didn't you go north to look for gold, like your brother did?" she asked, just to make conversation, when the silence had gone on too long and she started to feel lonely.

Will swept off his hat, as if in exasperation, then put it back on again in a motion just as brisk. "This is fine country right here," he said. "It has everything a man could ask for—timber, good soil, and lots of elbow room. Why anybody would want to turn their back on these good hills for a place where it's dark for six months of the year and the rivers freeze right down to the silt on the bottom is beyond me."

Bess looked at Will out of the corner of her eye, and her mood was thoughtful. He didn't have his brother's good looks, not that she could tell, anyway, but he was a man to stand fast and fight for what he wanted.

Which meant he was made of sturdier stuff than she was.

"Just what happened back there in the East that made you hightail it out to the far side of beyond, anyhow?" Will asked, showing that dratted intuition of his again.

"That was certainly a blunt question."

"Out here, we don't take the time to embroider our words and deck them out in fancy trim," he answered. "We just say what we mean, for the most part. It saves time."

Bess sighed. Sooner or later she'd have to confess anyway, so she might as well get it over with. "I was supposed to be married to a man named Jackson Reese," she said, sitting up very straight and not looking at Will. "It was the social event of the Christmas season. My wedding dress had real pearls stitched to the skirt—Mama had it made up in New York and we took the train there three times for fittings." Bess paused, for what she was saying was mortally hard to get out. "I guess none of that matters, about the dress and all, I mean. The point is, Jackson and my sister Molly ran away together, the morning of the wedding."

To Bess's abject surprise and mortification, Will pulled the wagon over to the side of the road and stopped the team with a forceful "Whoa!"

Bess trembled on that hard, cold wagon seat, wondering why Will had stopped their progress all of a sudden. Maybe he'd decided to put her out, bag and baggage. Maybe he'd decided he didn't want her, just as Jackson had.

"That man must have been the king of all fools," he said

quietly, putting one strong arm around Bess's waist and squeezing her against him once.

She wasn't frightened or insulted, for she knew the embrace was meant as a gesture of comfort, not familiarity.

Will cupped her chin in one hand and made her look up at him. "You remember this, Bess Campbell. What happened back there was their shame, your sister's and that bastard she took up with, not yours. If you're wise, you'll put it behind you and get on with making a place for yourself right here."

Bess finally nodded, not trusting herself to speak, and, mercifully, Will let go of her chin, took up the reins, and whistled to the team. Soon, they were jolting along the road again, and Bess remembered how tired she was. She yawned, leaned her head lightly against Will's shoulder, and drifted off to sleep.

He awakened her by drawing back on the reins sometime later, and yelling "Whoa!" again.

She started and looked around her, blinking. The sun was higher now, spilling dazzling spring light over the countryside.

Bess squinted and made out a small cabin made of logs, just like the ones she'd seen in picture books. Someone— surely it had been Will—had planted a sizable garden next to the house. On the other side was a clothesline with a faded quilt pegged to it.

Chickens squawked and fluttered in the dooryard, and a big yellow dog came bounding from the direction of the barn, which was much bigger than the house, with the mournful cries of several cows following after him.

Will had climbed down and walked around the back of the wagon to reach up for Bess, but he laughed when the dog hurled itself against him in glee.

"Does that creature bite?" Bess wanted to know. She had

no particular fear of dogs, but common sense told her to be wary of any beast that weighed more than she did.

"Calvin?" Will marveled, favoring her with yet another of those soul-wrenching grins. "No, ma'am, Calvin doesn't bite anybody but outlaws, tax men, and peddlers—do you, boy?"

Bess indulged in a little mild annoyance that Will was paying more attention to the dog than to her, then moved to help herself down from the wagon, since Will was too busy greeting the dog to offer a hand.

She started to descend, her back to Will, but her foot slipped. Suddenly, she felt Will's hands grasp her full hips, then slide slowly up to her waist.

Bess was mortified, not only by the intimacy of the contact, but by her own reaction to it. Why, she felt as though she'd stuffed herself with Chinese rockets, and now they were all going off at once.

One side of his mouth crooked upward in a half-smile, as if he'd read her thoughts, and she would have sworn it was on purpose that he let her slide along the length of his torso until she touched the ground.

He looked down into her eyes for the longest time, his hands lingering on her waist, and she found herself imagining what he'd look like with a trim haircut and a shave. The face in her thoughts made her heart thump with excitement.

Finally, Will stepped away and began unloading her baggage. Bess hurried away, 'round the back of the cabin, and found the privy.

When she was through, she came back to the front of the house again and, seeing no sign of Will, ventured to the open doorway.

He was stacking her things in the middle of the cabin's single room, a grim expression in his eyes. The trunks and cases made a convenient wall, it seemed to Bess.

She would sleep on the neatly made bed, with its polished brass frame and clean spread, and Will could take his rest on the bear rug at the other end of the cabin, in front of the fireplace. Yes, that seemed like an acceptable arrangement, at least until she decided whether to go or stay, and she said so.

Will looked at her incredulously, straightening his powerful back until he seemed to loom like the Grim Reaper.

"I beg your pardon?" he said, in a low but nevertheless dangerous voice. "Are you asking me to give up my bed?"

Bess remained in the doorway, thinking she might have to turn and flee at any time, and spoke with stalwart conviction. "It's no more than you expected that storekeeper to do. In fact, you berated him roundly for the oversight, if memory serves me correctly."

For a moment, Will was silent, ominously still. Then, remarkably, he slapped his sides and smiled. "The colonists had a custom they called bundling," he said. "We'll just practice that until Harlan gets here and makes it legal."

Bess refrained from pointing out that she had not agreed to marriage. She depended upon this man's hospitality and wasn't wont to offend him. "Bundling?" she echoed, in a squeaky and uncertain voice.

"Yes, bundling," Will answered, trying to make a sensible order of the baggage. "Stop dawdling in the doorway like you mean to bolt and run. There's beans and fatback on the stove, and there should be some coffee, too, unless some Indian came through and made himself to home while I was gone."

Bess swallowed, sought and found the stove with a tentative glance, and started toward it. She did not ask about bad-mannered Indians; she was still chewing on that other word he'd used, the one that concerned sleeping arrangements and sounded disturbingly cozy.

"What is bundling?" she insisted, lifting the lid off a pot of warm beans and bacon and nearly swooning under the wave of hunger that swept over her.

She'd found a bowl and ladled in some of the fragrant

soup before Will answered and, when he did, she started because he was right behind her.

"It's simple." He spoke quietly, reasonably, and yet there was an undercurrent of energy in his voice, too. Something elemental and manly, and better left alone. "In colonial days, when a man traveled a long way to call on his sweetheart, through perilous country and sorry weather, it wasn't a kindness to ask him to turn right around and ride home when the visit was through. So the girl's father would put a board down the middle of her bed for a barrier, and both the young lady and her suitor would be bundled up in quilts, tight as those Egyptian mummies you read about. That way, the two of them could lie there and talk the night through if they wanted to, but there was no question of fornication because they couldn't get themselves unwrapped without help."

There it was again, that impolite word. *Fornication*, she repeated silently to herself, in order to fortify herself against future shock.

Bess's hands trembled a little, as much from nerves as hunger, as she set her bowl on the table, which had been hewn from simple pine boards, and sat down on an upturned crate to eat. "It won't work, Mr. Tate," she said moderately, not daring to meet those mischievous eyes of his, or risk one of his knee-melting grins. "And I would think you'd have the sense to see it. Only one of us could be bundled, since there would be no one to wrap up the other."

She felt his amusement, then heard it in his voice.

"Well, then, I guess we'll just have to content ourselves with a board down the middle of the bed, Bess-my-love, because I'm not about to sleep on the floor."

Bess, who had been fairly gobbling up the succulent bean and bacon soup, at last dared to raise her eyes to meet Will's. "Fine. Then *I'll* sleep on the bear rug. Just don't present yourself as more of a gentleman than that dreadful storekeeper in the future, Mr. Tate, because you are no better."

She thought Will reddened a little, though it was hard to tell because of his bushy beard. "No lady will sleep on the floor under my roof," he said forcefully, "and that's final."

Bess decided it was futile to discuss the topic further, and so she shrugged. When nightfall came, she would simply sit up by the fire. Unless he was the worst kind of scoundrel, he would not force her to lie on the same mattress with him.

If he tried, she would just have to take her chances with the wild Indians beyond the cabin walls.

So it was that Bess tucked into the first warm meal she'd had in a day and a half of traveling. Will said he had chores to take care of, pointed out the woodpile, the washtub, and a precious bar of yellow soap, and went off to the fields.

Bess was weary to the core of her soul, and she yearned for a warm bath, but it was a while before she could bring herself to take the chance of stripping naked in a strange man's house. She built up the fire, though, and hauled water from the creek that flowed behind the cabin to heat on the stove. That done, she arranged her suitcases into a wall-like structure around the tub and finally sank, blissful and bare-skinned, into the water.

WILL WAITED AS long as he could, but when the sun was high, and hunger from a morning of plowing stony ground gnawed at his belly, he went inside the cabin.

There was no sign of Bess, who might have been a Christmas angel gone astray, with those eyes the color of cornflowers and that pretty pale hair. For a moment he thought she'd taken to the hills, and the disappointment nearly stopped his heart. Then he heard the softest of sounds—a delicate snore.

He approached the wall she'd made with her bags and peered over it, holding his breath.

There she sat, in the washtub, cross-legged and bare as a statue, sound asleep. The sight moved something deep inside Will's being, something rusted-over and cold, like a key turning in a lock.

Chapter Two

*J*ust looking at her sleeping there in the washtub, her blond hair all a-tumble and her sleek arms folded across her breasts, filled Will Tate with a hunger that was rooted in his very soul. It wasn't just that he wanted to bed Bess, though he definitely did, and the sooner the better—no, this yearning was something more.

He longed to hear her laugh and sing, and call him in for supper. He imagined looking across the table of an evening and seeing her there, smiling at him, the lantern light catching in her soft hair and flickering in her eyes. He savored the thought of her bringing him water in the fields and rubbing liniment into his back when his muscles got sore . . .

She opened her cornflower eyes and blinked, as if stunned to see him there. Then, with a frosty manner, she reached for a towel—a fancy one that Will didn't recognize—and covered herself.

"We are not married yet, Mr. Tate," Bess said, in a tone that could only be called saucy. "In fact, I have serious doubts that we ever will be, and I will be most grateful if you do not lurk about and spy upon me while I am attending to private matters."

Will was both annoyed and amused, and he marveled to himself that he'd gotten by without a woman's company for so long. Even though Bess was being distinctly testy, her very presence in that lonely place was a sweet wonder.

He turned his back, but only after pausing a few seconds to let her know he wasn't going to jump every time she said "grasshopper." Will had no desire to bully his bride, but neither would he let himself be henpecked.

"It's high time you had the noonday meal on the table," he said, glad she couldn't see his smile. "A man's got to eat, you know."

She sighed, and he heard soft rustling sounds as she dressed. The thought of her bare, clean skin, and the smooth, frilly things brushing against it made Will ache with sudden, blinding need—and that was further reason to be glad he'd turned away from her.

"I suppose you think I can't cook," Bess said, and he heard her bustling around amidst her trunks and boxes and satchels, opening this one, shutting that one. "You're probably telling yourself that I've been indulged all my life, and that I've never had to do a lick of work. Well, that's all you know, Mr. Tate—er, William. Our cook was called away last summer, because her sister had the grippe, and I took over Minerva's duties and fulfilled them so well that Papa and Simon swore they didn't know how they'd live without my biscuits."

Will tensed, though it was silly, since this Simon fellow was obviously two thousand miles away and thus in no position to offer significant competition for Bess's affections. "Simon?" he asked, making his way to the wash table, which was next to the cabin door. He stripped off his shirt and started to rinse the field dirt from his face and upper body, mostly to give himself something to do.

What he hadn't counted on was being able to see Bess clearly in the cracked shaving mirror affixed to the wall above the washbasin.

He forgot the mysterious Simon, for the moment.

Sweet Lord in heaven but she was a pretty thing; it fair brought Will's heart right up into his throat just to look at her. She was wearing a shirtwaist and black skirt, clothes too fancy and impractical for the wilderness, and Will thought he'd never in all his life gazed upon a fairer sight.

Bess caught him looking and frowned, and he quickly shifted his eyes to his own reflection in the murky mirror before him. He was amazed to see a wild-haired, bushy-bearded hermit staring back at him. He couldn't remember the last time he'd really taken note of himself, beyond bathing regularly in the creek and keeping his clothes as clean as he could, and the sight came as a profound shock.

Hell, Will thought, snatching a clean shirt from a peg next to the wash table, it was a miracle Miss Bess Campbell hadn't taken one glance at him and lit out for the tall timber.

Will turned, buttoning his shirt as he did so, and indicated her belongings with a nod of his head. "You wouldn't happen to have a good pair of scissors in there somewhere, would you?"

She smiled, brushing her pale gold hair and blithely interrupting Will's heartbeat again by lifting her arms to wind it into a plump bun at her nape. When she did that, her fine breasts jutted beneath her blouse and tempted Will so sorely that he had to turn away from her again.

"If it's a haircut you're wanting," she said to his back, "I'll be happy to oblige. It'll take me a while to find my sewing kit, I imagine." She was humming, clattering pans about on the top of the old, rusted-out cookstove Will's mother and father had brought all the way across the plains from Illinois, back in the early days.

He felt it was safe to look at her once more.

Bess was building up the fire and then peeping inside bins and barrels and sacks.

Miraculously, she soon had cornbread baking in the oven and canned sausage sizzling in a skillet.

Will watched her in wonderment. He'd known plenty of women in his time and had even been intimate with a few of them, though he truly didn't hold with fornication, but there was something different about Bess Campbell, something that just plain fascinated him.

For the first time in his memory, Will blessed his no-account dreamer of a brother for running off to chase yet another moonbeam. If John had stayed, after all, then Bess would have been *his* woman, and he, Will, would likely have spent the rest of his life lusting in his heart. And a few other places, too.

Make yourself useful, he chided himself.

He moved between the trunks, hoisted the tubful of bathwater—it was heavy, even for him—and headed for the dooryard. Once he'd flung the contents into the dirt, scaring the chickens out of three years' growth in the process, he returned to the cabin.

Will felt shy, all of a sudden, like an unexpected guest being cheerfully tolerated. Which was an odd thing, considering that he'd built the place with his own two hands and put down roots as deep as any of the tall Douglas firs growing on the hillsides.

"Where are we going to put all this stuff?" he asked, perhaps a touch too sharply, because he was feeling nervous. He meant the trunks and valises, of course—he'd never known a woman who owned so many things.

"We'll just leave it right where it is for the time being," Bess said pointedly, putting blue-enameled plates and mugs on the table with as much flourish as if she'd lived in that cabin from the day the walls were chinked against the cold mountain winds. "It'll serve admirably as a wall."

Will didn't want any walls between this woman and himself, but of course it was too early to say anything of the sort. "Did you make fresh coffee?" he asked.

Bess gave him a pert look that said he had sorry manners, and he probably did, compared to the men she'd known in Philadelphia.

"Who's Simon?" he inquired brusquely, remembering at last. He was glad of his beard, at least during those difficult moments, because it hid the heat burning in his face. Or so he hoped.

She lifted one side of her full, soft-looking mouth in a coy little smile. She took her sweet time getting the words out. "Simon is my brother."

The relief Will felt when she'd finally answered his question was out of all proportion to good sense—he drew back one of the crates next to the table and sat down heavily, for all of a sudden his knees had turned soft as bread dough. What the Sam Hill was happening to him, anyhow?

His brother had been right, Will decided, during that last, loud argument they'd had, just before John had headed north. He *had* been alone too long.

Bess gave him a look that fairly scorched his hide. "A gentleman never sits," she said tartly, "until any ladies present have been seated."

Will blushed again, under his dense beard, and his embarrassment stung. That made him angry.

He turned over his own crate, so abruptly did he rise, and stormed around the table to attend her royal highness. Once she was perched on the upended wooden box marked "Purity Salt," Will executed a slight bow.

Bess ignored him and began to serve herself rather generously from the plate of hot cornbread, the leftover beans, and the fried sausage. Will figured he could sit down, or he could starve, and it wouldn't concern her much either way.

He ate heartily, because he was ravenous and because he needed something to distract his attention from the beautiful creature sitting across from him. Why hadn't he noticed, back at Sickles's store, when Bess was curled up on those feed sacks, all dirty and rumpled, that she was like one of those fairy-tale princesses his mother used to talk about?

Well, she was *pretty much* like them, anyway. She was a trifle meaner than any he remembered from the stories, and as briefly as he'd known Bess, Will had already worked out that she wasn't the sort to lie around for a hundred years waiting for any man, prince or otherwise, to awaken her with a kiss.

No, sir. Bess Campbell was more the type to go out and find her own prince, knock him off his horse, and hog-tie him.

Will studied her through the thick lashes that had brought him so much teasing and grief when he was still a schoolboy, and smiled to himself.

After the meal was through, Bess made no attempt to start clearing away, and Will reasoned that she was leaving that task for later, when they'd had a sociable cup of coffee together. Lord knew, she'd said nary a word while they were eating, but that probably had something to do with eastern etiquette.

"John left a letter for you," he said, recollecting aloud. The words were out before he had a chance to assess them and, looking at Bess's sour expression, he wished he'd kept his mouth shut.

Since it was too late for that, he got up and went to the pine trunk at the foot of his bed. His clothes and personal possessions were stored in that chest, things like his parents' marriage picture and the small, well-worn Bible his mother had carried across the country in the pocket of her apron.

John's letter had worked its way down among things a bit, since he'd been gone for some weeks now, and it took a while to find it.

Will carried the sealed envelope over to Bess and set it down in front of her, where her plate had been before she'd pushed it aside.

She looked at that letter as if it might sprout legs like a bullfrog's and jump at her. Then, with shaky hands, she picked up the envelope and carefully tore it open . . .

BESS WISHED WILL wasn't standing there, watching her as she opened his brother's letter, but since she had her clothes on, she couldn't very well tell him to get out of his own cabin.

She bit her lip as she unfolded the single thick page inside.

Bess certainly hadn't loved John Tate—for mercy's sake, she hadn't even *known* him, really—but he was the second man in her life to ask for her hand in marriage and then abandon her, and that lent his words a certain bitter importance.

"My Dear Elizabeth," he had written, in a precise, formal, and very unfamiliar hand. "I apologize most sincerely for having to leave you before we stood up in front of a preacher, but I guess I wouldn't be much use to you even if I had stayed. I'd just be thinking about Alaska all the time, and the gold that lies at the bottom of those rivers and streams, and a pretty woman like you deserves better than me.

"Now, my brother Will here is a steady sort, and he's even fairly handsome under all that hair, and I know I can count on him to look after you. You could do worse than taking him for a husband, dear—by marrying me, for instance. Will is a good man, not fond of whiskey or wagering, and he doesn't even swear overmuch.

"The first thing I'm going to do, once I get settled, is send you a bank draft for as much money as I can piece together. That way, you'll have a choice—you can stay with Will and stake a claim to the three-hundred-twenty acres you're entitled to under the law, and have the wherewithal to make it productive, or you can go elsewhere and start new.

"Whatever you decide, lovely Elizabeth, I wish you well, and hope you will harbor some forgiveness in your heart for your errant friend, John Tate."

Bess closed the letter once she'd read it twice in an effort to make sense of it, and tucked it back into its envelope. Then she stood, without looking at Will, and started clearing the table.

"You'd best get back to the fields, William Tate," she said briskly. "You're burning daylight."

Will started to speak, stopped himself, then turned and left the cabin, letting the door gape open behind him. The big yellow dog came slinking over the threshold and threw itself down on the cold hearth to lie panting and watching Bess as she heated water for dishwashing.

While she worked, she thought about John Tate's words, and wondered for the thousandth time if there was something lacking in her, some trait that made a man want to stay with a woman.

Whatever that gift was, Bess thought sadly, her mother certainly had it. Her parents had been happily married for thirty-seven years.

For a moment, Bess missed her mother and father so much that she wasn't sure she could endure being apart from them. She lowered her head over the dishpan and sniffled, struggling to get control of herself before Will returned for some reason and caught her crying.

Laurel and Preston Campbell had been devastated when Bess announced that she was leaving forever, and Simon and his pretty wife, Jillie, had pleaded with her to stay. She'd get over Molly's betrayal someday, they'd said, and even forgive her flighty younger sister, and when that happened she would be free to fall in love with the right man.

Bess made a contemptuous sound, causing the panting dog to lift its head from its paws and study her for a moment.

"I'm never going to love any man again," she told the canine, "and I'm never going to trust another woman, either."

She saw the long shadow fall across the rough-hewn wooden floor before she heard the gruff voice.

"That's too bad," Will commented. "It's hard for anybody to make their way in this world if they don't let themselves believe in other people."

Bess brushed her cheek against one hunched shoulder before starting toward the door with the basin of dishwater. Will had the choice of stepping aside or getting run over, and in the end, he stepped aside.

All the same, he persisted, following her into the yard, standing in her path when she'd emptied the dishwater and turned to go back to the cabin.

She felt an incomprehensible urge to thrust herself into his strong arms, to let him hold and comfort her, and she resisted it with all her might.

To surrender, even if only long enough to cry on Will's broad and inviting shoulder, would be to trust, and she knew what pain that could bring, so she retreated a step and raised her chin a notch.

"I guess this farm must run itself," she said. "You seem to have all sorts of free time, Mr. Tate."

Will folded his arms and even through his beard she saw his jaw tense and then relax again. "I don't need you to tell me how to take care of this place, Bess—I've managed just fine without your advice all this while."

She plucked up her skirts in one hand and attempted to go around him, but he simply barred her way again. The urge to brain Will Tate with the empty dishpan was almost beyond her powers of restraint.

"What do you want?" she snapped.

"We're going to be husband and wife, you and I," Will declared, towering over her like one of the indomitable western mountains that seemed to fill that untamed territory. "We won't start off by hiding our feelings from each other."

Bess drew a deep breath and let it out slowly. She was exhausted from her journey, especially the last part, which had been made in a freight wagon, and every muscle in her body ached from the ordeal. But no part of her was sorer than her heart.

"I'll remind you again," she said, when she had brought her temper under control. "Our marriage is by no means a certainty. Furthermore, I will not be dictated to, one way or the other. My feelings are my own and if I want to hide them, I damn well will!"

Will stared at her in amazement for a moment, and she thought she saw something like admiration in his eyes, too, though she figured she'd probably imagined that part. "You're not like any other woman I've ever had the lame luck to run across," he said, and Bess couldn't tell for sure whether she was being complimented or insulted. His next words removed all doubt. "It's better to live in the desert and eat grasshoppers than get yourself tied up with a contentious female, according to the Good Book. Knowing you, even for this short time, has increased my appreciation for Scripture."

Bess threw the dishpan down and it clunked against a rock and bounced into the sweet, fragrant grass beside the footpath. "If you want to go and live in a desert, Will Tate," she hissed, "then you just feel free!"

Will bent, retrieved the basin, and handed it to Bess. "You're wrong to damn all men for what one polecat did to you," he said, with a quiet reason that made her ashamed of her outburst. "You'd best get rid of all that hate before it eats you up from the inside."

With that, he turned and walked away.

Bess watched Will as he went back to the field, shouldered the reins of the harness, and shouted an order to the horse. Gripping the weathered handles, he guided the plow forward, making a straight, clean furrow in the rich dirt.

Back inside the cabin, Bess sank down on the edge of Will's featherbed, feeling overwhelmed. Their exchange had confused and upset her, and yet it had stirred in her an odd, quiet elation as well.

She stretched out on the soft mattress with a sigh, not even bothering to unbutton her shoes and put them aside. She only meant to close her eyes for a while, and try to decide what to do.

Bess turned onto her side and yawned as she settled in deep. Will Tate, she concluded, was no prize, and at times he had the temperament of a bear with a burr stuck to its tongue, but at least he was straightforward. There could be little doubt of his beliefs, for he aired them readily, and he seemed decent and honorable, too.

She squirmed comfortably, noticing that the old quilt beneath her smelled pleasantly of sunshine and of Will's own distinct scent. Yes, Will was a gentleman, for all his frightening appearance; if he hadn't been, he probably would have flung her down somewhere and had his way with her by now.

Bess shivered. There were plenty of men who would do just such a despicable thing, especially in an isolated place like this, where there probably wasn't another human soul for miles.

FOR THE SECOND time in one day, Will entered his cabin and found Bess Campbell sleeping. He was both amused and exasperated—it seemed to him that the Lord was placing undue temptation in his way. First, he'd seen her naked, and now there she was, fully clothed, but stretched out on his bed, arms spread wide in unconscious abandon.

Will swallowed and let himself imagine, for a moment, what it would be like when he and Bess were married. *If* she agreed to become his wife.

Just thinking about the lush, delicious curves hidden beneath those costly clothes of hers made Will's blood turn hot, and his manhood was as hard as a chunk of seasoned firewood.

"God in heaven," he muttered, but he wasn't sure whether he was praying or taking the Lord's name in vain. He wondered if he shouldn't just go straight out to the creek and throw himself in; maybe that would calm him down a little.

Bess stirred and made a soft, whimpering sound, and Will thought he'd die of wanting her. He stood there, enduring, for a long time. Then, slowly, he turned away, grabbed up a couple of buckets, and headed for the creek.

He couldn't quite bring himself to jump in—that water came from melting snow high in the mountains, and it was colder than a politician's heart. Why, on Saturday, when he'd taken his last bath, he'd been numb for an hour afterward, and it had been about that long before his teeth stopped chattering.

Will filled both buckets and returned to the cabin, making as little noise as possible as he built up the fire and poured the fresh water into the reservoir on the side of the stove to heat. He made three more trips to the creek before he was satisfied that there would be enough for a real, civilized bath.

Bess slept, snoring a little, while Will moved quietly about the cabin. He took clean trousers and a shirt from his trunk, along with a hairbrush he hadn't troubled himself to use in some time.

When the water was hot enough to suit him, Will patiently filled the tin washtub Bess had used that morning and carried it outside and around to the rear of the cabin. The dog and half the chickens gathered in the tall grass to watch with interest while he stripped to the skin, stepped into the tub, and scrubbed from head to foot. He wished he could barber himself, too, but he didn't own a pair of scissors and he wasn't about to go ferreting through Bess's things looking for hers.

The chickens soon wandered off, bored, but Calvin lingered, whimpering low in his throat. Will guessed the animal knew somehow that his owner was smitten with a difficult woman and was sympathetic.

Will didn't own a towel, so after his bath he let the late-afternoon sunlight dry his skin. He had just pulled on his trousers, and was reaching for his shirt, when all of a sudden Bess came around the side of the cabin, headed toward the privy.

She started when she saw him, and laid one hand to her breast, and Will was so embarrassed he thought he'd never be able to face her again. It made no difference whatsoever that he had his britches on, or that she'd seen him earlier in the day without his shirt.

He blushed like a virgin.

Bess's eyes widened, then she burst out laughing. "If you could see your face!" she cried, in delight. Then she proceeded to the privy, humming to herself.

Will said a prayer of thanks that she hadn't caught him in the altogether, emptied the washtub, and carried it to the stream to be rinsed out. When he returned to the cabin, having taken his time in an effort to regain his dignity, he paused in the dooryard, stopped in his bootprints by the sound coming from inside.

Bess was singing—it was some silly little ditty about a girl giving her heart to a seagoing man—but it might have been the joyous caroling of an angel, the way it affected Will. The sound touched his spirit in a place so deep that tears burned his eyes.

He stood outside in the gathering twilight, holding the washtub in one hand and wishing with all his heart that he could step over the threshold of that cabin a suave and dapper man, like his brother. Oh, he'd attracted more than his share of the girls as a boy, Will had, but this was different. He was grown up now, big as a mountain and looking as though he'd never been barbered in his life.

God only knew how long he would have stood there, alternating between misery and foolish elation, if Bess hadn't come to the doorway and given him a curious look.

"Are you rooted to that footpath, William Tate?" she asked, in her crisp way. "Supper's about ready, and after that I'm going to take my scissors to that mane of yours. You do own a straight razor, I presume?"

Will felt more foolish than ever, and that was saying something, considering all he'd been through in the space of a day. It was downright consternating, the upheaval one female could cause in such a short time.

"What's for supper?" he countered, after an awkward clearing of the throat. He occupied himself with the process of hanging the tub on its peg on the outside wall of the cabin while awaiting her response.

"I made an oven-dish of the beans, and boiled up some turnips and carrots," she answered, lingering in the doorway until Will approached. "Fried chicken and mashed potatoes would have been good, but I don't believe I have the courage to catch one of those poor stupid creatures and chop off its head."

Having made this pronouncement, Bess turned and went back into the house, while Will reflected that to his way of thinking, she had the courage to do most *anything*. Hadn't she traveled most of the way across a continent, all by herself?

Supper was delicious—even though the food was necessarily simple, Bess had a knack for making everything taste good.

While he ate, Will came to the startling conclusion that he was happy. Until then, he hadn't known he wasn't, hadn't fully credited how lonely he'd been since leaving town life behind to prove up on a homestead.

After the meal, Bess cleared the table, then got out her scissors and ordered Will to pull one of the crates over by the fire. There was a lantern burning on the hardwood mantel, and she needed to see clearly.

Will sat blissfully, an old flour sack tied around his neck

for a barber's cape, while Bess snipped away. There was a small fire crackling on the hearth of the plain stone fireplace, and every once in a while she threw a handful of hair onto the logs to sizzle and shrink up to nothing.

When Bess was evidently satisfied that she'd shorn him properly, she started right in whacking off his beard. Will, having drifted into a half-sleep, jumped and started to bolt.

Bess laid a hand on his shoulder. "You just sit tight," she commanded. "You're going to look a lot better after this."

Will felt vulnerable in a new way; he was needing her company and her voice and her cooking too much. The realization made him peevish, coming on the heels of so many other realizations the way it did. "Just don't come at me with the straight razor," he grumbled. "I'm real choosy about who shaves me."

"That is evident, Mr. Tate," she said, removing the flour sack and going toward the door with it.

While she was outside, shaking out the improvised cape, Will went to the cracked mirror and peered warily at his reflection. His hair wasn't overly short, for it still touched his collar in back, and there was no arguing the fact that he looked better.

He stropped his razor, got out his shaving brush and soap, and filled a basin with hot water from the reservoir. Sometime during that process, Bess came back inside, found the broom, and began to sweep.

Will shaved, managing to cut himself a couple of times, but as he uncovered more and more of his old-time face, his grin got progressively broader.

When he turned around to face Bess, she dropped the skillet she was drying, and it made a considerable clatter on the splintery floor.

Chapter Three

While Bess had suspected that Will Tate might be a fine-looking man underneath his neglected hair and beard, nothing had prepared her for the way he actually looked.

He had a strong, square jaw, not the weak kind that some men hide beneath a beard, and a deep dimple in his chin. His dancing hazel eyes were full of laughter and mischief, and he was plainly much younger than she'd ever have guessed.

Embarrassed, Bess bent to pick up the skillet she'd dropped when Will had turned away from the mirror and confronted her with his clean-shaven and barbered self. It was curious, she thought, how her heart was pounding and those secret places inside her, places she hadn't really considered before, suddenly felt all achy and warm.

She straightened with dignity, pressing the skillet to her bosom like a shield with one hand and clasping the flour-sack dish towel in the other. Perhaps if she waved that towel, like a flag of surrender . . .

"Am I presentable?" Will asked. The question was guileless rather than artful; he really didn't know that he was breathtakingly handsome.

"Very," Bess allowed, though grudgingly, and the word came hoarse from her throat.

Will seemed gratified, and crossed the room to bank the

fire. "You'll want to start your sitting up long about now," he said, without looking at her. "Fact is, it's been a long day for me, and I'm ready to bed down."

Bess felt her face heat, and she was grateful that Will's attention was otherwise occupied. She glanced wistfully toward the bed, which she knew to be comfortable, and swallowed. Even though she'd fallen asleep that morning in the bathtub, and napped in the afternoon, she was still exhausted. The journey out from Pennsylvania to the Washington Territory had taken a lot more out of her than she'd ever dreamed it would.

She cleared her throat again. "You were talking about something called bundling before—exactly what does that entail?"

Will turned from the fire, casting a giant shadow on the cabin wall. Bess thought she saw the brief white flash of a grin, but she couldn't say for sure because he still wasn't looking at her. "You'd lie on one side of the bed and I'd lie on the other," he said, and he sounded as reasonable as could be.

"And what would be between us?" she pressed.

"We could put some of your baggage down the middle of the mattress, I guess, but there's really no call for that. I'm giving you my word that I won't touch you until we're married, and I've never gone back on a promise in my life. No point in starting now."

Bess believed him and, at the same time, she told herself she was crazy. Her own sister-in-law, Simon's wife, Jillie, had told her in all sincerity that men couldn't resist a woman who was lying down. They just had to jump on her, she'd said, though if a lady was fortunate, she'd enjoy it.

"I'm sure my reputation would be completely destroyed," she mused aloud.

Will turned down the single kerosene lantern on the table and the cabin was cast slowly into a sleepy darkness, broken only by the light of the dying fire. His chuckle was a distinctly masculine sound, and it both troubled and thrilled Bess. "There's nobody around here that would care much, one way or the other, about your 'reputation.' Besides, I reckon you probably lost that long ago, when you offered yourself as a mail-order bride and struck out for the romantic West."

Bess might have been stung by his assessment of her situation earlier, but supper and the peaceful task of trimming Will's hair had mellowed her temperament. She thought of the downtrodden Indians she'd seen after crossing the Mississippi River, the ugly weathered buildings marring the landscape, the multitudes of dead buffalo alongside the railroad tracks, slaughtered for sport, and Mr. Sickles, the filthy proprietor of a vermin-infested store.

"I would not call the West romantic," she said. She was still standing near the table, like Joan of Arc about to be tied to the stake. "But it's big, at least, with plenty of room for all kinds of people."

If Will thought it strange that she was chattering away in the darkness, he didn't give any indication. No, he just went to the bed, sat down on its edge, and kicked off his boots.

Bess looked away when he pushed his suspenders down off his shoulders and proceeded to unbutton his shirt.

"This is the last time I'm going to tell you, Bess," he said. "You're safe here. You can lie down and rest your bones without fearing that I'll take advantage of you."

Bess let out her breath in a long and somewhat forlorn sigh, then went to her mountain of baggage and opened a valise. From it she took her primmest flannel nightgown, her toothbrush, and a small tin of polishing powder.

"Very well," she said, as though granting him some great favor. "Now, if you would just get up and escort me to the privy."

The bedsprings creaked as Will stretched out his large, powerful frame to sleep. "Take the lantern and the dog," he said. "You're not likely to meet anything bigger than a field mouse out there, anyway."

Bess glanced warily at the canine and wondered if she could get through the night without relieving herself. The answer was no, and she was terrified to venture out of the cabin, but she also was too proud to beg Will to walk with her.

"You'll come for me if I scream?" she inquired.

Will yawned expansively. "On winged feet," he answered.

Bess put her nightgown and toothbrush on the table, along with the polishing powder, and took up the lantern instead. She struck a match to the stone face of the fireplace and lit the wick, then bravely headed for the door. The dog raised itself from its resting place, a patch of moonlight under the window, and followed her.

"You're more of a gentleman than your master," she told the animal, making no effort to keep her voice down as she raised the heavy crossbar on the door.

Beyond the walls of the cabin, the world was dark and large, full of looming shadows and curious sounds a city girl had no way of recognizing. Calling upon all her fortitude of spirit, Bess marched around the chinked log walls and headed for the outhouse.

She was on her way back, and congratulating herself on her stalwart nature, when she noticed that the dog had vanished. In the next instant, the chickens started squawking and there was cursing and crashing about inside the cabin as Will jumped up from his bed.

Bess saw a shadow rushing toward her and she stood there in the middle of the outhouse path, too terrified to move. A savage in ragged clothes stood before her, just for a moment, a fluttering, complaining chicken in each hand, and then bolted into the darkness.

The thief had already disappeared into the birch, fir, and pine trees behind the cabin when Will finally appeared, wearing only his trousers and carrying a rifle in one hand.

By some miracle, Bess found her voice. "You're too late," she said acidly. "Of course, if you'd seen fit to escort me, like a gentleman should, you would have encountered the Indian yourself."

Will cursed, scanning the tree line in the dim light of the moon. Then he took Bess's elbow in one hand and propelled her toward the cabin. "It's clear enough that he wanted the chickens, whoever he was, and not a yellow-haired white woman with a sharp tongue."

His words brought to mind every horrible story about captivity among the savages Bess had ever read or heard, and she started trembling so badly that Will had to let her arm go and take the lantern before she dropped it. "You needn't be flippant about this," she said, stumbling along beside him. "Furthermore, I believe I would do for a captive as well as the next woman."

Calvin began to bark in the distance, but Bess imagined it was all show. That mutt wanted them to think he'd chased the intruder off, though in truth he'd probably bolted into the timber at the first sign of trouble and cowered there until it was past.

They had reached the cabin door, God be thanked, and Will stepped back to let Bess go in before him. "The Indians around these parts are having enough trouble feeding themselves—they're not likely to be taking on slaves."

Bess shuddered, dizzy with relief at being safe inside the cabin, with Will there to protect her. "But why?" she asked. "I thought Indians were such legendary hunters."

Will latched the door, put the lantern back in the middle of the table, and hung the rifle above the fireplace before answering. "Last winter was especially hard, so there isn't much game this year. Also, they've had some trouble with a tribe from the north—the strangers come down from Canada every now and then and steal all their horses and women."

Bess went to Will's bed without hesitation, and without

removing her clothes; not even for the sake of personal honor would she have willingly strayed more than a few feet from the safety of his side. "Women?" she echoed, in a flimsy voice.

Will chuckled, as calm as if he handled an Indian raid every night of the week. "*Indian* women," he stressed. "Both tribes think 'Boston' females are too troublesome, even in prosperous times."

She sat on the edge of the mattress, on the side closest to the wall, and had the devil's own time unbuttoning her shoes because her fingers were trembling so much. "Wait until I write Mama and Papa and Jillie and Simon about *this* night," she said, painfully aware that Will had bedded down again, and probably had taken off his trousers before doing so.

What if she rolled over in the night, sheerly by accident, of course, and touched him?

He sighed again, the deep, lusty sigh of a strong man made weary by a hard day's work, and replied, "Just don't make one damn Indian into a full-scale massacre and scare the folks back home white-headed."

With that, he drifted off, leaving Bess to slide gingerly under the covers, fully dressed except for her shoes and the corset she'd removed that morning, on the occasion of her bath. It seemed that the cabin walls grew thinner with each passing moment, while the night sounds got louder.

In her vivid imagination, Bess pictured Indians in loincloths, with glistening coppery skin, gathering around a blazing fire and making plans for war . . .

She awoke to the sound of a skillet clanging against the metal surface of the stove top, amazed and more than a little relieved to find the cabin full of daylight.

The master of the house cracked several eggs into a pan and then turned his head to grin at Bess over one shoulder. She felt a lurch, seeing this new, clean-shaven Will, and her heart set itself to hammering again.

"Mornin'," he said companionably.

The door of the cabin was open to the fresh air and sunlight, and the good-for-nothing dog was back from its cowardly night wanderings, lying in comfort on the hearth.

"Good morning," Bess replied, trying to find the right balance between civility and improper friendliness. She'd never seen a man cook before, and it was hard not to stare—for more reasons than one.

Will poured a cup of coffee and set it on the table, and its scent wafted across the cabin to tease Bess. He tossed her another of his dangerous grins, and she made her way around the end of the bed and past her baggage to sit down at the table.

"I've been thinking," he said cheerfully.

Bess reached for the mug of coffee with shaking hands, feeling as unsteady as an old drunk after a three-day bender. "What about?" she asked, even though she knew beforehand that she'd regret the question.

"We can file for another three-hundred-and-twenty acres, once we're married," he said, expertly removing two slices of homemade bread from the oven, where they'd been toasting. "It would only take us a year or two to clear enough for another field of corn, and we could run a few more cattle, too."

Bess knew nothing about clearing land, raising corn, or "running" cattle, nor did she have much of a desire to learn, but she kept the fact to herself. "Who baked that bread?" she asked idly.

"Neighbor woman," Will said. "Her name's Mae Jessine."

Bess sat up a little straighter, intrigued. It would make things so much easier if there were another woman nearby, someone she could talk to and confide in, someone who could help her decide what to do. "I thought you said there weren't any neighbors."

"Well, the Jessines live ten miles from here, beyond the

next ridge," Will answered cheerfully, setting the fried eggs and toasted bread on the table, along with the familiar blue-enamel plates and tin utensils. "It's an overnight trip, so I don't see them much. Mr. Kipps comes through every other week or so—that's the circuit preacher—and Mae always sends some fresh bread along with him."

Bess sat up a little straighter. "Does that mean he won't be through—the minister, I mean—for another two weeks?"

Will sat down and helped himself to a plateful of food. He looked so different, so good, with his shorter hair and his smooth-shaven face, that Bess had to work hard not to stare. He shrugged. "Kipps'll be here when he gets here. Now that more and more people are coming in, he isn't so predictable."

Bess's stomach rumbled, reminding her that she was famished, and she took an egg and a slice of toast and began to eat. "Your brother said in his letter that he'd send me some money as soon as he got some," she announced. "If I decide to leave, maybe Mr. Kipps would see me as far as Onion Creek, so I could catch the freight wagon—"

Will put his fork down; his face grew hard and his countenance seemed to darken. "If you count on my brother for anything," he said, "you're likely to be disappointed. I'd have thought you would've guessed that by now." He paused and looked away, and a muscle in his jawline bunched and then smoothed out again. When he looked at Bess, his light brown eyes had lost their sparkle. "Should you decide you want to go, all you've got to do is say so, and I'll take you back to town and see you safely on your way."

Bess felt an ache inside, and wished she'd never left Philadelphia, never come to this far place and met up with Will Tate. Trial that he was, he would be a hard man to leave and, once gone, she expected she'd miss him for the rest of her life. She changed the subject. "Do you think that Indian will come back?"

SHE IS GOING to leave, Will thought grimly, as he stumbled along behind the plow that morning, heedless of the pleasant scent of the newly turned soil and the warm brightness of the sun. *Damn it, Bess is going to leave, even though she has nowhere to go.*

He glanced toward the cabin, his brow and chest wet with sweat, and was startled to see Bess coming toward him, making her ladylike way between the furrows with a ladle in one hand and her impractical skirts plucked up in the other.

Will's heart twisted, and he considered ignoring her, but instead he yelled "Whoa" to the horse, held the plow firmly, and watched her approach. It was what he'd dreamed of, a pretty woman bringing him water when he was working hard, but if she left, the memory would injure him over and over again during the long, lonely years to come.

She smiled. "I thought you might be thirsty," she said, holding out the ladle.

Will took it, saw that she'd spilled most of the water on the way, and gratefully swallowed what remained. "Thank you," he said, wondering when he'd started to care for Bess and wishing that he never had.

"You won't have to wait for Mr. Kipps to get fresh bread after this," she said. "I found some yeast in your supply cupboard, and I've got a batch rising right now."

Will wanted to touch her, just lay his fingers lightly to her smooth cheek or her shiny, silken hair, but he didn't dare. It would just be one more thing to remember, and mourn for, after she was gone. "That's fine," he said, and handed her back the ladle.

The happy smile wobbled on her mouth and then fell away.

That was another thing Will didn't want to think about: her mouth. He could imagine only too well what it would be like to kiss her there, to urge her lips apart and explore her with his tongue . . .

"Is something wrong?" she asked.

Will set his hands to the plow again, and was about to whistle to the horse when Bess laid her fingers lightly on his upper arm. He couldn't scare up a smile, so he simply raised one eyebrow as if to say, *What do you want?*

"I thought you said we weren't going to hide our feelings from each other," she challenged, in a voice so gentle that it made Will want to weep.

Of course he didn't do any such thing. He drew himself up and answered, "That was when I thought you'd be staying on."

She blinked, and Will reflected in wounded amazement that he wouldn't have guessed a woman's eyes could be so blue that it hurt to look into them.

"I haven't decided to go," Bess said, after a long and difficult silence. "I was just thinking out loud."

"You'll go," Will said, and this time he got a whistle out and the horse lurched forward. The plow swerved and made the furrow crooked before he got a good hold on it again.

Bess stumbled alongside him, heedless that the dirt was spoiling the hem of her pretty summer dress. "How can you presume to say such a thing when I don't know myself whether I'm going or staying?" she demanded breathlessly.

Will pretended not to look at her, though he was watching her out of the corner of one eye. "This is hard, lonely country, and you're a city woman," he said tersely. "You'd never last out the first winter, most likely."

Her cheeks reddened. "My being a 'city woman,' as you put it, doesn't mean I'm weak," she said, her strides long. "Damn it, Will Tate, *will you stop*?"

He stopped, and hope filled his heart—hope he couldn't stop himself from feeling.

She put her hands on her hips, the ladle jutting out from one, and glared up at him. "Life can be difficult in the cities, too, you know. There are outbreaks of typhoid, not to mention riots stirred up by union men. Folks get run down by trolley cars and carriages, bitten by rats, and shot by robbers!"

Will hardened his jaw briefly. "What is your point?" he asked.

Bess was seething. "My *point*, William, is that you home-steaders don't have a corner on trouble and hardship, and I'll thank you to stop acting as though you're the only person in the world who has to struggle to get by. We all do!"

He turned to begin plowing again, but Bess ducked under his arm and stood right in his path, between the handles of the plow, so close that she made his skin burn.

"If I choose to leave this place," she said, "it will be because I think it's the right thing to do, and not because I'm afraid of hard winters or Indians or anything else!"

Perhaps it was only her nearness that made Will lose his head, or maybe it was her saucy spirit, he didn't know. Between one moment and the next, he'd closed his big hands around her waist, hoisted her onto the toes of her high-button shoes, and bent his head to take her mouth in the most ferocious kiss he'd ever given any woman.

Bess stiffened, then dropped the ladle into the dirt, wrapped her arms around Will's neck, and kissed him back with an innocent passion that made his blood leap in his veins.

He probably would have lifted her into his arms, carried her into the cabin, and made love to her if it hadn't been for the braying of a mule and a familiar voice shouting, "Anybody home?"

With a ragged sigh, Will set a blushing, breathless Bess away from him.

"That'll be Mr. Kipps," he said hoarsely, unable to look at Bess because he was afraid he'd see relief in her face, or fury. She was probably ready to scalp him for being so forward, and she'd likely decide she had to ride out with the preacher when he left, just to safeguard her virtue.

BESS WAS DAZED; every nerve and fiber reverberated with the shattering aftershocks of the kiss. She was glad of the visitor's arrival, for if he hadn't come, she might have given herself to Will right there in the field, like some backstreet harlot.

She bent down to retrieve the ladle, then smoothed her hair and skirts with her free hand, working up a smile for the old man riding the mule. He was fat as a goose in autumn, with a bushy white beard and long white hair, and he wore a bowler hat, a worn but colorful serape, much-mended trousers, and moccasins.

"Looks like I didn't get here any too soon," Mr. Kipps boomed out, and then he threw back his grizzled head and laughed so hard that the plow horse nickered and tried to bolt.

Will calmed it with a word, but his face was a suspicious shade of pink and his whiskey-colored eyes were narrowed as he regarded the circuit preacher. "I'll thank you to explain that remark," he said, in a taut voice.

Bess elbowed him. It wasn't Mr. Kipps's fault that he'd caught them in an improper embrace, and besides, she already liked the dusty clergyman. "You needn't explain anything," she said sweetly. "You are our guest. You'll come in and make yourself at home, that's what you'll do. Will will see to your mule, and I'll set the table for the noonday meal. You'll join us, of course?"

Kipps looked at Will, raised one enormous white eyebrow, and with a visible effort suppressed a smile. "Of course I will," he said.

Bess glanced at Will, saw that his feathers had smoothed out a little, and felt safe in assuming that he wouldn't be rude to Mr. Kipps in her absence. She started for the cabin, calling back over one shoulder, "Don't be too long now."

Will had killed a chicken that morning and brought it to Bess and, with no small amount of trepidation, she'd dipped it into scalding water, plucked it, and cut it up for frying. The succulent pieces were sizzling away in a skillet at that very moment.

Mr. Kipps and Will both ate heartily of the meal—Bess had mashed potatoes, too, and made gravy—but it was the circuit preacher who did most of the talking. He related news of all the neighbors, saying Mrs. Jessine was about to have her baby any day and would sure be happy to have a woman about when she took to her childbed, and then made the blunt statement both Will and Bess had been waiting for.

"It ain't decent for you two to be living here alone, without benefit of holy words being said over you. Am I right in guessing that you haven't taken the trouble to get hitched?"

Will looked guilty, then exasperated. "There wasn't anybody around to marry us," he said. "She was sleeping on a pile of feed sacks when I found her, and old Sickles sure isn't empowered to perform a ceremony."

"All the same," Kipps insisted, pushing back from the table after a long siege, and laying gnarled hands to his large belly, "I can't leave this place in good conscience if I don't either bring the lady along with me or marry you up whilst I'm here."

Bess's heart started racing again, and she felt her cheeks turn pink. Suddenly shy, she averted her eyes, unable to look at Will.

"We have to talk about this," Will said. "Me and Bess, I mean. Alone."

When Mr. Kipps didn't take the hint and go outside so they could talk in privacy, Will reached across the table, clasped Bess's hand, and dragged her out into the dooryard.

"Well?" he whispered, flinging his arms wide. "What are we going to do? That's a man of God in there, and we can't ignore what he says!"

Bess folded her arms. "What are you suggesting?" she asked, even though she knew, and the idea made her weak and rather breathless. If she married Will, he'd kiss her, like he had in the field, and do other things, too. And she knew she'd like it.

"I want you to stay here and marry me," Will growled. "Damn it, you knew that, but you had to make me say it!"

Bess smiled. "That was the most inglorious proposal I've ever heard of, Mr. Tate—but I'll accept, on one condition."

A grin lit Will's face, but he quickly frowned it away. It seemed to Bess that he was holding his breath, at least until he said, "What condition?"

"We can't be intimate until we know each other better."

Will leaned close, so his nose wasn't an inch from hers. His pale gold eyes snapped with irritation and some other emotion that wasn't so easy to identify. "Just what is it that you want to know about me?" he demanded. "I'll be happy to tell you, right here and now."

Bess shook her head, stubbornly, and the fraction of a smile she allowed herself probably looked a little smug. "I'm afraid it's not as easy as that," she said. "I'm not going to give myself to a man I've known for one day, and that's final."

Will nodded angrily toward the field. "Not an hour ago, you kissed me as if you knew me pretty damn well!"

"Don't push me, Will. Either you agree to my terms, or I'll leave with Mr. Kipps."

He pushed past her and went back into the cabin, where the pious Mr. Kipps was waiting. "We'll be married," he said, sounding as if he'd rather be staked out over an anthill and covered with honey. "Just say the words and be done with it."

Bess interceded. "Now, just a minute, Will Tate. This is my wedding day, and I have to remember it for the rest of my life. I want to wear a pretty dress and fix my hair, and you'll go and find me a bouquet of wildflowers if you know what's good for you."

Mr. Kipps's bright blue eyes twinkled. "You heard what the lady said, Will," he remarked. "I'll see to my old mule, Miss Bess here will fancy herself up, and you'll pick flowers for the bride to hold."

When Will looked at Bess, his face softened all of a sudden, and she knew he didn't mind so much about the flowers as a person would have thought, listening to him before. He wanted her for a wife, even if it meant he had to wait for his husbandly rights, and the knowledge of that thrilled her.

She'd never felt this way about marrying Jackson Reese, she reflected, as she searched through her trunks for her loveliest frock, a pale ivory dancing gown with delicate embroidery edging the hem and the daring neckline.

When she was dressed, she brushed her hair, and pinned it loosely at the back of her head, so that it made a golden aura around her face.

A low whistle of exclamation made Bess turn toward the doorway and there, on the threshold, stood Will, with a clump of daisies in his hand and his heart in his eyes.

Chapter Four

*W*ill entered the cabin awkwardly, as though the place were new to him, and laid the bunch of yellow and white daisies on the table. His Adam's apple traveled the length of his throat, and then he let his eyes sweep over Bess's ivory dress and her soft, billowing coiffure, and swallowed again. "St. Peter will surely come up one short," he said hoarsely, "when he counts the angels tonight."

The words struck a chord deep in Bess's heart, in a region that had never been touched before. She'd heard enough compliments from men in her time, but most had been calculated for effect. Will's, she knew, was utterly sincere.

"Is it time?" she asked.

Will had washed, probably in the icy creek that ran less than a hundred feet from the house, and his work shirt was open to his midriff. "Yes, ma'am," he answered shyly, blushing and looking away. "It's time." With that, he knelt in front of the pinewood trunk where he kept his personal belongings and took out a clean white shirt. He set the folded garment on the foot of the bed and then dug deeper into the chest, finally bringing out a wooden matchbox. As Bess watched, he slid the box open and reached in for a small object. He closed his fist around whatever it was, shut his eyes briefly, in remembrance or perhaps prayer, and then put that same hand into his trouser pocket.

The brief ritual completed, Will rose gracefully to his feet again and favored Bess with a grin that struck her like a hard wind. "I'll just tidy myself up a little," he said, "and we'll be married."

The wedding took place outside, with the stream and the mountains and the newly plowed field for a church, and it was brief even though Mr. Kipps made an obvious effort to extend the event.

When he reached the part about the rings, Bess had none to offer, even though she'd come out west intending to be married. Will, however, produced a narrow gold band from his britches' pocket—no doubt this was what he had taken so reverently from the chest—and slid it onto Bess's finger.

Tears shimmered in Bess's eyes and her throat went tight, just for a moment, though she couldn't have explained either phenomenon for the life of her.

Finally, Mr. Kipps pronounced them man and wife, and generously invited Will to kiss the bride.

He did so, and with none of the shyness he'd exhibited inside the cabin, when he'd first caught sight of Bess in her wedding dress. In fact, Will kissed Bess almost exactly the way he had in the field that morning, and she thought she'd die of some combination of excitement and suffocation before he let her go.

"I'll make my camp out here, alongside the creek," Mr. Kipps said, after he'd shaken Will's hand in congratulations and offered a courtly bow to Bess. "Me and my ole mule, we favor sleepin' under God's bright stars."

Bess was about to argue that the visitor was welcome to sleep on the bear rug in front of the hearth, but Will stopped her from speaking with a firm pinch on the bottom.

"I haven't changed my mind, Will Tate," she whispered angrily a few minutes later, when they were inside the cabin with the door closed. "We're not consummating this marriage right away, and therefore there is absolutely no point in making that poor old man sleep on the ground!"

"That poor old man is tougher than boot leather and meaner than Geronimo, and anyhow he never makes his bed under a roof before the first snowfall," Will whispered back, sounding just as irritated. "Besides that, Mrs. Tate, I *will* be alone with my wife on the first night of my marriage, whether or not she allows me to touch her. Anything else would be downright embarrassing!"

Bess thought it was as good a time as any to change the subject. Besides, the bread she'd mixed up that morning was ready for the oven, supper needed to be started, and Will had plenty of chores to finish before nightfall. "If you wouldn't mind stepping outside," she said, turning away with a decisive flourish, "I'll just get out of this fancy gown and put on my morning dress."

She heard the door open and close behind her and was satisfied that she was alone. Humming the bridal march, and feeling happier than she would have admitted to anyone with less authority than an archangel, Bess undid the tiny pearl buttons at the front of her dress and stepped out of it. After that, she discarded the petticoats beneath and wearing only her muslin drawers and camisole reached up with both hands to let down her hair.

When she turned toward the main part of the bed, she gave a little cry and covered her chest ineffectually with both arms, for Will was standing there watching her, and grinning the broadest grin she'd ever seen on a man's face.

In the next instant, however, his features reflected a sort of solemn tenderness.

"Welcome home, Mrs. Tate," he said gruffly. "I've been waiting a very long time for you."

With those words, he turned from her, took off his good

white shirt, and hung it on a peg. The muscles of his back were clearly defined beneath the tan flesh, and Bess felt an overwhelming urge to touch his shoulder blades and kiss the place between them.

"Where did you get the wedding ring?" she asked, because she had to say something and there was nothing else she trusted herself to talk about in that fragile moment. "Was it your mother's?"

Will had donned his work shirt again, and he faced his bride, working the buttons as he spoke. "And her mother's before her," he said.

Again, Bess was touched on some fundamental level of her being. Jackson Reese would have given her a ring with diamonds, costing many times the price of the thin golden band her new husband had slipped onto her finger, but no gift could have been more precious than Will's.

She almost said she loved him, but then the dog began to bark, and Mr. Kipps's mule brayed, and the moment was lost. Will went outside,. muttering a curse, and Bess hurriedly put on the dress she'd worn earlier in the day.

At twilight, Mr. Kipps and Will came in to supper, the dog on their heels, and Bess proudly set out a fine meal of canned peas, cold chicken, reheated gravy, and her own fresh-baked bread.

Truth to tell, it nettled her just a little, the way Will acted that night at the table. He wasn't rude or anything like that, and he ate hungrily of the fare, but he talked mostly to Mr. Kipps about the current president and what ought rightly to be done about him. It was almost as though it had slipped Will's mind that there had been a wedding that day, and he'd taken himself a bride.

After the dishes had been cleared away, though, Mr. Kipps brought a mouth harp out of a pocket of his serape and began to play a spritely tune, and Will took Bess into his arms and high-stepped her all around the room. He didn't stop until she was breathless with laughter and so weak that she had no choice but to sag against him.

It was then that Mr. Kipps cleared his throat, murmured a discreet good night, and left the cabin, taking the dog with him for extra company. Apparently, the quality of the mule's companionship was wearing thin.

Very slowly, Will steadied Bess, and set her slightly away from him, though his hands lingered on her shoulders. He looked deep into her eyes for the longest moment, and light from the fire flickered darkly over his features.

Bess thought he was going to kiss her, and she wanted him to, but in the end he drew back.

"I'll be back sometime after you've gone to sleep," he said coolly. He'd been laughing moments before, but now it seemed that all sense of celebration had abandoned him. "Would you be wanting me to walk you out to the privy, just in case you meet another Indian?"

Bess wanted that, and more. She'd hoped that Will would lie beside her, and hold her in his arms, and help her get used to his nearness, but she was too proud to say any of those things. And although she was still as scared of the dark as she had been the night before, she wouldn't let herself ask him to escort her.

She shook her head. "I'll be fine," she said.

She went out, and as she made her way back, she saw the light of a lantern glowing in the gloom, and heard the clanging sound of metal against stone. What on earth was Will doing out there?

Bess suppressed her curiosity, along with the odd sense of disappointment she felt, and went on into the cabin. There, she blew out the lamp, exchanged her clothes for a nightdress, washed her face and polished her teeth, and wound her way through the piles of baggage to the bed.

She'd expected to drop right off to sleep, since the day had been a long and eventful one, but instead Bess lay there, wide awake, listening to the strange sound coming from the woods and wondering. To make matters worse, the cabin and indeed the bed seemed unbearably lonely.

Finally, Bess got up, slipped on her shoes without going through the arduous process of buttoning them, and pulled a wrapper on over her nightgown. Then, hair trailing in a single plait, she lighted the table lantern and set out to find Will.

Mr. Kipps was camped just where he'd said he would be, on the creek bank, and he'd built a little fire to warm himself. He was leaning against his saddle and playing a mournful song on his mouth harp, and Bess hoped he was too intent on his own musings to see her leaving the cabin.

Bess followed the light in the woods for what seemed to her an inordinately long time. Brambles caught at her wrapper and her hair, and more than once some night sound nearly made her jump out of her skin. By the time she reached the place where Will was working, she was in a somewhat fractious mood.

He was inside a cave of some sort, and by the light of his lantern and the one she carried, Bess saw that her husband was working shirtless in the gloom, swinging a pickax at a wall of solid stone.

"What in the name of mercy are you doing?" Bess demanded. Her patience was taxed to the limit and she could not find it within herself to be gracious, even though that probably would have been the wisest course, as well as the most Christian.

Will set down his ax and wiped his sweaty forehead with one filthy arm. "I might ask the same thing of you," he remarked, without rancor. "Wasn't it you who was afraid to walk out to the privy alone, just last night?"

Bess stomped one foot, and the lantern swayed dangerously in her hand. "Stop your hedging," she snapped. "I want to know what you're doing out here in this—this icy *pit,* on your wedding night!"

He shrugged, leaned down to catch hold of the handle on his own lantern, and then straightened again. "It's no colder than our bed would be," he said, "with you refusing to let me near you."

Tears stung Bess's eyes. She was indeed a living, breathing paradox, wanting Will to lie beside her on this special night and yet denying him the intimacies a husband expects from a wife. And she didn't understand herself any better than Will did.

"I'm afraid," she said, as surprised by the announcement as anyone. She hadn't consciously formed the words before saying them, but now they were out and there was no going back. "I'm afraid and I need someone to hold me."

Will came toward her, his expression unreadable in the darkness, but she didn't fear him. No, it was the things he made Bess feel that terrified her, the awesome needs and yearnings, the soaring joy and the heart-wrenching sorrow. In less than forty-eight hours, Will Tate had touched her most sacred emotions.

He took her lantern and extinguished the light, then did the same with his own. When he had set both lamps aside, he lifted Bess into his arms and started back along the pathway leading out of the woods, with the bright silver moon leading the way.

Even when they were inside again, Will didn't speak. He just set Bess gently on the bed, took off her unbuttoned shoes and tossed them aside, then left her. She couldn't see him for the baggage and the gloom, but she heard the clatter of the lid on the hot-water reservoir attached to the stove, followed shortly by a great deal of splashing.

She was lying back on a feather pillow, keeping carefully to her side of the mattress and wishing she'd just left well enough alone, when Will got into bed. Still without speaking, he gathered her close against his hard, smooth chest and rested his chin on the top of her head.

His right hand made a comforting circle on her back.

"You're a good man," she said softly, wanting to weep because she'd needed his tenderness so much and he was giving it with no apparent expectation of recompense.

Will's chuckle came from deep in his chest, and it was rueful. "There are surely times," he confessed, "when I wish I wasn't."

Bess had not wept when word came that Molly and Jackson had run off together, and that there would be no fancy society wedding, nor had she so much as whimpered during the long, frightening trip out west. Not even when she'd had to bed down in Mr. Sickles's dirty store, on a pile of feed sacks, knowing she was soon to be wed to a virtual stranger, had she cried out of the fear, remorse, and homesickness that nearly crushed her . . .

Now, of all times, when she was safe in Will Tate's strong arms, Bess let out a wail and began to sob.

Another man might have panicked, but Will was calm. He just lay there, wearing nothing but the bottoms of his long underwear, as far as Bess could tell, stroking her hair and holding her close.

Only when the storm had been past for some minutes did Will speak. "If you want to go back home to your folks," he said solemnly, "I'll understand."

Bess sniffled inelegantly. "I believe I'll just tarry right here a while, if it's all the same to you."

She felt his smile, like light warming the cool darkness. "I'd like to get on with some of that getting acquainted you're so set on," he said. "What exactly do you need to know about me, Bess?"

She laughed and socked him lightly with one balled fist. "All right, then, here's something. What *were* you doing in that cave out there in the timber?"

"Looking for gold. Or maybe silver."

Bess couldn't have been more surprised if he'd said he

expected to chip his way right through to China. "You?" She felt a little disappointed in him, though she was careful to hide the fact. "I thought you wanted to farm the land, and leave the mining business to your brother."

Will kissed the top of her head and, even though the gesture was purely innocuous, Bess felt a hot shiver go straight through her system and tingle in the tips of her toes.

"All I ever wanted was land and a good wife and as many babies as the Lord might see fit to send this way," he said, and he sounded sort of melancholy, like he thought he wasn't going to have those things. "John started that mine, before the wanderlust got so bad that he had to set out for the North country, and he even found a little ore—copper, mostly— but it was too slow for him. I figured if I had more to offer, you might decide to stay here and settle in with me."

Guilt and a piercing stab of something tender and fragile brought fresh tears to Bess's eyes. Will was an intelligent, insightful man; he'd guessed one of her reasons for not wanting to consummate the union too soon—if the two of them hadn't made love, the marriage could still be annulled.

Bess wriggled closer and kissed his warm, Will-scented neck. "Be patient with me," she pleaded. "I need some time to think, and get things worked out in my mind."

He made a comical growling sound, meant to convey his exasperation, and then turned onto his side and arranged Bess to fit against him, spoon-fashion. "Don't expect me to wait too long," he said in a rumbling voice, his breath warm on her nape. "Or I might just go crazy."

Bess's eyes were open wide with surprise, for she could feel Will's desire through the back of her nightgown, and she hadn't once imagined that he could be so big. When—and if—she gave her personal consent, it might be difficult to fit him inside her.

"Will?"

"Hmmm?" He sounded sleepy.

"Does it hurt?"

"Does what hurt?"

"When—when a man joins himself to a woman—isn't it rather a—a tight fit?"

Will gave a low chuckle, but his answer was gentle. "I reckon it's a little snug the first time," he said. "But after that, you'll like having me inside you. I promise."

She turned, propping herself on one elbow, to look him in the eye. "How can you promise a thing like that?" she asked, out of plain curiosity.

He gave her a nibbling kiss on the mouth that roused another ache in her personal parts.

"I know how to please a woman," he said.

Bess gave him a push and lay back down, though she didn't try to get beyond the warm, steely circle of his embrace. "I'd like to know how you learned, if you're so dead set against fornication!" she whispered, stung by the image of Will lying naked with some other woman.

He laughed. "I never claimed to be anything but a sinner," he told her.

His words were of no comfort to Bess, nor did they calm the minor riot going on inside her. If Will Tate did any sinning, it had better be with her, or she'd take off a strip of his hide.

"Bess."

She lay stiff in her bridegroom's arms, her back to his damnably strong chest. "Leave me alone," she said. "I want to sleep."

"No, you don't," Will answered with quiet confidence. "You want to know what there is to loving, besides taking me inside you." He turned her onto her back and kissed the hollow of her throat. "There's plenty, Bess."

She trembled, and it seemed to her that her skin was going to peel right off, she was so hot. "You promised, Will," she reminded him.

"And I'll keep my word," he assured her, but even as he said the words he was unbuttoning the front of her nightgown. And she couldn't do a thing to stop him, although she knew she was going to regret it if she let herself be wooed. "Relax, Bess, and let me show you what I learned in the big city."

She drew in a quick breath when he pushed aside the front of her gown, revealing one plump breast. He cupped her in a calloused hand and brushed one thumb over the nipple, and the pleasurable sensation made Bess groan.

Will bent his head over her, and touched his tongue to the sensitive tip, and Bess gasped and arched her back. She had been raised to believe that a man took satisfaction in these tussles in the night, while a woman merely did her duty, and nothing in her upbringing had prepared her for the things she was feeling then.

When Will closed his mouth around her nipple and began to suckle in a gentle but insistent way, she gave a soft, joyous sob and curved her spine into another arch, offering more of herself.

Will was a patient lover, however, and he took his time at that breast, then moved on to the other and attended it with the same languid passion. At the same time, he raised the hem of Bess's nightgown slowly over her knees and thighs until it was bunched around her waist.

She searched her soul for a word of protest, but there was none to be found. She wanted Will to show her more, to lead her to the unknown magic her body instinctively strained toward.

He parted her legs by sliding his hand between them, and she tossed her head from side to side in delirium when he began to caress the moist silk at the junction of her thighs.

"Will," she whispered, pleading for something she didn't understand. "Oh, Will—"

He caught her in a kiss, and at the same time burrowed

through to touch the place where her physical passion seemed to be centered. She moaned into his mouth and flung her arms around his neck and he plunged his finger inside her, while still teasing her with the pad of his thumb.

Bess was wild, rushing, careening toward some cataclysm of joy that she had never imagined before Will, let alone hoped for, and still he kissed her.

When she thought she would splinter apart into pieces, when she truly believed she could not feel more intensely than she did then, Will left her mouth, kissed both her breasts as he passed downward over the length of her body . . .

He withdrew his finger and used that and his thumb to part her, and then he nuzzled her ever so lightly with his lips.

Bess made a strangled sound and groped for him, finding his head, entangling the fingers of both hands in his hair.

Will circled the tiny, quivering piece of flesh once, with just the tip of his tongue, and then he began to suck.

Bess bucked under him, grasping the brass rails of the bedstead with both hands, unable to hold back the wild, pagan cries of surrender that rolled up out of her throat and over her tongue.

Something inside her was being wound tighter and tighter, and the pleasure was nearly unbearable, and yet Will showed no mercy. No matter how Bess twisted, he did not let her go, and an invisible sun took shape inside her, flared with sweet heat, and then exploded in a glorious burst of ecstasy.

Bess rode the tide bravely, though the cautious side of her wanted to hide from the dangers of the unknown, and moaned helplessly while her body buckled and arched.

Even when she was still, and Will had raised himself from her, Bess went right on reacting on the inside, for the tremors subsided slowly, leaving a series of small crescendos in their wake.

She knew Will desired her—she could feel the intimidating evidence of that—and she fully expected him to poise himself over her and make her completely his own.

But he didn't.

Instead, he just held her, and sighed again. Soon, he was asleep, his breathing deep and even.

Bess, on the other hand, lay wide awake for a long time, marveling at what Will had learned in the big city, and wondering what *else* he knew.

BESS AWAKENED WITH a sense of peaceful well-being, and the scents of coffee and frying bacon filled the cabin. She'd no more than stretched, however, when regret and embarrassment caught up with her.

She pulled the quilts up over her head and remembered, in the most abject misery, how she'd moaned and thrashed in Will's bed the night before. How on earth was she going to face him now, and maintain any semblance of dignity?

Will was whistling happily, and Bess blushed underneath the blankets.

She heard his boot heels on the floor and then, when she knew he was beside the bed, the whistling stopped. In the next instant, the sheet and quilt were flung back, and Bess was revealed, lying there with her bodice open and the hem of her nightgown around her waist.

"Good morning, Mrs. Tate," Will said cheerfully, and it struck her then that that infernal grin of his was not just mischievous but downright sinful. Why hadn't she noticed that before? "Time to get up and bid Mr. Kipps a fond farewell."

Awkwardly, and seething all the while, Bess struggled to right her nightdress. She didn't want to face the preacher, fearing that he must have heard her wanton cries of passion, even through the thick walls of the cabin, and wondered fleetingly if Will would believe she was sick.

His eyes danced with amused perception, as if he'd read her mind. He left the covers resting at the foot of the bed, ran his eyes along the length of Bess's body, leaving her every nerve thrumming with the reminder of all he'd taught her in the night, and then went back to his cooking and his blasted whistling.

Bess rose hastily, fearing that Mr. Kipps would come inside at any moment and catch her dressing, and threw on a brown cotton dress with a high, ruffled collar and a trail of tiny jet buttons going from the throat to the hem.

She had barely managed to brush and pin up her hair before the preacher knocked at the door, which Will had obligingly left open, and stepped over the threshold.

Bess tried, but she could not bring herself to meet Mr. Kipps's gaze.

They were almost through with breakfast, Will and Mr. Kipps talking the whole time like a pair of gossipy old women, when the preacher said something that made Bess look at him at last.

"You might go over and look in on Mae Jessine, Mrs. Tate, if you can manage the trip. She's going to have that baby any day now, and it would lift her spirits considerable to have another woman there to see to things."

Bess put down her fork, her eyes wide as she regarded the preacher and then Will. Did these men honestly expect her to officiate at a birth? Did they think she knew what to do, just because she was female?

"I guess we could manage that," Will said, raising his coffee mug to his lips and taking a sip before going on. "I've got most of the plowing and planting done."

Bess looked away, her cheeks warm, remembering the heat and softness of those lips, and the intimate places where she'd felt their touch. In the attempt to avoid meeting Will's eyes, her gaze collided with Mr. Kipps's gentle, knowing ones.

He nodded toward the bags and boxes, valises and trunks. "Mae is about your age, and about your size, too," he said.

"But the Jessines have seen some hard times, and she's been wearing the same dress ever since I've known them."

Bess got the hint, and she was more than willing to share her dresses with the less fortunate Mae, but she needed to clarify another point. "I don't know how to deliver babies," she said.

"It can be a right handy skill, out here in the wilderness," Mr. Kipps said, with implacable good nature.

Bess's heart plummeted to the pit of her stomach, leaving no room for any more of the delicious breakfast Will had made. She hardly heard Mr. Kipps's good-byes, or even her own, and when the preacher had ridden away on his mule, singing a hymn at the top of his lungs, she was still in something of a state. She kept dropping the dishes as she dried them, having to wash them again.

She started when Will stood behind her and laid his hands on her shoulders. He spoke in a quiet voice, but his words were blunt ones.

"Out here, Bess, we survive by helping each other. We'll leave for the Jessines' place as soon as I've finished with the planting."

Bess squared her shoulders and nodded, but she expected she looked a great deal braver than she felt.

Chapter Five

As it turned out, Will and Bess did not have to go to the Jessines', for two days after the wedding, their neighbors came to them, with their scant belongings carefully stowed in an aging covered wagon pulled by two mules and an ox.

When the sojourners arrived, Bess was in the process of unpacking her trunks, freshening the more practical of her garments by spreading them out on the grass to air in the light of the spring sun. Will was on the far side of the field, planting, but of course he left that off when he saw the wagon coming.

The Jessines were obviously even poorer than Mr. Kipps had intimated at the table—their clothes were ragged, and although both of them were probably in their twenties, like Will and Bess, they appeared to be twice that age.

Mr. Jessine was a wiry, sorrowful-looking man, clinging to a few tatters of pride. Mae was pregnant, and painfully thin despite her protruding stomach. Her skin was sallow and her brown hair lank and dull, though it was plainly clean.

She smiled sadly at Bess as Tom lifted her down from the high wagon seat, but seemed too shy to speak. Will nodded to Mrs. Jessine and shook her husband's hand. "Hello, Tom."

Jessine sounded as though he were on the verge of tears

when he replied, "We're givin' up on homesteadin', Will. Fact is, we're headed for Spokane, where I'm hopin' to land myself a job with the railroad."

Bess, who had never known true deprivation in her life, was suddenly embarrassed by her fine clothes, her good skin and shiny hair, and her fancy education. She put the feeling aside, however, and moved toward Mae, wanting to feed the other woman, to embrace her and tell her everything would turn out all right.

"This is my wife, Bess," Will said, when she reached his side. "Bess, Tom and Mae Jessine."

"Won't you come inside?" Bess said to Mae, leaving Tom to Will's care. "I could brew us some tea, and I baked a dried-apple pie just this morning."

Mae looked pathetically eager, and almost too weary to go another step. She stumbled once as she came toward Bess, and Bess automatically put a supporting arm around the other woman's waist.

"Tom and I don't want to be any trouble," Mae said in a small voice, once Bess had seated her on one of the crates that served for chairs. "We just thought we should stop by and let Will know we were leaving, so he wouldn't wonder. Maybe you could tell Mr. Kipps we went to Spokane, when he stops by again?"

"I'll be happy to," Bess said, keeping herself busy at the stove in an effort to bring the pity she was feeling under some control. At the same time, she was coveting a particular rocking chair that sat, unused, in an upstairs hallway of her family's house in Philadelphia. It had soft cushions, that chair, and wide armrests, and it would have been a comfort to Mae in her condition.

Perhaps her mother would ship it as far as Onion Creek, if Bess wrote and asked . . .

"You a store-bought bride?" Mae inquired.

Bess stopped, high color rising in her cheeks, and nodded,

still keeping her back to Mae. Before, she'd been trying to hide the pity she had yet to bring under control, but now she had a less selfish reason for not facing the other woman.

"I suppose you could say that," she answered, after a few moments.

"You couldn't have done better than Will Tate," Mae said, apparently seeing no shame in being a mail-order wife. "Now if you'd gotten his brother, John, that would have been a different story. He's got a smile like an angel, John has, but he's up to no good most of the time."

Bess had at last composed herself enough to turn around and face Mae. "The tea's almost ready," she said, sounding stupidly cheerful even to herself.

Instead of answering, Mae gasped and Bess watched in horror as the other woman's stomach contracted visibly beneath the worn blue calico of her dress.

Bess had always understood that the pangs of childbirth came on slowly, but it wasn't so with Mae. She doubled over, moaning in plain agony, and would have toppled off the crate if Bess hadn't rushed over and grabbed her shoulders.

"Come with me now," she urged, gently but firmly, helping Mae to her feet and guiding her to the bed.

There, Bess helped the woman out of her pitiful clothing, which was soaked through with bloody fluid, and put Mae into one of the pretty cotton nightgowns she'd brought from Philadelphia.

While Mae lay writhing and weeping on the mattress, Bess rushed to the door and called out to Will and Tom in the calmest voice she could manage. They had been tethering the Jessines' mismatched team next to the stream, but at Bess's summons they dropped everything and rushed toward her.

Tom, who had probably been through more suffering than any ten people Bess had ever encountered, turned out to be completely useless in the face of his wife's dire need.

He muttered something insensible, turned, and stumbled blindly out of the cabin.

Will, bless him, remained. He set his jaw and rolled up his sleeves, his eyes fixed on Mae Jessine. "Is there any hot water?" he asked in an even, quiet voice, and Bess couldn't help admiring his deep-rooted strength.

"I'll get some," Bess said, and hurried to obey.

Mae Jessine began to scream and arch her back in a grim parody of the pleasure Bess had felt in that very bed every night since she and Will had been married. They had not yet consummated their union, but Will had persisted in his skillful ministrations, and introduced his wife to a side of herself she had never known before.

Now, of course, things were tragically different. Bess rushed to the stove and began ladling hot water from the reservoir into a clean white basin. She was shaking so badly that half of it splashed onto the floor.

Mae shrieked, and a flood of fresh blood stained her nightdress crimson.

"Something's wrong," Bess whispered to Will. "You'd better go for a doctor."

He gave her a long-suffering glance, tinged with annoyance. "It would be plain to a blind man that something is wrong, Bess. And there isn't a doctor between here and Spokane. We're going to have to get through this on our own, you and me."

Bess was half-wild with panic. A part of her, one she wasn't the least proud of, wanted to run off into the distance, just the way Tom Jessine had done. On another level, Bess believed that she was strong enough to see the matter through, no matter what happened, as long as Will was there beside her.

Bess stayed, but tears of fear were trickling down her cheeks, and every time Mae screamed, the sound stabbed through her like a lance.

The rest of that day was hellish, and poor Mae seemed about to be ripped apart by the pain. Finally, though, just at twilight, a tiny, still figure slipped from her tortured figure into Will's waiting hands. The baby was dead, and the sight of its poor, colorless little form fractured something in Bess, something she feared would never heal.

Until that moment, she had not truly known, beyond a superficial awareness, how ugly and unfair life could be, especially in remote places like that one, where medical help was unavailable.

Mae was unconscious but alive, despite an unbelievable loss of blood, and whimpering softly. The merciless pain, and perhaps the knowledge of her loss, seemed to have followed her even into sleep.

Moving like a woman bewitched, Bess gently washed the child and wrapped it in a silken shawl she'd once worn to parties in that faraway world she'd left behind so impulsively. During those moments, she'd have given anything to be back home in Philadelphia, still blissfully ignorant of all the great griefs that could befall a person.

Will had gone out to speak to Tom, and Bess heard the bereaved father's cry of despair—it was a lonely, wolf like sound that she would never forget. When her husband returned to the cabin, Bess had bathed Mae as best she could and put clean blankets under her, and she was at the washstand, scrubbing her hands and arms with yellow soap. She hardly recognized the grim, frazzled woman staring back at her from the cracked surface of Will's shaving mirror.

He stood with his hands resting on her shoulders for a few moments, Will did, but then, probably guessing that no words had yet been invented to take away her horror or wipe the terrible memories from her mind, he turned away. After gathering the small, silent, motionless bundle up into his arms, he went out again.

Bess knew he was going to bury the baby, and she would

have sworn her heart actually shattered with the knowledge, right then and there.

Why had she thought, even for a moment, that she'd ever be strong enough, brave enough, for this wild, savage country?

It wasn't until Will had collected Bess, made her eat some of last night's supper, and led her to a bed he'd made for them both in the barn, that she gave in completely and dissolved into tears of fury and helplessness and brutal, stone-cold grief.

"That could happen to us," she sobbed into Will's shoulder, when she was finally able to form coherent sentences. "It might be *our* baby you're burying next time!"

"Shhh," Will said, holding her close. "Death can strike anywhere, Bess, you know that."

She shook her head, somewhat wildly. "In Philadelphia, we could have gotten a doctor!"

"Bess, please—you've got to stop tormenting yourself like this. What would or could have happened doesn't matter now; it's all over, and there's nothing for any of us to do but go on as best we can."

Bess was not mollified, but she was exhausted, and soon sank into a deep sleep fraught with dreadful nightmares. She dreamed that Will was shot by Indians, and that she held him in her arms while his blood soaked her bodice and skirts and turned the rich, newly tilled earth beneath them to crimson mud. In another, crueler scenario, they were happy, and the sun was shining, and there were two small daughters working with Bess in the garden, as well as two strapping sons trailing after Will in the fields.

Suddenly, a cloud passed over the sun, and the children closed their eyes, all four of them, and folded to the soil in a slow, graceful dance of death.

Bess awakened, shrieking, and Will had to hold her very tightly and talk very fast to calm her down again.

The next day, Mae opened her eyes, and when Tom gently

told her that the baby had never drawn a breath, and was indeed buried some distance from the cabin, in the shade of a cedar tree, her soft weeping made new bruises on Bess's battered heart.

Mae was soon up and around, though she was far from recovered, physically or emotionally—Tom was anxious to reach Spokane before all the jobs were taken, and no amount of pleading on Will and Bess's part would make him stay.

Will burned the old mattress, and made a new one by stitching two old blankets together and stuffing them with straw from the barn. His mood was grim and quiet, and it was plain to Bess that he'd already guessed the direction her thoughts had taken.

Still, she had to tell him what she meant to do, straight-out and face-to-face. She owed him that much, and considerably more.

She packed just one small bag—her other belongings were stored on a loft in the barn, to be sent for later—and gave that to Tom Jessine to load in the back of his wagon.

Then she went to the mine, where Will had been working the morning through, even though he still had planting to do. Bess knew he wasn't swinging that pickax out of any desire to find copper ore, but because he needed brutally hard, violent work to vent his emotions.

She paused in the yawning mouth of the mine, letting her eyes adjust, for even though Will kept a lamp burning, the place was thick with shadows.

Her heart rose into her throat when she saw Will, shirtless and drenched in sweat, driving his muscles to the point of exhaustion as he swung the ax, striking the hard stone over and over again. The sound rang with despair.

"Will," Bess said softly.

He stopped and lowered the pickax, but he didn't turn to meet her eyes.

"You going now?" he asked.

Bess nodded, her throat thick. "Yes," she said. "I left your mother's ring on the table." She stopped again, willing herself not to break down and cry. "I wouldn't have been a good wife to you, Will. I'm not strong enough, or brave enough, and you deserve someone who can stand up to life just the way you do."

Will ran one arm across his face and braced himself against the wall of the cave with his other hand, his head lowered. His voice was unusually gruff. "Farewell, then," he said.

Bess tried to speak again; there was so much more she wanted to say, but she couldn't get the words out. Nor could she hold back her tears any longer, so she turned and hurried away, the branches of trees and bushes slapping at her face and grasping at her clothes as she passed.

Mae and Tom had already said their good-byes to Will, and Mae was resting in the back of the wagon when Bess joined her there. The other woman had been scarred by her latest tragedy, of course; sometimes she wept disconsolately, or rocked an invisible baby in her arms, or simply stared off into space as if she were yearning to be called home to some better place.

That day, however, Mae seemed to be in a lucid state.

Now that Bess was aboard, Tom went around to the front of the wagon, climbed up into the box, and shouted to the team.

"You're a fool, Bess Tate, leavin' a man like that," Mae said from the pallet Bess had improvised for her earlier, on top of a crate full of tack and harnesses. There was a disturbing singsong quality to her voice, but that didn't lessen the impact of her words. "If you search from here to China, you'll never find anyone better than your own Will."

Bess was in no position to defend herself sensibly, since her emotions were still running riot, but she knew one thing: She couldn't endure the hardships that came hand in hand with homesteading. If she had to bury Will, or a child they'd created together, the sorrow would kill her.

"I know there's nobody better than Will," she said with a note of petulance in her voice. Bess couldn't figure why self-effacing, retiring Mae had chosen now, of all times, to become assertive in her opinions. "There's never been a better man and there never will be."

Mae made an exasperated sound. "What are you going to do after this? Run home to your fancy folks in Philadelphia?"

Bess bristled. "Of course not. I couldn't go back there to live—I've changed too much. I'm going to write and ask Papa for money, and when he sends it, I'll open a rooming house in Spokane, where I hope to find some degree of civilization." She envisioned herself as a spinster of sorts; she could never marry another man, loving Will the way she did, and the future looked long and lonely. All the same, being lonesome would be infinitely preferable to standing next to the grave of someone she loved and aching to jump in after him.

"I still think you're a fool," Mae insisted. She was fading, though, drifting off to sleep. Since Bess had given the other woman a good many of her clothes, Mae was dressed comfortably in a warm, soft nightgown.

Bess had last ridden over that rutted road with Will in his wagon, and the very jostling motion of the Jessines' old Conestoga brought back memories. She tried not to think about all she was leaving behind and to focus on the future, but that proved impossible.

They must have traveled for an hour or thereabouts— the progress was excruciatingly slow—when suddenly Tom shouted and the ancient wagon lumbered to a stop. Mae slept on, but Bess's eyes were open wide as she listened to the nickering of several horses. The hair stood up on the nape of her neck, but she forced herself to grope her way past nail kegs and garden tools to peer out through the opening in the canvas just behind Tom.

Six mounted Indians, clad in buckskins and wearing paint on their faces, blocked the wagon's passage. They were carrying guns, and their expressions were hostile.

"What do they want?" Bess whispered to Tom. She was too fascinated to be really afraid, for the moment at least.

"I'm not sure," Tom answered evenly, keeping his eyes on the Indians. His right hand clasped the barrel of the rifle he'd wisely stowed in the wagon box ahead of time. "They're not talkin' any language I recognize. Best you get back inside, though. Fair-haired women get carried off sometimes."

Bess shrank back into the shadowy confines of the wagon, biting her lower lip and waiting. Every nerve in her body was alive with fear, but not because of the threat of being captured by savages, horrible as it was. No, it was Will Bess was worried about, alone up there at the cabin, unaware of the danger.

By the sounds from outside, Bess knew the Indians were riding around the wagon in a circle, probably assessing it. When one of them thrust aside the canvas flap at the rear of the rig and peered inside, Bess started and slapped one hand over her mouth to stifle a cry.

Faced with the actual possibility of capture, Bess was flooded with insight. If these men carried her off—certainly Tom had a rifle, but he was badly outnumbered—there would be no chance that she would ever see Will again. Furthermore, other men would use her, and even the thought of being touched by anyone besides her husband was intolerable.

Bess closed her eyes and sagged back against a packing crate when the Indian moved away from the tent flap.

There followed more talk, all of it angry, in that strange, guttural language. Then, miraculously, Bess heard the horses retreating, and blood-chilling shrieks trailed back to her on the breeze.

She nearly broke her neck getting to the front of the wagon. "Did they leave?" she demanded of Tom. "Which way were they headed?" Despite her relief, Bess's head was filled with images of those renegades catching Will off guard in the field and killing him.

Tom had taken a kerchief from his hip pocket, and he mopped his sweaty face thoroughly before answering. "Not toward Will's farm," he said, thereby proving himself to be more perceptive than Bess would ever have guessed. "'Course, they could always double back. Why, I knew a fellow up in Kelly's Gorge who was just mindin' his own business when some injuns came on him unexpected. They done things to him that don't bear thinkin' about."

Bess grabbed up her valise and scrambled toward the rear of the wagon.

"I'm going back," she announced, after jumping down and walking around to look up at Tom, there in the wagon box.

"We can't turn around now," Tom protested. "And you sure as hell wouldn't be safe walking the whole way."

Bess's priorities had changed greatly, due to recent reflections, and she would not be swayed from her purpose. "I don't care about being safe," she said. "I love Will Tate and I'm going back to him, and no Indians better dare to get in my way, either."

After offering thanks for the ride and a heartfelt farewell, Bess started back up the long, rutted road that led to Will and all the dreams the two of them shared.

Tom shouted for her to come back, and even called her a cussed female, but Bess just kept walking, and pretty soon Mr. Jessine had no choice but to move on. After all, night would come in a few hours, and it was important to keep moving.

BESS WAS FOOTSORE by the time Will's cabin came into view, but when she saw her husband in the field, she threw down her valise and ran.

Calvin came bouncing out to meet her, barking joyously, and the sound made Will stop and turn to watch Bess stumbling over the neat furrows that lay between them. He didn't move or smile, and for an awful moment Bess thought he'd changed his mind and didn't want her after all.

When she reached him, she was amazed and touched to the core of her being to see that his wonderful, mischievous eyes were shining bright with tears.

Bess stood a little distance from Will, feeling shy and hopeful and terrified all at once. "I love you, Will Tate. I want to stay here, if you'll have me."

He smiled, and opened his sun-bronzed, dusty arms, and Bess flew into them, hurling her arms around his neck.

"Thank God," he whispered raggedly. "Thank God." Then he gripped Bess's shoulders and held her away from him. A tear made a streak in the layer of dirt covering his face. "I love you, Bess, with my whole heart, but there's one thing that has to be understood right up front. I've had enough of this waiting business—I want a real wife."

Bess blushed, but her smile was so wide it wobbled and threatened to fall away. "Well, that's just fine," she said, sounding tremulous and brazen, both at once. "I happen to be wanting a real husband."

At last, the familiar grin broke over Will's face. He left the plow, horse and all, and with a great shout of jubilation lifted Bess into his arms and carried her toward the cabin.

Bess was breathless, knowing what was about to happen, but practicality intruded. "Will, we met up with some Indians along the road. They had horses and they could be headed this way."

Will's long stride didn't slow up at all. "It's plain they didn't hurt you. Are Tom and Mae all right?"

Bess nodded, marveling at all she felt for this big man, covered in sweat and field dirt and grinning like a schoolboy. "The red men only wanted to intimidate us, I think. Or maybe they thought the Jessines had seen enough trouble already—that would have been clear to anybody."

A muscle bunched in Will's jaw. "More likely they didn't see anything worth stealing," he said. "If they were on horseback, they must have been northern Indians."

Bess swallowed, feeling perfectly safe in Will's arms, even though she knew that was, at least in part, an illusion. "Do you think we'll see them again?"

Will shrugged. The wind caught his battered old hat and sent it rolling across the yard, but he didn't make a move to retrieve it.

Instead, he carried Bess over the threshold of his house and set her on her feet with such suddenness that she swayed.

"Before we go any further," he said sternly, "I want to know what changed your mind. What brought you back here, Bess? Was it because of those Indians?"

Bess lowered her eyes for a moment, then met Will's gaze directly. "I didn't come back because I was scared, if that's what you're saying. No sane woman would have walked miles in the sun, with savages abroad, out of *fear*. No, Will, I came home because I realized that, whatever comes, joy or grief, I wanted to share it all with you. And if something bad was going to happen to you, then I wanted to be right here."

His stern face relaxed into another knee-melting grin. "In that case, Mrs. Tate, make yourself at home. I'll wash up a bit, and then you and I will begin our marriage proper-like."

Bess watched, fascinated and filled with love, while her husband took off his shirt, filled a basin, and splashed himself until he was at least partially clean. Then, to her surprise, he took her hand and led her outside, to a shady place on the far side of the cabin, where the grass was soft and fragrant.

"I want to love you here, Bess, this first time—on the land where we'll spend our lives."

She nodded, choked up with emotion and need, and

closed her eyes in blissful surrender as Will slowly unbuttoned the front of her shirtwaist. One by one, and ever so gently, he took away her garments and tossed them aside, until she stood bare and vulnerable before him.

His whiskey-colored eyes moved over her in a worshipful sweep, and then he kicked off his boots, unfastened his belt, and came to her as Adam must have come to Eve, so long before, in that distant garden.

His kiss was gentle but hungry, and his skin felt deliciously gritty against Bess's, and she wanted him more desperately than she ever had, even when she'd lain beside him in his bed, and he'd driven her wild with his kisses and caresses.

This was different, somehow holy, and Bess was transfixed with happiness as Will bent to kiss the bare hollow of her throat. She threw her head back, welcoming him, and her blond hair escaped its pins and tumbled down in a cascade.

Will kissed both her breasts, and made the nipples hard with wanting, and then his mouth came back to hers and together they made fire. Their tongues battled, and Bess felt herself being lowered to the summer-soft ground.

"I can't wait much longer," Will confessed raggedly, when a few passionate minutes had passed, "but I promise I'll be as gentle as I can."

Bess wanted to weep, so deeply did she love this fine man, and so tender was his concern for her. She tossed her head from side to side, her hair spread beneath them like a silken carpet. "No, Will—I don't want you to be gentle. I want to feel the full strength of your passion."

He didn't argue further, but simply positioned himself between Bess's thighs, found her entrance, and plunged inside her in one long, powerful stroke.

Bess felt pain, for Will was big and she had never received a man before, but there was a stirring of pleasure in it, too, a glorious sensation that started as a spark and grew quickly into a blaze.

She closed her hands hard on the sides of Will's strong jaws, drawing his head down and conquering his mouth with a primitive, fevered kiss.

Will groaned, and his magnificent body tensed upon Bess's. Then he began to move, slowly and rhythmically, in and out of her.

Bess broke away from the kiss, unable to restrain her responses any longer, arching her back and clawing at Will's shoulders in the ferocity of her wanting. She began to fling herself at him, and a loving warfare ensued, sweet and violent.

The odyssey ended at the exact same moment for both of them, with Will straining like a stallion claiming his mare, and Bess interlocking her legs with his and shouting his name in beautiful, shameless triumph.

They were both spent, and lay still while the sun waned and the first lavender shadows of twilight strayed across the gently swaying grass. Finally, with her head resting on Will's chest, Bess found the will to speak.

"What if those dratted Indians are watching?"

Will gave a shout of laughter and sat up, though he was careful to keep Bess within the circle of his arms. "Then they're damn rude Indians," he said. He kissed her. "Now, Mrs. Tate, I'd best get my britches back on and go bring that poor old horse of mine in from the field. You'll see about supper?"

Bess beamed at him. "Yes, *Mr.* Tate, I'll see about supper." She watched Will dress and walk away, though, before reaching for her own clothes.

Maybe she and Will had forty years of love ahead of them, she thought, and maybe they had a day, or an hour. Whatever time God had allotted to them, she intended to cherish it, and make the most of every precious moment.

Switch

Chapter One

"You're crazy," Jamie Roberts told her twin sister, Sara Summerville, orchestrating the statement with a pair of chopsticks.

Some of the other patrons of Wong's House of Eggrolls turned to peer at them from booths upholstered in cheap red vinyl. Sara folded her hands on the Formica tabletop, leaned in, and lowered her voice. "Maybe I am," she admitted, "but I'm also desperate."

Jamie was moved, her better judgment notwithstanding, by the note of true despair in Sara's tone. "We don't even look alike anymore!" she argued, in a loud whisper.

Sara tilted her gilded head to one side, a thoughtful expression on her face. "Of course we do, we're identical. You'd have to get a decent haircut, that's all, and maybe go a shade or two lighter. If you wore my clothes and makeup, everyone would think—"

"Now just a minute," Jamie broke in, a little frantic because she could feel herself being railroaded, just like in the old days. "It isn't that simple to take over somebody else's whole identity! Besides, if your life is so dull it's making you crazy, why would *I* want to live it?"

Sara's gold bangles twinkled in the dim light as she folded her arms. She was wearing a spectacular Armani pants suit, tailored to her trim figure.

Fate had been better to Sara than to Jamie, but then Sara had had a personal agenda since the age of twelve, and she'd taken a lot more risks between then and now. And stepped on a lot of toes, though Jamie preferred not to think about that, in the interest of establishing some sort of closeness with her sister.

"Dull?" Sara countered. "Jamie, Jamie, Jamie. I'm the widow of one of the richest men in the world. I live in Europe. I can do anything I want, go anywhere I want, buy anything I want. 'Dull' is the last word I'd use to describe the way I live."

Jamie thumped her nails on the table. Her blue jeans, worn sweatshirt, and sneakers offered a telling contrast to her sister's designer clothes. "Okay, then go do things and buy things and leave me out of it. Good grief, Sara. I manage a chain of tile stores for a living, and I inherited a lot of debts from my ex-husband. My Visa bill is bigger than the gross national product of Bolivia, and I haven't had a date in eight months. Believe me, you don't want this life."

"Who knows?" Sara speculated. "I might even improve on it a little. Come on, Jamie, this is important to me."

"Why?" Jamie was honestly puzzled.

"Because it is. Can't you just trust me for once?"

Jamie made a huffy sound. "The last time we switched, you flunked my Medieval Poetry class and came this close to enlisting in the Israeli army!"

Sara smiled wistfully at the memory and made no attempt to refute the charge. "That was in college," she said, after a few moments of reflective silence. "We're mature women now."

Now it was Jamie who sighed. "Almost thirty," she marveled, with a distracted nod. Willard Scott could announce their upcoming birthday on national television, along with all the other ancients.

Suddenly, Sara reached out, took Jamie's hand, and

squeezed it hard. "Please, James, do this for me. For the way things used to be between us. It's April now; all I'm asking for is a few months. Be me until September first, and let me be you."

Sara's childhood nickname for her tugged at Jamie's heart. They'd once been so close. But problems had arisen between them when Sara dropped out of college in their senior year and set out on a cross-country car trip with Jamie's boyfriend. They'd been estranged ever since—the whole thing seemed silly in retrospect—and they'd had little contact, except for the occasional stiff letter or impersonal card. Still, they were sisters—twins, no less—and Jamie wanted desperately to mend fences, to rebuild the old bond that had once allowed them to touch each other's hearts and minds, regardless of distance.

Besides, she'd already started thinking about her sister's palatial home just off the coast of France, on the sunny island of Tovia. Jamie had never actually visited. Alan, her ex, had kept her perennially broke, and besides she hadn't known how Sara would receive her. But she'd seen pictures of the place. It was like a Greek palace, with statues and a pool and a full staff of servants.

Jamie pushed away her half-eaten dinner. "There's more to this than you're telling me," she insisted. "You live like royalty. I'm definitely of the peasant persuasion. I can't believe you really want to exchange your life for mine."

Sara gnawed on her glossy lower lip for a moment. "I don't—not forever. I guess what it all comes down to is that I'm looking for a change and a challenge. Things are too easy for me. I want to see if I can survive in the real world."

"I need to think about this."

Sara's pensive expression turned to one of exasperation. "Oh, for heaven's sake, Jamie, you can be such a curmudgeon! You've been divorced for five years, and I'll bet you're still sleeping strictly on your own side of the bed.

Furthermore, I'll lay odds that you're watching Alan's favorite television programs, buying his brand of toothpaste, and sleeping in his T-shirts. Maybe you've even renewed his magazine subscriptions."

Jamie blushed. She *was* still sleeping on her own side of the bed, as if she expected Alan to reappear some night and crawl in beside her in his jockey shorts. "I have not renewed his subscriptions!" she blustered, deliberately failing to mention the TV shows, the toothpaste, and the T-shirts. "You make it sound as if I'm still in love with the man!"

"Are you?"

"Of course not!" She drew a deep breath. "Of course not," she repeated, more moderately. "Alan was, is, and always will be a jerk and you know it. I should never have married him in the first place."

Sara reached for her cocktail, forgotten until then, and twirled the tiny paper umbrella between two fingers. "That's exactly my point. You're still stuck in that awful part of your life, James. It's time to move on, shake things up, effect some healthy changes." She raised weary brown eyes—exact duplicates of Jamie's own except for the skillfully applied shadow, liner, and mascara—to her sister's face. "Now, if you don't mind, I'd like to go back to your place and get some sleep. I've got a major case of jet lag."

In spite of the thing with the Israeli army and a few similar experiences, Jamie felt real sympathy for her sister. It was going to work, she thought. They *would* be close again.

"Come on," she said, reaching for her purse. "I'll take the sofa bed, and you can crash in my room."

When Sara smiled, Jamie wanted more than ever to please her. "See? You're already warming to the idea of letting me be you."

"Don't push it," Jamie warned, but she smiled back at Sara as she said the words.

Fifteen minutes later, they were in Jamie's apartment, a two-bedroom with a view of downtown Seattle. While Sara languished in the shower, Jamie plucked Alan's old T-shirts out of the middle drawer of the bureau, hurried to the cleaning closet, and shoved them in the ragbag.

She was putting clean sheets on the bed when Sara came out of the bathroom, bundled in a short terry-cloth robe. Jamie was struck, in that moment, by the strange frailty she saw in her sister. There was a haunted look in Sara's eyes, and shadows tinged the delicate skin beneath them.

"You don't need to give up your room," Sara said, trying to smile, a pink towel covering her hair like a turban. "I'm not so fancy I can't sleep on a fold-out bed."

Jamie wanted to put her arms around Sara, but something in the set of her twin's shoulders warned against it. They'd parted on bitter terms, and it wouldn't be wise to push.

"Sara, are you in some kind of trouble? Is that what this is all about? If something's wrong, tell me. You know I'll do whatever I can to help."

Sara stood still in the bathroom doorway for a few moments, just looking at Jamie and saying nothing. Then she gave a nervous little laugh and tossed her head. "You're such a worrywart. Honestly, James, a few months of shameless self-indulgence is just what you need."

Jamie sighed and shoved splayed fingers through her tousled hair. The prospect was gaining appeal with every passing moment. She finished making the bed and sat down on the foot of the mattress. "Okay," she said, "suppose—just suppose—I agree to this wild scheme. I have to come back to my own life at some point, you know. What if I get here and find out you've messed it up?"

Sara looked around the small bedroom. All of a sudden, the place seemed as anonymous as a hotel room to Jamie, in spite of the familiar clutter.

"Anything would be an improvement, if you ask me," Sara

commented, setting her hands on her hips. "James, you're in a monumental rut, in case you haven't noticed."

Jamie felt heat flare in her face again. Nobody had ever been able to get under her skin the way Sara did, not even Alan. "Maybe I am," she said irritably, "but it's *my* rut. At least I know my way around it!"

Sara gave a long-suffering sigh, but her eyes were snapping with challenge. "Wow," she replied, with a wry twist of her lips. "What an accomplishment."

Once again, Jamie felt herself losing ground, and in her panic, she cried, "Do you think just anybody can manage a chain of tile stores?"

With a small smile, Sara held out one hand and admired her manicure. Her nails were perfect ovals, the same peachy-pink color as the inside of a shell Jamie had bought at a garage sale when she was eleven. She'd told everyone at school the next fall that her father had taken her and Sara to the ocean over summer vacation. In truth, he hadn't so much as written during that time.

"I wasn't planning to manage anything," Sara answered, with calm amusement. "I don't need to work at all, remember? I have plenty of money."

Jamie caught her hands together behind her back, hoping Sara hadn't noticed her own unfiled and unpolished nails. "You're forgetting one thing," she pointed out, as reasonably as she could. "I don't *have* plenty of money. And even if I agreed to change places with you"—she held up one hand against the bright light that was dawning on Sara's face—"which I haven't, I'd need a job and a home to come back to in September."

Sara folded her arms and tilted her towel-turbaned head to one side, eyes narrowed in speculation. Inspiration struck her visibly, after a few moments of silence, and Jamie waited, with equal measures of dread and excitement, for the newborn idea to be unveiled.

"I should have thought of it before," she said, drumming graceful, tapered fingers lightly against her upper arm. "I'll *rent* your life. It's a perfect solution."

Jamie figured she ought to be insulted by the suggestion, but in truth she was intrigued. Sara was an original thinker; you had to give her that. "What kind of money are we talking about here?" she ventured.

Sara considered briefly, then smiled a broad and generous smile. "A hundred thousand," she said. "After taxes."

Having been seated on the end of the bed all this time, Jamie bolted to her feet on a surge of shock and just as quickly sat down again. For several seconds, she was too stunned to speak, and when she did manage to say something, the words came out as one long croak. "A hundred thousand—"

"Dollars," Sara said triumphantly. "I'll have my accounting firm transfer the funds to your bank on September first."

Jamie felt faint. A hundred thousand dollars! She could pay off all the bills she'd been stuck with, travel, and finally start her own business with that kind of money. A small antiques shop, for instance, specializing in old toys . . .

"There's a catch here somewhere," she insisted, as her basically pragmatic nature reasserted itself.

Sara didn't challenge the accusation—didn't speak at all, in fact. She just stood there and smiled, knowing she'd won.

Jamie hurled herself backward on the bed, gazed up at the ceiling, and moaned with frustration. "All my life, I've comforted myself with the idea that, in spite of all my mistakes and failures, I was a person who couldn't be bought. But you've just met my price."

Sara was standing at the vanity table, looking into the mirror as she unwound the towel from her hair. "Everyone has a price," she said, in a distracted tone. "Don't be too hard on yourself, James. At least yours is higher than most people's."

Jamie wasn't comforted, and she still couldn't shake the feeling that she was standing at the edge of some kind of abyss. She *was* bored and lonely and tired of her life, however, and she couldn't remember the last time she'd taken a risk of any real significance. She was overdue for an adventure.

And she wanted Sara to be happy.

THE NEXT MORNING, Jamie awakened in her sofa bed and found Sara standing on her head in the doorway to the kitchenette.

"Yoga," Sara explained. "I do it every day."

"Great," Jamie replied, scrambling out of bed and stumbling into the bathroom. She was not a morning person, but Sara, she remembered with grim resignation, had always been full of energy from the moment her eyes flew open.

After showering and putting on jeans and a T-shirt—it was Tuesday, her day off from work—Jamie returned to the tiny living room to find that Sara had finished her yoga and exchanged her leotard and tights for a simple, expensive linen dress. The garment, probably just taken out of Sara's Gucci travel bag, was wrinkle-free.

"This is never going to work," Jamie said, jerking open the refrigerator door and burrowing among jars and bottles and bowls until she found a carton of cottage cheese with an expiration date she could live with. She found a spoon and swallowed two mouthfuls before going on. "We're too different."

Sara sniffed Jamie's breakfast, made a face, took a bagel from the bread box on the counter, and stuffed it into the toaster. "Of course it will work," she replied. "You want the money, don't you?"

Jamie couldn't deny that she did. She'd tossed and turned half the night, just thinking of the things she could do with such a staggering sum. "Yes," she said.

Sara took the cheese carton from her twin's hand and, nose wrinkled, dropped it into the trash. "Let's start with your eating habits," she said. "I would never touch this stuff. It isn't even the low-fat variety, for pete's sake."

After that, Jamie's refresher course in Being Sara began in earnest.

It started with the bagel, spread with a thin layer of jam but completely innocent of butter or cream cheese. Then there was a two-hour lesson in applying makeup in both day and evening versions. Following that was a session in a fancy salon, with an exclusive hairdresser who demanded references from his clients and accepted Jamie only because of Sara's platinum American Express card.

As she and Sara left the salon, Jamie caught a glimpse of their reflections in a shop window. It was like seeing a double image in a mirror.

Sara spent the afternoon drilling Jamie, teaching her the names of her servants, neighbors, and shopkeepers. Like Jamie, Sara didn't seem to have a lot of close friends, but that was probably a good thing under the circumstances. It would be very difficult to fool someone who knew Sara intimately.

"You'll have to be nice to the cat, too," Sara said that evening, as they sat at Jamie's kitchen table with the contents of Sara's purse between them. "His name is Lazarus, and he belonged to my husband." She shuddered a little, her eyes on the credit cards, documents, and cosmetics that had tumbled from her bag moments before. "Reprehensible creature."

Jamie allowed herself a half smile. "Who, the husband or the cat?"

Sara didn't meet Jamie's eyes. "The cat, of course," she said breezily. "Henri absolutely adored him, though. He even went so far as to mention the damnable thing in his will. As long as he lives, Lazarus must have all the cream and fish his evil little heart desires and be given the run of the villa, if you can believe it."

Jamie loved cats but because both Aunt Erlene and Alan had hated them, she'd never gotten one. It embarrassed her to realize she'd been living by other people's scripts all this time—wearing Alan's T-shirts for nightgowns, keeping to her own side of the bed, denying herself a pet. Most of all, though, she regretted letting the feud with Sara go on for so long.

"Lazarus won't be a problem," she said.

At last Sara looked directly at her sister again, with an odd, tense expression flickering far back in her eyes. "It means so much to me, Jamie, this time away. I really need a new perspective."

Once again, Jamie felt vaguely uneasy. She was in for some surprises in Tovia, she sensed that, but it was too late to change her mind.

"So do I," she said. Then, silently and with some chagrin, she added, *And I need the money, too.*

A week later, after spending all her free time on intensive training in the mores and manners of the impossibly rich, Jamie boarded a plane, wearing Sara's clothes and carrying her bags and passport, sank, knees trembling, into a seat in the first-class cabin, and asked herself what the hell she thought she was doing.

Once the craft was airborne, a flight attendant made the rounds, passing out champagne in elegant crystal flutes. Jamie took delicate but rapid sips, and after her second glass some of her nervousness faded away. By the time she'd finished a third, she believed she could bring peace to the Middle East without even breaking into a sweat.

The flight was fourteen hours long, and they touched down twice, once in New York and again in Madrid, with a change of planes, before making a final landing in Tovia. By then, Jamie's feet and ankles were swollen and she was so tired she could hardly hold up her head. She fumbled through customs, feeling a fresh rush of guilt when the officer compared her face with the one in Sara's passport, wielded his trusty stamp, and allowed her to pass.

Not surprisingly, since there were only about a quarter of a million people in all of Tovia, the airport was small, with a single baggage carousel. Jamie stood beside it, among the other passengers, and watched Sara's fancy leather bags make several revolutions before remembering that the luggage was supposed to be hers.

Awkwardly, she made her way through the dwindling crush of people and wrestled the suitcases off the conveyor belt. Just as she turned to scan the terminal for a porter, she saw a man striding purposefully toward her. He was handsome, with dark hair and eyes of a deep, anxiety-producing blue, and he wore an Italian suit, pale gray and exquisitely tailored. His aristocratic face was grim, but when Jamie met his gaze, he flashed her a quick white smile.

The experience was, for Jamie, like being struck in the stomach with a battering ram, but at the same time strangely pleasant. As he reached her and grazed her cheek with a brotherly kiss, she struggled to remember him from Sara's intense briefings.

He frowned, as if he'd already guessed that something was amiss, and took her bags. "I'm sorry Julian couldn't meet you himself," he said, and there was a stiffness in his tone and manner as he started toward the nearest exit, evidently trusting Jamie to follow him. "He must have been detained in Paris."

Julian? Sara definitely hadn't mentioned that name. "I see," she said. She was doing a pretty good job of imitating her sister, she thought, considering how tired she was. Jamie was teetering on the edge of a headache. She groped in the dark corners of her mind for the identity of the well-dressed Greek-god type schlepping her suitcases until it came to her.

This was Rowan Parrish, a former neighbor of Sara's and evidently a fairly close friend.

Once she'd determined that much, the rest tumbled after it. Parrish was thirty-five, divorced, and, like everyone in Sara's social circle, stinking rich. Although he was a member of the local aristocracy, he'd earned his fortune trading in Chinese artifacts, and he was an authority on antiques.

Outside, a shimmering black Rolls-Royce awaited them. The chauffeur—Sara had called him Curran, though whether that was his first or last name Jamie didn't know—got out of the car, opened the trunk, and stowed the bags as Parrish moved to take Jamie's arm.

She drew back and reached for the handle of one of the rear doors, only to remember too late that Sara would have waited for her escort to help her into the car. She checked herself, but out of the corner of her eye she saw Parrish watching her, the faintest line of puzzlement creasing his tanned forehead.

There was a brief silence and then, mercifully, Mr. Parrish opened the door himself. Jamie slipped into the cool, sedately posh interior with a grateful sigh. Curran took the wheel, and the other man, pensive again, joined her in the rear of the car, settling into the seat across from hers. The windows were tinted, soft classical music surrounded them, and the Rolls engine made a soothing sound, like the companionable purr of a great sleek cat.

Jamie sighed again and closed her eyes. She dozed, then awakened with a start, having no idea whether she'd slept for a minute or an hour.

She felt the car slow and saw a hint of high iron gates through the dark window. It was on the tip of her tongue to ask if they were almost there, but she stopped herself in time. Sara, of course, wouldn't have to ask such an elementary question, since the villa was her home.

"You must be exhausted," Mr. Parrish said gently.

Jamie felt something warm and soft brush against her heart. She and Sara had lost their mother when they were ten, and their father, an unlucky gambler with good intentions and a drinking problem, had shipped them off to his sister to raise. Aunt Erlene, who managed a tavern in a small town south of Seattle and lived in a two-bedroom trailer, had met their bus and driven them home in her smoking, chortling old boat of a car. They'd had enough to eat, and Erlene had seen that they studied, so they could get college scholarships and make something of themselves, but tenderness had been in short supply. Even after all that time, Jamie realized, she was still a sucker for a kind word and a little concern.

"I'll be all right," she said finally. They were following a driveway paved with white gravel, and in the distance Jamie could make out the crystalline sparkle of the Mediterranean. "How's Lazarus?" she asked, mostly to make conversation.

The blue eyes narrowed again, briefly, and then he dazzled Jamie with another unexpected smile. This one, however, had a slight edge. "Hale and hearty, I'm afraid, with all his nine lives still before him. He's well named, our Lazarus."

Jamie lowered her gaze to her hands, now knotted in her lap. Sara wasn't fond of the cat; she merely tolerated him. She had to remember that, if she was going to succeed with the masquerade and collect the hundred thousand dollars that would change her life.

"Reprehensible creature," she said, in the same tone she'd heard Sara use, and added an elegant little shiver for good measure.

By that time Mr. Parrish was gazing out the window, and he didn't offer a reply. Jamie yearned for the quiet of Sara's suite in the villa. All she needed to get back on track, she was sure, was a hot bath, something to eat, and about twelve hours of uninterrupted sleep.

The car came to a smooth stop and Curran appeared, momentarily, to open one of the rear doors and extend a gloved hand to Jamie. She let him help her out and stood still on the brick drive, gazing at the villa in pure amazement.

It was a great, sprawling place, made of some glittering white stone, with what seemed like hundreds of arched windows glistening in the sun. Although it was still winter in America, lush vegetation bloomed riotously on all sides here and the lawn was green and vast and rolling, like the golf course of some exclusive country club.

While Jamie hesitated, spellbound, a large black cat sashayed along a stone railing on the veranda, tail high and slightly bristled. He leaped onto one of the marble steps, landing with an audible thump because of his bulk, and approached the new arrival with an air of condescending charity.

"Reow?" he said inquiringly, haughty as a sultan encountering a slave in an unexpected place.

Jet-lagged and quite charmed, Jamie forgot herself and bent to pat his enormous silken head. "Hello, your highness," she said, with what surely seemed to him a fatuous and idiotic smile.

Lazarus purred, sounding like the engine of the Rolls, and wound himself around and between her ankles.

"Interesting," observed Mr. Parrish, from behind.

Jamie extricated herself from the cat, at the same time pretending she hadn't heard the remark, and proceeded into the villa at a brisk pace. She forced her tired mind to focus on the memory of Sara's sketches of the interior of the house.

The foyer was just as Sara had described it, a huge room with a black-and-white tile floor of the finest marble, a six-foot chandelier hanging from the domed and frescoed ceiling, a staircase fit for a grand hotel, Louis XIV chairs and tables, and paintings any museum would have been happy to claim.

Jamie tried to look bored. Turning to face her escort, she

held out one hand in a gesture of farewell. "Thank you for everything, Mr. Parrish. You've been very kind."

"Mr. Parrish?" he echoed, with anger catching fire in his eyes.

Jamie blushed, flustered. Another foolish slip. The man was Sara's friend, after all. She wouldn't have addressed him so formally. Putting one hand to her forehead, she managed a faltering smile, and the confusion in her manner was quite real. "I—I guess I'm more exhausted than I thought, Rowan," she said.

Just inside the front door, which still stood open, Lazarus sat grooming himself. He was possessed of a certain grand disinterest, ignoring both Jamie and Rowan. Jamie felt a profound hope that the animal would forgive her for snubbing him, after he'd offered such a generous greeting. Friends, she suspected, were going to be in short supply.

Rowan regarded her in a solemn and already familiar way. "Are you all right, Sara?" he asked.

The chauffeur came in before she had to answer, bringing the baggage, and a moment later, a maid hurried down the curved staircase, her color high.

"I'm so sorry I wasn't right on hand to greet you, Mrs. Summerville," the woman blurted, fairly choking on the words in her eagerness to get them said. "We've been busy making up your room, and of course now that Mr. Parrish is back from China, he'll be needing his regular suite—"

Jamie had expected to be addressed as Mrs. Summerville. It was the reference to Mr. Parrish's "regular suite" that threw her off-balance. Sara hadn't mentioned that he stayed at the villa.

"That's fine, Myrtle," Jamie said smoothly, starting up the staircase. Thank heaven, she knew the master suite was at the front of the house, with a terrace overlooking the ocean. "Please see that Mr. Parrish is comfortable."

"Yes, Mrs. Summerville," Myrtle replied. If she'd noticed

anything different about her employer, it didn't show in her plump, ingenuous face. "I could bring a supper tray upstairs, if you're hungry. If I know you, you didn't touch a bite of that awful airline food."

Actually, Jamie had wolfed down every morsel the flight attendant had put before her, but her stomach was empty again. "I'd like that," she said. "Thank you."

Jamie turned, before continuing upstairs, to look back over one shoulder. Rowan Parrish was still standing in the center of the foyer, staring at her thoughtfully. She gave him a cool nod, as she thought Sara would have done, and headed for her room.

She was in the private bathroom, with its fireplace, sweeping view of the sea, and gold-plated fixtures, running water into the enormous pink marble tub, when something struck the door with a solid thump. Jamie's heart had stuffed itself into her throat and triggered the flight-or-fight response, when Lazarus strolled through the narrow opening and greeted her with a matter-of-fact meow.

Jamie laughed at his audacity, and when she spoke it was in a conspiratorial whisper. "You shouldn't be here. After all, we're not supposed to be friends."

Lazarus positioned himself on the closed lid of the toilet and began another bath. Glad of his company, Jamie stripped off Sara's clothes and slipped into the tub.

She'd been there for about fifteen minutes when she heard the suite's main door open.

"I've brought your tray, Mrs. Summerville," Myrtle called cheerfully. "Will you just listen to me! I can't seem to break the habit of calling you that. I'd better get used to your new name, now that you're remarried and everything."

Jamie sank to her chin, closed her eyes, and seriously considered drowning herself. Among the other things Sara had neglected to mention, it seemed, was a brand-new husband.

Chapter Two

I'll kill her," Jamie whispered, the rush of her breath making glittering, iridescent canyons in the blanket of bubbles brimming over the edges of the tub.

"*Reow,*" said Lazarus, in what could only be interpreted as complete agreement, swishing his black tail back and forth and gazing at Jamie with unblinking yellow eyes.

"What was that, Mrs. Summ—Mrs. Castanello?" Myrtle called companionably, from somewhere beyond the bathroom door.

Jamie closed her eyes, fighting down a welter of emotions: panic, fear, and outrage that her own sister would set her up like this. "Nothing," she called back, in a high and slightly hysterical voice. *Just go away so I can think!* she added mentally.

When she heard the outer door close, Jamie sprang out of the tub like some sleek creature rising from the depths of the sea. Lazarus, startled by the noise and sudden motion, gave a meow of protest and fled.

After draping herself in a towel as big as a bedspread, Jamie padded into the suite and looked wildly around for the telephone. There were two, one on the vanity, one on the table beside the huge round bed.

Jamie had been intimidated by the bed in the first place; it looked like something out of a harem, covered in blue satin, as it was, and piled high with fussy pillows. Now that she knew a husband came as part of the package, her initial trepidation was rapidly turning to terror.

Reaching the vanity table, Jamie plunked down on the dainty bench and snatched up the receiver. She listened to make sure the line was clear, then punched out the correct overseas code, followed by her own number in Seattle.

"I'm sorry," responded a recorded voice, after two rings. "You have reached a number that has been disconnected or is no longer in service—"

She tried again, going through the sequence of numbers slowly, biting her lower lip. She'd misdialed the first time, she told herself. That was all.

The same recording twanged in her ear.

Numbly, Jamie replaced the receiver. Staring into the gilded oval mirror above the vanity, she saw Sara's face looking back at her, and a chill swiveled along her spine.

She'd known all along that Sara wasn't telling her the whole truth, but now it was beginning to dawn on Jamie that this wasn't just another of her sister's pranks. This wasn't high school or college. Sara had changed.

She, Jamie Roberts, had been had, and in a big way.

Even before she called the tile company where she'd been working for the last five years, Jamie knew what was coming. When her boss answered, though, she gave her name as Sara Summerville Castanello, Jamie's sister, and asked to speak to herself.

Fred Godwin sighed the heavy sigh of the long-suffering and badly treated. He was a loquacious sort—Fred never knew a stranger, his wife always said—ever ready to talk to anyone about anything. It didn't surprise Jamie that he confided so readily in her now.

"I'm sorry, Mrs. Castanello," he said, "but Jamie's re-signed and I don't have idea one where to find her. She just breezed in here, looking as if she'd spent the last month on some rich guy's yacht, and told me she was quitting. Wouldn't even wait for her paycheck. And after all I did for her, too."

Jamie closed her eyes, shaken, and leaned against the vanity, breathing deeply, willing herself not to lose it. "Did she say anything—anything at all?"

"No, ma'am," Fred said. "I couldn't get an explanation out of her, let alone two weeks' notice. I *will* say she seemed scared, and she was in a hurry, too—why else would she leave without her money? And what about her pension plan? Am I supposed to roll that over into some new account or what?"

"I don't know," Jamie said, fighting back the urge to blurt out, *Fred, don't you recognize my voice? It's me, Jamie. The person you saw was Sara.*

"You sure sound like your sister," Fred told her, cheering up a little. "Listen, you hear from Jamie, you tell her there's no hard feelings on this end. She was a loyal employee for five years, and I don't know what we're going to do without her. I guess she must have had a good reason for bailing out the way she did."

Tears stung Jamie's eyes, and it was all she could do not to sniffle. Fred had never told her he appreciated her. "I'm going to give you my telephone number here in Tovia. Please call me immediately, at any time of day or night—reversing the charges, of course—if you hear from my sister."

Fred accepted the number, said he hoped everything was okay, and rang off.

Jamie folded her arms on the glass surface of the vanity table and laid her head down on them. The anger she'd felt toward Sara earlier had turned to sick fear. Fred had said her twin looked scared, and the fact that Sara hadn't stayed to collect her paycheck certainly proved his assertion that she'd been in a rush. Even Sara, coddled and spoiled by a rich husband, must know that no working person with bills to pay would commit such an oversight.

After a while, Jamie began to get a grip on her whirling emotions. Although her instinct was to rush back to the airport, fly home to Seattle, and turn the whole city upside down, if necessary, looking for Sara, she knew the plan wasn't a good one. She needed a couple of days to think, to get her emotional equilibrium. Dealing with Sara's disappearance would call upon every resource she possessed, and she would have to do it all on her own, so she had to marshal her forces, make a plan.

For the moment, she was simply too tired, too shocked, to think clearly or to go gallivanting back over the top of the world to her own country. Furthermore, she had no apartment to go to, unless she missed her guess, and certainly no job.

She went over to the harem bed, pushed all the pillows onto the floor, and crawled under the covers. Tomorrow, she told herself, Sara would call, laughing, and say it was all a grand joke. Fred had been in on it, and so had the phone company.

"Not funny," Jamie murmured, as Lazarus curled up next to her, warm and noisy. Her consciousness caved in on itself and faded quickly to black.

"WAKE UP, DARLING," a male voice drawled. "Your prince is home."

Jamie opened her eyes and sucked in her breath. A man was bending over her bed, a handsome one, with chestnut hair, an aquiline nose, and hard gray eyes. She opened her mouth to scream, then remembered that she was married.

Rowan's voice echoed in her mind. *I'm sorry Julian couldn't meet you himself,* he'd said, in the airport the day before; *he must have been detained in Paris.*

The room was bright with dappled, moving sunlight, the

kind that is reflected off water. Jamie raised herself onto one elbow, veiling her panic, and squinted at the digital clock on the bedside table. Four-thirty-seven. Had she really slept almost twenty hours?

"How was France?" she asked, taking a chance.

"Paris never really changes," Julian said, turning away from the bed, to Jamie's vast relief. She hadn't decided whether or not to continue posing as Sara, but she knew damned well she wasn't going to sleep with this man to carry out the deception.

Julian was loosening his tie, and he kept his broad back turned to Jamie. His shoulders looked stiff under his expensive white shirt.

"What is Parrish doing back here?" he asked, in an undertone that revealed no emotion whatsoever.

Oddly, the mention of Rowan Parrish gave Jamie a degree of courage. She sat up in bed, well aware that she was clad in nothing but a twisted bath towel, and arranged the covers carefully. *I wish I knew,* she answered silently. "He's an old friend," she said, hoping the response was adequate.

Julian turned and looked at her with narrowed eyes. She would have sworn, just for that moment, that he despised her. It seemed strange, since they were, as far as she knew, newlyweds.

"An old lover, you mean," he replied, and each word struck Jamie like a small, smooth stone fired from a slingshot.

She didn't trust herself to speak and wouldn't have known what to say if she had, though color surged into her face. All she was certain of was that her first impression had been right: this marriage between Sara and Julian Castanello was not exactly a match made in heaven.

Jamie settled back against the curved, velvet-upholstered headboard of the bed, her mind racing even as she did her best to appear calm. She folded her arms on top of the covers and glared at Julian, waiting.

He sighed and shoved a hand through his lustrous, somewhat shaggy hair. "I'm sorry, Sara," he muttered. "I shouldn't have said that."

"No," Jamie answered, feeling self-righteous and completely confused, as well as terror-stricken. "You shouldn't have. What happened between Rowan and me is in the past."

What happened between Rowan and me is in the past? What in hell had made her say something like that?

"I just get nervous when he's around, that's all," Julian confessed, moving to one of the tall, arched windows to stare out at the view. Reflected light flickered over his too-perfect face. "I can't help wondering how much he knows."

Jamie's heart was hammering, and she barely restrained herself from asking, How much he knows about what? It also occurred to her that she might be better off to confess the truth to Julian right then, to tell him she wasn't his wife Sara at all, but Sara's identical twin sister. A nameless fear, one she couldn't explain even to herself, kept her from it. It didn't take a genius to figure out that something was very, very rotten in Tovia.

"Perhaps less than we think," she remarked.

Julian turned his cold, ruthless gaze on her. "Find out," he ordered, his voice low and yet sharp as a razor's edge. "Sleep with him if you have to, but *find out*."

Jamie averted her eyes and bit her lip, hoping Julian wouldn't see how revolted she was by this suggestion. "So much for the jealous bridegroom routine," she said, before she could stop herself.

He was on the bed beside her in the space of a heartbeat, kneeling on the mattress, his hand buried in her hair, wrenching at her scalp, his breath hot on her face and stale with the smell of wine. "Make no mistake, precious wife," he growled, his gaze alight with something that could scald, for all its coldness. "I haven't forgotten why we entered into this farce of a marriage, and neither will you, if you're as smart as you seem to think you are."

It was, incredibly, the depth of her fear that made Jamie brave. She was about to jam one knee into Julian's groin when he apparently read the intention in her eyes and withdrew. He leaped off the bed and turned, only to find himself confronted by a hissing Lazarus. The cat's ears were flat against his head, his teeth were bared, and the fur on his back and tail stood straight out.

Julian cursed and started to swing his foot at the animal, and Jamie cried, "Don't you dare hurt my cat!"

A profound stillness followed. Lazarus arranged himself, and Julian, straightening his tie and smoothing his hair, offered a strange parallel. After a long time, Julian looked at Jamie again, and it was as if he hadn't noticed her until then.

"*Your* cat? You've always hated that animal. What's going on here, Sara?" The low, even timbre of his voice was somehow more frightening than a shout.

"I've had a change of heart," she said coldly, trembling beneath the thin bedcovers. "Get out, Julian. I want to get dressed."

Another breath-stopping silence fell, during which Jamie feared she'd gone too far. Had she been too bold and inadvertently raised a challenge Julian's pride wouldn't let him ignore?

He looked at her with chilling contempt. "Wear something that will make Parrish want to confide in you—for old times' sake, if nothing else. I want to know what he's doing here."

Jamie didn't answer, or speak, or even nod. She just waited, and finally Julian went out, leaving her alone with Lazarus, her furry defender.

She bounded out of bed and dressed hastily in a black crepe jumpsuit from Sara's closet. She didn't dare defy Julian too openly when she didn't know what she was dealing with, and he'd already shown he could be violent.

Diamonds glittering at her ears and throat, Jamie was about to leave the suite when the phone made a polite but urgent jingling sound. She snatched up the receiver, knowing by that uncanny telepathy peculiar to certain twins that Sara was calling.

"Hello?" Jamie whispered, closing her eyes and holding her breath, praying no one had picked up an extension.

"I'm sorry about your job and your apartment," Sara blurted, half sobbing the words, "but I didn't have a choice. Don't forget your promise—if you do, we'll both die!"

It was over as quickly as that; before Jamie could say a word, the line went dead. Shaking, she lowered the receiver to its cradle and hugged herself, tears spoiling the eye makeup she'd applied so carefully.

By sheer force of will, Jamie pulled herself together. She repaired her mascara and eyeliner, squared her shoulders, and made herself leave the suite. It was a dubious comfort that Lazarus followed, his whiskers practically brushing her heels.

She found Rowan in the garden off the drawing room, quite by accident. He was standing next to a fountain, where a mossy statue poured water from a stone urn, gazing off into the distance as though he expected something, or someone, to appear on the horizon. Jamie could not guess whether he looked for salvation or destruction.

"Are you friend or foe, Rowan Parrish?" she asked, realizing only after the words were out that she'd spoken aloud.

He turned and regarded her, for the briefest of moments, with something that might have been tenderness. In the next instant, however, his face changed subtly. His expression was now closed, guarded.

"I might ask the same question of you," he said presently, raising his glass in an elegant salute. "To paraphrase, are you rich woman, poor woman, beggar woman—or thief?"

Jamie swallowed and looked away, injured by his words. The worst part was not understanding why the disdain of a stranger should hurt so much. "That was unkind," she ventured. His reply caught her by surprise.

"It was," he agreed gently. "I apologize. Which is not to say we won't lock horns again in five minutes. But then, ours was always a tempestuous alliance, wasn't it? Do you remember our picnic in that medieval ruin in the hills, Sara, when it rained and we got into a shouting match over whose responsibility it had been to check the weather forecast that morning?"

She didn't remember, of course, and Sara hadn't covered that particular part of her personal history. "Of course," she said, feeling an ache unfold in her heart because, even including the argument they'd evidently had, it would have been an inexplicably precious memory.

Rowan was silent, watching her again, in a way that made it seem that he'd already uncovered all her deepest secrets and was merely waiting for her to acknowledge them.

She almost told him who she was right then, almost blurted out that she and Sara had switched places, that something ominous was happening and she was afraid. In the end she stopped herself, because the odd, tender feelings Rowan Parrish stirred in her were, alas, no indication that he wasn't an enemy. It wouldn't be the first time, she thought cynically, that love had turned to hatred.

"Julian's back," she said, at long last, because she couldn't bear the silence and nothing else occurred to her.

"I know," Rowan replied, and the edge had returned to his voice. "Why are you standing in the garden with me, instead of welcoming your beloved husband back to hearth and home?"

Jamie shivered with the effort it took not to cross the small distance between them and slap the man with all the stinging force she could muster. She was fiercely glad she hadn't confided her secret.

"Why indeed?" inquired a third voice.

Jamie turned, startled, to see Julian striding toward her. He had exchanged his power clothes for slacks and a beige cashmere sweater, and he carried a cocktail in one hand and a wine goblet in the other.

Rowan said nothing, but simply toasted the new arrival with a somehow derisive lift of his glass. Jamie, flustered, feeling like the loser in some nightmare version of blindman's buff, snatched the wine from Julian's grasp. She had already swallowed a third of it before she took time to wonder if Sara would have chosen the cocktail.

"So nervous," Julian teased, stroking Jamie's back with fingertips that were still cold from the chilled goblet. "Do try to relax, darling."

Jamie took another gulp of the wine and stepped away from Sara's husband, just far enough to evade the touch of his hand. "I'm a little tired, that's all."

"Sara was in the States for a while," Julian commented to Rowan, with a sort of biting cordiality. Obviously, Sara was not the only one who had engendered Julian's dislike.

"I know," Rowan answered smoothly. "I met her at the airport."

Julian did not reply, but his gaze, as he glared at Rowan over the rim of his tumbler, was acidic.

"I don't believe you've mentioned what you were doing in the States," Rowan said. For the first time, Jamie noticed that he didn't have a recognizable accent, and neither did Julian. Either of them might have been from anywhere.

I don't believe you've explained why you're staying in this house, Jamie countered silently, but she couldn't ask without betraying the fact that she wasn't Sara.

She took another sip of wine. "I was visiting family," she said. She wondered how well these two men knew Sara, whether or not they were even aware that she had a twin sister. At that point, virtually nothing would have surprised her.

"Oh, yes," Rowan responded dryly. "I remember now. You were staying with your brother, James."

Sara had been able to slip a husband past her, Jamie thought, as the wine rushed to her head, but by God she'd have noticed a brother. Since she was still feeling her way in the dark, not to mention being a little drunk and jet-lagged in the bargain, she simply said, "Right."

As twilight settled over the garden, a chilly mist, faintly salted by the sea, came with it. Julian slipped an arm around her waist and ushered her toward the gaping French doors leading into the house. "Come along, darling," he said. "I wouldn't want you to fall ill."

"Heaven forbid," Rowan commented, and Jamie saw an almost imperceptible twitch along his jawline.

There was another brief, lethal stare-down, and for a second Jamie was afraid the two men would actually come to blows. In the end, though, Julian simply gave her a little push toward the doors.

She resented the gesture heartily, but there was no graceful way to fight back, so she let it pass.

"I'd like to see that medieval ruin you mentioned," she said to Rowan, in a bright voice, when the three of them had gathered in the drawing room to await the call to dinner. "Again, I mean."

Julian was on the hearth, adding birch logs to the fire, and he didn't speak or turn around. Rowan refilled Jamie's wineglass from a decanter on one of the tables, laying his hand to bottle and glass without looking, as easily as if he'd been master of that house in some previous incarnation.

"Again," he repeated, with just the slightest note of mockery. "Fine. We'll go tomorrow." Rowan glanced toward the man standing near the fire, making no effort either to project or lower his voice. "If your husband approves, of course. Would you like to join us, Julian?"

At last, Julian turned. The look he gave Rowan was hot enough to ignite the wine in Jamie's glass, make it flare like a torch in her hand. She retreated a step, unconsciously.

Once again, however, Julian was gracious. "I have business to attend to in Rome," he said. "I'm afraid I must leave tonight, directly after dinner."

Jamie took a sip of wine, speculating. Julian hadn't intended to travel to Rome until the moment he mentioned the idea, she decided. He didn't seem like the type to put on casual clothes, however costly, when he was planning to leave on a trip right away. No, he was trying to give her time alone with Rowan, so she could get the information he wanted. She just wished she had a clue as to what she was supposed to find out.

Rowan made a *tsk-tsk* sound. "A pity," he said.

Julian set his jaw, then started to speak, but before he could, Myrtle waltzed in, black uniform crisp, to announce that dinner was served.

There wasn't much conversation during the meal. In fact, if it hadn't been for Lazarus, who lurked under the table to garner pieces of broiled lobster from Jamie's fingers, she would have thought she'd become invisible.

Julian seemed to be in no hurry, but before dessert was served he made his excuses and left the table. Jamie silently thanked a benevolent fate that she and her "husband" wouldn't be spending the night under the same roof and attacked her chocolate mousse with relish.

Rowan's low chuckle startled her, lifting her heart at dizzying speed and at the same time piercing it like an arrow. "Some things never change," he said. "I must say, that's a comfort."

Jamie lowered her spoon. The kindness in his tone weakened her; she knew it was a trap, but she was drawn nevertheless. "Have so many things as all that changed, Rowan?" she asked cautiously, and with a gentleness she hadn't intended to reveal.

Again, his face hardened visibly. "Oh, yes," he answered gravely. "Everything has changed." With that, he pushed back his chair, rose, and left the dining room also, his dessert untouched.

The formal chamber seemed to yawn like some vast cavern when he was gone. Jamie's mousse lost its appeal, and she sagged back in her chair, despondent and so full of questions that she didn't know which to ask first.

Avoiding her room, where she might encounter Julian, Jamie found a lightweight jacket in one of the closets in a downstairs hall, slipped it on, and went out. Sara had warned her that the pathway leading down to the beach was steep, but the moon was almost full that night and Jamie could see clearly.

She walked along, hands plunged deep into the pockets of the borrowed jacket, to a small cove, framed on three sides with rugged, sharp-edged boulders.

Jamie sighed, feeling mist on her face as she stood watching the sea batter the mouth of the cove. The roar was deafening, and the force of the tide sent walls of spray high into the air.

Both she and Sara were in real danger, but Jamie had no idea how to save herself or her sister. She'd been forced into some deadly game, and no one had told her the rules. She didn't even know which side she was supposed to be on and she couldn't tell the good guys from the bad guys, if indeed there *were* any good guys.

Restless, yet somehow comforted by the churning, raging water, flinging itself into the little cove only to be trapped there, roiling like some devil's brew, Jamie climbed onto one of the boulders and looked down.

It was just the kind of thing the heroines of B-grade horror movies did, Jamie thought, even as two hands struck her hard from behind and she hurtled off the rocks and into the bubbling cauldron at her feet.

Being pushed was the first shock, and the icy temperature of the water was the second. Jamie flailed with terror as the current sucked her under, and a silent involuntary scream opened her mouth, stomach, and lungs to the furious sea.

She was going to die. That realization was the third shock, and the greatest by far. Jamie had never guessed, until then, just how badly she wanted to live.

She fought, but the water pounded her from above, and when she did manage to break the surface, the force of it slammed her against the rocks and she went under again. The scenario repeated itself as she struggled, over and over, to find air to breathe, but her strength was fading and after a while she couldn't tell which way was up and which was down.

Between one moment and the next, a delicious sense of warmth replaced the marrow-deep chill that had stiffened her muscles. The best thing to do, she decided, would be to fall asleep, to let the water take her. It was silly to keep fighting, wasn't it? She was so tired, and her lungs were bursting.

Something vaguely like a claw scraped her scalp, jarring her out of her dazed resignation, and then she felt fingers entangle themselves in her hair. A painful, blessed wrench followed, and Jamie's head was out of the water.

Air! She coughed and spat and sputtered and drew in great, greedy lungfuls of the stuff. Her rescuer—or her killer—gripped her by the shoulders and dragged her out of the freezing water.

"Don't kill me," she said, after throwing up salt water on the sand.

The light of the moon edged Rowan's face. "You're talking to the wrong man, love," he said, with a sort of gruff impatience.

When he was sure she was through emptying her stomach,

he hoisted her in his arms and started off into the darkness at a reassuringly brisk pace.

"What the hell were you doing out here in the dark?" he demanded, in a rasp underlaid with grudging concern. "Damn it, this place is dangerous enough in the daylight!"

"I was thinking," Jamie said, against the hard warmth of his shoulder.

"You couldn't prove that by me," Rowan retorted.

"Somebody pushed me. Was it you?"

"No," he said brusquely. "Didn't you see anyone?"

Jamie shook her wet head. She didn't want to trust Rowan, depend on him, care about him, and yet she felt herself leaning into his strength, taking comfort from it. "Just you," she replied. "It doesn't take a Perry Mason to theorize that you're the culprit."

They had reached a small stone cottage, on a bank overlooking the angry shore, and Rowan pushed the door open with one foot. Even though there was no fire and no light, Jamie felt warm. Even safe.

She had to be crazy.

"Here," Rowan said, setting her on a bed and shoving a blanket into her hands. "Get out of those clothes, and I'll build a fire."

Jamie peeled off the sodden jacket and once-glamorous jumpsuit with trembling hands. By the time she was finally able to wrap herself in the blanket, Rowan had a fire snapping on the hearth. She leaned toward the blaze, suddenly aware that she wasn't strong enough to walk, or even stand.

Rowan brought her whiskey in a disposable cup. "Here you are, little mermaid. Drink up."

"Was it you?" Jamie asked, her teeth chattering, as she raised the cup to her lips. "Did you try to kill me?"

"No," he said, and she believed him. There were 12-step groups, she thought, for women like her. He sat down beside her on the cot, or bed, or whatever it was. "Think about it,

Sara. If I wanted you dead, why would I have gone to all the trouble of pulling you out after pushing you in in the first place?"

Jamie was stumped. The whiskey was blending with her blood, warming it, flowing through her muscles and turning them to paste. "But you were there," she argued, clinging to the last shred of logic.

"I was following you."

"But you didn't see who attacked me?"

"No. There's a moon out, but there are clouds, too. A couple of times, it was so dark I couldn't make out my own hand in front of my face. I wouldn't have seen you flailing about in the water, in fact, if I hadn't been up on the bank and looking in just the right direction."

Jamie's thoughts were muddled, and she yawned loudly. "Thanks," she said. "For being there when I needed you."

Rowan touched her hair, or she thought he did, at least. He withdrew his hand so quickly that she might have imagined the contact. "Rest," he told her. "I'm right here."

She sighed and sagged against his arm and shoulder. "I'm not sure that's a comfort," she answered. And then she fell asleep, and when she awakened, it was morning and she was buried in warm quilts. A fire blazed on the hearth and the smell of fresh coffee filled the air.

Memories of the night before made Jamie sit bolt upright on the narrow cot. "What is this place?"

"Just the old fishing cabin," Rowan replied. "You've been here a million times. How do you feel?"

"As if I nearly drowned," Jamie said, drawing the covers up under her chin. Mentally, she added the cabin and the deadly tide pool to the list of things Sara hadn't mentioned during her briefings. "I guess it made me forget a few things."

Rowan crossed the room and handed her a mug of coffee, but the expression on his face was anything but friendly. "Like what you did with the jade goddess, for instance?"

Chapter Three

*W*hat jade goddess?" Jamie asked, with an innocence born of pure truth, as she accepted the coffee. "I don't know what you're talking about."

Rowan uttered a sigh and turned away. "Forget it. I should have guessed I wouldn't get a straight answer from you."

Jamie breathed in the aroma and warmth of the brew, stalling. She'd wanted adventure in her life, and now she was caught in the middle of some huge and very dangerous mystery. She hadn't been issued a rule book, nor did she know who her opponents were. Her situation was proof, if ever she'd seen it, that the old adage about being careful what one wishes for was right on target.

"Tell me about the jade goddess," she said, after a restorative sip of the coffee. Every muscle in her body felt bruised, and her lungs ached. She tried to make some kind of contact with Sara—they had sometimes been able to touch mentally, if not actually communicate in words—but there was nothing but deep, troubling silence. A void.

Rowan, who had poured coffee of his own and settled in a chair at the rough-hewn table, raised an eyebrow and gave her an ironic look.

Jamie was stung by his cynicism, but she forged bravely on. If there was another viable option besides putting one figurative foot in front of the other, it hadn't occurred to her yet. "Indulge me, Rowan. It's the least you can do, isn't it, after carrying me off, keeping me overnight, and thereby ruining my reputation forever?"

His expression became downright sardonic. "Ruining your reputation, is it? Ah, Sara, my darling, you are indeed a piece of work. You are a living, breathing scandal, and you have been since you swept poor Henri off his feet and became the mistress of all you survey. Spending a night in the cabin with me won't even make a ripple in your legend."

Jamie averted her eyes, the coffee burning in her throat. Rowan made Sara sound like a heartless, social-climbing, gold-digging bitch. Jamie's strongest impulse was to defend her sister, to refute his accusations, but she couldn't bring herself to do it. Most likely, Sara had known exactly what she was doing when she'd traveled to Europe some six years before, serving as secretary and companion to a wealthy old woman. Sara had told Jamie when they were children, still playing with dolls, that she meant to find a man with money someday, preferably an aging one, and marry him.

"People change," she said weakly, after a long time.

"Not you," Rowan replied, in a flat tone.

She shrugged and took a big risk. "You were in love with me once."

"I was a fool," he said. "You threw me over, don't forget. Henri was the better choice for a husband, by your calculations, being nearly seventy at the time, rich as hell, and in questionable health. And then there was the problem of my being a younger son. The family title and most of the estates went to my elder brother."

Jamie didn't reply. She loved her twin unconditionally, though she was sure everything Rowan said was true. He couldn't be expected to understand—perhaps no one could, besides Jamie herself—how the early years of deprivation, uncertainty, and shame had marked Sara. Granted, that didn't excuse her behavior; lots of people had difficult childhoods without growing up to be manipulative, self-centered, and generally thoughtless. It was just that no one who really knew and understood Sara could hate her.

Could they?

"What a shock it must have been," Rowan went on quietly, cruelly, "when poor Michael was killed and it all came to me."

"I should think it would have been more of a shock to Michael," Jamie answered. She didn't mean to be flip or disrespectful of the dead, but she wasn't going to be bullied either. "Did you kill him to get his money?" The words were out of Jamie's mouth before she'd even tried them out in her mind.

Rowan looked, for one terrible moment, as though he might spring from his chair, stride across the room, and choke her to death on the spot. He contained himself, however, with a visible effort, and remained where he was. Fury had drained all color from his face, and his eyes were no warmer and no calmer than the currents that had closed over Jamie's head the night before. "I loved my brother," he said finally, "although I realize you probably have no concept of what it is to care for another human being simply because they exist. Furthermore, I had no need of his money, since I've made a fortune of my own in recent years."

Jamie clasped the mug with both hands, to keep from spilling the contents. She had never seen such anger, such restrained fury, in another person as she saw in Rowan Parrish just then, and yet she sensed that he still cared for Sara in some deep and unwavering way.

"About the jade goddess," she prompted, wondering where this bold new side of her personality had been all these years. She could have used it when Alan was massacring her self-esteem, for instance, or when she'd been afraid to leave a job she'd hated.

Rowan put down his cup and folded his arms. A certain

cold resignation had crept into his manner, and he sighed. "You know it all as well as I do, but we'll go through the charade if you insist. The goddess is a priceless piece of oriental art, dating back almost a thousand years." He spoke in the tone of someone reciting a trite and dog-eared story that didn't really bear repeating. "I believe you stole it—with the help of your adoring bridegroom, of course."

The accusation struck Jamie like a blow, making her already-troubled stomach ache with the same violence as her muscles and lungs. Sara was capable of a lot of things, but stealing? The idea was too difficult and too painful to accept, and yet she couldn't help thinking of her conversation with Julian the night before. Rowan knew something, according to him, and Julian was willing to throw his wife to the wolves to find out what it was.

"I would never steal anything," she replied finally.

"Not even if your fairy-tale life had turned to sawdust? If, for example, you could sell a piece of ancient statuary for upwards of five million dollars on the black market and make it all better? Think of it: no questions, no taxes."

Five million dollars! The sum made the hundred thousand Sara had promised for Jamie seem like small potatoes—dirty ones, full of worms.

"Oh, my God," she whispered, as the truth of what Sara had done dawned on her in all its shattering glory. Sara and Julian *had* stolen the goddess. Furthermore, there was no hundred thousand dollars, because if Sara chose to disappear, and it seemed she had done just that, there would be no Jamie Roberts to claim the money. "I've been such a fool!"

There was bitterness but no trace of compassion in Rowan's voice. "Spare me," he said. "Julian is a world-class dirtbag, but he isn't smart enough to pull off a heist on this scale. I'd bet my ticket to heaven that *you* came up with the original idea—and the plans for carrying it out."

"You don't understand," Jamie protested, realizing, as she

started to her feet, that she was naked except for a blanket and she wasn't strong enough to stand. "I didn't—"

"Please," Rowan interrupted brusquely. "No protestations of innocence. I may be ill."

Jamie's frustration knew no bounds, and neither did her fury. If she told Rowan she wasn't Sara, and she still wasn't sure that would be a smart thing to do, he probably wouldn't believe her. He'd think she was just trying to get out of taking the fall for stealing his jade goddess!

"The hell with you," she said, and tried to get up again.

The room spun, tilted at a crazy angle, and righted itself with a jerk. Jamie crumpled back to the bed, moaning softly.

Rowan opened a chest and produced a pair of gray sweatpants and a maroon fisherman's sweater with holes in it. Still looking grim, he tossed the garments to her. "I'll step outside while you put these on," he said. "When you're decent, I'll take you back to the villa and call a doctor."

"I don't need a doctor," Jamie said. There were tears in her eyes, and she kept her head down so Rowan wouldn't see. "Just get out and let me dress."

He left without another word, which was both a mercy and a disappointment to Jamie.

Putting on the clothes, which were musty and much too large, was an exhausting process, far more difficult than it should have been. She was trembling, every inch of her body glistening with perspiration, by the time she gasped out, "All right. I'm ready."

Rowan appeared in the doorway, a dark shape framed in daylight. "What's the matter with you, Sara?" he asked, in a tone Jamie hadn't heard him use before. "You're shaking, and you're pale as death."

"I nearly drowned last night," Jamie murmured. "Such experiences upset me, as a general rule."

"It's more than that," he insisted. "Are you pregnant?"

"I wish I were," Jamie said, and he didn't reply.

Rowan carried her back to the villa, where their arrival produced an embarrassing flurry. Jamie was already feeling much stronger, but she pretended to be weak, letting her head loll against Rowan's shoulder and keeping her eyes closed. The last thing she wanted to do was answer a lot of questions.

It was as if Rowan could read her mind. As he carried her up the main stairway, he called down to someone, "Get the police."

"Why did you say that?" Jamie hissed, furious. It was enough that she was lying to him, to Julian, and to all the servants, about her identity. She didn't want to lie to the police, too.

"Don't worry, precious," Rowan replied acidly, a little breathless from the effort of carrying her across the landscape and up the stairs. "I haven't any solid proof against you yet, so you won't be arrested. Not today, at least."

"Or tomorrow, or next week," Jamie whispered angrily. "Because I didn't take your precious jade goddess!"

Reaching the door of the master suite, Rowan pushed it open with an unceremonious motion of one foot. "Coming from an inveterate liar like yourself," he said, flinging her onto the decadent bed and laying one hand to his heart, "I find that speech particularly moving."

"Is everything all right, sir?" It was Myrtle, standing in the doorway and wringing the hem of her apron between her hands. Jamie felt a flash of annoyance, since she was supposed to be mistress of the house.

"Everything is wonderful," she said, before Rowan could reply. "And Mr. Parrish was just leaving. Perhaps you wouldn't mind packing his bags for him?"

Myrtle turned crimson and flung a helpless, despairing glance at Rowan.

"Do as she says," he told the housekeeper quietly, without looking away from Jamie's face. "I'll stay at the cabin. In the meantime, call Mrs. Castanello's physician and ask him to stop by. I assume the police have already been contacted?"

"Yes, sir," Myrtle said. "They're on their way, and I'll ring Dr. Morrison right away." Having thus spoken, she departed, without a glance at Jamie.

IT WAS A grueling day.

The police arrived first, and Jamie recounted her experience on the beach in minute detail. Yes, someone had pushed her into the water. No, she hadn't seen anybody—except for Rowan Parrish, of course. It seemed a little odd that he was right there, didn't it?

The local constabulary didn't agree that Rowan's presence on the beach was odd. He'd saved her life, after all.

After two interminable hours, the police were satisfied that this was going to be a tough case, and they left, promising to check the sand for footprints.

Jamie just rolled her eyes at that. If the killer had left that sort of evidence behind, it would have washed away with the tide by then.

The doctor came next. He was a nervous, plump little man with florid cheeks and a bald, age-spotted pate. He examined Jamie's bruises, told her to rest, gave her a shot of something that made her entire body go limp, and departed. Only Lazarus, who had been watching the proceedings from his perch on top of an antique bookcase opposite the fireplace, remained to keep her company.

"*Reow*," he said, jumping down from his vantage point, landing with a resounding thump, and padding over to leap up onto the bed. There, he draped himself across Jamie's feet.

He was only an animal, but Jamie was glad of his presence. He was, she thought glumly, the only friend she had left.

She settled back onto her pillows, with a sound that might

have been either a sigh or a sob, and let the drug pull her under.

Jamie spent the rest of that day in bed, and all of the next, her arms, legs, and back so stiff she could barely move. On the third day, she got up, limped into the bathroom, and filled the tub with steaming-hot water. It was time to get back in action, though she had yet to decide what she would do.

The bath helped tremendously, and Jamie lingered for a long while, soaking away her aches and pains. Finally, she got out, dried off, and helped herself to lacy underwear, designer jeans, and a pink cashmere sweater from Sara's vast collection.

As she dressed, Jamie tried again to link herself with Sara, but there was only emptiness, and that frightened her more than anything that had happened since her arrival on the island. What could she do, call the Seattle police department and say, "I've lost telepathic contact with my sister"?

She left the bedroom, having purloined a lightweight leather bomber jacket from Sara's closet, and stepped out into the fresh April afternoon. A walk would clear her head, she decided. This time, though, she'd stay off the beach.

She was rounding the southwest corner of the house when Lazarus suddenly sprang out of a hydrangea bush to join her. He started down a path and Jamie followed, smiling a little. She would miss the cat when she went home.

The word *home* stopped her in the tracks of her borrowed sneakers. What if she couldn't go back ever? Suppose Sara, for whatever purpose, had made Jamie's life impossible to live? Just proving her true identity would be a challenge.

She might have cried, if she hadn't been so glad to be outside, in the fresh air and sunshine, and if Lazarus hadn't been capering along in front of her with an air of confidence.

The cat's path led through a thicket of weeds, but there was a good view of the sea, and the sky was that certain limpid shade of blue that always made Jamie want to take up painting. She was so enthralled with the scenery that she nearly tripped over Lazarus when he suddenly stopped and sat down.

"Most people walk dogs," commented a familiar voice. Rowan stood just ahead, an enigmatic smile curving his lips. Clad as he was, in boots, corduroy jeans, and a heavy gray sweater, he looked more like a fisherman than a nobleman and an expert on oriental art and antiques.

Jamie folded her arms and remained stubbornly silent. Rowan might have kept her from drowning, but he'd also made it clear that he believed she was a criminal. She wasn't about to get into another verbal sparring match.

"Feeling better?" He seemed determined to engage her in friendly conversation. It was a trap, she reminded herself.

"I think that's obvious," she said coolly.

Lazarus, the traitor, was looking up at Rowan and purring happily. It galled Jamie to realize that he actually liked this disturbing man.

"Has the conquering hero returned to the fold?"

"No." The question didn't trouble Jamie nearly so much as the prospect of having to deal with Julian again. Despite the alliance between Sara and him, he could definitely be listed in the Enemies column. In fact, Jamie had begun to think, darkly and in the very back of her mind, that it might have been Julian who pushed her into the tide pool. Of course, if she suggested her loving "husband" as a suspect, all the servants, and Rowan too, would probably testify that the master of the house had left for Rome right after dinner.

Lazarus made a squalling sound and darted into the underbrush, undoubtedly in pursuit of some small doomed creature. The sudden move startled Jamie and made her gasp.

Rowan immediately took a firm hold on her arm. "Take it easy, Sara. You look as though the devil just sprang out of the ground in a red mist."

Jamie was irritated by his assumption that he could touch her, and even more by the fact that she was enjoying even that small contact. She pulled free and started to walk around him.

He caught her by the wrist this time, and his grasp wasn't painful, but when she tried to yank her hand away, he held her fast.

"For God's sake, Sara," he rasped, "tell me the truth. Let me help you before something happens."

A shiver undulated through Sara's system and, though she tried, she was unable to hide it. She saw her fear reflected in Rowan's eyes.

She felt her resolve wavering, along with her courage, but inside her head a voice was chanting, *He's an enemy. He believes you're a liar and a thief. And even though he pulled you out of the water when you were ready to give up and die, he might have been the one who pushed you in. He could have staged the whole thing, in an effort to win your trust.*

"I can't," she said. "I can't tell you where the jade goddess is, because I don't know."

It was obvious, from the look on Rowan's face, that he didn't believe her. That was probably one of the reasons she was so surprised when he let go of her wrist and took a gentle grip on her hand.

"Come on," he said gruffly. "Let's go see how our ruins are holding up."

They climbed a grassy hillside with a spectacular view of the sea, moving ever closer to a stand of birch trees. Jamie's sore muscles protested the climb, but her heart was racing ahead on its own, like a spirited child hurrying toward a picnic.

Only there was nothing childlike about what was going on in Jamie's heart and in her body.

"Once," Rowan said, when they reached the tree line, "there was a Roman fortress on this site. The inhabitants would have been able to see for miles in every direction and bring the oil to a rolling boil in plenty of time to dump it onto the heads of any army foolish enough to attempt an invasion."

Grateful for the respite from Rowan's anger and mistrust, fascinated by the existence of anything so ancient, Jamie allowed her escort to pull her through the woods.

In a shady clearing, surrounded by trees and shadows, stood the remains of a stone structure. It had been a small building by modern standards, but virtually impregnable. Part of one wall still stood, dank and dark, with arrow slots high up, perhaps a dozen feet off the ground.

Jamie stopped, stricken by the odd, spooky magnificence of the place.

"Wow," she said.

"If I didn't know better," Rowan remarked, with neither affection nor rancor, "I'd think you'd never seen this place before."

Jamie stepped carefully through the rubble, needing to hide her face from him. "Let's pretend I'm a stranger," she said lightly. "Give me a guided tour."

He grabbed her, and wrenched her around to face him, and her breasts collided with his chest. "God help me," he muttered. "I'm sorry, Sara. I'm so sorry." Having made that cryptic statement and seen the shock in her face, he released her.

"You weren't going to hurt me, were you?" Jamie asked, though she knew the answer. The emotion emanating from Rowan a moment before had been passion, not anger. Even with her limited romantic experience, she sensed that much.

Rowan raked a hand through his dark hair. "No." He sighed. "I wanted to kiss you."

Jamie's pulse was hammering at the base of her throat. She took a step toward him. "Then do it," she said. She knew what she was doing was rash, but she didn't care. She yearned for

Rowan's kiss as much as she dreaded what it would do to her emotions.

"Sara!" It was a protest, a plea. "You have a husband, remember?"

She stood close to him and put her arms around his neck. She was free to kiss any man she wanted, but there was no convincing Rowan of that. Not without a lot of complicated explanations and an album full of pictures to prove Sara had a twin, anyway.

"I'm not asking you to throw me down in the grass and make love to me," she teased. "I just want one kiss. For old times' sake, if you will."

Rowan glared down at her for a long moment, but he didn't pull out of her embrace, and finally, with a low groan, he lowered his mouth to hers in a crushing, hungry kiss.

For Jamie, it was another drowning, except that this time she was swamped by joy, not frigid pounding surf. She felt excitement, fear, and a rush of adrenaline unlike anything she'd ever experienced before.

She stumbled a little when Rowan suddenly set her away from him.

"*Damn* you!" he bit out. "It's bad enough that I've made an idiot of myself over you. I won't be an adulterer in the bargain!"

Jamie's eyes burned, and her vision blurred. She was starting to care for this man, against her will and her better judgment, and he plainly despised her.

"Rowan, listen to me," she began, faltering, reaching for him with one hand and dying a little when he stepped back out of reach. "Please, I'm not—"

He turned on his heel and stormed away.

It was too much for Jamie; she sat down on a stone, covered her face with both hands, and cried. She cried because she'd lost her sense of Sara's presence in the world, because Rowan hated her, because she'd wasted so much of her life back in Seattle working at a job she hated. She might have gone on crying until she died, like some princess in an obscure fairy tale, if she hadn't become aware of something small and soft butting against her arm.

With a sniffle, she looked down and saw Lazarus on the stone beside her. How long had he been trying to get her attention?

"You again," she said with affection, and lifted the cat onto her lap.

He allowed himself to be held and petted, and the interlude was comforting for Jamie. She began to regain her composure.

"It just goes to prove," Jamie said, burying her wet face in the silky fur on his back for a moment, "that not all males are fickle. Too bad you're not human, old buddy."

Lazarus meowed companionably, as if offering a comment, and Jamie laughed.

"Hey," she said. "What's your sign?"

Five minutes later, satisfied that he had saved his adopted mistress from mental collapse, Lazarus jumped down off Jamie's lap and disappeared into the woods. She followed, walking slowly back toward the villa, telling herself that if she'd gotten over Alan, she could surely put this hormonal infatuation with Rowan Parrish behind her as well.

Dinner was ready when she reached the house, and Jamie was surprised to discover that she had an appetite. She was about to carry her empty plate back to the kitchen when a telephone jingled somewhere. Her sixth sense, never well developed, lurched into maximum overdrive.

Sara.

She heard the housekeeper speaking to someone and stood stiffly, waiting. Afraid to move.

Myrtle appeared in the doorway of the dining room, her normally rosy complexion pale, her lower lip trembling. "It's for you, Mrs. Castanello, a man in Seattle who says he's calling about your sister."

Jamie knew what the caller would say before she made her way into the hall and picked up the receiver Myrtle had left lying on a table. The housekeeper scurried after her, prattling.

"I never knew you had a sister, Mrs. Castanello."

Jamie was shaking. She thought she would be sick, right there in the hall. "Please be quiet," she snapped, before speaking into the telephone. "Hello?"

"It's Fred Godwin, Mrs. Castanello," her former boss said. "I'm afraid I've got some terrible news. Your sister Jamie was found dead this morning. She was murdered."

Jamie's knees gave out; she sank to the floor, still clutching the receiver, her stomach twisting itself around her heart and her windpipe, smothering her. She'd already known, on some level, that Sara was gone, but consciously facing the reality was another matter.

"Mrs. Castanello?"

Jamie made herself speak, at the same time brushing off Myrtle's attempts to help her back to her feet. She wanted to kneel, to pray that it wasn't true, to bend over and touch her forehead to the cool floor and bleed from every pore because half of herself had just been ripped away. "I'm—I'm here," she said. "What happened to Sa—to Jamie?"

"Apparently she was jogging along a country road—funny, because I never knew her to exercise on purpose. Anyway, somebody strangled her and left her in a ditch. The police don't have any leads as yet."

"Thank you," Jamie managed to say, clutching the edge of the hall table with one hand, hauling herself awkwardly to her feet. "I'll want to have my sister's body sent here, to Tovia. Can you tell me where she was taken?" She wrote down the numbers of the King County morgue and the Seattle police, which Fred obligingly looked up for her, said her good-byes, and hung up. Then, without further ado, Jamie fell into a dead faint.

Chapter Four

Fortunately, Jamie's state of shock was short-lived. Once she'd absorbed the first blow—Myrtle and the gardener had revived her after her faint and taken her to the drawing room settee to lie down—a strange, icy calm descended. Within minutes, she was on her feet again, calling the Seattle police from the hall telephone. She was put through to a Detective Stan Reeger, in the homicide division.

"My name is Sara Castanello," she said. The lie came to her lips with disturbing ease. "I'm calling from Europe. My—my sister was Jamie Roberts. When I asked for the detective in charge of her murder case, the operator put me through to you."

"I'm very sorry about your sister, Ms. Castanello," Reeger said, with the kind of gruff grace one might expect from a seasoned cop. "That was a real shame."

Jamie closed her eyes for a moment, her mind flooded with garish images of Sara, strangled and tossed into a ditch, limbs askew. "Did she suffer?"

Reeger hesitated. "It was a fairly quick death," he said at length. "But she would have felt some pain, having her air cut off that way, and I won't try to tell you she wasn't afraid. Anybody would have been."

"Do you have any idea who might have done this?"

"No, ma'am. I was hoping you could offer a few possibilities."

To Jamie's way of thinking, Julian was the prime suspect, but she wasn't ready to explain the circuitous route she'd taken to reach that conclusion, especially in an international telephone call. Rowan was probably right in believing that Julian hadn't been the brains of the operation, but surely the man wasn't stupid enough, or clumsy enough, to strangle Sara with his own hands. He would have hired out a nasty job like that, and it was a safe bet that he had an alibi for his whereabouts over the last twenty-four hours.

"I'll have to give that some thought, Detective Reeger," she said. "My sister and I have been out of contact for the last five years or so, and frankly, I don't know a lot about her life. In any case, I'll fly to Seattle as soon as I can and make the necessary arrangements."

Reeger cleared his throat. "There wouldn't be much point in that, Ms. Castanello. The medical examiner always does an autopsy in cases like this one, and it may be some time before the—er—remains are released for burial."

Jamie fought down a wave of nausea, picturing her sister's body lying gray and cold on some lab table. "You'll get in touch with me if you find out anything, won't you? It's an international call, so please simply reverse the charges . . ." Her voice faded away with the effort of trying to block out the terrible images in her mind.

The detective spoke gently. "I'll keep you posted," he said. "Just give me the number."

Jamie couldn't think what it was and she had to turn to Myrtle, who was hovering nearby, for that simple information. She recited the number into the receiver as the housekeeper told it to her. "And don't worry about the time difference," she finished. "If you find out anything— anything at all—I want to know about it immediately."

"Yes, ma'am. And am I right in assuming you'd be willing to return to the States if we should need your help with the investigation?"

"Just call," Jamie answered. "I'll be on the first plane back."

She replaced the receiver and leaned against the table for a moment, composing herself, gathering her strength. At some point far in the future, she supposed, everything would catch up with her, but for now she couldn't afford to fall apart. She was sure that whoever had killed Sara, or ordered her murder, had known his victim's true identity, and that meant he knew Jamie herself was an impostor. She was in as much danger as Sara had been, maybe more.

Jamie was in the foyer, about to start up the stairs, where she intended to pack for an immediate departure to anywhere, when the front door flew open and Julian breezed in.

Just looking at him, suspecting what he might have done to Sara, whether directly or indirectly, she wanted to fling herself upon him, screeching and clawing, and rip off whatever parts of his anatomy she could get a grip on. "Stay away from me!" she said.

Julian's smile was practiced and quick, but she saw the arrogance and greed in his eyes. "Is that any way to greet your long-lost husband?"

"You haven't been lost nearly long enough," Jamie replied, and proceeded up the stairs.

He caught up to her within a few strides, took her arm in a harsh grasp, and hustled her toward the second floor. She tried to pull free, but he was much stronger, and his fingers bit into the flesh of her elbow, bruising her, seeming to compress her bones.

Myrtle was still standing in the foyer, and Jamie called down to her in an even, reasonable tone, "Send someone for Mr. Parrish. Right away."

Julian half hurled, half dragged her along the upper hallway. Reaching the master suite, he shoved open the double doors and threw her inside.

"What the hell is going on here?"

Jamie supposed she should have been terrified, but her mind was calm, like the eye of some emotional storm. Grief and frustration and fear howled around her, but somehow she was keeping them at arm's length. "Sara's gone," she said. "Someone murdered her."

He closed the doors with an ominous click. "Since when do you speak of yourself in the third person?" he demanded. "If you're trying to convince me that you're cracking under the strain, forget it."

Jamie was grateful for his assumption, because she'd spoken without thinking. "I'm leaving," she said, opening a drawer and taking out a stack of designer jeans and tops and promptly laying them on top of the bureau. "This marriage is a charade and we both know it. I'm not willing to play the game anymore."

Julian didn't lay a hand on her, but she could feel the violence coiled within him, and if she hadn't been so numb over what had happened to Sara, she would have been mortally afraid. "Do you think you can back out so easily?" he hissed. "Because if you do, you really *are* losing it. You're in this as deep as I am, baby, and you're not going anywhere!"

"He knows," she said, taking a desperate gamble. "Rowan knows you and I took the jade goddess to sell on the black market."

Julian went white, even though he had to have considered the possibility before, and murmured a curse. "Did he tell you that?"

"You told me to find out what he knows, and I did."

"Why hasn't he told the police?"

"He has no proof," Jamie answered, still feeling nothing at all. She prayed the numbness would last until she was ready to deal with the permanent loss of Sara. "But he's working on it, Julian, and he means to nail us. The jig, as they say, is up."

She had to get away. Find a place to hide.

"You damn idiot," Julian breathed. "Parrish is trying to trick you into a confession, don't you see? It's guesswork, that's all."

Jamie nodded. "Yes," she agreed moderately, "but he guessed right, didn't he?"

Julian said nothing. He just turned and strode out of the suite, and Jamie went back to her packing. If only she could think of somewhere to go, she reflected, but no flash of genius came to her. She wouldn't be any safer on the other side of the world than Sara had been.

There was a polite rap at the door, and then Myrtle's trilling voice. "Mrs. Castanello? Mr. Parrish is downstairs."

"Thank you," Jamie replied, as the realization struck her that she'd just filled a whole suitcase with mismatched shoes and wire hangers. "Send him up, please."

Rowan arrived within a couple of minutes, not bothering to knock, his fine brow furrowed as he took in the suitcase and the crazy tangle of useless items inside it. "Sara—"

"I need to get away from here," she said matter-of-factly. "Please, Rowan, take me somewhere—anywhere—"

He crossed the room and gripped her shoulders. His touch, unlike Julian's, was gentle and lent her strength and a degree of comfort. "What's happened?"

"I'll explain everything, I promise. Just help me get out of this house."

Rowan released her. "All right," he said. He nodded toward the suitcase. "Dump that junk out, and put in some real clothes. While I'd love to see you running around the old family home in the altogether, it might shock the servants." With that, he went into Sara's closet, which was roughly the size of the suite of offices Jamie had worked in in Seattle, and came out with an armload of blouses, slacks, sweaters, and skirts.

"That's it?" Jamie asked, shock making her giddy. "Just

like that, you're taking me to your house? No questions? No gibes about counting the silver and locking up the artwork?"

Rowan smiled and tossed the garments he carried onto the suitcase. "I'll take care of all that later," he said. "Questions included."

"Julian will try to stop us."

His smile broadened. "I've been looking for an excuse to knock your husband out of his boots. Bring him on."

Jamie folded the items Rowan had selected for her, added jeans and T-shirts, nightgowns and underwear, tucked everything into her bag, and snapped the catches closed before she dropped her bombshell. "Julian is not my husband. However, feel free to deck him."

"Don't worry, I do." Rowan took the suitcase from her when she would have hoisted it herself and led the way through the doors and into the hallway beyond. To Jamie's secret relief, they didn't encounter Julian at all. He'd been a tough guy with Jamie, but apparently he wasn't so eager to tangle with Rowan.

A sleek silver sports car waited in the driveway, and Rowan tossed Jamie's suitcase into the tiny trunk before opening the passenger door for her. He cast one last look toward the house, obviously still hoping Julian would show up, and then got behind the wheel and started the engine.

"Wait!" Jamie cried.

"What?" Rowan asked impatiently.

"I can't leave without Lazarus."

"You'll have to," Rowan pointed out, shifting the car into reverse. "The terms of Henri's will forbid anyone to take him off the grounds without a very good reason, remember?"

Jamie bit her lip. "I don't care. I want him."

Rowan turned the car around and headed down the drive. "We'll settle this argument another time," he replied. "But you might just trouble yourself to explain your sudden attachment to that animal. You always hated him, and now, all of a sudden, he's your best friend. And exactly what did you mean back there, when you said Julian isn't your husband?"

She sank back in the small leather seat, closed her eyes, and sighed. The reality of Sara's murder was nipping at her heels; she would be dragged down soon, into a mire of grief she might never escape. "I can't talk about it, Rowan. Not until we're away from here."

He accepted her reply, apparently, for he didn't say another word for almost twenty minutes. Jamie was silent, too, feeling the fading sunlight on her skin, the salty wind ruffling her hair. Tovia might have been her own private paradise, she thought, if things had been different.

Finally, at dusk, Rowan brought the car to a stop at the side of the road. They were high above the villa; she could see the ruins in the woods and, of course, the sea. After turning off the engine, Rowan took her hand.

"Time to start explaining, my love. And leave out the lies."

Jamie sighed. There was a burning sensation behind her eyes, and her heart felt as heavy as a block of granite. She was beginning to mourn Sara—not the real one, of course, because she hadn't really known that woman after all, but the sister she'd invented for herself. The person she'd wanted Sara to be.

"You won't believe me. It's too fantastic."

"Convince me."

"I'm not married to Julian, because I'm not Sara. I'm her twin sister, Jamie."

"You're right, that's pretty wild. But go on. I'm listening."

"Think about it, Rowan. Sara hated the cat, and the feeling was probably mutual. But he and I took to each other right away."

"Stranger things have happened," Rowan said, but he spoke thoughtfully. Jamie knew he was taking in what she was saying, weighing the logic of it. She could sense that he wanted to believe her, whether he actually did or not.

"Sara's dead," Jamie said woodenly. "She was strangled sometime yesterday, on a rural road near Seattle. The police think her body is mine, because we traded lives."

Skepticism shadowed Rowan's face. "Convenient," he said. "If Jamie is dead, you can claim to be her and escape all the consequences of larceny on a truly grand scale."

Jamie hadn't anticipated that angle, and she was taken aback. When she finally replied, her voice was hollow. "Sara and I had the same blood type, and neither of us have ever been fingerprinted. But we didn't have the same teeth filled. I can prove I'm telling the truth. All I have to do is call my dentist."

"That's very good," Rowan admitted. "I suppose if I went to the trouble to check, though, I'd discover that your dentist's office burned down last month and all the records were lost."

She raised her wrist with a jerky motion and squinted at Sara's gold watch. "It's still morning in Seattle. Just get me to a telephone."

Rowan started the car, his jawline set tight, and pulled back onto the road. Within ten minutes, they passed between the towering brick gateposts of a sprawling country estate. He sped around the enormous circular driveway and brought the vehicle to an abrupt stop near the front step.

"I believe we have a telephone around somewhere," he said, shutting off the car.

Jamie got out without waiting for him to come around and open the door for her. "With your permission?"

Rowan had stopped to get her bag from the trunk, but he nodded toward the house. "My study is just off the foyer, on the left."

Jamie hurried inside. Her heart was still deadened, hollow and empty, but all of a sudden it was beating hard. She found the telephone on the corner of an exquisite antique cherry-wood desk and immediately reached an overseas operator. Since she had to get her dentist's number from Information, the call was just going through when Rowan came in. He'd evidently left the suitcase in the foyer, and his hands were shoved into the pockets of his jacket.

It would be too awkward to explain who she was, given the fact that everyone she'd known in Seattle believed she was dead, so Jamie introduced herself as Sara and asked that her late sister's dental records be sent to her in Tovia immediately.

"Jamie Roberts," the nurse mused. "That's the poor woman who was murdered, isn't it? What a shame; she was so young. I'm sorry, Mrs. Castanello. It must have been a terrible shock to you."

Jamie was looking at Rowan and winding the cord round and round on her index finger. "It was. About the dental records."

"I'm afraid we don't have them anymore," the woman said. "The police came by and picked them up this morning."

Some of Jamie's numbness gave way to dread, and the pit of her stomach constricted painfully. "I see. I suppose it was Detective Reeger?"

There was a brief, pulsing silence. "I don't think that was the name. Just a second, let me check my log book."

The nurse put Jamie on hold, and canned music filled her ear. She wanted to look away from Rowan's face but found she couldn't.

After several minutes, the woman returned. "According to my notes, Mrs. Castanello, Ms. Roberts's chart was signed out to a Detective Alex Martinelli."

A headache began to pound beneath Jamie's temples, and anxiety stabbed through her vitals like a lance. It was routine for the police to examine a murder victim's dental records, she told herself, but that didn't change the awful premonition she had. "Thank you," she said. After several attempts to return the telephone receiver to its cradle, she succeeded and reached into the pocket of her jeans for the numbers she'd written down earlier, while talking to her former boss. In a few minutes, she'd reached the Seattle Police Department.

After a moment's hesitation, she asked to speak with Detective Alex Martinelli. Rowan was standing beside Jamie, now, and frowning. She could smell fresh air, and the scent of soap on his skin, and she wanted him to hold her very close and for a very long time.

The operator paused, then confirmed Jamie's worst fears. "I'm sorry, ma'am. There is no officer by that name. Perhaps Mr. Martinelli is with another police force?"

Jamie shook her head, too dazed to realize, until after the fact, that the woman on the other end of the phone line couldn't see the gesture. "I—I must be mistaken," she said. "Could you please put me through to Detective Reeger?"

There were more electronic sounds, and then a male voice came on the line. "Homicide. Goodrich here."

Jamie repeated her request.

"Let me get your number," Goodrich responded. "Reeger's out right now. He'll get back to you as soon as he can."

"That's all right," Jamie said, in a voice she barely recognized as her own. "I'll call later." She hung up, pushed her hand through her hair, and looked straight into Rowan's eyes. "Well, it wasn't a fire, like you said. Just a common, ordinary con job."

"What happened?"

"Somebody pretending to be a detective named Martinelli picked up my dental records. I think it's safe to say we'll never lay eyes on them."

Rowan sighed. "If what you say is true—and believing you, my darling, is a little like poking a hand into the fire after sustaining a third-degree burn—there would still be

Sara's records. All we have to do is find out who her dentist was." He put a gentle, undemanding arm around her waist. "In the meantime, guilty or innocent, you're obviously at the end of your tether. I want you to lie down on that couch over there by the hearth. I'll get you some hot tea and then build a fire."

Jamie's defenses were weakening. "I'm not Sara," she said, because she needed him to believe her, to be on her side.

Rowan squeezed her hands, then raised one to his lips and brushed a light kiss over the knuckles. "Wouldn't it be wonderful if that were true," he said.

"Did you hate her so much? Sara, I mean?"

"Oh, it was much worse," Rowan said, with sorrow and irony in his eyes, even as his mouth shaped itself into a faint smile. "I loved Sara. And I must still be obsessed, or I would have left you with Julian. God knows, the two of you deserve each other."

Jamie turned away and moved slowly toward the couch he'd pointed out. It was no use trying to convince Rowan that she wasn't Sara, no use at all. Even if she did manage to produce dental records, her own or Sara's, he'd probably just think she'd tricked him somehow.

Something in the timbre of his voice stopped her, though she didn't turn around to meet his gaze.

"There *is* one thing that makes me think you might be an impostor," he said. "Remember that reference I made to our picnic at the ruins—when it rained and we argued because we each thought the other should have checked the forecast?"

"Yes," Jamie whispered. She still didn't face him, because she knew she couldn't endure the contempt and pity she expected to see in his eyes.

"It never happened."

Startled, she whirled. "Then why—"

"Strange as it sounds, when I first saw you, standing there by the baggage carousel at the airport, I was struck by some difference in you that I couldn't quite put my finger on. I had the whimsical thought that you might be a stranger, maybe an actress who bore a strong resemblance to Sara, or even someone who had had cosmetic surgery for the purpose of looking like her. I tried to trip you up a couple of times, but I finally decided that my theories, while entertaining, were simply too farfetched. That's when I came to the conclusion that you were laying the groundwork—by acting vague and pretending to remember things that had never happened, I mean—to stage some kind of spectacular mental breakdown. Amnesia would be a bit of a stretch, outside a soap opera, but you always had a flair for the dramatic. Or Sara did, if you do indeed have the extreme good fortune to be someone else."

"What are you going to do with me?"

"For now, I plan to protect you." He pressed her gently onto the couch. "I'll be back in a few minutes."

Jamie couldn't have moved if all the draperies on all the windows in the room had burst simultaneously into flames. The inner resources that had sustained her up to now had ebbed away, like a low tide, and she wanted to curl into a fetal position and sleep for days.

She was staring into the empty hearth when Rowan returned, carrying a china tea service on a tray. He set everything down on a small table near the couch and went to build the promised fire.

"Sara wanted so much," she mused, speaking as much to herself as to Rowan. "That was the problem, you know. She wanted so much more than most of us do."

Rowan looked back at her over one broad shoulder, still crouched next to the fireplace. "What did Jamie want?" he asked.

Jamie's smile trembled on her mouth, fleeting and slippery. "A husband who loved her. Her own dusty little antiques shop. And a few babies."

"A nice dream," Rowan acknowledged.

"What about you? What do you want most in all the world?"

He considered, then said without rancor, "To turn the clock back to the day before I met you and head in the opposite direction."

Jamie would never know what made her ask the next question. Some defiant, self-destructive impulse, probably. "And to find the jade goddess? That's why you were staying at Sara's house when I arrived, isn't it? You were looking for it."

Rowan got to his feet and touched an empty space on the mantel. "Yes," he admitted. Then he sighed. "It's very unlikely that I'll ever see the goddess again," he went on, after a few moments of thoughtful silence. "I just want to prove that you and Julian stole the piece."

Somehow, without being aware of it, Jamie had poured herself a cup of tea. She lifted the drink from the tray with a small start of surprise. "This vendetta of yours is mostly about revenge, then," she said.

"It's about justice," Rowan retorted.

"You should have protected her better—the goddess, I mean."

A corner of Rowan's mouth lifted in a faint and sardonic semblance of a smile. "So now it's my fault she was taken, and not that of the thieves? Strange reasoning, Sara-Jamie."

She put down the cup and saucer with a clatter. "Don't call me that!"

Rowan looked as surprised as Jamie felt, though he didn't speak. The protest had risen without warning from some deep part of her unconscious mind, like a scaly dragon breathing fire.

"It's not as if Sara and I were the same person," Jamie said, foundering. She was frantic and afraid and desperately alone, and words she wouldn't have spoken under other circumstances tumbled from her lips. "Being a twin can be very difficult, you know. Sometimes, it was as though I didn't exist at all. There were moments when I honestly believed I was nothing more than a reflection of my sister. And you can stop thinking what you're thinking, Rowan Parrish, because I'm not crazy and I'm not trying to convince you that I am!" She tapped one temple with an index finger. "No extra personalities in here," she rushed on. "Just plain old plodding Jamie Roberts, who thought she wanted an adventure!"

"Stop," Rowan said gently.

She began to sob. "I loved my sister!" she cried, as Rowan sat down beside her and pulled her into his arms. "No matter what she was, or what she did, I loved her!"

He held her long after she'd fallen silent, long after the fire on the hearth had cooled to embers, long after twilight had sent long purple shadows creeping through the windows and across the floor.

"Come along," he said finally. "I'll tuck you in and we'll work things through in the morning."

She clung to him with both hands, something she'd sworn she'd never do again, with any man, after Alan had taught her the finer points of heartbreak. "Don't let me go," she pleaded hoarsely, no longer caring if he thought she'd lost her mind; maybe she had. Maybe she really was Sara Castanello. Maybe there had never been a Jamie Roberts at all. . . .

"All right," he assured her. "All right, love, I'm here. Don't be afraid."

Don't be afraid. Jamie might have laughed if she hadn't known how she would sound. Hysterical, at best. Stark raving mad at worst.

"Just hold me," she said. "Please." Hold me forever, keep me safe, change the world so nothing bad ever happens again.

"I will," Rowan answered, rising to his feet and pulling

Jamie with him. He lifted her easily into his arms, the way he had done the night she'd almost drowned. "I will."

He carried her up a flight of stairs and into a large bedroom furnished in antiques. It was Rowan's room, Jamie knew. She was glad. She wanted to be close to him, for just this one night. She yearned to lie in his arms, whether he made love to her or not, and pretend it was she, Jamie, that he meant to hold, and not the memory of Sara.

Rowan laid her on the bed and dimmed the lights. He undressed her gently, without fumbling, as gracefully as if he'd done it a thousand times before. Then he took off his own clothes, crawled into bed, and drew Jamie back into his arms.

It was bliss, a quiet, magical time out of time. The jade goddess wasn't missing, and she'd never met Julian Castanello, and Sara wasn't dead. Best of all, Rowan cared for her, Jamie.

"Make love to me," she said.

She felt his lips, warm and soft, brush her forehead. "I'd like nothing better, but I'm afraid I'm not quite scoundrel enough to take advantage that way," he told her, with a rueful chuckle in his voice. "Wish I could summon up a little villain, but there it is. I'm a knight who was never issued his shining armor, but a chivalrous fellow nonetheless."

Jamie smiled into his bare shoulder. "If you insist on being honorable, I suppose there's nothing I can do," she said, snuggling closer. And even though she still wanted him, a small, achy corner of her heart was warmed by the knowledge that he did not take loving a woman lightly. "Good night, Sir Rowan."

He laughed, and the sound was low and richly masculine. "Sleep well, milady," he replied.

Chapter Five

Already dressed when Jamie opened her eyes the next morning, Rowan sat beside the bed, legs outstretched, his aristocratic face solemn with contemplation. Seeing that she was awake, he gave her a brief, cryptic grin that was probably intended to serve as a "good morning."

There had been a similar scenario with Julian, right after her arrival in Tovia, and Jamie was tired of dealing with fully clothed males while she had only bedsheets to cover her. "Stop looking at me that way." Her suitcase was on a bench at the foot of the mattress, and she wriggled toward it on her knees, using the bedclothes for a shield.

"What way?" Rowan hadn't moved.

"Like we spent the night engaged in wild passion. We didn't."

"So I noticed," he said ruefully.

Jamie got tangled in the covers, lost her balance, and toppled forward, affording Rowan an embarrassing view of her bare backside. She righted herself as quickly as she could, face crimson, and narrowed her eyes, silently daring him to mock her.

He looked away for a moment, probably smoothing the amusement from his face. Then, finally, he rose to his feet. "I'll leave you to get dressed," he said. "After that, we'll figure out what to do about Julian."

Jamie gulped and her heart tripped, like a skater thrown

off-balance, and went spinning. "About Julian? Does that mean—"

Rowan touched the tip of her nose, and though the gesture was innocuous, a surge of sweet well-being rushed through Jamie's spirit. "It means I believe you. You're not Sara."

"But, how—"

His pressed the same fingertip to her lips. "It was the way you lay in my arms last night, the way you breathed and moved, the way you fit against my side. Beyond that, I can't explain. Maybe it's just that I want so much for you to be real."

Tears burned in Jamie's eyes as she realized that the undeniable attraction between them was still about Sara. If Rowan wanted her, Jamie, it was because she had her sister's face and body. She bit her lip and nodded, since that was all she could manage, and he left the room.

Jamie washed her face in the adjoining bathroom, brushed her teeth with a new brush that had been laid out for her, and dressed quickly in black slacks, a gray-blue fisherman's sweater, heavy socks, and sneakers.

She didn't see any of Rowan's servants as she descended the stairs, and that was a relief. She'd spent the night in the master bedroom, and even though nothing had happened, Jamie was old-fashioned enough to be embarrassed by appearances. No one who knew she'd shared Rowan's bed—everyone in the house, probably—would believe the truth.

Jamie found the dining room by following the scent of bacon. Rowan was already there, seated at the head of a beautifully carved table. "I've decided that Julian has no reason to kill me," she announced, going to the sideboard and helping herself to a plate. An appealing array of food had been set out in chafing dishes, including southern-fried potatoes, crepes, biscuits, sausage, and bacon. There was fruit as well, along with yogurt and dry cereal.

Rowan rose from his chair, out of courtesy, and then sat down again. "Considering that he probably tried to drown you the other night, and that he either murdered Sara himself or ordered it done, that's a remarkable conclusion. Were you hurt when you jumped to it?"

Jamie summoned up part of a smile and joined him at the table. Her appetite was nonexistent, given all the shocks and traumas of recent days, but she needed to keep her strength up, so she nibbled. "We agree that Julian and Sara must have stolen the goddess. When I alluded to what they'd done yesterday, he didn't trouble to deny it. Still, if he had Sara killed—and I believe he did—he not only knows who I am, he can also be fairly certain that I don't know anything at all about the theft. So why should he worry about me?"

Rowan chewed and swallowed a bite of bacon before replying. "Because there's one thing he can't be sure of, Jamie. He's probably terrified that Sara told you the whole sordid story. He might even think you and Sara were trying to put something over on him, to cut him out of the deal somehow."

"But if they've already taken the statue, fenced it, and divided the money . . ."

"I've been thinking about this most of the night," Rowan said, when Jamie's words fell away for lack of momentum. "It occurred to me that maybe things never got that far. Something went wrong, I'm sure of it. Patience isn't Julian's long suit. If he had his half of the loot—the equivalent of roughly two-point-five million dollars—he'd have vanished by now."

"That would raise questions about Sara's murder. His disappearing, I mean."

"Would it? Don't forget. As far as the police are concerned, they found the body of Jamie Roberts, not Sara."

"Almost the perfect crime," Jamie mused. "If I'd drowned in that tide pool, people would have thought it was an accident. Julian, as Sara's husband, stood to inherit whatever she had."

Rowan shook his head, and Jamie thought she saw something like guilt flicker in his eyes. "Sara didn't have anything for him to inherit, really, besides the proceeds from selling the jade goddess to some crooked art broker. The villa itself belongs to Lazarus."

"The cat?" Jamie marveled. She'd known about the codicil in Sara's first husband's will, assuring Lazarus of a home and a constant supply of gourmet food, but she hadn't guessed that the animal might actually own property. "How is that possible? Lazarus is one smart kitty, but he can't manage an inheritance."

"He doesn't have to," Rowan said, clearing his throat. "Henri appointed me trustee before he died. I manage the whole shebang, as you Americans say."

Jamie sank back in her chair, momentarily surprised. Then she remembered how Myrtle had deferred to Rowan and called him sir, as though he were master of the house. His knowledge of the villa had struck her more than once, too. It was a vast place, with a complex layout.

"Is that why Sara came to Seattle?" she asked, with exaggerated calm. "Because you, as trustee, told her to leave the villa?"

Rowan looked patently annoyed. "Use your head, Jamie. Why would I have given Sara the boot and allowed Julian to stay?"

She didn't have an answer.

"In any case," he went on, with an effort to moderate his tone of voice, "Henri made a provision in his will that allowed Sara to live there as long as she wanted. She had an income most women, even in her social circles, would have considered more than adequate."

Jamie braced herself to learn something else about her sister that she hadn't known. "But?" she prompted.

Rowan sighed. "But she had a problem."

Jamie thought of her father, for the first time in a long while. She remembered his rare calls from Las Vegas or Reno, the lies and the promises that were never kept. Both Jamie and Sara had expected, against all reason, that he'd come home one day, land some kind of job, and make a home for them. It hadn't happened, of course.

"Sara was gambling."

Rowan nodded grimly. "She and Julian met in Monaco, a few months after Henri died. I suspect that was when Sara's pet vice became a slavering monster. It isn't too great a stretch to imagine that when her income was consumed by gambling debts she cooked up the scheme to steal the goddess. She knew it was here, that I was planning to take it to my gallery in Hong Kong. We'd talked about antiques and artifacts often when we were dating, and she even went on a few buying trips with me. She was well aware that the goddess was valuable."

Jamie felt a flash of jealousy, imagining Rowan and Sara traveling together, but she quelled it by reminding herself that she was supposed to be in mourning. She wondered if she would grieve, once the numbness passed, for the stranger who had been her sister.

"Why were you taking the goddess out of the country?"

"The piece was Chinese. I thought it belonged in the Orient."

"Were you and Sara having an affair? Is that why she was here and saw the statue?"

"Aren't we full of questions today?" Rowan responded, but his tone was good-natured and there was tenderness in his eyes. "The answer is no. Sara was married, and I do not sleep with other men's wives. Or at least if I do, I don't make love to them."

"It's that chivalry thing again," Jamie said. She was pleased by his reply and didn't try to hide it. "You are a very unusual man, Rowan Parrish."

"And you are a very lovely woman. Be forewarned, Jamie Roberts. When this is over—when I've dealt with Julian and you've had some time to get your emotional bearings—I intend to seduce you."

Jamie blushed because she wanted to surrender and she was sure it showed. Still, she wouldn't allow herself to think anything real or lasting could ever develop between the two of them. Rowan had loved Sara once, and Jamie didn't want to spend the rest of her life wondering if he was simply using her as a substitute. She had no desire to be a reasonable facsimile of someone else; her adventures in Tovia had taught her that, while she definitely wouldn't wish to change lives with anyone, there was no going back to her old ways of doing things. No more sleeping in her ex-husband's T-shirts and going around half-conscious, waiting for something to happen. When and if she got out of this confusing situation, Jamie promised herself, she would make her own magic.

Rowan pushed away his plate. "In the meantime, though, I have business in St. Rupertsburg, our capital city. I want you to come with me."

Jamie had no intention of turning down a viable opportunity to stay alive, but the idea of hiding out went against the grain. She'd spent her whole life as a coward, a hostage to her own fears about taking risks, but she had a different philosophy now. She meant to take an active role in everything that concerned her.

"All right," she said, somewhat primly, as if she'd been given a choice instead of a polite command. "I'll go, but I won't skulk about like some criminal." A plan was forming, in the dazed, shock-muddled recesses of her mind, but she wasn't ready to share it. "How can I solve my problems if I run away from them?"

"Sometimes flight is the only prudent course of action. To paraphrase, 'She who fights and runs away—'"

"She who fights and runs away," Jamie informed him, "loses the war."

"Not necessarily," he countered. "That isn't the way the saying goes, remember. You're overlooking the part about living to fight another day." Seeing that Jamie had pushed her plate away, he rose and came to stand beside her and offer his hand. "Come along, milady, and we'll see what we can do about keeping you alive."

Telling herself she was a fool, that when she could finally slough of Sara's identity and take back her own she would have to leave Tovia forever, Jamie gave Rowan her hand.

St. Rupertsburg was a small city, by most standards, but it was quaintly beautiful, full of stone buildings with tiled roofs, terraces, and courtyards, all poised at the edge of the sparkling sea like eager swimmers about to plunge in. Steep hillsides, thick with olive groves and vineyards, curved around the place like a mother's arm. A vast, rambling medieval keep loomed above it all, at once ominous and benevolent.

Jamie, riding in the passenger seat of Rowan's sports car, drew in a sharp breath.

"How could anyone ever leave such a place?" she whispered. "It's surely enchanted."

Rowan might not have heard her comment if the car's top had been down, but the afternoon sky was cloudy so he had left it in place. He chuckled, and there was a light in his eyes when he glanced at her. "It is beautiful, I'll grant you that, but there are no resident wizards and no dragon slayers. We're on our own, princess."

Jamie's unfeeling, frozen heart began to thaw in that moment, and the process promised to be painful. "I'm scared," she confessed. Her idea had solidified a little on the three-hour drive along the coast to St. Rupertsburg, but

the plan she'd formulated was a dangerou[s]
knew Rowan would reject it out of hand.

He reached across to squeeze her fingers firmly in his own. "Me, too," he answered. "Let's make a bargain. I know you can't forget what happened to Sara, but for the rest of the day, let's put Julian and the jade goddess out of our minds and try to enjoy the city."

Jamie nodded, but she couldn't quite smile. "It's terrible, Rowan," she confided miserably, "but I don't feel any grief for Sara. I don't feel anything at all, except fear. It's as if she was only some woman I heard of once, or read about in a newspaper. A stranger."

Rowan didn't reply. They were entering the narrow brick-paved streets of the city, and he concentrated on his driving.

Jamie gazed at the buildings and the people. They appeared oddly dreamlike. She wondered if they were real, if she herself was real. Should she look into a mirror? Would the image she saw there be her own?

Rowan wove expertly through traffic that included every conceivable make and model of car and more than one donkey cart. At last they stopped in front of a spectacular old hotel with rows and rows of balconies overlooking the sea.

A cheerful parking attendant opened Jamie's car door and helped her out, and Rowan slipped from behind the wheel. A bellman appeared immediately to collect Jamie's suitcase, and that was when she noticed that Rowan hadn't brought any luggage.

He spoke to the two hotel employees in turn, handing each of them a bill, and then put his hand on the small of Jamie's back and steered her into the lobby. It was an elegant room, full of crystal and mahogany; priceless oriental rugs graced the floor.

Rowan didn't even glance toward the registration desk but headed straight for a bank of elevators on the far side. "I

...or arrived, and they stepped inside.
"...y aristocratic of you," Jamie replied. "Are we ...perating on the old hide-in-plain-sight theory? Julian must know about this place."

He waggled a finger at her. "Have you forgotten our agreement? We're not going to worry about Julian until tomorrow, remember?"

Jamie sighed. She had a headache and a strong hunch that her horoscope, should she work up the courage to read it, would say, Run like hell!

"Right," she grumbled. "Why should you turn a hair? It's *me* Julian wants to kill, after all."

Rowan cupped her chin in his hand and looked deep into her eyes. "And if he succeeded, I would die, too. From the loss." He bent his head and kissed her lightly on the mouth. "I've fallen in love with you, Jamie Roberts."

No, Jamie thought despairingly. You may think you're free, but you're still under Sara's spell. You don't really want me, you want a reincarnation of her.

She shook her head. "Don't say that, Rowan. Please."

The elevator stopped and the doors opened, but Rowan didn't step off, nor did he allow Jamie to do so. He braced his hands against the wall of the cubicle, effectively trapping her between them. In the hall, an elderly couple looked at them curiously as the doors closed again.

"Why not?" he demanded. "Why can't I say I love you, Jamie? Tell me."

She swallowed hard and wrapped her arms tightly around herself. "Because you don't, not really."

Rowan reached out with one hand, never looking away from Jamie's face, and found the ornate STOP knob above the elevator buttons. She wondered distractedly if he had radar or something.

"What makes you say that?"

Jamie drew in a quick, deep breath, and let it out again in a mournful sigh. "We don't really know each other, Rowan. And things have been happening so fast that no one could begin to sort them out without a lot of time and effort." She hesitated, biting her lip. "When you look at me, you don't see me, Jamie Roberts. You see some fantasy version of Sara. As much as I care about you, I can't spend my life posing as someone else."

Rowan started to speak, then stopped. He released the STOP button and pressed the number for the top floor. His stride, as he stepped off the elevator and started down the hall, was rapid, but he didn't seem angry. To Jamie, he looked preoccupied.

She followed him to the white double doors of his suite and waited in silence while he produced a key from the pocket of his slacks and worked the lock. Beyond the threshold was a large living room, furnished in what appeared to be French antiques. There were lots of tables and mirrors, and colorful fresh flowers were everywhere, filling the air with a symphony of scent.

At last, Rowan spoke again. "I'll show you to your room," he said, and started across the lush white carpet toward another set of double doors. He pushed one open and gestured for Jamie to step through before him.

She found herself in a sumptuous bedroom with a white marble fireplace and a terrace overlooking the sea. Jamie felt a silken rope wind around her heart and squeeze tight. "It's beautiful, but—"

He silenced her with a light kiss on the mouth. "I'll take the other room, Jamie. I'm not going to pressure you; you must know that."

Jamie nodded. She couldn't quite make herself tell him that she not only wanted him to share her bed, to hold her and protect her as he had the night before, but to be her lover.

Not after the speech he'd made about abstaining from sex until everything was settled and she'd gotten her emotions under control, and not after turning away his declaration of love.

"I know," she said, and she sounded disgustingly timid, even to herself. Realizing that she was wringing her hands, she wrenched them apart.

Rowan touched her face gently, then withdrew. "I have some things to attend to," he said. "We'll have dinner when I get back and then go to the theater, if you feel like it."

She honestly tried to smile. "I could use a little entertainment," she said. "But I don't think I brought anything suitable to wear."

A corner of his mouth lifted, and some sad, gentle emotion moved in his eyes like a shadow. "No problem. There's a very good shop downstairs in the lobby. Buy whatever you want."

The idea of wearing a dress that she'd chosen herself appealed to Jamie, even though she would have to use one of Sara's credit cards to buy it. It would be a small step toward reestablishing her own identity. "I've been managing tile stores in Seattle for five years," she joked. "And I haven't had much leisure time. I'm a little out of practice when it comes to picking out dresses for dinner and the theater."

"You'll manage, I'm sure," Rowan replied, with tender humor. "Be careful, my love. If you leave the hotel, make sure you pay strict attention to everything that's going on around you."

She saluted. "Yes, sir," she said.

He laughed, kissed her again, more lingeringly this time, and then left her alone. His absence seemed to suck the oxygen out of the bedroom, and Jamie stood staring after him like a fool, warning herself not to fall in love with him.

The message wasn't getting through; she knew that by the ache in her heart and the weakness in her knees. Even if she managed to survive this extraordinary adventure, how would she ever survive losing Rowan?

She would, she insisted silently, the nails of her right hand digging into her left palm as she clasped her hands together in an unconscious gesture of entreaty. She had to become herself, in a way she had never been before. Only then could she find a man who loved her for being Jamie Roberts.

After some deep breathing and fast talking, Jamie freed herself from the attack of romantic paralysis and went into the echoing marble vault of a bath that adjoined the bedroom. There, she splashed water on her face, used one of the elegant little packaged toothbrushes waiting on the glistening cabinet housing the sink, and combed her hair with her fingers.

Without Sara's makeup and carefully arranged tresses, she thought, with a slight lift of her spirits, she was beginning to look like herself again. Now all she had to do was figure out who the hell she really was.

The suitcase full of her sister's clothes was delivered just as she was about to head downstairs, purse in hand, and explore the shop Rowan had mentioned. It suddenly seemed repulsive, the idea of wearing a dead person's garments, and she shuddered a little as she stepped onto the elevator.

The hotel's boutique was brimming with splendid things, and Jamie tried on several outfits before she selected a short dress of silk crepe. It was midnight blue and drop-dead sexy, with a scattering of tiny rhinestones across the bodice. After charging her purchase and having it sent to Rowan's suite— the clerk didn't bat an eye at this request, Jamie noted, but then it probably wasn't unusual for Mr. Parrish to entertain a woman—she went out into the late-afternoon sunshine.

It was late April, and a soft, balmy breeze fluffed her hair and caressed her skin. Jamie was feeling better—she hadn't realized how it was getting her down, living in costume like an actress playing a part in a movie that never ended—and she wanted to buy fresh makeup and some casual clothes.

From the hotel she went to a nearby department store, where she bought some new things to wear and had a make-over at one of the cosmetic counters, buying new makeup instead of her old brand. She left just as the store was closing, her arms full of packages.

Jamie had entered the store by a different entrance, and for a few moments she stood on the sidewalk, bewildered. The sense of disorientation only lasted until she rounded the corner and saw the sea glittering in the late-day sunlight, and then she walked with a brisk step, thinking of the glamorous evening ahead. Just for that one night, she would take a vacation from her problems and indulge in the pretense that she and Rowan might actually have a future together.

When the limousine nearly struck her down in the crosswalk, Jamie thought at first she was only dealing with a careless driver. She was struggling to keep from dropping her bags and boxes, and muttering, when suddenly the rear door sprang open and a man leaped out—a man she remembered seeing inside the department store earlier. Before Jamie understood what was happening, he grabbed her by the arm and flung her into the car, leaving her purchases scattered on the pavement.

The inside of the vehicle was sumptuous and very dark, because of the tinted windows. The man shoved the barrel of a small handgun into Jamie's face and said, "Don't scream."

Bile rushed into the back of Jamie's throat, scalding, and she swallowed. It hadn't occurred to her to shout for help; she'd been thinking, ludicrously, that she would never have guessed it was so easy to kidnap someone. It had happened in the space of seconds, with no opportunity for struggle, and if anyone else had seen what was going on, nobody rushed to the rescue. Several horns had honked behind the limo, but that was probably only because the other drivers wanted the way cleared.

She straightened her clothes—Sara's clothes—and even though it was insane, under the circumstances, she felt a twinge of sorrow for the lost things in those bags and boxes. "Let me out of the car this instant," she said.

"Anything you say, lady," the stranger answered acidly.

"Who are you?" Jamie demanded.

"Nobody you know."

Fear was beginning to penetrate the haze of shock and general emotional befuddlement that had been plaguing Jamie since she learned of Sara's death. She tried the door handle, and her captor immediately shoved the pistol barrel hard into the side of her neck.

"I'd hate to mess up a nice car like this," he said, as though he were reprimanding her for parking in a private space or failing to return a library book on time, "but I'll shoot you if I have to. Don't make me prove it."

Jamie nodded. Carefully. "Just put that thing down," she said. "Please."

He lowered the gun to his ample lap. He was a dark-haired man, stocky but not obese, and well-dressed. Jamie sensed that he was strong as the proverbial bull, and her chances of getting away from him were nil.

"Is this what happened to Sara?" she asked, surprised by how calm she sounded. She'd thought she was screaming.

His answer was chillingly simple. "Yes."

"Oh, God," Jamie whispered, covering her face with her hands for a few seconds and fighting an onslaught of sheer hysteria. "You killed her—you personally killed my sister?"

"She wouldn't tell us where she put the jade goddess," he said, as though that were reason enough for any sort of reprisal, even something so brutal as murder.

"You would have killed her anyway," Jamie murmured, seething and shaken. She wondered if this monster would shoot her if she threw up all over his fancy car. "And you plan to do the same thing to me."

The man shrugged. "You'd talk too much afterward," he said. "We can't have that. So let's just get down to business. Your sister gave you the goddess when she landed in Seattle, and you hid it. I want to know where."

Jamie closed her eyes briefly and drew a deep breath. "Sara didn't confide in me. I've never seen that damn statue, and I wish I'd never heard of it, either."

"You've only just started wishing that," her companion said, settling back against the leather seat with a lusty sigh and gazing forlornly through the darkened window.

A chill tingled along Jamie's nerve endings. They were leaving the city behind, heading back along the coastline in the general direction of the villa. Rowan would learn she was missing soon enough, because the purse she'd dropped with her parcels contained a key to his room at the hotel, and he'd have a fair idea where to look for her, too, she supposed.

"I suppose you work for Julian," she said evenly.

The man laughed. "Not exactly. He and the girlfriend owed me money. The girlfriend, she came to me and said she could get a certain piece of oriental art that I happened to want. We worked out a deal, and she and Julian lifted the statue from Rowan Parrish's house." The mirth drained from the round face, replaced by a look of cold fury that made Jamie's very bones seem to draw inward, shrinking from him. "I don't know why I'm telling you all this, when you already know what happened. They tried to put something over on me. I guess they planned to sell the goddess at a profit and buy me off with part of the proceeds. I didn't go for it."

"So you murdered Sara."

"She could have saved herself, but she spit in my face when I asked her about the goddess. Nobody spits on Charlie Beech. Nobody."

Tears filled Jamie's eyes. Oh, Sara, she thought miserably, Sara.

"Sara didn't tell me where she put the statue," she said, after drying her cheeks with the back of one hand. The motion was quick and furtive. "Did you think to ask Julian, her partner in crime?"

"That slimebag? Yeah, I asked him. He said he didn't know, and then darned if he didn't meet with the damnedest boating accident you could imagine. It was right out of an Arnold Schwarzenegger movie."

Once again, nausea roiled in Jamie's stomach. She hadn't liked Julian, but she certainly wouldn't have wished him dead. It was a tragic irony that beautiful, privileged people, like him and like Sara, would actually commit crimes and endanger their own lives for the sake of greed.

"You sound proud of yourself," she said coldly.

"Oh, I am," Charlie answered. "I'm a master at what I do."

"A genuine hit man. Wow, I'm honored."

"You're a smart-ass," he countered wearily. "And you're also as good as dead."

Chapter Six

Don't panic, Jamie warned herself silently, as the expensive car sped away from St. Rupertsburg. She tried hard to make contact with that mysterious part of her mind that had occasionally linked her, however tenuously, with Sara. It was as though the whereabouts of the jade goddess lay hidden somewhere in her unconscious, despite the fact that her twin had never mentioned the object or even hinted at its existence.

Not that it would do her any lasting good to find the statue, she reflected, staring thoughtfully at the back of the limousine driver's head. Charlie Beech meant to kill her, one way or the other; he'd already admitted that. Still, if she could turn the statue over to him, it might buy her some time. And the longer she could stay alive, she reasoned, the better her chances of escape.

"Where did your sister hide the jade goddess, Ms. Roberts?" Charlie asked at length, when they'd traveled quite a distance without speaking. His bored, desultory tone was terrifying for its lack of expression alone. "Tell me and save yourself a lot of suffering."

Jamie's stomach clenched as she imagined the ordeal that might lie ahead, but she was angry as well as frightened, and her anger sustained her. The icy coldness of the emotion kept her from being reckless.

"I don't know, but I have a theory."

Charlie turned his bulk, his silk suit making a whispery sound against the leather upholstery. "I'm warning you right now: no tricks. And no stalling tactics. I'm in deadly earnest here."

Jamie ran the tip of her tongue over her dry lips. "Do you want to hear my theory or not?" she asked evenly.

Charlie narrowed his eyes speculatively. "All right, spill it."

"There is an old fortress on one of the hills behind my sister's villa. She used to go there with someone she cared about, and I think it was a special place to her. It would have been like Sara to bury the goddess somewhere on the grounds or hide it in a hollow spot in the wall that nobody else knew about." Jamie's speculations stemmed from vague memorylike images flickering on the inside of her skull. The pictures became clearer with every passing moment. "Yes," she whispered, amazed. "Sara hid the statue somewhere in those ruins!"

Charlie leaned forward and tapped on the glass separating the back seat from the front, in order to get the driver's attention. The chauffeur lowered the barrier and turned his head. "Yes, sir?"

Jamie was stunned. It was Curran, Sara's driver, who, with Rowan, had met her at the airport the day she arrived in Tovia.

"The lady thinks we'll find what we're looking for in the ruins above the villa."

Curran nodded. "Very good, sir," he said. He met Jamie's eyes, squarely and with mild defiance, before turning his attention back to the road.

Charlie closed the divider with a press of a button on the armrest.

"Julian sneaked back and pushed me into the tide pool that night," Jamie muttered. "He must have suspected I wasn't Sara."

"See?" Charlie said, with a mocking smile. "You're just too smart for your own good."

Jamie didn't answer. She certainly didn't *feel* smart; nobody with half a brain would have gotten into such a mess in the first place. If she'd listened to her own instincts, she'd still be in Seattle, working for Fred Godwin and wishing something interesting would happen.

In which case she would never have met Rowan Parrish. She still didn't know whether falling in love with him had been a plus or a minus. No matter what happened when she and Charlie and Curran reached the ancient fortress, there was no happy ending on the horizon.

She settled back against the seat, closed her eyes, and tried to summon more images to her mind, but it was no use. All she could picture was Rowan's face—a face she might never see again.

Charlie was reading a paperback novel about space aliens when she finally stole another glance at him. He must have ice in his veins, she concluded, to sit there flipping pages and moving his lips, seemingly without a care in the world. No doubt kidnapping and murder were common notations on his To Do list.

It was dark by the time the villa came into view. Curran flipped off the headlights and steered the limo skillfully onto a tree-lined lane Jamie had never noticed before. The track was narrow and unpaved, and the big car jostled on its shock absorbers as they climbed.

The ruin was eerie in the light of the moon, and Jamie's legs trembled as she got out of the car. Unless she got very very lucky, very very soon, she was going to die in this dark place.

"How do you expect to find anything now?" she asked, hugging herself in an effort to ward off the evening chill and the fear.

Curran handed her a flashlight, but it was Charlie who spoke.

"*We're* not going to find anything. *You* are."

Jamie heard a faint rustling in the bushes, but her hope of salvation died a borning. Just a rabbit or a squirrel, she thought. Then a whimsical voice made an announcement inside her head. *We regret to inform you that Sir Galahad won't be riding to the rescue tonight. He's otherwise occupied. You're on your own, kid.*

She pointed herself toward the ruins, sent a quick prayer heavenward, and stumbled forward. The beam of the flashlight wove crazily over the stones, caught on a pair of jewel-bright amber eyes. Lazarus!

Jamie took some comfort in the animal's presence, and she was glad that Curran and Charlie apparently hadn't noticed him. Too bad, she thought, with the whimsy of hysteria, that she couldn't borrow one of her feline friend's nine lives.

The ground was rough and uneven, scattered with stones both large and small. Jamie nearly fell several times, but each time she righted herself and forged on.

Sara, she pleaded silently, help me.

There was no blinding flash of light, no voice from the heavens. All of a sudden, though, Jamie knew where the goddess was hidden. The location of the cache was as clear in her mind as if she'd put the statue there with her own hands.

She went straight to the towering wall and pried at a loose stone, cursing when she broke a nail. "Help me, one of you," she snapped. "The statue is behind this piece of rock."

"This had better not be some kind of trick," Charlie warned.

Jamie stepped back as Charlie moved past her to the wall, intent on his treasure. He worked the stone free with a pocket knife and had just reached inside the cache when

Lazarus came hurtling down out of the darkness. The cat landed on Charlie's head and shoulders, screeching like a banshee, claws extended, all four paws working with a terrible, swift grace.

Charlie shrieked and fought his attacker in vain, and Jamie dropped the flashlight and fled into the shadows.

"Get him off me!" Charlie screamed.

Jamie crouched behind a rock and saw Curran take a small pistol from the pocket of his coat. At first she thought he meant to shoot Lazarus, and she cried out and started to bolt from her hiding place. Curran fired, Lazarus yowled shrilly and streaked off into the darkness, and Charlie crumpled to the ground.

Curran took the statue from his employer's limp hand and straightened. He looked lean and wolflike, framed in the great silvery circle of the moon, and Jamie held her breath. He seemed to be able to see her, even in the darkness.

"I don't kill women," he said. And then he turned and walked away, leaving Jamie crouched behind her stone and Charlie lying in a heap in the ruins. Curran got back into the limousine and simply drove away.

Jamie had been sustained and protected by a state of ongoing shock, but now that the worst had passed, leaving her alive in its wake, she fell apart. She slid down onto the ground and wept with great, violent, gulping sobs that made no sound at all. At some point, Lazarus returned and settled himself against her side, purring like a rotary engine.

A prickle at her nape alerted her, even before Lazarus stiffened beside her and shrieked like a panther. Jamie turned, horror pooling thick in the pit of her stomach, and looked up to see Charlie leaning against the rock she'd taken refuge behind. His leering face was torn and bleeding. He reached one awkward, crimson hand toward her, and she screamed and bolted off.

Charlie loomed there, like a well-stuffed scarecrow, illuminated by the moonlight. His eyes glittered, and he took a step toward Jamie, stumbled, and fell.

She ran blindly into the woods behind the fortress, her heart pounding in the back of her throat, afraid to go toward the villa in case Beech and Curran had posted an accomplice somewhere on the grounds. Gasping and whimpering in terror, she ran and ran—there were no other houses in sight—until her strength was gone, and then she collapsed onto the cold ground.

Rowan and the police found her just after dawn, sitting with her back to an old moss-covered gravestone that stood alone in the middle of a clearing.

Rowan knelt beside her in an instant, checking her for injuries, saying her name over and over again. Not Sara's, but her own. Then he wrenched her into his arms and embraced her fiercely. "It's over now," he said. "It's over."

Jamie luxuriated in being held, in being safe, with her lungs still drawing air and her heart still beating. Her mind was surprisingly clear.

"We found a body in the ruins," Rowan told her, after a long time, holding her gently by the shoulders and gazing deep into her eyes. "What happened?"

She gave him an abridged version of the story, from the moment she was snatched in the crosswalk in St. Rupertsburg to her frantic, mindless flight into the woods. One of the policemen made notes while she talked; another produced a blanket, which Rowan wrapped tightly around her.

"Curran took the goddess," she finished, getting to her feet with a lot of help from Rowan and clutching the blanket close like a cloak.

"I don't give a damn about that," Rowan said. "You're safe. That's all that matters."

A black, silken form brushed against Jamie's ankle, and

she looked down to see Lazarus there, purring. "Here's the male of the hour," she said. "My hero."

Lazarus demurred. "*Reow,*" he said, with rare humility.

Jamie laughed and bent to sweep him up into her arms and then, leaning just a little on Rowan's strength, she walked down the hill to the sprawling villa overlooking the sea.

"I'M SORRY YOU didn't recover the goddess," Jamie said, hours later, when the police were gone and she was ensconced in Rowan's house and bed, being shamefully pampered. She was wearing silk pajamas—his—and there had been a constant flow of tea, sympathy, and chicken soup all day long.

He touched her face. "Oh, but I did," he answered gruffly. "She's right here, wearing my pajamas."

Tears pooled along Jamie's lashes. "I love you," she whispered.

He kissed her. "And I love you."

Jamie drew back, albeit reluctantly. "I'm going to need some time."

"Before we make love, or before we get married?"

The thought of being Rowan's wife made her heart swell with a strange liquid warmth. "I want to make love now, today," she told him brokenly, slipping her arms around his neck, "but I can't marry you, Rowan. Not until we're both sure who I am."

Rowan's eyes were dark with tenderness and sorrow, but he nodded. "I know exactly who you are," he said. "But I can wait until you make the same discovery."

She kissed him and fell slowly back onto the pillows, and Rowan fell with her. The kiss intensified until Jamie's very soul seemed to burn, and she surrendered long before she'd been conquered.

Their lovemaking was bittersweet and violent, born of joy, tinged with the shadow of the inevitable parting. Jamie writhed in Rowan's arms, arching her back when he opened the pajama top and laid claim to her breasts, first with his hands, then with his mouth.

The sensations were exquisite, and Jamie pitched beneath Rowan, wanting more, demanding more. She sobbed, when he finally thrust himself far inside her, and raised her hips high off the bed, trying to consume him, to draw him, body and soul, into her uttermost depths.

He groaned and kissed her, and the motions of their two bodies became more and more frantic with every passing moment. Finally, with a single hoarse cry that came not from one but from both of them, they entered into a fusion so complete, so elemental, that Jamie knew they would never really be separated again, no matter how many oceans might lie between them.

When it was over, and they lay still in each other's arms, breathless and exhausted, Jamie wanted to take back what she'd said about needing time. It would be so easy to stay, she thought, to marry Rowan, to bear his children and share his passion for antiques and art.

She couldn't. She owed herself, and Rowan, much more than a marriage of impulse. If she was going to wed this man, or any other, she wanted the relationship to last. The best way to ensure that was to wait and think, pray and heal.

They made love often, and with heart-wrenching urgency.

After a week, Jamie returned to Sara's villa alone, intending to say good-bye to Myrtle and the others and hoping for a few minutes with Lazarus. The cat didn't put in an appearance, though she searched all his favorite places in and around the house and even walked up to the ruin on the hill.

There was no sign of him anywhere. Sadly, Jamie gave up and returned to the villa, where a taxi was waiting. She'd refused to let Rowan drive her to the airport, knowing she wouldn't be able to bear telling him good-bye.

They'd parted with a kiss and a promise that morning, on Rowan's front walk, and Jamie had driven away without looking back.

She meant to keep going, keep searching, until she found the real Jamie, the best Jamie, the Jamie she was meant to be.

Chapter Seven

The gallery was exclusive, with an intimidating facade and real gold lettering on the leaded display windows. Through the glass, Jamie could see a lovely old harp, a china doll in an ornate wicker carriage, and a black cat bathing itself with an air of snooty decorum.

She smiled and tapped her fingers against the window, and the cat looked up at her with shining golden eyes.

Lazarus. She hadn't seen him in six months. What was he doing in Hong Kong?

A tiny silver bell tinkled overhead as Jamie opened the door and entered the antiques shop.

Lazarus hopped down from the window with a resounding thump and trotted over to her with a meow of greeting. She crouched, heedless of her white linen suit, to pet him and murmur the kinds of silly, senseless things cat lovers say to their favorite felines.

"May I help you?" someone asked.

Jamie looked up. At first, she thought the words had come from a life-sized bronze statue of a Chinese warrior on display nearby, but a small birdlike woman with gray hair peered around it. She was exquisitely dressed, with the look of perpetual surprise that often comes with multiple face-lifts.

Jamie raised herself, somewhat awkwardly, with Lazarus

cradled in her arms like a fat, furry baby. "I'm looking for Rowan Parrish," she said, in a careful voice, not wanting to betray how important her errand was. "Is he in?"

"He's in the office, buried in paperwork," the woman said, offering a manicured hand. "I'm Doris Shaw, Mr. Parrish's assistant. If you'll just give me your name—?"

"Jamie Roberts," she replied, without a trace of the hesitation and doubt that had plagued her in Tovia.

Doris looked at the cat and made a *tsk-tsk* sound, but her manner and tone were benevolent and Jamie liked her. "You'll spoil your lovely suit, holding that old reprobate. Will you just look at him! You'd think it was his due to have the rest of us pay court to him!"

Jamie laughed and nuzzled Lazarus's head. "Lazarus is royalty," she said. "Naturally, he commands the proper respect."

Doris smiled, shook her sprayed and coiffed gray head, and excused herself. Jamie put the cat down gently and tried to brush the fur off her suit.

She didn't hear Rowan enter the room, didn't know he was there until he said her name. She lifted her eyes at the sound of his voice, found his beloved face, and felt her heart turn over. Her love for him had grown and ripened in the time they'd been apart.

"Hello, Rowan."

He was thinner, and his aristocratic features had taken on a cragginess that only added to his appeal. His eyes were full of wary hunger as he looked at her, but he made no move to come closer. "You look wonderful," he said hoarsely.

Jamie took one tentative step, lost her courage, and stopped. She'd done a lot of healing and growing in the past six months, and if Rowan rejected her, she knew she would recover. Still, it would be devastating to lose him and the life they might have together.

"Thank you," she said, her voice trembling a little, like her knees. She cleared her throat and blushed, running through a litany of motivational clichés in her mind: *Now or never . . . no guts, no glory . . . no pain, no gain . . .* "Rowan—"

"Yes?" He still didn't move, damn him. He wasn't going to make it easy.

"I was wondering if you'd be interested in hiring an apprentice," she blurted out. "I've been working with antiques for months now, and studying on my own, and I think I could be an asset—"

"I'm not looking for an apprentice," Rowan broke in quietly, and for Jamie the world stopped turning. Then he smiled. "A partner would be nice, though."

Jamie stared at him, confounded, trying not to hope and already in over her head. "Are you saying—"

"I'm saying that I love you, Jamie Roberts. I want you to share my life, as well as my business."

With a soft cry, Jamie launched herself into his arms. "I accept!" she cried jubilantly, and Rowan spun her around in celebration, nearly overturning the bronze warrior. "Oh, Rowan, I love you, I love you, I love you!"

He laughed and kissed her hard.

"What is Lazarus doing here?" she asked, when she could catch her breath. "I thought he couldn't leave his estate."

Rowan smiled down at her, holding her close. "I'm afraid poor Lazarus fell on hard times. The villa had to be sold for debts and taxes, as it happened. Our friend here had to depend upon the kindness of his neighbors."

Seemingly unembarrassed by the mention of his reduced circumstances, Lazarus climbed back into the front window and began to bathe himself again.

Jamie laughed, completely happy. "I've been thinking about you ever since I left Tovia," she said.

"And I've been thinking about you," he replied. "Let me show you some of the scandalous things I imagined us doing together."

Warmth flooded through her. "How could I refuse an offer like that?"

Rowan smiled, took Jamie's hand, and led her toward a rear stairway, and she knew without being told that he lived upstairs and he was taking her to his bed. Somewhere in the back of the gallery, a door clicked as Doris let herself out.

At Avon Books, we know your passion for romance—once you finish one of our novels, you find yourself wanting more.

May we tempt you with . . .

- **Excerpts** from our upcoming releases.

- Entertaining **extras**, including authors' personal photo albums and book lists.

- Behind-the-scenes **scoop** on your favorite characters and series.

- **Sweepstakes** for the chance to win free books, romantic getaways, and other fun prizes.

- Writing **tips** from our authors and editors.

- **Blog** with our authors and find out why they love to write romance.

- **Exclusive content** that's not contained within the pages of our novels.

Join us at
www.avonbooks.com

An Imprint of HarperCollinsPublishers
www.avonromance.com